THE FOX AND THE DRYAD
A ROWAN BLOOD NOVEL

KELLEN GRAVES

CONTENTS

Author's Note

This novel is Fantasy-Romance for a New Adult audience, and contains tropes commonly found in that genre. Such tropes include but are not limited to:

- Themes of anxiety, depression
- Sexual harassment and intimidation
- Themes of gaslighting
- Crude language
- Descriptions of body horror, gore
- Themes of emotional abuse/control by a parent
- Unhealthy behaviors involving drugs and alcohol
- Scenes of consensual sex

Pronounciation Guide

Beantighe *(Ban-tee)*
Felme *(Fell-ma)*
Larissa *(Lah-riss-ah)*
Lillis *(Lil-iss)*
Lusia *(Loose-ia)*
Malric *(Mal-rick)*
Maura *(More-ah)*
Mavera *(Mah-vare-ah)*
Neda *(Neh-da)*
Persea *(Purr-say-ah)*
Reta *(Reh-tah)*
Sídhe *(shee)*

Title Reference

He/She/They
Lord/Lady/Gentle
King/Queen/Danae
Prince/Princess/Daurae

"At last the right companion is coming," said the musician, "for I was seeking a human being, not wild animals." And he began to play so beautifully and delightfully that the poor man stood there enraptured, his heart filled with pleasure.

While he was thus standing there, the wolf, the fox, and the hare approached. He saw well that they had evil intentions, so he raised his shining axe and placed himself before the musician, as if to say, "Anyone who wants to harm him beware, for he will have to deal with me."

The Strange Musician
Children's and Household Tales
Grimms' Fairy Tales 1857.

MALRIC

Moon-eared witches were such assholes.

Moon-eared, arid, iron, whatever they called themselves—human witches were absolute assholes, every single one.

Perhaps the only bigger asshole was the one who kicked Malric's drunk ass out of the party room, clamping a charmed get-home-safe bracelet on his wrist that read his thoughts and knew exactly where to take him. He stumbled the entire way, tugging on the circlet, groaning and begging it to find literally anywhere else to drag his sorry ass than that place.

It wasn't home. It hadn't been for months—if it ever had been at all. Especially not since that final confrontation with Marie that liberated him to bounce between the human and fey worlds. Constantly seeking a place to crash until he overstayed his welcome and went searching for somewhere else. Maybe it was only because he didn't have anywhere to stay that very night that the bracelet sent him off to the last place he wanted to be. Perhaps he should have been nicer to the cutest moon-eared witch he'd seen in the darkness. Maybe he'd have been able to go home with them, instead.

But, no. Malric was towed back to the d'Alarie family estate.

How long had it been? He hadn't avoided all of his family entirely, just enough to skirt the attention of his mother. It had to have still been at least a month. Maybe two. When did Felme have her art gallery exhibition again? He'd gone home with her and the others to drink in secret after that, hiding in Neda's private library so their mother wouldn't notice Malric was there. Whenever that was. Oh, gods, he couldn't think straight at all.

Approaching the family estate was always bittersweet, traveling from his eyes to his mouth and down his throat to settle in his gut like a rock. Maybe like suffocating mud and clay. Perhaps ice littered with nails, where it slowly thawed and pricked Malric's insides for every hour he remained past the front threshold.

Before he'd claimed his freedom, Malric really thought it would be easier to come back for visits, knowing he wouldn't be forced to stay. He thought that ball of frozen nails would cease if he ever returned, because there would not be that same dread of being trapped again in that house. Not knowing what would be asked of him. Whether or not the night would be his or his mother's. But that was a foolish thing to think, and Malric should have known better. He would always exist within the d'Alarie estate with a stomach full of nails.

Stumbling up the drive, the house's warm electric lights burned like lanterns used to, though without the friendly flicker of flames. Something about electric light was so cold—though perhaps not as cold as the ones used in the human world on the other side of the veil. A part of Malric wished the fey had never adopted electric light at all—before realizing, it could always be worse. He didn't want to think about what would happen if the known-for-dramatics high fey ever evolved enough along human invention to get their hands on uninhibited social media access. The daily gossip pamphlets sold on the street were more than enough already.

The front door still responded to his touch, inviting the first nail in his stomach to poke. A reminder that his mother still expected him to return home at some point, return back to the nest where she could pluck his feathers, ground him, remind him why it was a mistake to ever leave at all...

Malric touched his thumb to the lever, and invited himself inside to scowl at the garish interior that seemingly changed every time he went to visit. An ongoing symptom of his perpetually debt-ridden mother's need to keep up appearances amongst the fey nobles who attended her revels. They hardly ever visited the home itself, though—otherwise they would see how it lacked enough beantighe or fey servants to keep the dust off the mantles, the laundry washed and sorted, lavish meals on the table. Still, Marie d'Alarie insisted, since they descended from a powerful Sídhe family, they must put on the airs of one and the same.

When Malric first left, the house resembled a Victorian Queen-Anne. That night, it was much more with the times according to the rest of the Autumn Court—a horrible mix of Edwardian and Art Deco, of which Malric only recognized because his human friend Bianca made him attend a Halloween party dressed as some human named *Gatsby* after watching a documentary about him and his wealth.

Malric hoped to slink down the front corridor and past the sitting room for the stairs, not wanting anyone to know he'd stopped by at all—but, of course, his timing was impeccable as he stumbled across a gathering of his siblings, all nine of them, clustered on the sofas and drinking tea from the table in the center. Illuminated by both the electric lights and the fire burning in the hearth, he saw all of their faces, counting them in habit, before feeling relieved when his mother was indeed not seated amongst them. Still, nine faces turning to acknowledge him all at once might as well have been a summoning ritual in itself, thrusting an ounce of sobriety into his blood. Or perhaps it was just panic.

They sipped spirits with their tea, but the mood in the room would have implied otherwise. It was more like they'd just returned home from a funeral with the way they spoke in low, hushed voices, lacking any of the normal boisterousness of a gathering without their mother involved. Malric had to swallow the urge to ask if Marie had finally croaked.

"Look who's back," Mavera said first, and Malric grimaced, leaning against the entryway as the floor turned beneath his inebriated feet. His sister's reddish hair glowed orange in the fireplace, Maura's twin features glowing the same where he sat alongside her. Both of them moved with synchronicity, angular faces tilted toward him, sharp brown eyes searching him up and down as if they shared the same critical mind. "The prodigal son returns."

"So soon with the bible stuff, Mavera," Malric teased, then flashed his charmed bracelet from the club. All of his siblings rolled their eyes in tandem, like it was the least surprising thing ever. He couldn't blame them. It was perhaps more of a surprise that was the first time it'd happened since his liberation—gods knew it was nearly nightly before that. "I simply got put into time-out."

Lusia leapt to their feet, next, long brown hair pulled back into a braid that whipped Malric in the face before he was taken up in a long hug. They were thinner than the last time he saw them, making him frown and hug them tighter. Patting him on the back, they offered him a meal so he wouldn't be hungover in the morning, and Malric tried to refuse, but they waved him off, muttering something about how it was about time to start breakfast for mother's plaything, anyway. He didn't have a chance to ask what that meant before Neda and Felme offered to join Lusia in the kitchen, hurrying away without meeting his eyes for long—which was Malric's first sign there was something he wasn't being told. Something more than normal, at least. He and his siblings normally didn't hesitate to imbibe in gossip as much as they did tea and whiskey, it being one of the few traits they inherited from their mother.

"Is mother home?" he asked as three bodies vacated through a side door toward the kitchen. Mavera shook her head, then glanced at Maura perched on the couch next to her. They exchanged a horrible little smirk that only further confirmed Malric's suspicion, though he juggled whether or not it was worth asking. The room still spun, his head was starting to hurt, his anxiety was at an all time high like a mouse hiding from a fox in a field. He was eager to hurry up the stairs to his bedroom, which he was sure had gone untouched since the last time he slept there in secret. Just until the charmed bracelet let him leave again with the sunrise.

"Mother is still reveling," Mavera finally answered, flipping a long strand of hair over one shoulder. "Who knows when she'll be home."

Malric eyeballed everyone's outfits, narrowing his eyes when he recognized the consistent classical designs. Exactly how Marie d'Alarie had everyone dress for her fetes in the woods, as if tapping into ancient fey roots. Lots of flowery embroidery, layered and loose fabrics cinched strategically down the silhouette, long sleeves ending in points, high collars, hair pinned back with pine needles and acorn bundles. It was then he also sensed the stench of rosemary on the air, like residual perfume he knew to come only from that clearing in the trees.

"Why are you all dressed like you were reveling with her?" he played coy, anyway.

"Because we were," Persea grumbled, pouring himself a new cup of tea from the tray, before adding half a cup's-worth of pine whiskey to top it off. His wavy, reddish-brown hair was pulled back in a golden pin matching those in the hair of Larissa and Reta on the couch next to him, matching makeup on their three faces making it harder than normal to tell the triplets apart. "Again."

"Again?" Malric crossed his arms with a smirk, unable to resist the flicker of satisfaction that came with those words. To know he'd gone another night without even knowing there was a revel at all, when he used to be required to attend each and every one of them. "What's got mother in such a festive mood? Did you three finally get moved to revel-performances? Persea,

Larissa, Reta, singing for all of mother's most affluent friends—"

"Mother has a new toy," Mavera interrupted, still wearing that foxlike grin as if she'd been waiting for exactly the right moment to say it. He almost asked what she meant, but then recalled what Lusia said before leaving toward the kitchen. *I've got to start breakfast for mother's new plaything...*

"A..." he attempted, but it wouldn't come. A new toy.

"Your replacement," Maura answered for him, wearing the same sly grin as his clone. He sipped his tea after uttering those words, perhaps to allow them to really settle into Malric's mind, and then his heart, and then his gut, where the ball of frozen nails sank a little deeper to bite into him. It suddenly made sense why Lusia and Felme and Neda all jumped up to leave the room so quickly. Why Persea spoke of the revels with such resentment, when he normally didn't give them a care at all. Why Reta and Larissa remained completely silent right next to them, and even Lillis on the neighboring couch just focused on their drink.

The children of the d'Alarie family were known and celebrated for their artistic abilities amongst Autumn Court nobility, and only partially because of Marie d'Alarie's nighttime revels. A long lineage of masterpiece-makers, blessed by Danu herself. Their family, claimed to have performed at the Bricriu's ancient feast, to such adoration from the guests they were invited to join the many branches of the de Bricriu Sídhe family tree.

Malric had been known for his dance. Maura and Mavera for piano; Lusia for culinary abilities; Felme for painting; Neda and his poetry; Lillis for their acting; Persea, Larissa, and Reta for their singing voices. A family of artists, forced to bend to the beck and call of a mother who told them where to be, when to be, how to be, always asserting the dire importance of performing and taking joy in their gifts at every opportunity. Otherwise, if Danu didn't see their appreciation, the gifts might be taken away.

More realistically—if Marie d'Alarie didn't get enough attention from her affluent friends, she might wither and die like a flower in winter. And it worked, for years and years and years, until her children grew into adults and they finally realized, perhaps they were not chosen by the goddess at all. Perhaps it was only Marie's doing, to feed her own unquenchable thirst for commendation.

Of Marie's ten children, only four ever refused her demands and left to find their own lives to lead. To seek their own agency to claim. And each time, Marie d'Alarie simply found something to replace them. Some low fey from another court, another country; some human beantighe, some foundling who needed patronage; some innocent creature who didn't know what they agreed to, not knowing they would never get what they were offered, as Marie just promised to make them as perfect and beautiful as the child she'd lost... until that child inevitably returned, unprepared for the outside world. Unprepared to uphold their own agency, as if by their mother's own design. And then that replacement would simply... go somewhere else, no longer having any reason to stay once Marie's prodigal child returned back to where Danu had pinned their fate.

Of the four who left, three had returned to reclaim their fates. Some took longer than others, some even left and came back more than once—but they always returned.

Only one had not yet come crawling back—and he stood in the doorway facing his siblings, six months into his freedom. Freedom that came at a high cost. Freedom that was not as lavish and delightful and delicious as he always hoped it would be, but only Felme, Lusia, Neda would ever know that. His other three siblings who had left and come back, left and come back, who knew how impossible it was to find a new life outside the d'Alarie home without anything to start with. A secret they would keep so as to not accidentally influence any of the others from trying, one day. Anyone else might be more successful. And if they weren't— the secret group of those who'd failed would simply grow a little bit bigger until one finally did.

From the beginning, Malric knew his mother would

inevitably replace him, too. Especially once he was away long enough for her friends to ask questions, for Marie's excuses to fall flat. *Whatever happened to your son, the dancer, who used to perform at the revels for us? Is he still away at whatever-place-you-claim-he's-visiting? Will he be back home, soon? Oh how we miss getting shitfaced and crossfaded and sucking on each other in the forest clearing while someone dances for us like a trained dog...*

Malric knew it would happen, eventually. He always thought it would come as a relief to hear when it had been done, like proof he was succeeding in being free, proof he was causing his mother grief by keeping away for a long enough time—but instead, Malric felt only the sharp pinch of a thawed nail in his gut.

"Well, who are they, then?" he asked despite the discomfort. "Are they a fey? Some noble who's trained as long as I have? Do they hold up?"

Mavera and Maura exchanged another cat-like smile. Lillis snorted a curse into their tea. The triplets exchanged pale looks, as if sharing silent thoughts the same way Mavera and Maura seemingly could. Gods, Malric hated the clones the most.

"No, they're not a noble fey~" Mavera practically purred, trailing a finger over the rim of her teacup before taking a sip.

"A low fey, then," Malric insisted.

"Not exactly."

Malric scoffed through a bitter smile. "You're not telling me some beantighe dances as well as I do—"

"Not a beantighe," Mavera giggled. "Or even a foundling. But... still a human."

Malric watched her for a long time, waiting for her to laugh and admit the joke. But she didn't. She just waited, wearing her shit-eating smile like his discomfort was exactly what she needed to lift her spirits.

"What, from...? Across the veil?" he finally asked in disbelief. Another unexpected nail thawed in his stomach. "What is mother doing making deals with other-siders like it's the fucking dark ages?"

"You seem upset." Maura smiled. Malric narrowed his eyes in threat.

"Well—are they dancing at her revel right now? Maybe I'll go—"

"They're upstairs. In your bed."

Malric glanced up at the decorated copper ceiling, then back to his siblings.

"In my room?" he asked flatly.

"Mother doesn't let him go home in the dark." Mavera tapped a sugar spoon on the edge of her cup after pouring herself more tea. "He sleeps in your bed after every performance."

Another stab in Malric's stomach. Deeper, that time, feeling real enough that he almost touched to see if it broached skin. He scoffed again in disbelief, glanced up at the ceiling one more time, then rolled his eyes and turned for the stairs. He wanted to see it for himself.

The hallway of the second floor was dark, and he grabbed the single oil lamp sitting on the side table to light his way. Even with the newly-glamoured interior and unfamiliar wallpaper, he knew which room was his, counting in the back of his mind until he found the black-painted double doors and copper filigree doorknob.

He thought of all the things he would say to whoever was stupid enough to be on the other side—except that upon grabbing the knob, it burned his palm with the heat of iron, leaving decorative motifs printed in his skin. Hissing and reeling, he waved it back and forth to put out the invisible fire, before flattening his face against the crack between the doors to peek inside. It was strange to be on the opposite side looking in, when he'd spent so much of his life right on the other side searching outward.

Through the crack, illuminated by a line of light from his lamp, Malric spotted a bright red bundle of berries draped over the knobs on the other side. Rowan berries. A simple, protective door knob charm to keep fey like Malric out. Oh, gods—that human who took his place—were they an arid witch? Would Malric's mother really be so foolish as to bring an arid witch into the family house? To make a fey deal with them?

Malric was smug about it for exactly one moment—to think only a human witch could ever stand a chance at impressing like Malric did at the revels—but then his stomach turned over at the thought of his siblings. Were they safe? Had their mother thought it through at all?

Worse—the thought of someone, a total stranger, sleeping in Malric's bed... staying in his room, familiarizing themself with the interior like Malric once did, perhaps even with the personal things Malric left behind, in that place he'd always considered more a prison than a comfort... How ironic they would place a charm to keep fey out, when all Malric ever wanted was to get away. Perhaps they just didn't know any better; perhaps it was still too early in their deal with Marie to know how impossible it would be to leave when they realized what they'd done.

Growing more annoyed by the minute, Malric returned to the stairs and wobbled down them, fully prepared to get an ax from the tool shed and break the door down—but Lusia accosted him with snacks, first. Then drinks. Then tea, then conversation. As if they knew what he was about to do; as if, for some reason they wouldn't say, they didn't want Malric to break down the door and see the person who replaced him in dancing for his mother. Who would be receiving all of Malric's hard-earned praise, love, adoration... when they were only a human. An idiotic human, at that, to ever agree to any kind of deal made with Marie d'Alarie.

THE SOUND OF SOMETHING CLANGING AGAINST GLASS woke Malric from a fitful sleep, dreaming of claws and teeth and coppery fur, of the night he first left home, of the couch he cried on in the human world until the sun came up and he could finally sleep.

His head throbbed. He ran fingers back through his hair and

flinched against the sunlight. The charmed bracelet was gone from his wrist, having detached itself with the coming sun only to bang against the window in an effort to return to the club it originated from. Malric, meanwhile, blinked away exhaustion to clearly see the copper ceilings of the sitting room overhead, vaguely recalling how long he and his siblings gorged themselves on more alcohol and tea and gossip until he finally passed out. And they just left him there. Out in the open like that, without a blanket or anything. Maybe he shouldn't have been so insulted—the ensured drama of Marie spotting him would have definitely been something memorable.

Groaning, he finally sat up, rubbing his eyes before rolling to his feet to open the window and let the cuff out. It zipped into the sky, but he didn't linger to watch. He knew exactly what those charms looked like while flying away, and he really should focus more on his own escape, anyway.

Scratching the back of his neck and yawning, he frowned at the flowery burn on the palm of his hand from the charmed door-knob of his bedroom. He listened for any other noise in the house, deciding he had at least a few minutes to find something to eat before his mother or anyone else found him. Didn't Lusia say something about cooking for his mother's plaything?

In the kitchen, he drew water from the clanging faucet, throwing back a glass full enough that it spilled down his chin. He was in the process of chugging a second one when something suddenly rushed through the swinging door at his back, racing into the kitchen—and then right past him, out the back door in a flash of sky blue. Startled, Malric choked, coughing into the sink before glaring out the window at whoever had swept past him without even saying hello—

Strawberry-blonde hair, as long as a high fey's and pulled back into a ponytail whipping with every slam of their feet on the grass. A sky-blue sweatshirt, sleeves pushed up to their elbows, thick hood flopping in rhythm with their hair. Torn black jeans and Converse sneakers. An expensive-looking black backpack not fully cinched shut, the mouth of it gaping open with all the movement. From it, a flash of red tumbled out—and Malric realized with a jolt who they must be.

He pushed away from the sink and took off in chase. Out the back door, across the patio, onto the grassy courtyard—but by the time his bare feet were stained green from running, the human was already long gone. Breathing heavy, Malric lumbered to a stop as he reached the clump of dropped berries, frowning and kneeling down over it. Red rowan berries, tied off with a string of small bells and a little bag of coarse salt.

Using a stick, he lifted the witchy bundle, turning it back and forth all while denying what he felt to be curiosity. He truly could not understand how Marie could be so arrogant to think she could pull one over on a human witch—but then something caught his eye, and his heart drummed with heightened intrigue he could no longer deny.

The thumb-sized bag of salt was cinched shut with a warm yellow ribbon. The shade of yellow, specifically, made Malric's thoughts swirl, and he carefully thumbed over one end of the ribbon until finding what he was looking for. The embroidered initials *BV.*

"Bianca," he muttered in disbelief. *"Madame Ochre.* I thought you didn't fuck with high fey?"

Bianca Vásquez, one of only a few human folk-witches who knew Malric as a high fey, who Malric could trust implicitly, who was the first one to take him in after he left home. The witch who finally convinced him to leave at all. One who didn't formally practice arid magic—the opposite of opulent fey magic—and was instead trained in human charms, folk remedies, theology. She who wouldn't step foot near the veil, let alone a deal with Marie d'Alarie.

Marie's new dancer wasn't the witch, themself—but surely Bianca didn't know she was making charm bags for someone way in over their head with the fey, either. Surely...

No, no, *no*—Malric didn't care. He wasn't going to get

wrapped up in it. Bianca could make charms for whoever she wished, and Malric wouldn't say anything unless she was in direct danger, herself. He was not going to wrap his friend up in his mother's affairs. He was not going to wrap *himself* up in his mother's affairs. He was going to leave the d'Alarie estate, disappear for another three months, maybe hop-skip over to Europe for a while, maybe go check in on that cute guy he met in Korea a month earlier...

He was not going to waste energy on his replacement. On a stupid human who clearly made stupid deals and thought they could rely on folk charms to protect them.

It was their own fault, their own fate. Maybe Malric should be thanking them—without their agreement to dance for Marie d'Alarie, she might still hope Malric would return home one day, too.

It was not Malric's business. It was not his problem.

He was not going to think about it again.

But curiosity—no, not curiosity, just *concern*—enchanted him one last time, holding the rowan charm on the stick, wondering if there were any others left in his room that could be traced back to Bianca. Upon returning silently to his bedroom, though, he found no additional charms—only a tray of untouched food made by Lusia. Ruffled blankets. The window, hanging wide open. And—spots of bright blood on his pillow. Maybe from a nosebleed. Maybe from a split lip. Maybe just a papercut.

Malric wouldn't think about it.

He wouldn't think about why his replacement felt the need to set protection charms on the door while they slept in the first place, as Malric's siblings were no one to worry about. Especially if they were, apparently, extending kindness by preparing meals for them, or any of the other plethora of things they always did with someone's replacement. Ensuring they had everything they needed, while keeping their distance to ensure Marie didn't catch wind of kindness.

Malric wouldn't think about how, about *why* there were spots of fresh blood on his pillow. Or the way the dancer raced past him in the kitchen, then full-tilt into the woods, as if catching Malric's eye for even a moment terrified them.

Malric wouldn't think about it. He wouldn't think about a human who got themself into the same mess he himself fought for years to gather the courage to finally escape.

He wouldn't think about it—until it was the only thing he could think about at all.

2

MALRIC AND THE WITCH

There were innumerable things Malric preferred about the human world—the quick ways to find and talk to someone, easy-access public transportation, how soft and squishy humans were without true names to protect them against compelling enchantments... but at the same time, gods, there were a thousand other things Malric couldn't stand.

The crowded streets. The pollution. The honking of cars and squeaking brakes—of which had only just started finding popularity in the fey world, though they were only just dabbling with the rumbling, horn-honking nightmares that was a human Model-T of the early 1900s.

But there were a few things that, despite those dislikes, made up for it. Things that made the human world the place where Malric found the most peace while living his best life away from his family, in addition to the reason he was harder to find on that side. First and foremost—human beings, themselves, especially those in-tune with magic and the fey world, who were gods' gift to pathetic wanderers like fey lord Malric d'Alarie.

With two hot coffees and a blueberry scone in tow, Malric had to use his foot to push the elevator button, and then to knock on Bianca's door. He thought she would be excited to see him, since he was technically her biggest customer—but when the door opened, his friend's expression plummeted, just as quickly pinching into a scowl before she unleashed on him without warning.

"Absolutely *not!* Get out of here, Malric! I don't have time for you right now!" she cried, clumsily pushing him back into the hallway, then in the direction of the stairs as if the elevator wasn't an option. "Come back in the morning! No, not the morning—the afternoon! No—just wait until I text you!"

"What! Bianca!" Malric complained, digging his heels into the floor, though it didn't matter much as he easily had a foot of height over her. He tried to garner context by the way she looked —dark hair curled and pinned up nicely, smelling of expensive perfume, even donning sparkly earrings in the lobes Malric always forgot were even pierced—but his disdain of being rejected got in the way of logical thinking. "I brought coffee! To apologize for last time!"

"It's—7 P.M.! Get out of here! I have a date—coming over, damnit!"

"It won't take long! This is a matter of love, too—you know!"

"The hell does a fey prince know about *love!*"

"Plenty! And, damnit—stop calling me a prince! *You're going to get me in trouble!*"

At the end of the hallway, she nearly shoved him down the stairs, but Malric side-stepped out of the way at the last second. It nearly sent Bianca tumbling to her end, and Malric abandoned the drinks and snack in favor of saving her. Even though she was being rude as hell.

"Damnit—now I have to go change again. God, I hate you so much," Bianca moaned, her nice shirt donning a new coffee stain down the front.

Malric followed as she turned back to her door, apologizing with enough insistence that she sighed and invited him inside. Bianca knew she was the only human Malric would ever apologize to, it being a sign of a high fey's submission and all. Malric could get Bianca to do almost anything once he pathetically *apologized* or *thanked* her for something, the two biggest no-nos in human-fey interactions. Still, he tried not to take advantage of that trick too much, despite it coming in handy.

"How can I help?" he went on as soon as they were inside. "I know you're the witch here, but maybe I can hide that stain in your shirt—"

"Yes, but then the stain would still be there," Bianca grumbled, already stripping it off to rinse in the sink. Malric leaned against her counter in the cramped space, folding his arms politely to give her peace while scrubbing. Bianca's kitchen hadn't changed at all since the last time Malric visited, which might have only been a few weeks earlier, though it all blurred together so readily. It was easy to lose track of time moving between the veil, though the d'Alarie house's proximity to such a large tear between worlds at least meant the passage of time between human and fey wasn't so noticeable as upon journeying farther away would be.

While Bianca didn't live with excessive amounts of money, her work at the biochem-istrology-sciencology lab in the city certainly paid the bills, and more. Her apartment, a modest one-bedroom in downtown Seattle, certainly didn't come cheap, and didn't have a particularly fancy view from the balcony, but damn if it wasn't cozy. Most of that came from Bianca, herself, and her propensity for stubborn cleanliness, comfy blankets and pillows always in reach, hot water always pre-boiled in the kettle for tea, on top of the collection of vintage occult tapestries and prints framed on the walls, and the table and shelves of herbs and crystals for making charms.

"Who are you going on a date with?" he asked, trying to make nice. "Is it that same gal from the last time I was here?"

Malric had met Stella the night of her and Bianca's first date—when Stella hit him with her car while dropping Bianca off at home. Oh—why did that stir up something in his memory, making his stomach flutter? What color had her hoodie been, the one he got a bloody handprint on...? She was even a dancer at one of the local schools—was there any chance she knew his mother's newest toy?

Bianca threw him a scrunched look of annoyance, but he was far away in his own mind, staring at her, making possible connections like clipping a thousand barrettes into his hair one at a time.

"Yes, it's the same girl," she sighed. "We're going to a show, and this was the only nice shirt I had."

"That's not true," Malric encouraged, shrugging away from the counter. "I'll help. Come on. What kind of show are you going to? She's a dancer, right? Is she performing? Actually, now that you mention it—"

"I don't know. Her school's sponsoring some theater thing and she has free tickets," Bianca interrupted, knowing Malric's games, knowing how he could twist a conversation into asking her for something. Normally she played along a little more.

Malric's eyes sparkled, but definitely not for reasons Bianca would ever guess. *Stella, the dancer, and her hoodie, and Bianca's charm, with his mother's dancer... Stella might have introduced Bianca to them, then maybe they asked for the charm, and then Bianca would have made it for them, and if they went to the same school Stella did...*

Bianca noticed Malric's intense focus, scrunching her face further before throwing the damp shirt at him in annoyance.

"No! *No!*"

"You don't even know what I—!" Malric choked on a laugh.

"I don't care! Why are you even here!"

"I was hoping—"

But a knock came at the door, followed by a click of the latch, then a subtle squeak and the jingling of witch-bells on the knob as it was pushed open.

"Um... hello?" the guest called out, before poking her head inside. Malric knew it was Stella right away despite their first, and only, brief yet highly dramatic introduction. She was hard to miss with her grown-out, hot-pink butch-cut hair, intense blue eyes, and admittedly intimidating physique. Malric knew she had to dance demi-pointe by the size of her arms and thighs, alone. What else could she be throwing around other than little en-pointe partners?

Stella stretched her gaze into the kitchen, spotting Malric, then a shirtless Bianca. Her eyes narrowed back on him. "Bee? Everything... alright?"

"Hi," Malric said with a handsome, completely innocent smile. "Madame Ochre is not currently taking customers. She has a date, tonight."

Stella rolled her eyes like she still couldn't stand him. She must have remembered how Malric kicked in her front bumper. She surely never figured out who drunkenly poured sugar in her gas tank, though, to keep the bloodthirsty vehicle off the road for good.

"Is he coming with us?" she asked. "I only have tickets for you and me."

"He's not coming," Bianca said like a promise, sidling past Malric to peck Stella on the lips and mumble about getting a new top. Stella teased that she preferred Bianca the way she was, and Bianca flushed red before hurrying away. The moment she was gone, Stella turned right back to Malric with a look that edged on accusatory.

"What are you doing here?" she said. "Bianca told me she kicked you out."

"Um, actually..." Malric pointed at her, but hadn't thought of how to finish that sentence, yet. She raised an eyebrow, and he quickly corrected himself. "I was... I was wondering about that dance school you go to, actually. Artemis something or other, right?"

By the look on her face, *other* was correct. Malric tried to keep his polite smile. "I actually am a trained dancer, you know. Ballet, like you. I'm sure Bianca has already told you how good I am—"

"Yeah. She said you gave it up."

Malric frowned. Obviously Bianca would say something like

that, especially since Malric had never told her exactly what he traded in order to escape Marie's grasp once and for all. Maybe she thought the reason he never danced anymore really was because he hated it, not because...

His thoughts tangled in an instant, a reminder of how difficult it was to contextualize that term of the deal. Just like everything his mother did, being able to speak out loud about it was nigh-impossible, in order to make it even more difficult for her victims to seek help.

"Erm, I'm interested in visiting your campus to see what classes are like," Malric stretched the truth. *In order to see if my mother's new dancer attends any classes there...*

"Oh god," Stella sighed, running fingers back through her bright hair and glancing with a look of desperation toward Bianca's closed bedroom door.

Malric's smile just strained slightly in frustration. Stella was hugely muscular and could probably snap him in half over one leg, and her personality was equally guarded against people she didn't care for. That much was plain as day. And while Malric couldn't comprehend why anyone wouldn't like him, he also knew he'd have to play by her unwritten rules if he ever wanted to find out if his mother's dancer attended the same school as her—and if she, herself, had been the one to introduce Bianca to them.

"What show are you going to see?" Malric went on. "Bianca said it was at your school? Are there any more tickets available?"

"I don't think so. Opening night isn't until tomorrow, tonight's just for Artemisia students. And I only have tickets for me and Bianca, so—oh, thank god."

Bianca finally emerged from her room, looking shy as the blouse she wore was clearly too snug for her preference. But Stella, as if she hadn't just been having the most frustrating conversation ever, lit up and gasped dramatically, immediately spilling compliments all over Bianca like she was walking gold and jewels. Malric wasn't expecting it—just like he wasn't expecting the way his heart warmed at the sight of his friend blushing and smiling like she wasn't entirely sure Stella was real.

"I won't keep you," he said, despite there being a thousand more questions he wished to ask. He even bit back the nasty urge to compel Stella into giving him her own ticket so he could search for the dancer at the show—because seeing Bianca so flustered, holding Stella's hand, biting back a smile as Stella helped her into her coat... damnit. Alright. Malric could wait one more night.

"You can stay if you need to," Bianca offered as Stella opened the door for her. "But only if you behave, alright?"

"I always behave." Malric smiled. "Did you already put all my things away?"

"Oh—yeah, I did, sorry. They're in the laundry room, in a basket on the top shelf. But I just hung new witch bells and salted the door and windows, so you should be alright for a little bit. *Do not carve anything into my door again, Mal, I swear to god—*"

"Yes, *alright*." Malric put his hands up with a defensive pout. His eyes flickered to the door where his attempt at a protection sigil had been plastered and painted over multiple times on the back, though always bled through anyway.

"See you soon," Bianca wished him farewell, and Stella nudged her out the door. Malric let them go without any further trouble, though his insides stewed with the feeling of being left out. He nearly called out something sarcastic to get the last word, but paused as they chatted while waiting for the elevator.

"Do you want to stay over at my place, tonight?"

"Don't you have class in the morning?"

"Nah—they still haven't replaced Madame Cruz, so we get another week off. Come on, it'll be fun. And I won't have to worry about you and that guy."

"He and I never—"

"No, I mean—he's got terrible vibes. Really, really awful vibes. Like when someone hates cats."

Bianca laughed. She laughed in a way Malric had never heard

before, and it shoved all the urge to bother them down farther until he couldn't reach it.

"Sure, but only if Briar won't mind."

"I have a feeling he won't even make it back."

The elevator dinged, and the women stepped inside, cutting Malric off from whatever else came next. Still, he lingered by the door, gazing down at where the print from his bedroom door knob was still burned into his hand.

His thoughts turned slowly when he finally stepped away, churning in the background as he made himself at home in that one-bedroom apartment he'd come to know almost as well as the place he grew up across the veil.

Human folk magic consisted of a little bit of tangible human aridity, intangible fey opulence, and charms formed through manifestation and intention. Spread so thin across every sort of magic there was, it was far less saturated, far less effective than an arid-ogham circle carved into the floor might be—but Malric didn't need anything more powerful than simply diluting his scent. He only wished to go unnoticed.

Moving around as much as he did already helped with that, crashing on the couch of a human folk-witch helped even further, simply because Bianca's apartment was already filled to the brim with every sort of charm to protect against high fey, low fey, wild fey, as well as ghosts and things called *demons* and *evil spirits*. Malric always knew humans feared everything they couldn't understand, and in the beginning would tease Bianca about it endlessly, until she turned it right back around because high fey technically feared many of the same things, just with different names. Based in different theology and ideology and culture. Malric stopped teasing her after she threatened to manifest a Winter Court blue wraith to come and freeze his dreams while he slept.

Malric returned all of his tucked-away charms to the door, the windows, the floor, under the couch where he normally slept while staying over. Baubles brought from the fey world, baubles bought in the human world, hand-crafted magic objects made by Bianca, even burning a special herb-stuffed candle that made his nose and skin itch. All of it, just enough to disappear from anyone who wasn't specifically looking for him. Just enough to exist under the surface of the tide, just in case his mother came looking.

When the charms were set, Malric threw all of his favorite pillows and blankets on the couch. He collapsed into them, grabbing the charging phone he only used when staying with Bianca and opening the browser to do a search.

Artemisia ballet school.

The very first result was a job listing for a ballet dance instructor, at the very same Artemisia College of the Arts in Seattle, Washington. Malric's eyes skimmed over the link just long enough for a smile to cross his mouth.

"Oh."

3

MALRIC AND THE DANCER

Malric woke early the following morning. When Bianca still wasn't home, he sighed and mumbled a weary *'good for her'* to cover his envy.

It didn't take much to convince the dean of *Artemisia College of the Arts* that Malric was the exact person they needed to fill the vacancy posted on their website—even without any proper qualifications to show. Human ones, at least. It only took a little flick of Malric's voice into one of compelling intention to steer the dean in the right direction, after bypassing the application process entirely and arriving on-campus to speak to him directly. Malric still hadn't quite figured out how to compel over the phone—not to mention, he liked looking into someone's eyes the moment they realized his words were made of honey and impossible to resist.

Artemisia College of the Arts wasn't exactly what Malric was expecting. In his own ballet studies in the Summer Court, he lived on campus in a dormitory, the school was large enough to essentially be a town in itself, there were strict dress codes and uniforms and requirements of one's appearance. But at Artemisia—it was hardly any different from Bianca's alma mater, walkways crowded with exhausted-looking students of all backgrounds and clear degree goals. Artemisia was not only for dancers, but for painters, musicians, philosophers—and Malric couldn't help but smile, strangely enamored at the idea of how all of his siblings could have attended school together, instead of spread out across Alfidel and abroad. Perhaps that would have reduced the odds of their inevitable fates.

Locating the massive practice room shown to him the day prior, Malric hovered right outside with his gaudy quilted Versace bag thrown over one shoulder. If his mother's dancer, the one with the clearly expensively-made backpack, was anywhere nearby, they would certainly notice Malric's own.

Pulling off his sunglasses, he regarded the students lining the bars inside, dipping and bending and stretching to warm up for class. They mumbled to one another in annoyance, clearly having thought class would be canceled again that morning, only to get a last-second email that they were expected for attendance. Stella was amongst them, stretching in the back corner and towering over the peachy-blonde en pointe dancer alongside her. Malric ignored the complaints, just scanning their faces until he realized, that en pointe dancer with Stella, near the back of the room—

Ah. His heart skipped.

"Found you," he whispered, hooking the ear of his sunglasses over the collar of his shirt and pulling the glass door open.

The chatter died down as he entered, shoulders back and chin high, looking hot as all hell and knowing it. He'd done that on purpose, not wanting any reason he wouldn't be the center of attention on arrival. Normally that was standard for him—but that time, he had a slightly nobler cause.

Compared to the glamour he normally wore in the human world, that morning his auburn hair was a little shinier, his skin a little smoother and brighter, his eyes a little bit greener, his mouth a little more captivating, allowing a little more of his fey features to shine through and dazzle anyone who looked—all the while still glamouring other details so no one who knew his real face would be able to recognize him on sight. The small improvements seemed to work, a few students sinking out of their stretches, as if in awe. Whispers emerged as others stood up a little straighter, fixed their hair in the mirrors, elongated their legs like they wanted Malric to see. But the one person Malric was hoping to *really* notice his arrival, instead of swooning on sight, just frowned in the back corner and turned to say something to Stella. Stella, who hadn't noticed Malric enter either, turned to look—and her mouth dropped open in disbelief. Malric had to resist smirking and waving his fingers at her.

"Good morning," he greeted in his smoothest, most evocative tone. "I'm your new dance master, starting today. You can call me Mal."

The cries of adulation didn't come like he hoped, but he wouldn't let it bruise his ego. His eyes just flickered back to his mother's dancer in the far corner, who didn't give Mal a second glance, just focusing on their warming stretches. Compared to Stella's gaze of pure resentment, he might as well have been smiling and swooning, after all.

"I was told you have class prefects who help with instruction. Or, erm—were they called assistants? *Tee-Ays?* Where's mine?"

Stella grumbled something, then shrugged from the bar and approached. Malric grimaced, and it seemed to amuse her.

"*Enchanté,* Master Mal," she said, offering a girlish, sarcastic curtsy. "I am happy to take the lead on today's class so you can see how Madame Cruz ran it."

"... Yes, thank you. And your name is?"

"Kiss my ass," Stella muttered, before turning to address everyone else. Malric might come to secretly like Stella.

"Barre." Stella clapped her hands together like it clearly wasn't her first time taking charge. The room went from students to dolls in an instant, feet kicking off warmers, jumpers stripping to reveal shoulders underneath, bodies claiming spots perpendicular to the bars before dipping into a simultaneous routine. From a speaker system on the wall, a classical score played, and Stella snatched the attendance sheet from Malric. As she began marking names, he put his hand out, snatching it back.

"Will you introduce me?" he asked, knowing it would be the easiest way to learn his mother's dancer's name. Stella snatched the clipboard right back with a grunt, and they started at the first bar.

Human ballet and fey ballet weren't all that different in the grand scheme, though Malric had never stood in a human classroom, before. He'd been told such practices mimicked those of high fey, since high fey were the ones to introduce ballet to humans in the first place—but the students of Artemisia were nothing like Mal expected.

It was humans who originally split roles between *female* and *male,* but Artemisia seemed to follow the standards of fey ballet where *anatomy* actually played little role in whether a person danced demi or en pointe.

Meanwhile, fey had always followed strict rules for what was considered *beautiful* on stage, which humans mimicked on their own—but Artemisia had a swathe of diversity in that room alone, all gliding through steps with matching grace. Malric observed a broad range of heights, limb lengths, body structures, even one dancer who utilized a prosthetic leg and another whose partner supported them upright through the movements. Not in the way of a pas de deux, but existing in the same mind, sharing their intentions. It captivated him for a long time, before finally moving on to continue down the line.

Name after name, Stella introduced him. Every time, Malric nodded and smiled politely, unable to resist his eyes flickering constantly back to where his object of curiosity remained disinterested as ever. Something about it annoyed him. Something about it excited him. A part of him wanted to just stand there and be ignored while watching them in their natural element—but Stella kept moving him along, and he had his own part to play in the act.

While his critiques started small, it wasn't because he was hesitant to offer them—rather because he simply couldn't hold them back any longer.

Elongate your spine. Stop slouching so much. Your arm is stiff. Why are your legs trembling? Stop making that face. Next time wash your hair before coming to class. What in gods' names are you wearing? Your legs are very nice, but that doesn't make up for your bad posture...

All the way around the room, Malric's filter loosened as he found something to say to every single one of them. It filled him with a sort of adrenaline he hadn't felt since his own studies. Who would have thought he'd love criticizing humans so godsdamned much.

And then, the moment he'd been waiting for—he finally reached the back corner, where Marie's dancer was illuminated in a brief morning light through the tall windows. They didn't even look when Malric and Stella approached, though Malric knew he was finally impossible to ignore.

The dancer wore skin-tight leggings and a cropped white shirt, a golden body chain dangling from their neck and looping over their chest to cinch at the small of their back. It took everything in Malric not to grab and tug on it. The only thing distracting him from actually doing so, was realizing they wore a silver Vivienne Westwood bangle on the same hand holding the bar. Why did that feel like direct flirting?

For barely a moment, the dancer's blue-gray eyes flickered to meet his, and Malric had to resist smiling in satisfaction. They looked away again just as quickly, sweeping from third into fourth position. Malric couldn't resist watching their slender leg elongate and bend back into the curve of their waist; their extended arms, one hand forming a gentle fan in the air while the other clung to the bar with a slightly trembling grasp before dipping and gliding fingers over the floor...

"Your breaths are uneven," he said, unable to resist. "Exhale when you extend, inhale when you bring the movement back in again."

The dancer still didn't meet Malric's eyes, but his jaw twitched as it clenched. Malric, eager for any additional reaction at all, propped a hand against their stomach. They stiffened in an instant.

"Tighten these muscles, here. Then your other movements won't be so stiff."

Their jaw tightened more, then they jerked away. But instead of looking at Malric, they sought out Stella. Stella sighed.

"Master Mal, this is Mx. Briar Hunt."

"It's nice to meet you, Mx. Hunt—though you look a little unhappy to be here. Am I bothering you?"

"That's just my hangover." Briar smiled, though it was stubborn. Malric smirked in reply, silently accepting whatever challenge was being extended.

"Late night?"

They opened their mouth to answer, but met Stella's eyes again. Stella was giving them a look that said *reel it in*.

"Ah—were you at the opera show last night, too?" Malric baited instead.

"No."

"Oh—do you not like opera?"

Briar made another face. He shrugged and looked away.

Malric had to resist touching Briar's back again, instead letting his eyes linger. They were petite, nearly a foot shorter than he was, but with long limbs for their frame. Everything about Briar was narrow and compact, but at the same time, carved with strength given to someone who started dancing before their first growth spurt. Up close, Malric appreciated the color of their hair —like fallen leaves, not totally blonde, not completely red. Their eyes were like stormy winter clouds, like lake water reflecting a blue sky. Their features were just as delicate and lovely as the rest of them, even when narrowed in annoyance at him. He might have even preferred it like that—something about disgust excited him.

"Do you have any more critique for my form, Master Mal?"

Briar asked outright, avoiding Malric's eyes again. Malric wished he could see them, wished he could know exactly everything Briar was thinking.

"I'm sure I can find more if I continue watching," he answered coyly. A muscle twitched in Briar's cheek as he clearly withheld some comment he wished to make. Malric wanted to tease it out more than anything, touching Briar's back again and urging him to lean into arabesque. "I know you must be better than this stiff attempt at warming up, Mx. Hunt."

"I'm not," Briar practically growled, pulling away from Malric's hand. By then, other students noticed how Malric lingered with Briar, and what Malric could only call conspiratorial whispers emerged from distant mouths.

"Then I'll be sure to give you all the attention you need going forward," Malric gave him his most handsome smile.

Briar suddenly went still. Malric assumed he'd been stunned by Malric's beauty, but it was as if he'd gone catatonic. Stella attempted to nudge Malric forward, trying to encourage him to continue down the line. He almost protested—but something caught his attention out the window. A magpie on the railing, with white eyes and a sprig of rosemary in its beak. Around its neck, a bronze pendant dangled, resembling a fox mask.

Stella made a sound like she thought the bird was cute, but Briar petrified in an instant. He knew what that bird was, clearly —and so did Malric, though he wouldn't show it. No, he just threw his arms up at the bird, laughing as it squawked and flapped away.

But in the brief moment Malric turned his attention, Briar pulled away from the bar, gathered his things, and hurried from the room before anyone could stop him.

Malric watched him go, pinched by annoyance. Malric had followed Briar to the human world with the sole intention of seeing him up close, to see who exactly his mother thought to be perfect enough to replace him at her revels... but his first impression was disappointing. Had he made a mistake? Sought out the wrong person? But then why would his mother's magpie have come to make a summons?

Perhaps the only way to know for sure... was to attend one of his mother's revels and see for himself. To memorize the dancer who'd taken his place in the clearing, to entertain Marie d'Alarie's guests at her beck and call. He would risk his mother recognizing him, but... perhaps it might be worth it. Malric wanted to see who took his place in that cursed clearing, more than anything else.

4

MALRIC AND THE REVEL

Some Danian scholars, worshippers of Danu, claimed dance was what first teased the veil open—a human and a high fey turning, twisting, floating in tandem with one another without any awareness of the mirror's edge on the other side. And the veil, so enamored by the two of them individually, wanted to see what would happen if they danced hand in hand, instead. So desperate to witness such a lovely visage, it rent itself apart, and so aridity and opulence enmeshed for the first time.

Malric used to dance with the intention of rending open the veil for himself just as well. Both to find someone who could meet his ability as a dancer, but also to escape the pinching, prodding, insufferable demands of his mother, temptress of all nobility and purveyor of all things artistic. With ten children under her belt, it should have been easy for Malric to disappear within the tide of his siblings—but too badly had he wanted to find his partner, through the veil or otherwise, that he accidentally caught the eye of his own mother and came to regret it even centuries later.

It wasn't technically his first time attending one of Marie's revels as an audience member—his siblings had been called to perform on occasion depending on if a special guest attended, or if Marie simply felt compelled to show them off—but that was the first time Malric would be one of those wearing a mask. It was surreal, and a little nauseating, to claim one of the fox masks dangling from the array of ribbons on the edge of the clearing, hanging from the thick branches overhead. Pulling it over his face, he fell into instant anonymity just like every other attendee who donned the same. Still, he was sure to glamour his voice, just in case there was any reason to speak. He might go unrecognized behind the mask, but his voice would sell his secret in an instant.

He wore something subtle enough to not stand out, decorated enough to not look out of place. His golden-brown vest was embroidered with stalks of wheat, cinched over a ruffled ochre blouse with bronze buttons down the high collar. It would have been easy enough to glamour something to wear—but he hadn't been invited to a formal event worthy of such dolling-up in a long time, so he took advantage of the things he had but hadn't been able to enjoy. Ah—perhaps *invited* wasn't the proper term for why he was seated at a d'Alarie revel, donning a fox mask. But then again, no one was ever *invited* to the revels—nothing with so much wine, gossip, and debauchery ever left any kind of paper trail of its existence.

He found a place to recline. His nest of pillows and blankets wasn't right in the center with the best view—but he didn't humble himself to sitting on the sidelines, either. He wanted to see the dancer up close. He wanted to know if it really was Briar Hunt whom he'd seen in the practice room earlier that morning. A part of him was still skeptical.

But that night in the revel clearing, with its circle of cushions and blankets, cakes and candies, standing candles and lanterns illuminating the darkness, air rich with the smell of rosemary and mint—he witnessed Briar Hunt emerge from the edge of the trees, demure and breathtaking even as they simply took their place in the grass, string instruments swelling to life off to the side of the audience.

Just like in the dance studio, their hair was the color of early fall leaves in the morning. Malric's eyes lingered too long on their waist, hands tingling as he recalled how it felt to touch his palm to the small of their back and feel the tensing muscles hidden there. He watched their legs, how the points of their toes never faltered while dancing gracefully over the expanse of the forest clearing. They performed with the grace of a high fey, making love to the orchestral music swelling between the trees like someone begging Danu for fresh water in the desert. Briar Hunt moved with the elegance of water over moss, of a beantighe's chiffon veil caught on a breath of wind. And Malric was instantly enchanted, no differently than if the human had gripped his true name and twisted it into a sensual bow around his throat.

It was no wonder his mother chose them.

As the only thing at the fete not wearing a fox mask, eyes lingered on Briar's pretty face like wild creatures eyeing a rabbit. They wore a sheer bodice adorned with leaves sprawling over their chest and stomach, spilling into a knee-length skirt made of more threaded greenery and layers of flowing fabric. Malric knew it was the ensemble of a fey ballet—*Gairdín an Tseilg, Garden of the Hunter*—and he was even more impressed that they knew the dance. No—did they? Or did whatever glamoured their outfit also glamour their thoughts, to pretend they were familiar? If anyone attempted to interrupt before Malric was satisfied, until the end of eternity—he would turn their bodies inside out to feed to the knots of the trees.

But even eternity would have come too soon, and would have been as grating as the dancer's natural end. Music swelled before tumbling, the third act of the brief tale told, falling, falling, falling until trailing off as Briar gazed longingly up at the sky with arms extended. Awaiting their applause, their praise. Breathing heavily, but hardly showing it on their calm face. Malric was enamored even by the way their chest rose and fell, accentuating the silhouette of their shoulders and waist. He recalled how that moment always felt—the relief of being finished, the anticipation of what would come next.

How strange, to be on the opposite side of that feeling.

It was no wonder at all why Marie d'Alarie, collector of beautiful things, had chosen Briar Hunt to take Malric's place.

And Malric—would give that human anything. Anything at all. A witch, after all—one who used their body to enchant, compel, steal the hearts and words of every single magical thing that witnessed them. In all of his wealth and power and affluence, would Malric ever have enough to own them?

Briar finally bowed, keeping his eyes low, never smiling or stepping away from the conclusive spot of grass beneath their feet. He wasn't given a chance to flee, before three high fey leapt from the audience and rushed to him, adoring him, fawning over him, then pulling him every which way by the arms. Malric knew how that felt, too. He understood the same expression Briar wore after taking that final bow—empty, hollow, disappearing from one's own body just to survive the next hour until the admirers would grow bored and one could make their escape. Never once realizing exactly how breathtaking they'd been, as there was no joy in performing at one of Marie's woodland revels.

Malric never thought anyone else would understand that feeling—but watching Briar's face, it was clear. Malric took a sip from his wine, clutching a fistful of the pillow beneath his hand as unexpected emotions overwhelmed him.

He remained where he was as Briar was roughly won over by one of the pleading, doting fey ladies, stumbling over his feet on the flattened grass toward a nest of pillows on the edge of the clearing. Malric just watched; it was all he could do. He just watched as they practically pinned Briar against the pillows, cooing over him, pinching his ears and feeding him fruits, pouring wine into his mouth despite his brief attempts to turn away. Malric held his breath as one of them grabbed Briar's face, arching his head back and forcing him to drink until he choked.

Malric had no reason to stay longer, but he couldn't bring himself to leave. Even if he wouldn't be the one to walk Briar home, or back to the veil, or to the d'Alarie estate if that was where he truly slept after performing like his siblings claimed—

Malric simply couldn't bring himself to leave Briar alone, even if there was nothing he could do. Even once the audience interest waned and Briar finally managed to stumble away, Malric just watched over the rim of his glass.

Briar would at least make it home for the night—but then Malric noticed a handful of other fox masks turn in the direction the dancer had escaped. Turned, then hesitated, then rose to their feet to follow. Four of them, heads bowed and moving carefully as to not draw attention to themselves.

Finishing his glass of wine, Malric tossed it away and moved with all the silence of the mask over his features and the opulence in his blood. Stepping from the fray into the trees, he kept to the side of where the others had entered, searching for movement in the darkness.

"Come on, little bird—open your mouth. Have a taste. You'll feel much better—after eating some of this special fruit."

"You stitched up your ears—after all the work we went to trying to fix them?"

"Why won't you tell us your name? Would you really rather us compel you into answering?"

"Careful—*hrk!*"

Malric leaned around a tree at the sound of grunting, followed by the thud of a body hitting the earth—only to bite back a sound of surprise to find the willowy rosefinch with a fist extended, having just socked one of the high fey in the mouth. They were only half dressed, jeans hanging open over their stomach as if interrupted right before they could button them. Their bare chest was flushed from the exertion of the dance, rising and falling with heavy breaths and shiny with sweat.

Time moved slowly as the others grabbed the dancer, shoving him against a tree and pinning him into the bark as he thrashed and bit, snarling and hissing, but never uttering a single word. One of them grabbed his jaw just like in the clearing, prying their mouth open to shove a fairy-pink strawberry inside. The human just spit it back in their face.

The fey lord shoved his mask away in a rage, reeling his hand back to strike the dancer in rebuttal—but Malric leapt from his hiding place, grabbing the lord's wrist and twisting it backward. The fey lord yelped, crying out and turning to grapple at Malric for mercy. Malric just met his eyes—then bent his hand back farther until the bone snapped.

The lord shrieked, knees buckling, begging Malric to let him go, to show mercy, to not tear it off—but Malric barely heard him, realizing just then the dancer was already taking off into the woods.

"Wait!" he called on impulse, throwing his victim away and moving in chase. At the last second, Malric spotted Briar's sneakers abandoned in the dirt, cursing and scooping them up in his hurry.

After following for what felt like an eternity, eventually even the dancer grew too tired to keep running, resorting to a rapid walk on the path, instead. They constantly threw a look over their shoulder to where Malric followed a dozen feet back, lifting their shoes into view.

"You should really put these on!" Malric called out. "I'm not gonna bother you, I promise!"

But the dancer never stopped. Never even slowed down. Just hurried ahead, constantly glancing over their shoulder, clinging to their backpack like they were afraid Malric was going to rob them.

"Why don't you—!" But Malric was cut off when someone suddenly came hollering from the trees, tackling him to the ground and attempting to rip his mask off. Malric cursed, grunting and kicking them in the stomach, sending his attacker rocketing back into the brush with a pathetic whimper. Groaning, Malric lifted his head again to search for Briar Hunt—but the bird was long gone.

Frowning down at the shoes in his hand, Malric's mind raced. Behind him, the revel continued stronger than ever, guests riding the high of witnessing something so beautiful perform in the clearing. Malric understood. Malric understood everything. His own heart pounded when he thought about it—but for more reasons than just Briar's talent. Because of all the things Malric saw of himself in the human whose wings had been clipped, forced to dance on the whims of Marie d'Alarie. Just like he once had.

Sighing, Malric knelt down to tuck Briar's shoes into the grass alongside the path he would take back home in the morning. It wasn't ideal, but he would at least find them before passing back through the veil. Malric's ears rang the whole time, unable to step away from the hiding place at first. Just staring at those shoes, dirty with mud and grass. Recalling how Briar was only half-dressed as those fey lords bothered him. How he looked so worried as Malric followed behind him.

Malric always knew his mother would find someone to replace him at her revels—but he never expected such an intense guilt to come the moment he put a name and face to that reality.

5

BRIAR

Briar couldn't move his hands. No—he couldn't move any part of his body at all. Dangling off the ground, arms extended over his head, legs pinned together as if his bones had fused into a singular line, he knew that view. Gazing over the clearing where he was forced to dance on the fey lady's demand, always summoned by the same magpie who would tap on Briar's window early in the morning, or follow him home late at night.

Nearly perfect.

I'll do better next time.

He opened his mouth from his place in the sky to announce it, even though he wouldn't see the face of who he intended it for in the darkness—but when he attempted to speak, there were no words, only a tangle of something solid and creeping up the back of his throat. Choking him, tickling the inside of his windpipe until he retched backward, coughing and coughing until spit dripped from his mouth.

No—not spit. It was cloudy and golden-tinged. It was sticky and stretched in long strings. And, captured within it, writhing spiders, leaves, butterflies, and at the tail end of the suffocating blob, an entire robin strangled by the syrupy liquid emerged from the back of Briar's throat and dangled from his lips with twisted wings and *disrupted feathers. He couldn't even scream—there was too much growth claiming the inside of his lungs to inhale at all.*

BRIAR WOKE WITH A GASP, INHALING SO ROUGHLY HIS back arched and his eyes bulged in a rush of panic. Collapsing back to the bed, he clutched his chest, then his throat between the subsequent hyperventilation. He squeezed his eyes closed and blinked away tears of horror as the dream quietly unhooked itself and drifted away. Just like it always did. The same dream, but painted with different brushes. The same dream like a theatrical performance, but the lines changed every night, always reflecting something that came any time before closing his eyes.

But because he was so used to those nightmares, he knew it would pass quickly. The knot of emotions would pass quickly, within only a few minutes. He only needed to close his eyes and breathe. Relax. Return to his body and the real world.

Except he wasn't in the real world. Well, no—he was, but at the same time—he might as well have not existed at all.

He would never get used to waking up in that bed that wasn't his. The one given to him, but wasn't his. And never would be, if he could help it. He wasn't sure how long that would last, though, since it was quickly becoming the only place he could actually get a good night's rest. How ironic.

That fey lord's bedroom, in the fey world, in some place called the Fall Court—no, the Autumn Court. Briar couldn't forget the fit the fey lady threw when he called it the *Fall Court* that one time.

Sitting up, Briar groaned at the throb in his sore muscles. Stretching his arms over his head, he glanced around the room to see if anything had been disturbed while he slept, just like every other morning. Nothing was astray. Nothing was touched. The barricade he put up against the double doors remained right where he left it, having to resort to drastic measures since losing his rowan berry charm. He wouldn't take any risks.

Climbing from the bed that was far too plush, far too comfortable, Briar took one step on the floor—and ate shit, hitting the hardwood with an embarrassing yelp of surprise. Groaning, he rubbed the back of his head before stretching out his leg to observe the swollen joint of his ankle, recalling exactly what had happened the night before. How he'd twisted the already-angry injury in the clearing, then was forced to run barefoot back to the house after those fey bastards accosted him like they always did after a dance.

"Fuck," he whispered like a curse, considering massaging blood back into the swollen joint, only to hiss and pull his hand away in regret. Resentment grew like a rose in his chest.

Yanking the borrowed nightshirt off over his head, Briar hobbled in his underwear to his clothes piled at the foot of the bed. Pulling them on, they smelled of rosemary and sweat, just like every other time. Running fingers through his hair, it was tangled and littered with pine needles and fern drops, just like every other time. Scraping nails down the side of his neck, the gold-chain necklace still encompassed his throat, just like every other time. And, just like every other time, he tried to yank it off. To surprise it, thinking it might actually work that time—but the gold was stronger than it looked. That necklace that shackled him to the fey lady, to their agreement, that glamoured his ensembles every time he crossed into the revel clearing, which also somehow injected choreography into his mind without consciously realizing it. As if glamouring his memories, his body, to move to music he'd never heard before. Every time he was forced to dance a fey ballet he didn't know, he felt like clawing off all his skin right afterward.

Digging the crunched pack of cigarettes from his jacket pocket, Briar lit one while pulling the furniture away from the wall. His sore feet throbbed as he walked on them, cursing himself for leaving his shoes behind. Would he really have to go all the way home on the ferry without any goddamn shoes on? Maybe it could be worse. God, it could always be worse. He really should stop jinxing himself like that.

But it was too late—the universe took the jinx and formed his nightmare from wax right on the other side. The fey lady stood waiting for him the moment he opened the doors to leave, and Briar nearly screamed at the sight of her.

Just like every other time she stood before him, the woman appeared as the queen of the wilis, Myrtha, from Giselle. That ballet that had been Briar's tipping point, where she found him crying backstage after the final curtain. Still in his white tutu and pointe shoes. Approaching him like the queen, the forest queen of the dead, offering him the only thing he'd ever wanted. Something so simple—but terrible, he later learned. *I want to dance for someone beautiful.*

I can make you perfect. I can make you the most beautiful thing on two legs...

"Good morning," she smiled, alluring and beautiful just like all the other high fey Briar had had the misfortune of crossing paths with during his five months of hell. There was something so surreal about her bright red hair brushed into a romantic bun; her smooth, tan skin decorated with the same thick stage makeup he recognized of the performance costume, making her green eyes stand out; that perfect replica of Queen Myrtha's tutu framing her curvy silhouette. Mature in appearance, but at the same time, far too young to apparently be a mother of so many adult children. Fey magic, fey glamours—perhaps it was the same trick Briar's necklace used to glamour him in performance outfits at every revel.

The fey lady plucked the cigarette dangling from his mouth, dragging it down to ash on her own lips without breaking eye-contact. "I thought you might join me for breakfast."

Briar wanted to scream at her to *fuck all the way off*—but he knew better than to use that language.

"I should be getting home," he said with a painfully-forced polite smile. "I appreciate your offer, my lady. I look forward to dancing for you again, next—"

"If you will not dine with me, then still hear what I meant to say," she said, stopping him short as he attempted to slide past her. He halted where he stood, but didn't meet her eyes, just staring at the floor. Waiting. Knowing what she was going to say. "I see how much you are struggling, Gentle Briar. A reminder—my offer still stands. Bring me someone to take your place, and I'll offer your reward despite failing to offer me mine. I will consider our deal realized and complete."

Briar let the words linger. He still didn't look at her, though he eventually nodded before hurrying away. That bitch. That bitch. God, he hated her so much.

She offered it with that same condescending smile as all the times previous, as if she knew exactly what Briar actually heard when she said them. *Loser. Failure. Pathetic. Incompetent. A poor excuse for a dancer. Gods help you if my son ever comes to witness you dance; he would surely be so insulted, he would snap both your legs in two.*

"I'd like to see him try," Briar muttered as soon as he escaped the clutches of that terrible, horrible, miserable house. Even barefoot, even limping slightly with every hurried step, it was all better than remaining in those walls for even a moment longer.

But then something caught his eye as he reached the mouth of the trail into the woods, and for the first time ever, he stopped to look. He barked a laugh, pushing hair from his eyes with a sigh. His dirty sneakers, hidden beneath a bush. Waiting for him.

It was dangerous to accept gifts from the fey—but god knew, Briar was already too deep in the shit to care about what else could possibly happen to him. He kicked the sneakers on with no fear.

Down the woodland path, he passed the revel clearing empty of any sign of the previous night's party, just like every other time. And just like every other time, Briar couldn't escape that sinking anxiety that he only ever imagined dancing for them. Only ever imagined the fox faces watching him, adoring him, complimenting him—

He grabbed his bandaged ear, squeaking when it hurt worse

than he expected. It was definitely real. It was all real. He wasn't imagining anything.

Crossing through the veil was like getting kicked in the chest, but Briar was beginning to love the feeling. It meant he was back in the real world where things made sense. Still, every time he successfully scrounged around well enough to find that trick of the light, like a shimmering mirage floating as high as he was tall, he worried passing through would launch him somewhere else, entirely. Every time he felt the chill of Possession Sound on the other side, he breathed a deep sigh of relief.

That time, too, he emerged on the very edge of the Saratoga Woods of Whidbey Island. Right on the beach, always within reach of where he entered. Always going through in the same place, always emerging slightly off to the side with no way to anticipate where or how far. He forced himself to avoid thinking about the implications of that, too. He lost enough sleep considering everything else, he didn't need to also worry about how, one day, he might emerge somewhere he didn't know at all.

He didn't care. He couldn't afford to care. Briar just wanted to get the hell home again.

Limping up the beach, he found his bike buried beneath the same bushes he always hid it under. Tightening the straps of his backpack, he grabbed the bike and dragged it through the undergrowth up to the road, kicking his sore ankle over the seat and pushing off to make the three mile journey along the coast toward the Clinton ferry. There were tears in his eyes by the time the familiar lights came into view, both from the cold and his goddamn ankle, but he just bit back the pain and cursed that fey bitch to hell the entire time. As always, it only sort of helped.

Sweeping in right as the ferry was boarding, Briar said hello to the same ferry supervisor he always said hello to at the asscrack of dawn, never asking questions or even showing an ounce of curiosity about what could have possibly gotten Briar so grouchy, dirty, bruised up over night.

God*damn* Briar was tired.

. . .

BACK ON LAND, HE FINISHED OFF ANOTHER CIGARETTE by the time the bus came, staring straight ahead the entire time he waited because he was sure there was a face twisting in the bark of a sidewalk tree and he really didn't want to know. Especially not after his dream the night before, especially when he knew acknowledging wild fairy things in the real world only invited more to harass him as if they could smell the fey deal on him. As if they could smell the veil between worlds on him, always bothering him most right when he passed back home again. He learned quickly to just pretend they didn't exist at all. Hopefully the thing living in his room and keeping him awake every night had finally moved on, too.

Claiming a seat on the bus, he had just enough battery on his phone left to let Stella know he was on his way home and to wait for him before leaving for class. She sent him back a scolding text asking where he'd been, how worried she'd been, how he better move his ass or else they would be late, and he just sent back a smiling angel emoji before closing his eyes and resting his head against the seat.

His ankle throbbed. His entire being throbbed with an ache he couldn't shake off. The fey lady's words refused to leave him alone.

My offer still stands. Bring me someone to take your place, and you will never have to dance for me again.

It would mean giving up. It would be failing. It would mean admitting he wasn't, and never would be, perfect like she wished. It should have been so simple. It should have been easy. Briar had no idea the first time he made that deal with her.

Sneaking another cigarette in the ferry bathroom, blowing smoke through a crack in the window, Briar considered how offering another sacrificial pig might save him. Perhaps someone else would be able to offer the fey lady what she wanted, because clearly Briar couldn't. After five months of torture, if he hadn't already, he wouldn't in the future.

Still, the thought of handing someone over to take his place dancing in the revel made his heart squeeze. He didn't know if it stemmed from guilt, or shame, or perhaps just—the way he felt like he deserved it, in a way. He deserved to suffer, to be miserable, to be in pain, to spend the rest of his stupid life striving for perfection because that really was what he needed to get what he wanted. To get the attention of the one person he'd always wanted to get it from.

Perhaps Briar deserved to suffer a little longer when he was so willing to throw his life away for something so fucking silly.

6

BRIAR AND THE WIRRY-COW

Briar made it back to the apartment with just enough time to spare for a lightning-quick shower and a sweep of blush to give color to his cheeks, kicking his feet into clean pants and a plain shirt. Stella harped on him the entire time, standing in the doorway to his room with her arms crossed like a disappointed older sister, but Briar just smiled and fluttered his eyelashes innocently. She assumed he'd gone drinking and hooked up with someone—which wasn't completely out of the realm of possibility, especially in those previous few months. It was less embarrassing than the truth, at least. *Who, me? Going home with a random stranger? Not keeping track of how many drinks I had at the club? I know, I know, I'm so irresponsible, but it could always be worse, right? I could have sold my soul to a fey she-wolf who gets in the way of getting laid...*

It normally didn't, but Briar was quickly reaching his breaking point. And upon reaching a breaking point, there was nothing more satisfying than intentional self-destruction to bring that rock-bottom hurtling closer until finally smashing into the ground. Once he hit the bottom, there was nowhere else to go but up, right? Things would get better once he hit his lowest. He just had to get there as fast as possible. He was tired of the descent, already.

But the plummet remained endless when he realized the thing living in his room had not, in fact, moved on. Despite avoiding his own bed for three days straight between sleeping at the fey lady's house or sleeping in a stranger's bed after a late night drinking. Briar was exhausted. Briar wanted a chance to lay down on his own goddamned pillows without his dresser drawers rumbling then slamming, curtains thrashing around, bed sheets tangling then pulling off his body. Had he not been ankle-deep in fairy bullshit already, he might have attributed it to a ghost, but a ghost would have been better. At least then he would know the source was semi-human. Like it could be reasoned with. It gave him quite the new perspective on ancient people trying to make sense of the afterlife, though.

AFTER DOING HIS BEST TO ATTEND CLASSES THAT afternoon—most of them, at least, allowing himself to be picky because his mood could not actually be worse—Briar finally, *finally* gave in and sought out Stella's new girlfriend for help. Again.

The first time he and Bianca met, it was when he'd gone with Stella to pick her up from her apartment. After learning she had certain skills in certain protection-charm-related-acts, and after a few long, *long* days of trying to resist, he meekly sent her a formal email asking if she could make a special charm just for him—that same one he lost in the fey world only a few days prior. At least Briar wouldn't be a *total* stranger showing up at 9PM on a weeknight.

Still, he hesitated outside her door with a hovering fist, trying to fight back the embarrassment of what he was about to do, period. In his mouth, a cigarette burned on the last of its life, nicotine swirling in his blood in an attempt to falsify confidence. He needed it to admit to someone else that he thought there was a ghost-fairy-poltergeist creature keeping him up at night. What if Bianca asked more questions? What if she tried to dig into how Briar knew as much as he did about fairy bullshit at all? And he got all tongue-tied just like every other time trying to explain why he was gone all night, or had to suddenly cancel plans, because the fey lady was demanding a show?

It ended up not mattering, because the elevator at the end of the hallway suddenly dinged, and two people walked out arguing about something while carrying paper bags of groceries. Briar turned quickly, even more embarrassed at the thought of being spotted hovering outside a random apartment door—but then he realized he recognized the shorter, curvier one approaching on the left. She recognized him, too, looking surprised before smiling. But Briar was distracted by the man alongside her. Wasn't that... the new dance instructor? Damnit—what was his name again?

The man met Briar's eyes with initial annoyance, before stopping in his tracks and staring, unblinking, at where they loitered outside Bianca's apartment door. Briar looked away in a flash, unsure how to handle that look of surprise on the man's face. *Damnit, damnit, what was his name again??* He really had been a little bit drunk that first day of class, and then he skipped the second class that morning—and Briar couldn't remember anything except that he hated the guy, though everyone else in his class thought he was super hot and intimidating, for some reason.

Ah, no—maybe not *for some reason*. It was actually extremely obvious.

"Hi, Briar," Bianca greeted on approach, clearly restraining a soft panic. "Is everything alright? Is Stella—?"

"Stella's fine," Briar insisted right away, putting his hands up. "Um... I'm actually... She actually doesn't know I'm here..."

He looked at the floor, then back to the man still paralyzed a few steps behind Bianca, like he didn't quite know how to react to Briar being there, either. Briar just looked back to the witch whose expression held way too much gentleness for someone arriving at her doorstep so late at night.

"I... I was hoping... you could help me, again. Uh, I think there's a... a ghost, or... some kind of fairy thing... haunting my room. Uh, maybe you could make me another charm like the one last time...? Erm, and maybe another one of those, too, since I lost it..."

"Oh!" Bianca and the man exclaimed at the same time, making Briar jump. Bianca shoved her bags into the man's arms, then grabbed Briar's hand, looking at him like a kicked puppy she wanted to wrap up in a blanket. "Of course! Please, come inside, I'm happy to help however I can."

"Thanks," Briar offered a tiny nod, picking at his nail beds like he always did. He should have known to wear the spinner ring. He wondered if Bianca would let him smoke in her apartment.

Bianca opened the door with a familiar clash of bells on the opposite side, inviting Briar to follow. Briar did, but had to step back out of the way just as quickly as Bianca swept past him to steal the bags from Mal still in the hallway.

"*Mal!*" Briar exclaimed without thinking, only for his face to flare hot as Master Mal grinned like a goddamn idiot in reply. Bianca just nudged Mal back out the door again, though, before closing it and locking him out. She gave Briar a polite smile as Mal pounded on the door and complained, before patting Briar's fidgeting tangle of hands in reassurance.

"He'll be alright. He knows I don't let him hang out when doing private work. Come on, I'll make you some tea."

BRIAR ALREADY KNEW WHY STELLA LIKED BIANCA SO much, but was continually reminded whenever he sat in her apartment. Bianca was inherently *warm*, and inviting, and something about her made him want to burst into tears and spill everything that'd ever hurt him in his entire life. As if revealing all of his worst memories would allow her to sweep them away like some sort of comforting fairy godmother.

But Bianca was also a grad student studying biochemistry or

biobiology or bio-geometry-astrology-medicine-ology—Whatever it was, it was proof she was smarter than Briar could ever imagine to be. But even when Briar asked her about it, she never talked like she thought so, herself. She didn't even hold back on using big, science-y words like she was talking to a baby. She used all the big words but gave enough context that he sort of understood what she was going on about, and even that in itself made him feel like she was his new best friend, too. He would never forget their first conversation, burned into his memory the exact moment he knew she was safe for his best friend to date:

"Do you dance as well?" he'd asked.

"Oh, definitely not. I'm more of a pipettes and petri dish kind of girl."

"Very cool. I like those little drinks you get at Club Baxter that come in test tubes, which means we have a lot in common..."

A witch and a biochemist who made perfectly-brewed tea and pillowy pumpkin cookies. Stella really lucked out.

Bianca eventually settled on *wirry-cow* for the thing harassing Briar at night, interviewing him like a doctor trying to get a diagnosis for some unknown ailment. She seemed most perplexed when Briar described the creature's tenacity, even when he stayed away for days at a time; according to her, his absence should have starved the thing out and forced it to move on. Briar tried not to let it get to him. He forced himself to stay silent about the fey lady, though knew there had to be some kind of connection. That veil-stink that was all over him all the time, that he never seemed to be able to wash off.

The witch gathered him a little velvet bag of coarse rock salt, an iron horseshoe, and a very impressive clear quartz cluster as heavy as a honeydew. With it, she wrote instructions on a little recipe card before pausing and including a few bags of sleepytime tea, lavender incense, and finally, a replacement doorknob charm made of rowan and salt like the one he'd lost.

"Wow," Briar croaked once the gift box was handed to him. "How much do I owe you?"

She smiled, thanked him, and shook her head at his offer of payment—but then paused, biting her lip before glancing back to the door where a persistently needy Master Mal whined and begged on the other side.

"Actually..." She mumbled, then sighed. "Let me just... get a second opinion, just in case. Brace yourself."

"Huh?" Briar asked, but she was already unlocking the door and poking her head out. She and Mal exchanged a few words that sounded something like *"What name are you using?"* before the pathetic man was let inside. He smiled in some sort of mysterious self-satisfaction Briar didn't even want to try and understand, though it felt in-character considering how he'd acted during their first class together.

"You weren't in class this morning," Mal said in way of greeting. Bianca gave him a strange look, but Briar was too busy locked in a staring contest with Master Mal in front of him.

"So... are you a witch too, or something?" he asked flatly.

"Not a folk-witch exactly, no, but—I taught Bianca everything she knows."

"Oh," Briar said, raising an eyebrow at the *'folk-witch'* distinction, wondering why it was made at all. "What, so you're a wiccan or something?"

"A what?"

But Bianca elbowed Mal in the side before he could say anything else, like a restart button. Mal cleared his throat, finally shirking off his thick wool jacket and draping it over the back of the closest chair. Briar realized it was Prada, and was weirdly impressed—until he realized the white, blocky pullover he wore underneath was Supreme.

"So, you have a wirry-cow problem, Briar?" Mal asked, stepping forward and rifling through Briar's box of things. Briar might have pulled away, had he not been immediately captured by Mal's cologne.

"Is that Chanel?" he mumbled, and Mal's pretty hazel eyes

lifted to meet his. He glanced down at his sweater, before his mouth quirked into an uneven smile.

"Actually, it's Supreme."

"... I meant your cologne."

"Oh. I'm impressed," Mal laughed, tapping the side of his nose. Briar blushed without knowing why. He looked away as Mal continued sifting through his witch offerings.

"Those fuckers really are the worst," Mal went on, back to the wirry-cow. Briar noticed how he barely glanced inside the box longer than he had to, though, eyes spilling up Briar's arms, over his own Givenchy sweatshirt under his jacket, then lingering at the base of his throat all while speaking. "Horseshoe, nice. Salt, quartz, good, good, anti-boggart precautions should work just fine... Ah, you could also try inviting brownies in, they'll chase it out while keeping your room clean for you. Technically wirry-cows are just nastier versions of boggarts, which are just brownies who became naughty after feeling unappreciated, so you'll have to make sure you reward the next ones a little better..."

Briar made a face like Mal was out of his mind.

"What for?" he asked.

"What?"

"That face. What's that face for?"

"Oh..." Briar huffed, turning away again. He'd never met anyone who flustered him so goddamned much in so little time. "I don't know, I'm just... not used to all of this, I guess..."

Mal's hazel eyes burrowed into him like he knew Briar was lying —but Briar *wasn't* lying. Even just getting that doorknob charm from Bianca had been surreal enough. He'd only just recently become familiar with high fey, specifically, more than he ever wished to be—and adding knowledge of other little fairy bastards roaming around in the human world didn't help his nerves. Especially those little fairy bastards who bothered him more than anyone else, who lived in his room and followed him home and tied knots in his hair. It was hard to shake the instinctual wrinkling of his nose when people talked about fairies and ghosts and demons and all those things with such sincerity, even though Briar had been made very aware of their existence in recent months. Perhaps it was a defense mechanism. He wouldn't have to ever acknowledge how stupid he was for making a fey deal with something he thought didn't exist, if he continued to pretend that to be the truth.

Mal grabbed the recipe card from Briar's box, pausing for way too long a time while staring at the page before a lightbulb went off and he wrote down a series of numbers. Oh. A phone number.

"Call me if your little bugbear gets out of hand despite these charms, alright?" he said. Briar took the scrap of paper handed to him.

"Bugbear...?"

"Cuter than *wirry-cow*, isn't it? They hate *wirry-cow*. You would, too, if the other option was *bugbear*."

Briar wasn't sure how to feel about Mal, especially when he kept saying batshit things like *that*. He met Bianca's eyes for a brief moment, then folded and tucked the card back into his box of trinkets. Thanking them, he nodded and made his way to the exit, only half surprised when Mal followed him all the way out, then continued down the hallway, even as Bianca hissed for him to stop being so clingy.

"Another late night last night?" he asked on Briar's heels.

Briar adjusted the box in his arms as he approached the elevator doors as quickly as he could. He ignored that question, propping the rattling box on his hip to push the button. He nearly lost his grip, but Mal scooped it up to safety just as quickly, and Briar finally had to look at him again with an awkward—exasperated—smile.

"Yes. I wasn't feeling well this morning."

"I didn't embarrass you the other day, did I?"

Briar frowned.

"No."

"I was sure that's the reason you didn't come to class this morning."

"It wasn't."

"Do I intimidate you, then?"

"What? No," Briar scoffed. He strummed his fingers in agitation against the box as the elevator took its sweet time ascending to meet him.

"Then you'll be there tomorrow morning?"

"In the class I'm enrolled in?" Briar scowled. The elevator finally dinged and he hurried inside, adjusting his grasp on the box again and frantically pushing the *close door* button before Mal could follow him in.

"I'd love to talk more about that necklace of yours, sometime."

Those words stopped Briar's heart dead. He lifted his eyes to meet Mal's, finding him suddenly smirking, leaning against the wall with his arms crossed.

"You've got yourself in some nasty fey deal, don't you?"

Briar's arm snapped out as the doors were closing, shoving them back open. He grabbed Mal by the front of the shirt and wrenched him into the elevator, making the man yelp and stumble as if he didn't expect it. Briar's brain just boiled, shoving Mal against the wall as the doors slid shut. It was only because Mal was caught off guard that Briar was able to manhandle him at all —or perhaps the strike of adrenaline from hearing those words. Just the acknowledgement of the permanent necklace made the gold chains burn into his skin, reminding him.

"What did you say?" he asked breathlessly. Without thinking, he dropped the box of Bianca's trinkets and yanked down the collar of his sweatshirt. Revealing the necklace entirely, Mal's eyes sparkled with curiosity. "You know what this is?"

Mal's hand slowly extended, pressing the emergency stop button on the elevator. Briar never took his eyes from those staring right back at him. Not even when warm fingers lifted to tuck under the dangling chains around his neck, sending goosebumps down his arms.

"This is more a shackle than a necklace, isn't it?" Mal asked in a low voice. "I suspected something when that opulent-kissed magpie landed outside the studio window, like it was looking for you. And now here you are, begging Bianca for protection charms while wearing something like this around your neck..."

Briar forgot how to breathe. He gripped Mal's shirt so tightly, his fingers started to go numb.

"How do you know?" he asked. His voice cracked without permission, spoken through a tight throat. Mal's eyes flickered up from the necklace back to meet his gaze, more intensely than Briar expected. If he had been able to breathe before then, that look would have stolen it right away.

"Do you need help?" Mal asked. Briar's grip on his shirt trembled.

Beneath their feet, the elevator shuddered. Something from the button panel beeped, and then the lift groaned and started downward again, ignoring Mal's push of the stop button. It knocked some sense back into Briar's body, and he jerked backward, releasing his grasp. His fist left a wrinkled clump of fabric behind on Mal's chest.

Sweeping the box of charms off the floor, Briar kept his eyes down.

"No," he finally said. "I don't know what you're talking about."

They reached the bottom floor, and Briar slid through the doors the instant they cracked open. Behind him, Mal didn't follow—just called out one last time:

"Let me know how that wirry-cow treats you!"

Blood filled Briar's cheeks in mortification. He rushed the main doors and escaped out onto the street, where he finally inhaled a real breath for the first time. He touched the spot between his collarbones where the pink pearl dangled from the fey necklace, warm where Mal had held it. It tingled against his touch; his heart thudded, his stomach lurched. No one had ever touched it gently like that, almost in appreciation. Until then, he'd always asked his one-night stands to try and break it off. Otherwise, he kept it hidden under his clothes. Even Stella had never seen it.

But Mal touched it with a knowing hand, as if—as if he really did know what it was. As if it was familiar to him, like he knew the line between appreciating its beauty and respecting the danger of it.

The thought alone—the thought there was anyone else in the world who knew what Briar was dealing with—felt just as equally beautiful and dangerous in his gut.

7

MALRIC AND THE WALK

Malric painted the protection charm on the back of Bianca's door again, but glamoured it to go unseen unless she specifically went looking for it. It would only last as long as Malric was there to up the magic every morning, and would become visible again the moment he moved on for more than a few days. He already had his mental apology drafted up for when that day came.

It was strange, but at the same time, wholly familiar and comfortable to be in Bianca's apartment, again. He didn't even mind sleeping on the couch all that much, though he never missed the chance to steal her bed when she spent the night away with Stella. She always came back complaining about her sheets smelling like him, and he would wash them like he always did.

To avoid driving his roommate entirely up the wall, Malric spent his free time around teaching class organizing Bianca's things, cleaning up her workstation, refilling her spell ingredients from local shops around town. Bianca, the folk witch who practiced both her mother's New England magic and her father's brujería of Puerto Rico, of which some parts could be combined, and others were kept separate. A delicate, sometimes contentious balance of two crafts that complemented one another in many ways, but also couldn't be separated from the fraught history of how they were used against one another. Malric loved getting into bidding wars online for rare brujería books owned by old white ladies in Kentucky, loved the wicked sparkle in Bianca's eyes when he told her the money used to buy it wasn't in a real bank account and the payment would bounce in another few days.

When Malric wasn't carving protection sigils in the back of her door, or scamming people online, or refilling her jars of mustard seed, he was checking the salt bags and lines around the windows, the horseshoe over the front door, the rowan-berry painted circles around the doorknobs and window latches. He was making his corner of her front room comfortable, just the way he liked it, scrounging through every place she hid pillows and blankets until the cushions were as comfy and luxurious as possible; stuffing the fridge with expensive groceries, mostly cakes and candies and other treats with his name written on every one; scouring the internet for videos of previous Artemisia school performances, originally in an attempt to spot Briar in any of them, but inevitably getting drunk and loudly criticizing the forms of everyone on stage. Perhaps being a dance instructor really was meant to be his calling in life.

BRIAR WAS MISSING FROM CLASS AGAIN THE FOLLOWING morning—and then the morning after that, and Malric was growing impatient. That was, until he felt that little shift in the air; until he found the piece of charmed glass, stolen from the d'Alarie estate, hanging in Bianca's window donning a crack spider-webbing across the surface. A sign that something related to that energy had come near—or, at least, something related to that energy passed through the veil, within reach. He knew without having to ask—it was likely Marie's summoning Magpie.

If there was only one place he would be able to witness the rosefinch dance, whether they liked it or not, he'd take the opportunity to do just that. He needed a new piece of charmed glass, anyway.

MALRIC ARRIVED EARLY TO WITNESS THE REVEL'S entertainment. That time, he wore a low-cut maroon blouse printed with golden leaves down the front, cinched by a wide belt around the waist that gaped the fabric to show off most of his chest. Around his neck and down the front of his body, disappearing into the shirt, a body chain adorned with dangling acorn charms, not much different from the one Briar wore in their first day of class together. He wondered if Briar would notice.

In first position, waiting for their cue, Briar stood in the center of the clearing with arms raised toward the night sky. It provided the audience a chance to fully appreciate the ensemble glamoured over him by the necklace he wore—that same necklace Malric had seen, touched, understood the very instant he saw it first in Bianca's apartment, peeking out from under the collar of Briar's shirt. That shackle Briar was forced to wear, proof he was owned. Proof he was imprisoned.

That necklace glamoured them in a bell-skirt tutu in blush pink, panels of draped chiffon hanging off the shoulders in sleeves, sparkling with soft gold beading and embroidery that trailed down the sides of his legs despite no tights visible covering his skin. He wore his hair long and loose, as was tradition in high fey ballet, adorned with pink flowers woven between the strands in tiny braids. All of it, glamoured by the necklace, except perhaps the slippers on his feet stained by the grass.

After much consideration, Malric was beginning to wonder if the veil made Briar's movements more stunning while he danced, which would explain why his demonstration in the first and only class they shared wasn't anything *special*.

Yet, right there, Briar soared between steps and glided between movements with the classical music in the corner of the tree line, nigh a shift in his weight or a flicker across his expression. Perhaps the peach-haired gentle was less a thing of beauty in his normal life, prone to lies and nastiness just like every other human Malric had ever met. But instead of annoyance, he only felt the intrigue grow hotter in his chest. A part of him wanted to confront them —or would it be more satisfying to massage that perfection out of human-world Briar, instead? Like tearing a carcass from a hungry dog. How satisfying would it be, to coerce Briar to dance for him and not Marie—

Malric's heart skipped as the landing of a grand leap summoned a twist of something across Briar's expression, before snapping back again as if it never happened. No one else seemed to notice, but Malric's thoughts came to an immediate halt. Resting the side of his face against elongated fingers, he watched more closely from that moment on. Never again did Briar's pretty features shift from the calm serenity of someone dancing with ease—but that split-second crack had burned itself into Malric's mind. He recalled how tightly Briar gripped the bar in their first class together, enough that the rest of their body trembled—they weren't dancing on an injury, were they...?

Just like the last time, the moment the music faded, a dozen fey leapt to their feet for a chance to drag the dancer to their side of the circle where they could *ooh* and *aah* over him like a porcelain doll. And, also just like the last time, Briar let them. Malric's eyes just lingered on his round ears the whole time, recalling what those fey had said the last time, the blood on Malric's pillow the morning he and Briar first crossed paths. Curious, he searched the crowd for the culprits from the last time, next, spotting them down the way pretending like they hadn't even noticed the dance had ended.

Those who won the tug-of-war on the dancer's arms pulled him onto the blanket nest right alongside where Malric sat by himself, and Malric had to resist turning to look. He strained his ears to listen, but quickly realized Briar had no intention of speaking out loud that night, either. Smart. Briar was so smart, and Malric couldn't help but recall that previous claim of *"I'm not used to all of this"* in Bianca's apartment—before the mirth faded as he wondered how much of what Briar knew was from experience, rather than friendly advice. It made that look on Briar's face when Mal asked '*do you need help?*' even more unsettling.

Someone else approached, and despite wearing the same fox mask as all the others, Malric knew who she was in an instant. He knew by her body language, the smile she wore, but most of all— that thick smell of rosemary that followed anywhere she went. Out of the corner of his eye, he distinctly saw the way Briar stiffened and petrified the moment Marie d'Alarie spoke, as well, and Malric wished he could reassure them that he felt the exact same way. Going absolutely still at the mere sound of her voice, not wanting to be noticed, wishing to disappear into the background if at all possible.

"Aren't they lovely, my gentles?" she asked with honeyed words, reaching down to stroke a piece of Briar's long hair. "Have you ever seen a more beautiful human dancer?"

"They're perfect, madame," someone answered, touching Briar's face. Briar just stared straight ahead—which happened to be right where Malric was seated on the cushions alongside them. Briar probably didn't even realize they stared directly at anyone at all, but Malric felt every single moment those blue eyes locked on him. He silently encouraged it, sipping slowly at his wine. *I'm a safe place to linger. Gaze at me all you like. I won't do anything to surprise you. For as long as you need...*

"Nearly perfect," Marie laughed lightly. Goosebumps flushed Malric's skin. He'd heard those words before, he knew how they stung. "I'm hoping they one day become flawless under my watchful eye. Maybe then they can amount to something on both sides of the veil, hm?"

"You're so benevolent, my lady. I never would have thought to give the time of day to a human dancer. Especially after witnessing your son, previously. Is he well?"

"He's more than well," Marie said with the practiced speech of a proud mother. Malric had to resist smirking, knowing she chose her words carefully to avoid any outright lies. "He has so many talents, and is journeying elsewhere to discover what else he may excel at."

"Oh, I cannot wait to see him dance again the moment he returns to the Autumn Court."

"Until then, we will continue to appreciate Gentle Briar in his stead," Marie cooed, and Malric's stomach turned at the sound of Briar's name on her tongue. It was a cardinal rule of her revels never to speak another's name out loud—and to share Briar's so thoughtlessly, when they themself wouldn't even speak a word in an attempt to protect themselves, it was enough to make Malric sick. "As they once told me—all they ever wanted was to dance for someone beautiful, and now they are able whenever I allow them. It is the grace I extend to any and all artists, you know, especially those within whom I see greatness waiting to emerge."

Malric couldn't resist glancing in that direction—and he met Briar's eyes. They remained empty, staring straight ahead, but something swam in their overcast depths. Something of fear and anxiety, spilling from those wide, unblinking eyes to even flush his cheeks with restrained emotion.

"Oh, will they dance again for us tonight?" one of the guests asked, draping herself over Briar and caressing his face, his hair. "Just one more performance for us before the night ends, madame?"

"Perhaps—"

"We shouldn't overindulge in something so sweet so quickly, my lady. Otherwise they might rot us from the inside."

Malric didn't realize he spoke until all eyes were on him, including his mother's, who regarded him with question. She clearly didn't recognize him right away, especially beneath the mask, especially since they had not crossed paths in months—but Malric knew it was a thin line to walk. He would have been better off not saying anything at all—but he couldn't stop himself. It was all he could do, or else he might actually snap and throw Briar over his shoulder to run away with.

He couldn't allow them to force Briar back to his feet when he was already exhausted. When he had already done his part of the night. When Malric couldn't get that brief memory of how his expression cracked when he landed on his ankle, wondering if there was something more to it.

"Let us allow the bird to rest for now; perhaps then, they will be able to perform flawlessly the next time you grace us with another fete," he went on behind a casual sip of wine.

"Ah… of course," the first guest said with a polite smile. Malric just continued smiling at Marie, who, eventually, nodded as well and commented on his graciousness.

"If rest was all they needed to be perfect, they surely would have shown it by now, however," she left with one final tease, and everyone laughed to sate her, including Malric. Everyone except Briar, who had finally pulled his eyes away and stared down at his lap. Clutching the skin of his thighs through the glamour of his skirt, as if even such a powerful magic necklace couldn't trick his mind into finding enough corporeal fabric to grip and anchor himself to.

WHEN THE EXCITEMENT DIED DOWN, WHEN THE FEY who fawned over him finally lost interest, Briar did exactly what they had the previous time—crawled silently to their feet, slipping into the trees directly in line with where they sat. Malric waited a few moments that time, too, before finishing off his wine and quietly following. That time, he made sure to do so before anyone else could sneak up on the rosefinch and harass him, first.

Sifting through the undergrowth, Malric finally spotted them a distance away, standing completely still, naked amongst the trees. As if wishing to disappear into them, as if wishing he might turn into one of them for himself. Or, perhaps, simply straining his senses to see if anyone followed.

Briar's nakedness implied they'd left the edge of the revel clearing, that circle of thick rosemary where the necklace knew to glamour their performance ensembles, leaving them nude to the air and any peering eyes. When Malric danced for his mother, he never had to wear a glamour for his own dress, and wondered why Marie had done so with Briar. To be naked while he danced, then while physically accosted afterward, then having to rush and pull on clothes all while never knowing if someone followed him into the trees, all with only a tricky psychic spell between his skin and strange high fey hands...

Malric's insides twisted at the implication, wondering if anyone had ever taken advantage of that window of vulnerability, not unlike the group of fey who'd attacked him the previous time.

Clenching his fists and keeping his breath low and silent, Malric waited until Briar finally moved, again. The woods were quiet enough, there were no footsteps crunching over roots in search of him, so Briar found the courage to bend over and rustle around in his things. Crouched behind the bushes, Malric saw brief glimpses of a t-shirt tugged on over strawberry-blonde hair, followed by a puffy sherpa jacket, then jeans dragged on over legs. It was then he swore he heard something else from the bird frantically pulling their coverings back on—and that was the sound of sniffling. Whimpering. And then Malric couldn't hang back any longer.

As he approached, a small, practically nonexistent sob broke from Briar's mouth, followed by a shuddering breath as he dragged his hands over his eyes. With his back to Malric's approach, Malric could watch unnoticed as Briar's hands shakily untied the ribbons of his pointe shoes. The first slid off with ease. The second, however, came with more sharp breaths and trembling hands between ticks of hesitation.

Finally, Briar cursed at himself, and then at every fey at the fete, wiping his nose on the back of his hand and pulling off the second slipper. Beneath it, tight bandages clutched the arch of his foot, relentlessly snaking up around his ankle to support it as much as layered cloth bandages could. He cursed again and again and again while forcing his sneaker over the swelling joint, angry tears spilling down his cheeks as Malric could only watch, having turned to cold stone at the sight.

Marie forced Briar to dance on an injured ankle—or, more simply, Briar simply had no choice at all.

"Did you hurt it just now?" he blurted, and Briar practically screamed, whirling around. His hand flashed to grab a fallen branch, extending it like a sword between them, only to stumble back to his ass in the mud. The pitiful threat combined with Briar's puffy eyes and tear-stained cheeks only made Malric feel worse.

"You sleep at the d'Alarie manor after dancing, don't you? Let me walk you there."

Briar's delicate features crushed into annoyance, or maybe it was anger, and he snapped the branch in Malric's direction again in warning. Malric put his hands up, trying to prove he was unarmed and trustworthy. According to Briar's expression, though, Malric might as well have been a snake reeling its head back to strike. He almost pulled off his fox mask in an attempt to help the situation, but stopped himself mid-movement.

But then Briar attempted to rush to his feet, moving too quickly and nearly buckling to the dirt. Malric moved without thinking, leaping forward with arms extended to catch him before he fell. It left Briar speechless—well, in a different way—still white-knuckling his tree branch before slowly turning back to Malric with wide eyes. As if the mere touch of Malric's hands— terrified him.

"I'm not going to hurt you," Malric whispered with sincerity. "I just want to help you."

Briar's mouth moved like he was going to say something—but then closed again before he did. It pulled the air from Malric's lungs, like he couldn't breathe in anticipation. He wanted to hear Briar's voice more than anything, in that moment. He wanted to know what they would say to him, a fey reveler, masked and with pointed ears like knives.

His eyes flickered to Briar's own ears again, healing injuries visible with the glamour stripped away. Red and angry. Still donning butterfly bandages.

"Please," Malric attempted again softly. That time, he stepped back slightly, but left his arms extended for Briar to cling to, if they so wished. To his surprise, Briar did, having to balance on his one good ankle while the other hovered off a bent knee. His touch trembled, clinging to Malric's sleeve as his expression contorted in a mix of embarrassment and what could only be self-hatred.

"Why?" Briar finally uttered, quiet enough that it could have been the wind. Malric might have been tricked, had he not been watching Briar's mouth so closely.

That single word, said so weakly, with so much exhaustion, made Malric's heart wrench in his chest. He put a gentle hand on Briar's back, leaning closer.

"Because dancers look out for one another."

Briar looked at Malric again; their expression was so intense, gray-blue eyes shimmering like rolling storm clouds deciding between rain or snow or lightning. Malric thought he might fall into them, swim in them—then maybe he would finally understand everything Briar hid behind the wall he built to protect himself from—

From high fey like Malric.

Once again, Briar said nothing. He turned his eyes down. He turned his head to avoid Malric's gaze, but didn't pull away, perhaps only because he knew he couldn't. He even tossed the branch off to the side, and Malric took the chance offered.

Turning his back—despite having a strong gut feeling there was a knife or two tucked into Briar's backpack—he crouched low. After a long moment of consideration, Briar actually hopped closer, then hesitantly dragged himself onto Malric's back with a soft exhale of exertion.

Malric gently bucked forward, just enough to hike Briar higher up on his hips. Briar's arms instinctively snapped around Malric's neck to gather his balance, before quickly pulling back again with another small sound—that time of embarrassment.

Malric just chuckled under his breath, told Briar to hold on, and started through the trees. Back toward the house, where he would drop Briar off, and turn in the opposite direction. Knowing that the dancer, while nowhere near safe, would at least be able to sleep... soundly.

"Do people bother you often on your way back?" Malric asked, referring to the previous incident. He fully expected Briar to remain silent, and Briar did, but Malric didn't take it personally. "I saw your ears... Next time, I'll bring you a paste to help them heal without scarring."

Briar's hands on Malric's shoulders twitched.

"I don't want it," Briar mumbled, once again no louder than the breeze.

"Why not?"

Briar's grip tightened again.

"I don't accept fey gifts."

"Ah," Malric smiled over his shoulder, but Briar moved his head out of sight. He glanced over his opposite shoulder instead, then back over the first, though Briar just kept dodging. Malric couldn't help but laugh. "Smart."

Behind them, the revel continued as it always did, filling the forest with laughter and music that slowly dwindled the farther Malric traveled down the path. When they fully escaped the fingers of light and lingering voices, Malric spoke again.

"You dance for the lady of the revel, right?" An obvious thing to say, but Malric didn't know how else to broach the subject except by playing dumb. Gods knew Briar Hunt wouldn't be forthcoming with information in the human world any time soon, either, so Malric was going to take any little chance he could get on either side of the coin.

"... Obviously," Briar whispered Malric's thoughts, and Malric chuckled again. Maybe Briar had never heard a fey lord laugh casually, because their grip on his shoulders lightened just slightly. Malric took it as invitation to try some more.

"What made you decide to dance for her?"

Briar was quiet for a long, long time, but Malric matched it. He was learning that Briar Hunt would always speak, eventually, if Malric just gave him enough time to decide what words to say.

"I... wanted to dance for someone beautiful."

The wind. Those words, on the breeze, carried by the same silent storm that existed behind Briar's eyes, spoken with a mix of intensity and a sort of horror perhaps only Malric could understand. He nodded.

"Right. For people like me, right?"

Oh—Briar actually laughed, though it only lasted for a split second.

"I don't think any of you are beautiful."

"Don't say that so loudly," Malric teased. "Lady Marie d'Alarie would be insulted."

Briar stilled, then surprised Malric when he leaned forward slightly. Malric had to resist turning away, assuring himself there wasn't enough room through the side of the mask for Briar to see any of his features underneath.

"What is it?" he asked when Briar didn't speak. Briar wiggled slightly in uncertainty, and Malric bounced him in encouragement.

"I..." Briar whispered. "I didn't know... that was her name."

"But you knew the name *d'Alarie*, didn't you?"

Briar didn't answer. Malric frowned. That time when he glanced back, he caught sight of Briar's face, though it didn't notice him. It was busy scowling down at Malric's shoulder.

"No?"

Briar shook his head. He looked almost embarrassed.

"Don't be," Malric answered his own observation, and Briar's pretty eyes lifted to meet his, again. "Fey are more protective of their names than anything else."

"I know that."

"Oh, you do, do you?" Malric teased.

"... Yes. I—I'm very good friends with a powerful witch, so

don't even think about trying to trick me, I can turn it right back on you again two-fold."

It was the longest sentence Briar had spoken on that side of the veil, and perhaps it was only Malric's silent awe that kept him from bursting out laughing. Bianca, the powerful folk witch, who could turn a fey's trick back on them two-fold... ah, the more Malric thought about it, the more he decided he didn't actually want to test that theory. Bianca could definitely be nasty if she needed to be.

"I wasn't, but now I definitely won't," Malric assured him, and the way Briar actually relaxed his grip on the back of Malric's tunic was... endearing. Malric let out a breath, watching it steam and swirl on the air. It would only get chillier from there, with the tear in the veil keeping the area warmer than normal. That same tear Briar would race through again in the morning to get back home.

Malric almost took a roundabout way to the estate house's back courtyard, wanting to draw out their time together as much as he could, but he also didn't want to risk Briar noticing and accusing him of being tricksy, after all. Still, when they reached the edge where thinning woods met grass, Malric couldn't help but feel a little disappointed that their time had been cut so short. He had to remind himself they might cross paths again the following morning, if Briar decided to show up to class. Even though it would be different, under different circumstances, Malric would still be able to keep an eye on his dancer. On both sides of the veil.

The moment the house came into view, Briar kicked off of Malric's back and hit the dirt. It caught Malric off guard, barely catching his own balance as Briar shoved away and rushed over the grass. He limped the entire way; Malric would have been able to catch up to him easily, but something kept him rooted where he stood. Perhaps it was the way the dark house intimidated him, perhaps it was the thought of Marie noticing him and calling him out when Briar could still hear—

Perhaps it was the way, despite everything, Briar still ran from him like he bared claws and snarling teeth. It filled him with heavy ice. Heavy ice littered with nails, meant to pierce his insides slowly and one by one, every time Briar accepted his mercy with so much reluctance, and ran away the moment he thought he could.

Malric closed his eyes. He clenched his fists, then touched his shoulder where Briar had clung so tightly to his tunic. Had it really only been for balance—or because he was terrified of what Malric was going to do to him? Did he doubt Malric was going to actually take him to the manor? Was that why he dropped and ran in an instant...?

Malric shouldn't blame him. Malric shouldn't even *care* what Briar thought of him. Malric wasn't actually there to be Briar's friend, he was only there because of a misplaced obligation to help him escape Marie. Malric shouldn't care about what Briar thought of him, specifically...

A thawed nail pressed through the inside of his stomach. At the memory of Briar's eyes, staring at him, wide with fear; the feeling of his fist clutching the shoulder of Malric's tunic, as if he was used to high fey offering kindness only to turn it on him again without warning.

He thought about their confrontation in the elevator outside Bianca's apartment, how Briar had looked so shocked and *scared* the moment Malric acknowledged his fey necklace. Touched it, fondled it, like it was nothing to be afraid of. He wondered if that necklace had been Briar's first exposure to a high fey's offered gift, only for it to turn into a trick once he was sold on the deal.

I wanted to dance for someone beautiful...

Malric pressed a hand into his stomach. He wanted to bury it into his guts and rip the nails out himself, one by one. He didn't want to feel that strange disappointment, that strange self-consciousness, that horrible sense of dread any longer. Why did those words cling to him, hooking into the deepest parts of his being, as if speaking to a part of him he'd long forgotten? A part he'd long abandoned the more Marie made her demands of him and his talents—a part that once dreamed of dancing so beautifully, the veil gifted him a perfect partner from the other side?

Malric—wanted to earn Briar Hunt's trust, no matter which side of the veil he stood on. To earn his trust, to learn exactly the terms of the deal he'd made. To touch him, one day, without that look of fear in his eyes—both as Mal the dance instructor, and Malric, the fey lord, son of Marie d'Alarie. Maybe then, Malric could free them. Malric could save them from the same fate he himself had fallen to, trading away any chance to ever dance again, to ever find that veil-partner from myth, in exchange for a chance at freedom. Those terms that would follow him until the day he died, or inevitably returned to Marie just like his siblings had.

Dance for anyone other than me, ever again, and you shall become one with the copper fauna. Of they behind whom we hide our faces; of teeth and shadowed paws. Of your roots and starving for rabbits.

"Malric," a familiar voice said his name, and Malric turned. The last person he expected to find was Felme, approaching while pulling off a fox mask of her own. He let out a relieved breath through his nose, running fingers under his own mask and pushing it back, tangling in his hair.

"Hey, Fel," he sighed. "Mind doing me a favor? I need another piece of glass from the attic, for a protection charm back on the other side."

"I'll do you better—how about a drink?"

"Oh—gods yes," he groaned, throwing his head back and making his sister laugh. Ah—he hadn't heard that sound in such a long time. Why did it make his heart pound?

8

MALRIC AND THE PAINTER

Despite being the oldest, and on the outside, always appearing the most well put-together, Felme's bedroom was easily the messiest. It was the only space where weekly servants weren't allowed inside to clean, and followed a system of organization only she herself understood. Being the artist requiring the most hands-on crafts in the family, though, perhaps it made sense. Lusia came in right behind her as the culinary genius.

Felme offered him something to drink after closing the door, and Malric thanked her, busy gazing at the dozens of paintings-in-progress at one end of the room. Landscapes, still lifes, even a royal-portrait-in-progress. Malric hadn't realized the newest Tuatha dé Danann had already been born.

Felme approached and handed him the drink. He took it, unable to ignore how his sister's hands moved stiffly, rubbing them together before pulling a sheet down over the royal portrait, specifically. She knocked a few slender paintbrushes to the floor as she did, but didn't bother picking them up. Malric wanted to assume Felme's stiff hands were from the nighttime chill outside, but knew better. He and everyone else knew the tremors in her hands were from overuse, from that unspoken expectation that she would spawn masterpieces on canvas any moment she wasn't otherwise eating or drinking or sleeping. Malric just exhaled through his nose, closing his eyes and pulling Felme into a silent hug. Neither of them were particularly touchy like that, but being the two oldest had its perks. Shared physical vulnerability was one of them.

"We haven't had a chance to just... chat, yet," she said, pulling away before pouring her own shaky glass from the crystal carafe by the window. "I wanted to ask how you've been enjoying your freedom since you last visited."

"Hm," Malric breathed into his glass, taking a long drink. "Better than in the very beginning, I guess. Still hard. Still... uncertain, I guess..."

He hated admitting it out loud—but once again, Felme was the only one he felt like he could be honest with. Being on his own was *hard*. Being a high fey whose only learned skill was *dancing ballet* was *hard*, if not impossible in the human world. He could get away with compelling humans into feeding, housing, clothing him if he really wanted to, but what sort of meaningless existence was that?

He didn't even know what else there was to do, though. What, get a job? Have a *career*? Technically he'd done that, already, with his new gig at Artemisia. He chuckled into his glass with another swallow, before flicking his eyes to the other end of the room, knowing Briar was in his bed on the other side. Why did that make his heart race?

"I always thought the second time would be easier than the first," his sister sighed, taking a seat in her squeaky painting chair. Malric sat cross-legged on the floor next to her, examining the painting of the landscape she hadn't covered up.

Felme held the record for attempts to leave—sitting at three, total. Still, she had returned every time, for one reason or another. For reasons Malric never understood, until he was in her same position.

Sitting in silence, Malric couldn't help but watch how her

fingers twitched on her knee, even while resting limp. As if the tendons in her forearms plucked themselves on instinct, so used to holding a brush or a palette that they weren't sure what to do with themselves when empty.

"Did your hips ever heal?" she went on.

"Yeah, after a few weeks," Malric nodded, placing the empty glass on the wood floor before reclining back with a sigh. He let the hard floor stretch out his back, though felt a ghostly pang in his hip at the reminder. "Found a good healer over here, and smoked a lot of weed over there."

"You're still friends with that human folk-witch, aren't you? What was her name, again? The one whose apartment I stayed at that one night..."

"Bianca, yeah. I'm actually crashing with her right now. She's as hospitable as ever."

"Be sure to give her a gift in thanks."

"She wouldn't take it—knows the old warnings way too well."

Felme laughed. "I think your dancer does, too. They never speak or eat at mother's revels, so long as they can help it. I don't know if they've ever eaten anything Lusia has prepared for them, either, but they keep trying. Gods know the guests manage to shove plenty of food and drink into his mouth anyway, but..."

The way she trailed off, gazing down at her drink as the surface trembled beneath her unsteady hands.

"You're not... thinking of returning, are you?" she asked, voice quiet. "I was surprised to see you at her revel... I don't think she noticed you, but... I knew it was you right away. You watched Briar dance far too closely. I hope you're not letting yourself get drawn back in, enough that you make poor decisions..."

"What? Me, making poor decisions?" Malric asked sarcastically, before running his fingers back through his hair in consideration. "I don't have any plans of coming home anytime soon, no. But... godsdamnit, I don't like her having Briar, either."

"Briar." Felme smiled. "I always liked his name. Like something from a storybook."

"I think it's actually from a human fairytale," Malric breathed, gazing up at the ceiling. He wondered if Briar could hear their voices through the wall, quiet and low. He wondered if Briar slept well after dancing, or if he tossed and turned. "*Sleeping Beauty*, who pricks her finger on a spindle and is cursed to sleep for eternity, unless her true love comes and kisses her, or something."

He thanked Felme as she poured him another drink, sitting up just enough to take a sip.

"You know... he's being harassed by a wirry-cow on the other side of the veil. Do you happen to know anything about that?"

Felme frowned as she thought about it, before shaking her head. "Perhaps traveling back and forth between the veil is attracting wild things to follow him home."

"That's what I thought, too," Malric returned back to the floor, absentmindedly swirling the amber drink in his cup over his chest. "But apparently, no matter how long Briar stays away, it's always still there when he gets back home. Most wirry-cows would starve-out by then."

"Do you think mother has something to do with it?"

Malric groaned quietly, squeezing his eyes closed and pressing the bottom of the glass to his forehead. "Would it be any surprise? She seems to have gone completely mad, anyway. Making a deal with a human dancer on the other side is wild enough. I wouldn't put compelling a wirry-cow past her."

"But why?"

"Who knows."

Felme gazed down into her own drink for a long time, not unlike she used to when searching for inspiration for her work. Perhaps the moonlight struck the golden liquid in a way she liked, memorizing it to paint, later.

"We've been extending kindness to him, just like all the others," she said, as if wanting Malric to know, specifically. Malric remained silent. He wasn't sure why she thought he would care, but... it still softened his worry, just a little bit. "Neda seems to have made the strongest connection with them, though even then it's thin. They once asked him where they could find a new blanket."

"Wow, how brave."

Felme laughed, throwing back the rest of her drink.

"After watching him dance, tonight, it really breaks my heart. He dances beautifully, don't you think? But mother will never tell him that. She'll keep him for as long as she possibly can."

"Sounds familiar."

Felme smirked, gazing into her drink again like a scrying mirror. Trying to find answers where there weren't any, sucking down more and more alcohol as if clearing the surface would allow some other divine reflection to show through and offer exactly what they needed.

"Perhaps... she knows we're all on our last leg," Felme finally said, and it made Malric go still. He sat up, crossing his legs and looking at her in question. "She won't be having any more children anytime soon, and none of her friends will allow her to mentor their own children, perhaps because they see how she treats her own. Soon enough... there will be nothing left for her to show off."

"What do you mean?" Malric asked. His eyes flickered to Felme's hand again, heart thudding in his chest. Felme took a long drink, finishing her second glass in one go. She paused for another moment before answering, licking her lips.

"Maura and Mavera spend every night writing and practicing new scores on the piano; some mornings, their fingers are too stiff to even hold a fork. Lusia grows more malnourished by the day, because they don't care to cook or eat for themself any longer; they only ever cook for Briar, or when mother makes them. Neda is hardly present during the day, always staring off into space or sleeping for all hours, searching for writing inspiration. Lillis doesn't leave the house since that night they forgot their lines on stage and that gossip pamphlet called them *washed up* the next morning. Persea, Larissa, and Reta hardly speak at all, thinking they have to save every ounce of their voices for mother's choir performances. And I…" she trailed her finger through a wet spot of paint on her easel, smearing the pigment between two fingers. "My hands may have another hundred paintings in them, but I'm slowly losing my eyesight. It's irreversible, unless I reduce the strain on them. Which is out of the question, because who then will provide work for mother to present in her galleries across the Autumn Court?"

Felme turned to meet Malric's gaze—and Malric saw every single year of his sister's life in them. In the bags under her eyes, growing old despite her youth. She should have another hundred, two hundred years in her before even considering herself used up, but just like the rest of them, she'd been wrung out of everything she ever had to offer. Never given a chance to be anything other than mother's prestigious, genius painter of the world's beauties.

"Maybe that's for the best," Malric spoke without knowing what he would say, next. He just let the tangle of emotions in his stomach, his chest, form words as he listened. "If we were to all leave at once, what would she do, then? She would not be able to hurt any of us any longer—"

"She would only hurt other people like Briar," Felme smiled weakly. "Don't you think? Imagine how she might even enjoy it more, to find people more easily exploited than we are. No wonder she loves Briar so much—he is trapped in a deal with her. She will dance him to death, and then find another just like him. And then they will have the same fate—to dance until they die, trying to earn whatever it is mother promised to give. And then another will come after that, and another. Sacrifice begets sacrifice."

Malric felt like he'd been kicked in the back. He turned back to his drink, hunching over it, closing his eyes and breathing through his nose. Briar, without ever knowing it—had proven to Marie how easy it was to prey on humans in grief. They proved how easily Marie could get her hands on an artist she wanted, and then keep them for as long as she wanted. Felme was right—even if all of her children grew incapable of meeting her demands, or left on their own volition, she now knew exactly how easy it would be to cross through the veil and find someone else to replace them. Someone who would beg for her help, until it was too late to change their mind.

"There has to be something we can do," Malric muttered, equally for Felme and his own ears to hear. He squeezed the crystal glass. "We cannot allow that woman to continue exploiting people like this... to steal the only things they've ever found joy in, to use for herself and her own social climb..."

"How do you stop a hungry fox without getting eaten, yourself?" Felme muttered. "Perhaps you poison it."

Malric pressed his lips together. He thought of Briar being accosted by those fey lords after his dance; he thought of Briar being forced to eat and drink wine and fruits; he thought of Briar's persistent fear and distrust of everything Malric did, despite trying to prove himself a friend.

"Perhaps you break their jaw," he muttered. "So that they cannot eat even as they starve. Maybe then they will see exactly how unwanted they are, when no one else will offer to feed them, either."

"Well," Felme breathed. "If you figure out a way to break mother's jaw... I know eight others who may be willing to turn the other way."

Malric downed the rest of his glass. Outside, the sun was on the edge of rising over the horizon, and he knew he had to go in order to avoid bumping into Briar, let alone his mother on her way back from the revel.

"When mother brought Briar as your replacement, you know, I got curious about something... ah, about what happened to the people she originally chose to replace me when I left all those times," she said, and Malric nodded. "Well—I tried to find out.

And then I tried to find out about the ones who replaced Neda and Lusia, too."

"And?"

"And..." she bit her lip. "I still don't know what happened to them. I can't find much about any of them, really, since mother never formally patronized them, and she doesn't record her fey-human deals with the town oracle... It's like they disappeared, or... or never existed at all..."

Nails—frozen in Malric's stomach. One, two, three of them pinched at those words. He glanced back toward the wall between him and Briar asleep, soundly, safely, in his bed on the other side. But for how much longer? How much longer until Briar would choose that bed on purpose, because otherwise he would never get a sound sleep in the human world?

Disappeared?

"I'm going to help him," Malric admitted to Felme, who looked the exact opposite of *surprised*. "I've already... injected myself into his life in the human world, in a human disguise. I won't let mother keep getting what she wants."

Felme nodded. "Just be careful," she added in a whisper. "Our mother is a fox who is always starving. Never fully sated, no matter what she's given."

"Gods know," Malric mumbled, downing the last of his drink before getting to his feet.

He said goodbye to Felme, offering her a hug and wishing her well. She offered to attend more of their mother's revels going forward, both to keep an eye on him and on Briar, especially if Malric insisted on getting involved. He almost asked her not to, not wanting her to get wrapped up in anything he would summon on himself—but the thought of someone trustworthy there with him, watching his back as he watched Briar's, was a reassuring thought.

Before he left the house, there was one last thing he needed—and he found it in a picture frame. A tintype photo of the entire family on the fireplace mantle in the sitting room, where Malric had been glamoured out of view, leaving a gap between Felme and Larissa. How many times had that same photo lost the visage of Felme, of Neda, of Lusia, whenever they left? Only to show them again as soon as they returned?

Frowning down at it, Malric ground his teeth together. He popped the tabs on the back, shaking the frame's guts into his hand. He gazed at the photo a moment longer, before shaking his head and tucking it back into place without the sheet of glass covering the front. A piece of glass, naturally charmed by simply existing in that house for so long. A perfect replacement for the one that'd cracked in Bianca's window.

Leaving the house, he cast a final glance over his shoulder at his window on the upper floor, a part of him wondering if there would be any lights as Briar woke early to escape—but it was dark, lifeless, motionless as death. A house full of residents, unmoving, unwelcoming. Miserable.

He clutched the glass in his hand tighter, before closing his eyes. He forced himself to relax, before he would accidentally hurt himself. Still—one thought pervaded.

Malric would be the one to steal back whatever his mother fed on—or break her jaw so she might starve, herself.

9

BRIAR AND THE VISITOR

*T*he skin of Briar's feet ached, just like they always did when he walked through the wild trees to the edge of the fey lady's revel clearing.

Lady Marie d'Alarie. That fey lord's voice reverberated through the sky, before manifesting as a fox trotting along at Briar's feet in the dark. His fur was the same dark, coppery penny-color as the lord's wavy chestnut hair. The same color as Master Mal's short, wolfish hair. Something about it made Briar feel safe, to have such a little creature there to wander the grounds with him.

He hated the fey lady's grounds. He hated the clearing. No— Marie d'Alarie's grounds. Marie d'Alarie's clearing. From the sweeping yard of lush green grass, to the autumnal trees of the forest encircling the back courtyard, to the wintry chill that nipped at every inch of bare skin despite no snow ever falling. As if it all fell on the human side of the veil, instead, when the Pacific Northwest was always thought to be temperate. Maybe something about that opening in the veil messed with the weather.

Encircling one side of the clearing, Briar practically had the line of trees memorized by then. There was a myriad of strange growth in the woods near the veil, but those ones there, in their little grouping, were so interesting. They existed all in states of spring bloom. Fresh green leaves of a maple tree; aromatic pink flowers of a cherry blossom tree; the soft, evergreen needle clusters of a white pine; white petals of a spring-snow crabapple; the purple tendrils of a flowering lilac... Briar's mom would have been impressed with how he could name every one of them, from one end of the line to the next. She would be thrilled to know he'd paid more attention than she ever thought while gardening together every spring. He should have told her much sooner how much he used to love planting in the soft, chilly dirt with her every March. He was never actually as grouchy as he looked. It was something he missed more than anything, especially once their weekly phone calls drifted into every other week, then once a month, as Lady d'Alarie's demands grew ever more onerous.

The fox at Briar's feet came to a stop in front of an empty spot, and Briar paused with it. He always wondered what would grow there, what sort of tree the fey lady had planned for her collection—and that time, he was blessed with a peek. He couldn't resist his curiosity at the sight of something the color of paperbark maple poking through the grass.

But the moment he knelt in front of it, the fox lunged and buried its teeth into Briar's hand. Briar cried out, snatching himself away—but he lost his balance, and the moment his hand fell into the center of the plot, something slithered out and wrapped around his wrist. It snagged tight, burying into Briar's flesh like an encircling rope—then dragged his hand into the dirt, hard enough that he slammed all the way to his shoulder.

Gasping in panic, Briar planted his opposite hand against the grass to push back—but just as quickly as the first was swallowed, that arm was claimed by the earth, too. Thrashing backward, he begged for the fox to help him—but the animal only buried its teeth into the curve of Briar's round ear, tearing it away with a swing of its head. Briar screamed, and the earth took advantage of his open mouth. Ropelike strands of wiry roots shot over his chin, spreading down his throat to loop around the root of his lungs—and pulled. Like an anchor buried into sand, it wrenched Briar face-first into the grass, where more fibers and scratchy rocks infiltrated his mouth, his lungs, filling every inch of his skin like a stuffed toy. Pulling, tearing, filling him without any chance to catch his breath; darkening his eyes until he saw nothing; filling his ears with the sound of shifting dirt and clay and gravel and worms chomping through the earth—

He woke with a jolt and a gasp on the floor of that bedroom that wasn't his. Curled on his side near the door hanging open at his feet, which terrified him even more than being interred in the earth ever would. Before a single additional thought formed, Briar rammed his foot against the door, slamming it with an echoing *bang* throughout that miserable house.

Slumping back to the floor and closing his eyes, he fought to catch his breath. He clawed at his throat, coughing and hating how gravelly the inside of his windpipe was. It was then he realized, it wasn't only the inside of his throat that scratched—there was dirt over every inch of him. In his hair, his mouth, coating his borrowed nightshirt, embedded under his fingernails. He scrambled upward, choking on another gasp and frantically brushing himself off. No, no, no—it was only a dream. Just like all the other times he woke up covered in dirt—it was only a dream. It was only a trick. Just a fey trick. It was only his imagination, maybe the necklace made a mistake with its glamour...

He didn't want to call it sleepwalking. He didn't want to call it his imagination. So he just called it what it was—*fairy bullshit.*

Gathering himself, he shoved the thoughts away like he always did. He brushed himself off as much as he could, ignored the fucking *miserable* ache in his ankle, and gathered his things in the dark. He pulled on his sneakers, wrapping the laces around his injury like a makeshift splint. It only had to last until he made it through the veil. He'd danced on worse.

· · ·

THE D'ALARIE ESTATE WAS QUIET, EMPTY THAT morning, perhaps because of how early it was. The sun wasn't even up, but Briar still pushed himself harder than ever to cross the back lawn as fast as he could despite the pain in his ankle and the weight in his chest. He just wanted to escape potential eyes. He didn't need anyone to see him limping, like an injured doe hunted by wolves.

Through the veil. Onto the beach. Uncovering his bike from the trees and pedaling as fast as he could to the ferry.

I wanted to dance for someone beautiful. Those words spoken to that fox-lord struck Briar like sudden lightning, and he nearly threw himself into the sound. What was he, fucking stupid? How could he say something so moronic, so mortifying, especially to a total stranger? A *fey lord*, at that?

By the time he made it back to the city, and then to his apartment, it edged on five in the morning and he felt it in every single bone. Inside, he tripped over Stella's shoes, and then he tripped over a pair of pink Doc Martens, knowing right away Bianca must have spent the night. Good for them. Briar was jealous.

Throwing his bag down in his room, he face-planted into the pile of blankets on his bed, releasing a muffled scream of frustration in the least dramatic way possible. Once his lungs emptied, he slumped to his knees over the side, glaring at the dusty lavender fabric of his duvet with nothing but resentment. There were more muddy hand- and footprints across the top, a reminder of his cow-bear, wirry-bug, cow-gart roommate's insistence despite doing all the things Bianca told him to in order to evict it. Groaning again, Briar pressed his face hard enough into the blankets to nearly suffocate. He almost did. The temptation was so sweet.

But then his phone pinged, summoning him from the mire and forcing him to search through his bag. He didn't recognize the number on the screen, but the words in the message told him who was on the other end right away. He sighed, slumping to the floor and leaning back against the bed to answer.

Bianca isn't home. Is she with Stella?

who is this?

Take a wild guess.

how did you get my #?

Defensive much? I'm stalking you.

Briar grumbled, tugging the elastic from his hair before sending back an annoyed reply.

bianca is here. dont message me again

How's your wirry-cow treating you?

Briar almost ignored him. He almost responded a generic *'fine,'* but held his head in his hand while reading the words, feeling the exhaustion in his body, the throbbing of his ankle, the eyes of his family in the photo on his dresser as their voices echoed in his head the same way they used to every Sunday when they facetimed one another. *How are things going? Are you doing well in class? How is dance practice? Do you have any roles in the next season production?*

"Damnit," he whispered, then raised the phone over his head and snapped a dim photo of the mud on his duvet. He sent it.

i did everything Bianca said but its still here

Mal took a long time to reply, and Briar took the pause in conversation to save his contact information. When Mal finally replied, Briar sighed again.

I can stop by this morning and bring the big guns.

oh would a gun work?

Ha ha. No. Maybe. I don't know. I'll bring something extra special.

you dont know where i live

Stella dragged me into your apartment after hitting me with her car.

THAT WAS YOU??????

its your bloody handprint on my hoodie??

Your hoodie? It's ten times bigger than you are.

she gave it to me

couldnt get the stain out and i thought it was cool

Alright, weirdo. Who's the witch here, again?

Briar smirked. No—he hated that Mal made him smile at all, damnit. Still, he had to resist telling the man to buzz off, taking a look at the handprints again to remind himself of Mal's potential usefulness. Even if he was annoying as hell.

can you make it before class starts?

Oh, are you coming to class today?

I was sure I'd scared you away for good.

changed my mind. nvm

I'll come right now.

DO NOT COME RIGHT NOW

I'll come at 8.

ok

> What are you doing right now that's so important?

> what are you, a cop?

Briar smiled to himself. He hated that.

In the meantime, he took a shower to wash the sweat and dirt off his face and out of his hair. He made toast with jam, then spent more time than usual adhering to every step of his neglected skincare routine, even applying a full face of makeup because otherwise his nerves were going to eat him alive. Mal, Master Mal, was coming to their apartment... to take a look at Briar's wirry-cow problem. Was that okay? Should he have told Stella? Surely Bianca wouldn't be friends with him if he really was a weirdo, right?

No, it was even anything to do with *Mal*—it was the thought of how, by inviting the man over, Briar was admitting he needed help. There were things he couldn't handle on his own. He... needed someone to help him.

Wow—what an awful fucking feeling.

I wanted to dance for someone beautiful.

"Fuck," he whispered, glaring at himself in the mirror after pulling his hair out from the back of his top.

I want to dance for someone beautiful. I want to be the most beautiful thing on two feet. I want to impress Leon Heller enough that he'll only pas de deux with me; enough that he won't accept that scholarship to St. Tomassin, and instead stay at Artemisia with me...

Marie d'Alarie, the fey lady, agreed so easily, almost *eagerly*, that night she approached him backstage. Briar really thought it would be that simple. He'd been sure of himself and his ability to dance—but had since learned. There was nothing in the whole world the fey lady considered *perfect*, except perhaps her own son whom Briar had replaced at the revels. Who would break both of

Briar's legs, surely, if he were ever to witness their poor attempt at performing...

A vicious, self-cannibalistic cycle. The more Briar danced for the fey lady at her parties, the more sleepless nights he carried in his bones, the more injuries he stacked on top of one another, the more exhausted he grew—the less enchanting he was, both in her presence and in Artemisia's practice rooms. The more he made a fool out of himself with every class he had to sit in the back of, or skip entirely, or barely hobble through. The closer he came to losing the opportunity to dance at all, as the rest of his general studies fell to the wayside and more and more he fell behind on assignments and studying and keeping his grades up—until soon, he wouldn't be eligible to audition for any season production roles at all.

All for a single chance at catching Leon Heller's eye.

I wanted to dance for someone beautiful.

Briar hated himself.

His phone pinged a few times as the group chat woke up and shared pictures of breakfast, gym selfies, asking if someone could interpret their dreams, gossiping about the new instructor who replaced Madame Cruz. They had no idea. Briar considered dropping the news that Master Mal was also a bonafide devil-worshiping witch—or something adjacent—but knew that would only excite everyone more. Mal was egotistical enough, maybe it was better for the sake of the world not to feed it more than necessary.

Not much later, a knock came at Briar's door, and Stella poked her head inside to express how happy she was that he was actually home in time to make it to class.

"Have fun while I was away?" Briar asked, flicking his tongue between two fingers as Stella smirked at him.

"Yes, and she's still here. Want some breakfast?"

"What, you didn't love her into a coma?"

"... Hold on. Now that you mention it, I didn't check to see if she was conscious."

Briar laughed as Stella went back into her room, followed by a series of high-pitched moans and sighs as an answer to his question. Apparently Bianca was not only coma-free, but wide awake.

He wore an oversized Palm Angels t-shirt, fitted Thom Browne chino pants, and white Doc Martens, shoving the rest of his practice clothes into his shoulder bag. In the kitchen, Stella whistled amidst the smell of pancakes, and Briar finally spotted Bianca on the couch scrolling her phone. He offered her a polite hello, and she beamed at him in a way only someone still in their afterglow could. When a knock came at the door, though, followed by a sing-song announcement of who it was, the air in the room dropped into exasperation. Briar surprised himself by laughing out loud.

"Don't worry, I invited him," he reassured them. The witch's eyes went wide, Stella leaning out from the kitchen to stare at him in disbelief, but Briar just smiled awkwardly and hurried to the door before the loudmouth on the other side woke the whole floor.

"Wow, you actually opened the door," Mal smiled on the other side, looking particularly smug—and surprisingly well dressed, enough that it halted the sarcastic reply in Briar's mouth. Mal seemed to notice, even stepping back and extending his hands to show off. "I dunno, I think I've outdone you again, today."

"I can still kick you back out," Briar warned, turning his nose up and turning back into the apartment. "I'm sure Stella would be happy to help me."

"Bianca would defend me," Mal replied.

Briar glanced at where Bianca sat on the couch with a cute, but clearly very confused smile, just looking between Mal and Briar again and again like she really couldn't believe they had made peace behind her back. Briar nearly assured her "peace" was going too far, and the only reason he'd ask Mal for help instead of her was because... well, he didn't know. He just remembered how Mal touched his necklace in the elevator, how he spoke with such certainty, knowing exactly what Briar had done without ever having to ask... and perhaps the thought of not having to admit to anything was more appealing, even if it meant having to rely on someone who wore *Supreme.*

"Everything okay?" Stella asked under her breath, offering Briar some coffee in his favorite kitschy grandma-mug. She said it in that way he hated—but then felt guilty for hating. That tone full of worry, and a little bit of pity, because she knew he wasn't in his right mind despite his best efforts to keep the truth from her. She thought the reason he was up at all hours of the night, drinking more, going home with strangers, napping during the day, missing class, donning heavy bags under his eyes, was simply... nightmares. Stress, maybe, considering upcoming auditions for the spring show. Maybe still trying to get over his crush on Leon, which he thought he'd been doing better to cover up. Bianca had promised to keep his request for protection charms secret, though he didn't know how trustworthy she was, especially when Stella could be very convincing. More than anything, he just didn't need Stella thinking he was going out of his mind. He didn't need his mental state being passed off to his moms, with whom Stella had way too friendly of a relationship over DMs.

At the thought, he adjusted the collar of his shirt to make sure the chains of the necklace were hidden.

"Everything's fine," he finally answered with a calm smile. "I've been getting cramps in my arches lately, so I asked if Master Mal could give me any advice. He wants to see where I practice. Come on, my room is this way."

He motioned for Mal to follow, and Mal did, like a good dog who also liked keeping secrets. He smiled just a little too much at the thought, in fact, and Briar wanted to squash that sentiment as soon as he had the chance. *Sharing secrets doesn't make us friends. It doesn't mean I trust you. I never tell more than just a white lie to my friends, especially Stella...*

He grimaced. Behind him, Mal followed a little too closely, clearly excited to see the wirry-cow skulking around in Briar's room.

"I brought the guns," he said as they reached the end of the hallway.

"The what?" Stella asked from the kitchen, and Briar bit back an unexpected laugh before inviting Mal into his room.

It had been a long time since Briar let anyone except Stella into his room. He always went with other people for one-night stands or after parties, never inviting them back to his own space. To invite a stranger inside, even one who might be able to help with his wirry-cow problem... perhaps even his fey lady problem... it made his skin crawl.

Still, he thought about a chance at getting a single good night's rest, when the fey lady wasn't stealing it from him in other ways. He closed his eyes and breathed in deep, then silently stepped out of the way for Mal to take stock of the bedroom.

Briar pointed out the salt, the crystals, the horseshoe, and everything else he'd done by Bianca's instructions as Mal put on a facade of exaggerated observation, touching his chin and nodding thoughtfully. Briar picked at his cuticles as the man wandered the entire room, spotting all the places Briar had shoved clutter in a mad-dash to clean up just an hour earlier. Mal paused at the pile of makeup and skincare products on the vanity, then touched the string lights dangling from rusted hooks in the brick wall, even peered out the dirty window as if the rickety fire escape on the other side would give him any kind of clues. Briar almost said something, almost accused him of being extra nosy on purpose, when Mal spoke first.

"What's this?" he asked, pointing at a wood box on Briar's dresser.

"That's... where I hide my weed and cigarettes."

"Oh?" he asked, grabbing the box without Briar's permission and cracking it open. To Briar's disbelief, he helped himself to a cigarette inside, lighting it and taking a drag.

"Hmm..." Mal inhaled a lungful of smoke before releasing it in a single cloud like a movie star. Briar almost clobbered him, but he turned and pointed at something else, first. "And that?"

"That's—! It's nothing, just some kitsch. Did you seriously just—"

"What about this?"

Briar groaned. "That's just some shit from online."

Mal pointed at a photo of Briar's family, from the previous summer when he visited them at home in California. "Who are they?" he asked.

Briar's rage tempered in an instant, as if embarrassed to be so angry in front of them. He returned to picking at his nails, shearing off a layer of pink nail polish as he spoke.

"My parents and my sisters."

"Where's this?" Mal pointed to the next photo.

"Cape Disappointment."

Mal found Briar's closet, stepping inside and flipping on the light. He had enough forethought to hold the cigarette out the door, at least. Briar would have skinned him alive, otherwise.

"Quite the designer collection you have, here," he called out, pinching the sleeve of his baby camel Eskander jacket. "How do you afford it all?"

"I'm a dance mentor for some kids with rich parents on the weekends," Briar said. "Or—I steal it."

Mal threw him a look like he didn't know whether or not Briar was being sarcastic. Briar wasn't about to tell.

Mal took another drag off the cigarette, turning back to the room.

"Where'd you get these?"

Briar skimmed over the awards his mom placed on his bookshelf the day he moved in. He never touched them again after that, letting them collect dust, despite the sweaty anxiety they gave him every time he made eye-contact. To take them down would make him feel terrible; leaving them up only made him self-conscious. But maybe that was exactly why he left them there, to always be reminded of how he used to be something special. How, maybe, if he was ever able to impress the fey lady, he might become something special again.

He cleared his throat.

"I actually am good at dancing, you know. I win—erm, I won a lot of competitions growing up."

"Oh?" the corner of Mal's mouth quirked. "I wouldn't have known, considering how you never come to class and show me."

Briar frowned. He peeled another layer of nail polish off in agitation.

"Are you just going to keep wasting my time, or what?" he snapped. "I thought you said you could help me with my problem—"

"I am helping you with your problem." Mal smiled like it was obvious. It only made Briar more annoyed, but once again, he wasn't able to explode before the man just turned to continue whatever he was doing. Briar would wait until they made eye-contact again. He wanted to see Mal's face the moment he screamed for him to get the fuck out.

Mal, completely unaware of his impending doom, trailed his fingers through a forest of ribbons dangling from Briar's line of pointe shoes on the wall behind the door. He tilted his head in curiosity, and Briar didn't want to hear him ask, so he offered the information on his own. He made sure to sound annoyed as he did, though.

"Those are slippers from every final performance I've done."

"There are so many," Mal offered an impressed smile over his shoulder, and Briar was surprised by the sincerity of it. Mal tugged on the first pair of ribbons. "What're these from?"

"It should say on the bottom."

"Ah," he found the handwriting on the heel, moving down the line. "*Coppélia... Romeo and Juliet... The Nutcracker...* ooooh, *La Sylphide,* one of my favorites."

"Mine, too."

"Who did you play? Surely the sylph, herself."

"Erm... one of Effie's bridesmaids."

"Hm," he sniffed. "A poor choice. What about in *Coppélia?*"

"One of the townspeople who dance with Swanhilda..."

Mal frowned. He looked genuinely annoyed. "Romeo and Juliet?"

"Um, Benvolio."

"What, en pointe?"

"No, he's demi."

Mal's annoyance grew.

"Oh, but—" Briar offered before realizing what he was doing. For some reason, he suddenly wanted to insist he wasn't always dancing in the background. "Um, in our last show... I was Giselle. Only an understudy, technically, but I was able to dance in the finale..."

Mal gave him another look—but that one was different. It wasn't sarcastic, or teasing, or even particularly impressed, it was simply—regarding. Up and down Briar's entire body, as if trying to imagine it, or maybe just sifting through his ghost. His being. What was it about those words that sparked such deep-set curiosity in that man's face?

"I'm sure you were stunning," Mal finally said, but his voice was more thoughtful. More serious. Briar smiled sarcastically, about to tell him he wouldn't know, he'd never seen Briar dance— "If you were cast as Giselle, I know you must be stunning. Even as an understudy."

The words lingered. Oh—did Briar's heart skip? Such a simple statement wiped any and all vitriol from his blood. In any other circumstances, he might have burst into tears. If he had the emotional energy to spare, he might have taken Mal's handsome face and kissed him in appreciation.

He never thought such a small sentiment would mean so much, especially after so many months of being told, of really believing, he was nothing special at all.

"Where are those shoes hanging?" Mal went on as the silence lingered. "I'd like to kiss them in appreciation."

"Oh..." Briar rocketed back to reality, and the lump that lived in his stomach returned with him. He formed a lie that was a little too easy to tell. "I, um... haven't had a chance to hang them up, yet."

No—those slippers were buried on the edge of the revel circle, just outside the edge of rosemary. A show of his agreement to their deal. He'd done so that very same night he danced the Giselle finale with Leon; that same night the fey lady, donning the visage of the wili queen Myrtha from the same ballet, approached and asked *what such a pretty thing had to be so sad about...*

"Tell me where they are, I'll do it right now," Mal smiled, wiggling his fingers hungrily. "In fact, I'll pull down all these others to make room for them. Dancing as Giselle is something to be proud of."

Briar wanted to argue, to make up another lie, to change the subject, but the necklace around his throat was suddenly heavy. He touched it beneath his shirt, before biting his lip and glancing at the photo of his family, then the row of dangling pointe shoes, then back to Mal.

"I..." he started, but that familiar twist of his thoughts arrived —the same one that came whenever he spoke a little too closely to the truth of what he'd done. Even trying to write it down in the beginning had all been for naught, as whenever he attempted to conceptualize his fey deal in any way, shape, or form, his mind would tangle up like ancient roots until he forgot what he was talking about.

Mal noticed. That intensity from the elevator returned to his expression, and Briar's breath caught. Mal reached out to slowly close the bedroom door with a click of the latch, then took a step closer.

"Where are they, Briar?" he insisted in a low, dangerous voice. Stepping within reach, his hand brushed against where Briar touched the pearl on his necklace. It was then Briar sensed the lightest hint of rosemary on Mal's clothes, and his throat closed off to escape it. But he didn't move, just stared at the man looming over him.

"I..." he attempted, though it hardly came out as a rasp. "She... has them. I... I gave them to her..."

"The fey lady you made your deal with," Mal's voice lowered further, clearly meant just for Briar. Briar could only nod. He wanted to look away as well, almost too embarrassed to remain standing, but Mal's eyes had a way of trapping him. "What are the terms of your deal?"

Briar's mouth dangled open, empty of an answer. He just shook his head, relieved when Mal nodded slightly.

"You can't talk about it?"

Briar nodded. Mal's thick brows furrowed, finally releasing Briar from his gaze to hook a finger under the necklace, pulling it out to regard it more closely.

"There are ways to get around a secrecy curse," Mal said it like a promise, and Briar let out a relieved breath he didn't realize he was holding. "But until then... I think you should know, your wirry-cow might not be totally unrelated."

"Why does that not surprise me?" Briar grimaced. Mal raised his eyebrows in question, and Briar finally managed to pull away from their close quarters. The second he did, he really could breathe again, though found the air surprisingly chilly on the other side. "Ever since I made my deal, weird fairy things have started following me everywhere. It's almost worse than the deal, itself."

"What form does the wirry-cow take when you see it?"

"What do you mean?"

Mal sat on the edge of Briar's bed, running his hand over the dirty prints left on his duvet. "Wirry-cows take on the form of a person's worst fear. What do you see when it shows itself?"

Briar fidgeted with his hands again. He didn't know if it was anxiety or embarrassment returning to him, but he at least knew better than to meet Mal's eyes and end up trapped all over again.

"Um... the queen of the wilis, from Giselle. Erm—that's... that's what she looked like when she... when Marie d'Alarie, she..."

"Who? The fey lady?"

"Um, yes—I don't mean the queen literally, of course, but... that's what she looked like when we first made our deal, and that's how she always looks when she talks to me, even in the fey world... so... So it's really awful when I see her in that corner at night, because... because I never know if it's the wirry-cow or actually her, you know?"

He was talking too much, saying too many embarrassing things, but to his relief, Mal just nodded the whole time. Briar risked glancing up at him, and fell for his trap in an instant. Unable to look away, all he could do was smile awkwardly.

"Do you... really know about them? Fey deals, I mean."

Mal nodded.

"Then... can you help me?"

"Do you want my help?"

The question was so pointed, moreso than when Mal asked in the elevator—*"Do you need help?"* As if Mal had slapped him, rather than asked something so simple. So simple—but at the same time, so complicated, as Briar had spent the last five months navigating his mistakes all by himself in fear of people thinking he was out of his mind, or making things up, or just trying to get attention. And on the off chance someone actually did believe him—to have to admit what he'd done, and for what reasons, was enough to make his heart stop out of pure mortification.

"I—"

A sudden knock came at his door, and Stella gracelessly announced it was time to go on the other side. Briar could have thanked her. Briar could have cursed her.

Either way, he was forced to sit with that question for the rest of the morning. It burrowed into his being, stretching long tendrils out in every direction, trying to find a single reason why those five words intimidated him so much.

10

BRIAR AND THE WALTZ

Master Mal loved giving critique—especially to Briar, for some reason, which only pissed him off. He intentionally did everything opposite what the new instructor said, keeping his expression blank, or innocent, or confused, hoping to break the man entirely. But Mal's nerves were made of steel—or maybe he just knew what Briar was doing, and liked the game, too. All the while—Briar just couldn't stop thinking about their brief exchange in his bedroom that morning.

Do you want my help?

Did they? Briar—didn't know. Briar had done so well to avoid asking for help outside of random charms from Bianca, both unable to fully speak the terms of his deal with the fey lady, and also being too goddamn mortified to even consider admitting what he'd done. That stupid, embarrassing thing he'd done, what he'd thrown his life away for, only to be tricked like he deserved to be. Was Mal any different? Would Briar ever feel like he could tell Mal anything, even if it meant possibly getting the help he needed...?

Briar fled the moment class ended, claiming he was going to be late for English and rushing off before the instructor-witch had any chance to try and stop him.

He did actually go straight to his next class—but that morning, and in the classes following, Briar heard nothing. Saw and perceived nothing, except those words Mal spoke to him. Those five words that brought Briar's world to a halt, words he couldn't believe were so difficult to internalize. *Do you want my help?*

No. Yes. Briar didn't know—his heart just pounded endlessly every time he thought about it. He kept trying to text Mal to give him an answer, or maybe ask a question, or anything else—but couldn't get more than a few letters into a message every time he tried, and could only pray Mal didn't notice every time his *"Briar is typing..."* bubble popped up on the other side of the screen.

Briar just needed to clear his head. He needed to relax. He needed to just... distract himself long enough to think clearly. To think ahead. To figure out every single possible consequence of saying... *yes.* Of saying *no.*

After his final class, as the winter sun set earlier than ever, Briar coasted his bike back to the dance studio on the other side of campus. He locked the bike on the rack with only one long-abandoned, flat-tired bike, pulling his scarf closer to his mouth and using the fob on his lanyard to unlock the doors to the empty studio building. The motion-detection lights spotted him, flickering to life as he passed beneath them. He quietly greeted the ghosts of the ancient building, apologizing for waking them up so early into the night. They would understand why he was there; god knew they were the most common audience members whenever people danced in the practice room. They might even recognize him from that morning. Another reason he preferred human ghosts to fairy wirry-cows.

Unwrapping himself from his scarf, jacket, hoodie, boots and double-thick wool socks, Briar made himself comfortable on the floor against the mirror, pulling out a new pair of black en pointe slippers he saved just for private sessions, as well as elastic ribbons, scissors, dental floss, darning thread, and needles. He settled into a familiar routine, hating how his heart fluttered at the thought of, perhaps, being able to dance through a single pair of shoes in the studio instead of staining them in grass.

Sewing elastic into the heel and wings of the arch; cutting and half-shanking the sole; cutting and re-sewing the upper edge of the vamp seam; taking out any remaining aggression by applying his weight to the folded slipper to break in whatever stiffness remained.

Wrapping his toes in tape, he triple-wrapped his fucky ankle, last, before finally rising to his feet and carefully rolling his foot, his arches, his ankle, then stretching downward to slip the shoes on. He practically sighed in relief, rolling through the motions of demi-pointe to en pointe a few more times to loosen the vamp stitching and settle the arch of his foot into place. He took a few minutes to stretch against the ballet bar, elongating his hamstrings, his thighs, his arms and legs. Finally—he pushed wireless headphones into his ears, summoning Swan Lake. A dance everyone knew from the first day they were finally cleared to pull on pointe shoes.

The studio fell away beneath him; Briar closed his eyes, sinking into the initial swell of the orchestra, allowing his movements to bloom into choreography he had memorized like each syllable of his name. Hardly needing to think about every step that came next, sweeping and turning through each without pushing his stiff, sore legs too hard with each movement. Keeping himself on the ground, moving like water through a string of bells on a rainy day despite how hard it poured from the sky. Easy. Careful. Gentleness extended to the audience, even if that night it was only ghosts hiding from the lights in far corners of the room.

God—it was liberating to dance just for himself, again. In the low light of the studio room, thick clouds and snow on the other side of the high windows kept the ambiance relaxed. The lights in the hallway on the other side of the doors flickered dark again. Briar danced with ease, moreso than whenever he stood in front of peers, in front of an audience, in front of the fey lady and her revel guests, not minding if his steps elongated slightly too much and missed the next note, simply letting the music flow through his limbs until he gathered the tempo again.

The tight bandages around his ankle did everything they could, though he had to swiftly side-step whenever needing to apply his whole weight to the injury in question.

He swept nearly through the first scene of act one before sensing another presence in the room—and hands suddenly tucked into his as he solo'd the pas des deux. His eyes fluttered open, mouth dropping wide as, in front of him, Leon Heller smiled, then laughed while pulling Briar in every direction. It hadn't been more than a few weeks since Briar last saw Leon in person, it wasn't like he could forget what the man looked like— but still, existing so close to him, so suddenly, rushed Briar's body with a surge of inebriating wine, sparks of hot fire, a torrent of acid rain settling in the back of his throat before dripping into his stomach and making it turn in uncertainty.

Leon, who wasn't so handsome it made him intimidating; Leon, with his wavy blonde hair only ever brushed into submission for performances. Whose scruffy chin and cheeks made him look older than he was, hiding the boyish features of a dancer who had to shave for performances. Who could pass as slender from a distance, only to demonstrate the strength in his muscles the moment his hands took a partner by the waist and lifted them overhead. Who Briar had to lift his chin to meet the eyes of, whose cheerful smile melted Briar's insides until there was hardly anything left except ambrosial warmth and comfort.

"Leon?" Briar asked breathlessly, partly convinced it was only a dream. "Wh-what are you doing here?"

"I was dropping Madison off with the dean for an enrollment interview," Leon grinned. Briar's insides turned to mush. "Saw the studio lights were on. Wondered who could be here so late. Maybe I should have known."

Briar's face erupted into flames. He claimed one of the pods from his ear in order to better make conversation—but Leon took it from him just as swiftly, tucking it into his own ear to share in the orchestra. Closing his eyes, he smiled to himself, then nodded.

"I thought so," he said. "I can always recognize the first waltz. Mind if I join you?"

Briar couldn't help but smile, allowing himself to settle back into the ease of the movements again, that time providing Leon with the slightest amount of trust to balance what he'd been carrying alone, before. It was—easy to dance with Leon. But at the same time, Briar couldn't help but feel his heart squeeze, his lungs open and close in what had to be a panic.

"I was actually... going to text you later," Leon went on, only making Briar's anxiety more palpable. "I have a favor to ask."

Briar couldn't think of how to respond. Leon continued without prompting.

"It's just that... I need your help. We're doing La Sylphide's pas de deux for the Tomassin charity gala in a few weeks... and you're the only person I can think of to help me."

"Oh—" Briar breathed—though it may have been more of a wheeze. He used the following steps of the dance to bide his time. "H-help you?"

Leon smiled handsomely, boyishly, down at him. He moved Briar in a way that was both leading and following, just like Briar remembered. His hands, gentle when they needed to be, firm every other time, always keeping Briar exactly in line with where he needed to go.

"I, uh... need you to dance with me. Remember when you understudied for Kara? Tell me you remember the choreography."

"Dance?" Briar came to a sudden halt. "With you?"

Leon chuckled. He turned Briar this way and that, before bringing him back around again. "Where are you confused?"

"Um—sorry," Briar laughed awkwardly, bowing into arabesque and using it as a chance to think. Every thought, all at once—it was a trick. This was a trick. He wasn't who Briar thought. It wasn't really him. This was too good to be true. It couldn't be happening. Not like that. Not after everything he'd done to have exactly that... "I... would love to dance with you again, Leon."

Even if it was a trick, even if it was only a dream...

"Great!" Leon grinned, pulling Briar in close after a turn, and Briar's breath caught. "Our next practice is this weekend; I'll text you more information about it, alright? Thank god for you, Briar."

Briar's face erupted hotter, if that were possible. He thought his skin might melt away, even pressing his fingers to his cheeks to try and hold it in place. It didn't matter—someone called out Leon's name from the outside hallway, and Leon made a sound of acknowledgement. He settled Briar back on his feet, then, charming as ever—took Briar's hand and kissed the back of it. It wasn't anything more than playfulness, but—Briar lost all his ability to think straight.

"I should get back to Madison, but I'll text you, alright?" he said. "It'll be fun to dance together, again."

"Yeah..." Was all Briar could manage, before something struck him, lunging and grabbing Leon's hand at the last second. He made up the first thing to come to mind, knowing Stella wouldn't mind an impromptu date opportunity, at least. "Um—we're going ice skating in a couple of days. Do you want to come?"

Leon grinned, and Briar couldn't help but smile in relief, too.

"Yeah! I haven't been since last winter's production." He said, referring to how Artemisia cast would go ice-skating before the first practice of the winter production, surfing before the spring production. Leon might have said something else, but Briar's ears were nothing but singing angels.

"Yeah, I'll text you." He smiled, forcing himself to release Leon's hand before it stood out how snugly he clung to it. Leon waved goodbye, hurrying through the clanging doors, and Briar recognized the voice of Leon's sister, Madison, on the other side. He wondered if she would recognize him, too.

Briar's world spun. All those things he'd done to try and win exactly what was being dropped right in his lap—all that time spent dancing for the fey lady at the revel, all the sleepless nights, all the harassment from those high fey, all the pain he'd endured... none of it mattered. But he wasn't angry, no—he was relieved. Maybe he wouldn't have to do it again. Maybe he would simply be able to... forget any of it happened, and simply claim his time with Leon for himself. On his own accord.

Briar bit back a smile. He hopped a few times on his toes in excitement, before turning and giggling and running his fingers back through his hair in pure elation.

He didn't stop smiling as he pulled off his slippers and got dressed again. He didn't stop smiling even as the air was bitter and harsh outside, breath thick on the chill.

The only thing to make his heart sink—was the sight of a magpie perched on the seat of his bike as he approached outside. A magpie with white eyes and matching wing-tips, a fox-mask pendant dangling from its neck. A call from the fey lady, who once promised Briar the ability to get exactly what he'd just been given on his own.

A fire sparked in Briar's chest. He raced toward the bird, throwing his hands up and scaring it off. It squawked and flapped backward, complaining at him and swooping to try and peck some of his hair free, but Briar just swung his bag at the bird and told it to *go to hell*. The moment it disappeared into the dark sky, though, the adrenaline trembled, then sank. His grin followed, and he couldn't help but wonder... if it would really be that easy. If anything in his world would ever be *easy* ever again...

The sudden anxiety ate at him all the way home. All the way up the elevator to the apartment, which was empty with a note on the fridge from Stella. *Staying late with Bianca. Don't wait up.*

Briar took a shower. He thought about going to the revel, anyway, even though he would definitely be late—but then did his best to steel his nerves and reassure himself everything would be fine. He didn't need that fey woman. He didn't need her fey magic. He didn't need their deal any longer.

But then he opened the door to his bedroom—and saw her,

in her Myrtha ensemble, hovering in the corner of the room. Staring at him, with eyes glowing through the darkness. He quickly flipped on the light, just like every other time, and she vanished.

Still—he didn't move from where he stood. His resolve cracked, on the verge of crumbling as he wondered the consequences he might have completely ignored. Perhaps he never should have spurned her call. He never should have scared her bird away and assumed he was safe to leave when he wanted, even if he was being given everything he'd ever wanted. Would she understand? Wouldn't she understand?

All he knew was—he suddenly didn't want to be home, just in case she came looking for him. Not alone, not when it was dark outside. Not when the fey lady could come looking for him, not when the wirry-cow in the corner was surely still there, only stifled by the overhead light. He could go and apologize to her in the morning, as soon as the sun rose. He would answer her next call, if one ever came.

He changed his clothes. He dug through his bag, grabbing only his ID, credit card, and phone.

Briar just wanted to be somewhere else. Anywhere else. Somewhere he wouldn't be found, not when he'd been given something to be happy about for the first time in months. He just wanted to enjoy it, revel in it.

Damnit—his ears hurt. His ankle hurt. His chest hurt. His feet, his heart, his ego—it was all too frail to keep his body upright. He just needed to disappear for a few hours, where no one would recognize him or want anything from him at all.

❧ II ❧

BRIAR AND THE WILI

The bass thumped through Briar's bones. They vibrated beneath the pulsing music, buzzing the anxiety out of his muscles as the third long island iced tea prickled his skin and numbed the pain in his ankle. He wore his favorite teal-blue Marc Jacobs mini skirt with rainbows on the ass, paired with a black Dolce & Gabbana crop top, intentionally showing as much skin as he could so he wouldn't be tempted to step anywhere outside until he really meant it. So if he got a little too drunk and someone he didn't choose tried to shepherd him into a cab, he would feel the bite of the winter air and realize something was wrong. He just had to cup his hand over the top of his drinks, never put them down, and remind anyone who looked at him a little too long that he had a switchblade tucked in his waistband. He would love to finally get to use it.

Despite the precautions, it was easy for Briar to slip into dancing, grinding, feeling up on anyone who would consent to it. He would cup their faces and kiss them gently, then roughly, then laugh sharply when one or two strangers would pull him into the back hallway and push him into the wall and really kiss him. He never fucked in the club bathroom—yet, at least—but just experiencing anyone who wanted to experience him back was exactly what he needed to feel sweet emptiness, to exist as nothing and something at the same time. Just a mouth to kiss and a waist to grab and, if the person he found was a good enough kisser, legs to open later in the stranger's bed. A single offering of peace and anonymity in a world he wished to disappear from.

He was in the middle of disappearing into some dumb jock's minty breath and lip balm when something suddenly caught his eye—and stopped him short. On the other side of the dancefloor, like a beam of light in the darkness, a woman stood dressed in a white bell skirt, a white bodice, donning a white flower crown that matched the wings sewn into the small of her back...

Pulling away, the man grabbed Briar in confusion—and Briar instinctively smashed the heel of his palm into the man's nose. He wasn't thinking—he was drunk, maybe a little crossfaded, he couldn't remember, but Myrtha—no, Marie d'Alarie, the fey lady who owned him—had found him, even in his best attempts to disappear.

He managed a raspy *"sorry"* to his victim before stumbling away, grabbing his head and trying to blink the personage away. It was only his imagination. The wirry-cow, even though he'd never seen it leave his room, before. But even the fey lady had never cornered him somewhere in the real world—at least not like that. Not in the middle of public, in the middle of a club.

Seeking out somewhere dark, quiet, private, Briar stopped at any lonely corner he could find—but she was there, every single time. At the end of the long corridor to the bathrooms, near the front coat check, behind the bar, everywhere he looked. All he could do was shove people out of the way as he hurried back in the opposite direction, holding his head, anxiety rising like bile in the back of his throat. She'd found him, despite his attempts to hide. She found him, even though he only wanted one night.

In another corner, he grappled for his phone, managing to snap a shaky picture. Wanting to prove it was his only imagination —but he couldn't get his screen brightness up enough to see it. It was too blurry to make anything out. His hands wouldn't stop shaking.

He had to prove to someone else that she was real, though. Or simply show someone else there was nothing there, so they might comfort him. His first thought was to send it to Stella, inebriated mind racing, not thinking clearly, dropping it into the first conversation open on his phone and hitting *send*.

But the moment he did, the stench of rosemary flooded his nose, and he dropped his phone. Searching in every direction, he no longer saw her, that false queen of the wilis, only smelled her. That awful scent that always filled the revel clearing, the one he smelled so strongly that first night she approached him backstage after his dance with Leon. Where he first thought she was a friend still in costume, only to realize he didn't recognize her face. The bodice of her ensemble was made with real lace and expensive silk. The flowers in her hair and in a sash over her chest were fresh and real. The branch in her hand was genuine rosemary, bundled together in shimmering string.

Briar panicked. He just had to get out, get away from her, from the darkness and the flashing lights and the pounding music that made it impossible to think. But in his panic, his drunkenness, he couldn't find his way back to the front. Back to the coat-check. Instead—he left through the first exit he could find, straight out into the cold with nothing to protect him against the chill.

It was snowing when he burst into the back alley, his footprints the first to disrupt a new frozen carpet gathering on the concrete. He shuddered, throwing his arms around himself and immediately turning to grab the door and rush back inside, but he was locked out the moment it clanged shut. Cursing under his breath, he turned in every direction until he spotted the sidewalk next to the main road—but there was something silhouetted in the streetlamps on the other side of the mouth of the alley, blocking his way.

He could only stare at her. His hands flashed to his pocket, searching for his phone, wanting to take another picture—realizing he had left it where it fell inside. He was going to be sick.

Putting his hands up, he searched for his mouth over all the emotion clouding his thoughts.

"Stay away from me," he managed, thick clouds of steam puffing from his breath as he did. "I don't—I don't need you anymore. I don't need our deal anymore, I want—"

"Oh?" the figure asked. Illuminated from behind, her white skirts were bright and celestial. She stood en pointe, even while claiming a few steps toward him. He stumbled backward in response, nearly falling to the snow—only for his wrists to be suddenly grabbed in her hands, not even seeing her move. It should have been impossible to be so fast—but she grabbed him, pulling him close. With eyes wide and nostrils flared, Briar had never seen anyone so angry before in his life.

"You humiliated me," she hissed. "You were meant to dance for me tonight, Briar Hunt."

"How—" he begged hoarsely. "How did you find me?"

"What, my own little dancer?" her tone shifted instantly, cooing at him. Icy cold fingers trailed down his cheek, then his jaw, curling under his chin. "When you did not come to dance for me tonight, I grew worried. I knew you had to be dead, or close to it, to have the nerve to deny me when I summon you."

Briar gulped, but the lump in his throat was thorny. Shaking, he returned to his feet, never taking his eyes off her.

"I'm—I'm sorry, my lady," he said breathlessly. He wanted to insist on his original declaration, that he decided he didn't need her anymore, he could make Leon notice him all on his own—but the smell of rosemary was too thick in his nose. Her eyes, green and bright even in the low light, burrowed into him. He could feel the leaves of her thrush scraping against the side of his bare leg. "I must not have seen your bird—"

"Just because you can lie to me, does not mean I recommend you do," she answered with enough ice Briar felt it crystallize in his blood. "I know you saw my messenger, Briar, and I know you turned the other way."

"I—"

"Not only have you failed to live up to my expectations, now you are being purposefully disobedient," she continued, clutching his face in clawed nails and making him yelp. He grabbed her wrist in an attempt to push it away, but her hand held fast. "Need I remind you what will happen if you refuse me, again? Do you remember?"

Briar tried to swallow again, and nodded weakly. She nodded back expectantly, and Briar wet his lips.

"I—I will *'become as the trees, to witness the perfection of another... to—to learn what I myself couldn't do'...*"

"That's right," she said, looking down her nose at him with a small smile. "Either you dance when I call you, or you bring me a replacement. Do you remember that mercy I extended you, as well?"

Briar nodded again, as much as her grip on his face would allow. She leaned in close, breath as cold as the air around them.

"If you truly mean it when you say you wish to end our deal... then send someone in your place, and you will be free. But you alone are not the one to determine when our terms are void. Do you understand me?"

Briar tried to speak, but only flinched when her nails buried into his cheeks.

"It's that simple, Briar; I will show you grace, despite never receiving that one perfect dance I wanted. Tenderheartedness has always been my weakness, you know, especially when faced with such pitiful artists such as yourself. You are not the first human who has disappointed me—I know better than to ever put too much faith in the likes of you."

Briar squeezed his eyes closed, then cracked them open to gaze up at her. Like a towering fox, she smiled down at him like a meal to be eaten.

"Come when I call next, or send your understudy," she reiterated. "Else you shall know what it means to become as the trees, Briar."

She suddenly pulled Briar forward, pressing their lips together. Briar grunted, shoving away in an instant—but she was gone the second he gathered himself. As quickly as she'd moved to grab him, she'd vanished, and he was the only one left in the alleyway. Even the snow beneath where she'd walked, where she'd stood while holding him—was undisturbed.

He thought he might be sick. Breathing heavily, he pressed his face into his hands, then ran his fingers back through his hair— only for strands to tangle on his nails, as if broken, hooked, rough to the touch.

Pulling them back again, he stared in horror at the sight of fibrous tendrils emerging from under his fingernails, splitting them, pushing through his skin like flowers through grass. From their buds, leaves unfurled. More and more and more, no matter how frantically he tore at them, ripping the twigs growing from his skin and taking fingernails with them.

Whimpering in fear, he could do nothing when the same burning, tingling sensation of something spreading under his skin grew in his legs, up his stomach, and then in the back of his throat. His ears clogged, his lungs buckled beneath the weight of branches entangling within his ribcage, searching for a way free, searching for sunlight, only to crawl up his airway and erupt from his mouth.

Buckling to his knees in the snow, Briar heaved, gagged, clutching at his throat before desperately tearing at handfuls of branches and leaves blocking his airway—but they grew too fast. They devoured him from the inside like a plague, knotting and tangling and squeezing and suffocating him—until he felt the exact moment they infiltrated his heart, and tore it in half.

12

MALRIC AND THE PLEA

Malric knew what it looked like when Marie was angry—but he'd never seen the facade of a perfect revel hostess come so close to cracking when she finally realized Briar Hunt was not coming. He wasn't only late, wasn't just lost on his way—he had no intention of arriving at all.

Malric might have been more than amused at the thought, if he wasn't so suddenly worried about *why*. Did something happen?

Or, worst of all—was he completely fine, and only rebelling? Malric didn't know if that scared him or turned him on more.

Glancing over to where Felme sat with Mavera and Maura, they all stared straight ahead and sipped their wines to also pretend nothing was amiss, despite Marie storming into the woods to search for her missing rosefinch dancer on foot. The moment she was gone, Malric leapt to his feet and skittered around to the first tear in the veil he could find for himself, wanting to find Briar before his mother did.

Unfortunately, the veil spot he chose spit him out farther from the beach than where he hoped to end up, and trying to make his way back to the ferry was a real pain in the ass. It didn't help that, as he hurried, he tried calling Stella and Bianca both fifteen times each, only for Stella to inform him she didn't know where Briar was when she finally answered. Malric paused a little too long when she asked if she should be worried—and it was amidst that pause that Malric received a message that would haunt him. A blurry image from Briar's number, depicting a ghastly ballerina staring at him from the darkness of a club. Queen Myrtha of the wilis, just like in Giselle. What was it he said about the queen and Malric's mother...?

"Shit!" he hissed, hopping back on the call with Stella and telling her to do what she could to find him. She hung up in an instant, and Malric knew he had a better chance of finding the rosefinch with Stella's help.

When he finally made it to the ferry, when he finally made it into the city, Bianca sent him a location of where they were going —though it took a lot of pestering for her to do so. It was only when Malric implied there might be something else going on that she gave in and sent him the pin. He arrived before they did, and, not wanting to wait, compelled the bouncer to give him entry to the club.

Briar shouldn't have been too hard to find, but the loud music, flashing lights, cramped bodies definitely didn't help. Malric searched the lower floor, the dance floor, then the second level, all while using the photo on his phone as a point of reference. As soon as he found the exact spot Briar stood before snapping the photo, though, he only grew more annoyed when the dancer wasn't there waiting for him. He nearly turned to look somewhere else, when something crunched under his foot. Scooping it up, Malric's breath caught when he recognized Briar's phone case with the flowers and cherubs on the back.

"Fuck," he muttered, looking in every direction again before pinching his eyes closed. Fuck, fuck *fuck, fine, alright!*

Shoving his way through the crowded bar area, he found a dark corner and huddled into it, back turned to the rest of the world.

The d'Alarie family were not Sídhe. They did not each have

unique abilities like those other more powerful fey—but that didn't mean special traits didn't come to them. They were still descended from another powerful Sídhe family, one they shared the fox crest with. One they carried other, smaller abilities from.

Malric closed his eyes, breathing in deep through his nose.

He knew if Marie really was close by, she might be able to find him, too, if he utilized opulence like that. He'd been so careful to avoid using too much of his family magic at any one time for that exact reason, but—but Briar might be in trouble, and Malric had to find him. He had to find his rosefinch before Marie had them to herself for too long. He didn't want to imagine what she might do in her anger.

Channeling what he could claim from the veil existing all around them, Malric clutched the phone case tighter. He flared his nostrils and squeezed his eyes shut. He focused on Briar until the rest of the club fell away, leaving only the thudding of the overhead base pounding through his chest. When his eyes opened again, the world had dimmed, except a single trail of cloudy light showing Malric exactly all the places Briar had gone, where reality had kissed his existence just long enough to remember the taste. It would fade soon enough, just like it always did—but the fact there was any sign of him at all meant Malric couldn't be that far behind.

Following the cloudy path, every one of his other senses were dulled in the process. He hadn't tracked anyone opulently in so long, he even felt how it sucked the energy from his body, not unlike running a marathon without training for months. But Malric didn't need a lot, he wouldn't have to track for long. He just needed to get close enough to find him, wherever he was.

Back through the crowd. Wandering around to the bar, back through the corridors where Malric had already checked, weaving through bodies on the dancefloor, toward the front entrance then back again, Malric retraced his own steps, as well as Briar's. He knew he was on the right track as the light condensed into a sharper line, like a floating string of energy more focused the younger it was. Briar was close, they were so close.

When Malric finally pushed open one of the back doors, he glanced up and down the alleyway in confusion. The string, brighter and more laser-focused than ever, led him right that way —but there was nothing in the alleyway except fresh snow...

"Briar!" he choked. There, a few feet down the way, someone was curled up under a thin blanket of snow. Every one of Malric's senses rushed back into place, nearly knocking him off his feet. His heart erupted into his throat, and he threw himself into the cold.

"Hey, hey! Briar! Hey!" he exclaimed, dropping to his knees and pulling Briar's motionless body into his arms, his chest, fighting to lift him up off the cold ground. He hurriedly stripped off his own coat to wrap his dancer in, rubbing up and down Briar's bare arms before pulling him closer to search for any signs of life. Thankfully, Briar's breaths came in low and fast, his body was still warm, there was the flush of chilled life in his cheeks.

"What the hell are you doing out here?" Malric demanded. "Wearing so little? Are you stupid? You could have frozen to death..."

He trailed off as soft words escaped Briar's lips, having to lean closer as he wasn't sure if he was just imagining them. But as his ear hovered alongside Briar's mouth, Malric heard them. Tiny, breathless, pathetic.

"...your help. I want your help..."

Malric almost grumbled 'what do you think I'm doing?' in reply, before stopping himself. *I want your help. I want...*

"Oh," he whispered, but his following words disappeared before he could speak them. Clenching his jaw, he pulled Briar closer, pressing his face into their soft hair. "She found you first, didn't she?"

But Briar still didn't say anything, except those repeated pleas. *"Help me. Help me. Please, I want your help..."*

"I'll help you," Malric promised, quiet enough just for Briar.

To keep for himself in whatever exhausted, numb dream he wandered through. "I was always going to help you, whether you liked it or not, idiot."

And then—Briar's cold lips turned upward, in the tiniest smile of relief Malric had ever seen. He went still just at the sight of something so small, so pitiful. As if Malric really was the first person who had ever even noticed something was amiss, and then offered to help. He couldn't stop his hand from reaching out—and gently touching Briar's face, pushing loose hair from his eyes.

No—that wasn't true. Stella knew something was wrong. Bianca knew something was wrong. Surely, everyone else in Briar's life knew something was wrong with him—but Malric was the first person Briar had ever admitted defeat to. Why did that only make Malric angrier?

"I'm going to help you," he promised again, softer that time. "I won't let her hurt you like she hurt me, Briar Hunt."

WITH BRIAR DRAPED IN HIS ARMS, MALRIC KNEW THE moment his dancer emerged from the cold place holding them down when they started shivering. When their teeth chattered loud enough to be heard over the voices in the club Malric wandered through, trying to find the coat check so he could make sure Briar had all their things to go home with.

"What are you doing?" Briar's exhausted voice finally poked through as they waited—before tearing suddenly from Malric's grasp, hitting the floor and scrambling away with a gasp. They clawed at their face, their mouth, scraping nails down their arms and neck—before staring at Malric with wide eyes, who stared right back in shock.

"Um?" Malric huffed. "Are you good?"

"I—" Briar rasped. He dragged his hands up and down his arms again, perhaps on instinct, perhaps in shock. What exactly did he think he was going to find? Only when he realized there was nothing there did his face flush red, turning quickly to snag his jacket from the clerk offering it, shoving his arms through the sleeves and hurrying out the front doors. Malric called after him in annoyance, but it didn't matter—Briar walked straight into Stella, who looked fucking furious.

Malric could only sigh as she and Briar got into it instantly, Stella screaming at him for making her worry, Briar shouting back for her to keep her voice down, it wasn't that big of a deal, he was completely fine.. Bianca, meanwhile, just looked like a tired mom who'd lost her kid in the grocery store, wobbling to where Malric stood off to the side lighting a cigarette.

"Share," she sighed, and he offered her a drag. "Thanks for finding him."

Malric nodded, keeping his eyes on Stella and Briar as Stella threatened to grab them by the scruff and throw them into traffic. He let out a long sigh, cold steam on his breath even thicker than the smoke he exhaled.

"Briar made a fey deal with my mother."

Bianca went stiff. When she finally turned to him, her eyes were the size of the obscured moon overhead, mouth hanging open about the same.

"They... what?" she croaked. As if she couldn't believe it. Malric just pinched his eyes closed, nodding and taking another drag off the cigarette. Trying to claim any warmth he could from it, though his insides remained cold as ever.

"I think... they're the one she took to replace me, Bee."

"When you stopped dancing for her?"

Malric nodded. Bianca watched him for a moment longer, before turning slowly to keep her eyes on the fighting friends, too.

"How did she find him?" she asked.

"I'm not sure," Malric muttered, flicking ash off the cigarette. "She's attracted to grief, though. I can't imagine it was hard. You know anything?"

"Not really." She shook her head. "Briar has always been nice enough since Stella and I met, although... always kept to themself, too."

"Yeah."

Bianca let out a frustrated breath through her nose. She wore that expression Malric had come to know well, when she was deep in thought, whether trying to deduce something scientific or related to her own witchery. That face she put on when someone approached with a particularly difficult curse they needed break-ing; when someone at the lab was bothering her enough she mentally brought it home to stew over all night long.

"I'm going to help him," Malric offered, in an attempt to ease her obvious worry. "I won't let my mother hurt him."

He thought Bianca would be relieved at that, but that pinched look of concern on her face didn't change. It didn't even twitch, and Malric had to wonder if... she didn't quite believe him. But then she surprised him, taking the cigarette back and inhaling a long burn.

"Are you sure that's alright?" she asked quietly. Malric almost argued, thinking she was implying he wouldn't be able to— "She'll find you again, Mal. You'll be right where she can find you again..."

Malric's defense fizzled, like the air had been knocked out of him. Oh. Bianca was worried about him. Why did that suddenly make it hard to think straight?

He took back what remained of the cigarette. He watched Briar and Stella continue arguing, though they were reaching the point of mutual tears and exclaiming how much they loved each other. He couldn't help but smile to himself, shaking his head.

He knew the risks of getting involved with Briar, especially with Briar and their deal with Marie. Malric knew it would put him directly in the line of sight of his mother, whose entire wish was likely to get Malric right back into the revel clearing. Maybe she never intended on Briar being the perfect bait, but at the same time—she probably knew exactly what she was doing, picking the prettiest human dancer she could find and biding her time. Malric got that from her, after all. Being attracted to pretty things on nice legs.

But Malric wouldn't let his mother hurt someone else outside of the family. Not again. Not someone like Briar, who was still so young, who still had that spark of passion for the art left. Malric wouldn't be able to live with himself if he knowingly allowed Marie d'Alarie to snuff another artistic flame, just like she had with him. Just like she had with all of the d'Alarie children.

Claiming the last burn of the cigarette on a long breath, he tossed it to the snowy sidewalk and crushed it under the toe of his shoe.

Despite all of that, he couldn't deny the stab of thawing nails in his stomach.

13

MALRIC AND THE WIRRY-COW

The adrenaline mixed with tears mixed with alcohol and whatever else Briar ingested at the club all combined to make one very, very sleepy rosefinch on the train, who swapped from draping over Stella's shoulder to drooling on Malric's lap while Stella and Bianca took pictures to use against him, later. Malric pretended to tease, too. In reality, he was just happy to have Briar close by at all. He couldn't shake the memory of that face, that pleading voice—*help me. Please, I want your help...*

Malric's finger curled through a strand of Briar's damp hair while Stella and Bianca weren't looking, resting his cheek on a closed fist and unable to resist just... staring. At this person unconscious over his lap, who was normally so thorny and abrasive. Who would have thought someone as rough as Briar Hunt could be so squishy when drunk off their ass. Malric was only a little bit jealous—he hadn't been that drunk, himself, since... well, since he first learned of the human dancer sleeping in his bed.

When the train reached their stop, Malric would have carried Briar himself, had Stella not grabbed and flung her friend over one shoulder like a shepherd and a lost lamb. Briar's eyes didn't even open, though he mumbled something that sounded like threats, or maybe just warnings he was going to puke. Neither came to pass, as he slumped back into unconsciousness the moment they emerged into the cold night air. It was still snowing by the time they made it to the sidewalk, and Malric kept glancing back at Briar on Stella's shoulder. His bare legs, especially, were hard to ignore. For a lot of reasons. Gods—if Malric ever crossed paths with Briar in a dark, crowded club or bar, he wasn't sure there would be much to convince him to behave. Something told him Briar wasn't exactly an angel in those situations, either.

Back at the apartment, Stella dumped Briar into her own bed as Bianca offered Malric the couch, and Malric just thanked her, before grimacing at the thrifted, threadbare piece of furniture in the front room. Still, he was polite as ever—unusual for him, which was confirmed by Bianca's narrowed eyes of suspicion. He just narrowed them back and motioned for her to join her lover in the bedroom.

The moment Briar was snuggled in bed like a kitten between two cats, Malric forewent the couch in favor of the kitten's own bed. He recalled what it looked like from the first time he visited to address Briar's wirry-cow problem, recalling the thick duvet, the ocean of pillows, and... the dirty hand- and footprints over the lavender fabric. The wirry-cow, sniffing around, leaving its mark even while Briar wasn't home. That meant it wasn't just a passing omen, it wasn't just a wild thing catching wind of a random person's grief. No—it was either trapped, or it was compelled. Malric was curious to know which, though a part of him had a good idea the queen of the wilis was somehow involved.

Closing the door behind him, Malric took a moment to observe the room as it was. Dim without the corner lamp on, only low light from the street through the window casting any kind of visibility. Even then, it was ominous. The perfect amount for dark shadows to fester in the corners, along the floor, under the bed. He entered deeper, keeping his eyes focused on anything that might move within the stillness.

Trailing his hand through the dangling ballet ribbons like the vines of a weeping willow; drawing his finger in an invisible line down the polished metal of the footboard; brushing his hand over the top of the duvet and wiping away most of the dust left behind by the wirry-cow's most recent visit, Malric memorized every single detail of the room he possibly could without digging around. Without leaving any trace he'd been there at all, recalling how awkward Briar had been when they were there together, the first time.

In his search, Malric tried to uncover any additional clues as to what interested Marie with Briar Hunt in the first place—but he came up short every additional minute that passed. From everything Malric could see, from what he'd witnessed, Briar was simply...

Briar was a beautiful dancer—but so were others. Briar was smart and clearly wanted the perfection offered by Marie, but—so would anyone else. Briar wasn't particularly decorated with more accolades or performances under his belt than anyone else at his stage, his name wasn't known in famous circles, he didn't even have a huge following on social media, or anything like that—so why would Marie choose someone like him to replace someone like Malric?

A surge of unexpected defensiveness came over him, but not in regards to himself—in regards to *Briar*. For Marie to prey on someone so simple yet talented, someone so smart yet so naïve, it was even more malevolent than Malric ever thought. Of course Marie would target someone who could perform well, but at the same time doubted their own abilities. Just enough to believe it when Marie refused to call them perfect, but assured perfection was within reach. Of course she would prey on someone who was just like everyone else, to reduce the odds of someone in Briar's life noticing something was amiss and trying to intervene.

Malric smirked bitterly. He thought of Bianca, first—then of himself, then even of Stella. Marie would regret preying on Briar Hunt, as far as he was concerned.

Kicking off his shoes, Malric collapsed onto the bed. Crossing his legs, he settled back into the pillows, bending his arms behind his head and making himself comfortable. The blankets smelled of stale detergent and fresh shampoo—and Briar, themself, which Malric only realized then he'd come to learn. He couldn't help but smile at the glow-in-the-dark sticker stars on the ceiling overhead, at the crystals dangling from the window that would surely catch the morning light, at the faint sound of cars on the street and a whistle through a crack in the old windowpane. He wondered what Briar thought about while laying in bed—at least, before his deal, before the wirry-cow started bothering him. Then Malric wondered what Briar thought about while laying in *his* bed back at the d'Alarie estate—and had to push the thoughts away before he got angry all over again.

Staring at the ceiling, he realized Briar had the constellation for *vulpecula*, the fox, right over his bed. Unable to resist smiling to himself, Malric let his arms unfold over either side of him, stroking the soft blankets beneath his hands and closing his eyes.

"This bed is far more comfortable than mine back in the Autumn Court," he whispered. "It would be a shame for you to lose another night from it..."

"I knew you would come back to see me soon, Malric."

Malric's blood ran cold, but he didn't move. He kept his eyes on the ceiling, holding his breath as, out of the corner of his eye, a figure manifested out of the shadows. He knew what he would see the moment he turned, so he didn't. It'd spoken in his mother's voice.

"Why are you lingering here?" he asked, still refusing to meet its gaze. The wirry-cow struggled to maintain a solid form because of it, unable to feed off the fear in Malric eyes.

"You came to me, málda."

Malric chewed on the inside of his cheek. He wasn't expecting a wild fey to know that nickname, let alone speak it with the same stomach-turning sweetness as Marie always did. It told him more than the wirry-cow probably expected, however, and Malric finally exhaled through his nose.

"Tell me who sent you here," he compelled, only meeting the wirry-cow's eyes long enough to enchant it. Just long enough to make his nerves heighten, hating the image of his mother within arm's reach, wearing the same thing she did the night Malric left home for good.

"I sent myself," the wirry-cow replied. An obvious truth hidden in a false lie.

"So Marie sent you?" he clarified. The wirry-cow shimmered in the corner of his eye again, and Malric knew he would starve it to death, slowly. His mother was definitely his biggest fear, the wirry-cow had that much right—but it wasn't just her appearance that made his heart race. This wisp would never be able to mimic what made Marie d'Alarie actually frightening. "What for?"

When it didn't answer, Malric sighed and gave it something to chew on. Meeting its eyes, he compelled it again. *"Tell me why Marie sent you to attach to the human who sleeps in this room."*

"I would rather he sleep where it's safe," the wild thing answered with a sly smile, and Malric unraveled that response as thoroughly as if Marie had actually said it, herself. *I would much rather keep Briar within reach, at home, on the fey side of the veil. I hate that he goes home to his own bed at all. The fact he stays after each performance isn't enough, I want to keep him forever...*

Malric only knew because he'd been victim to that same sentiment his entire life. Coming up against a nightly curfew no matter what age he was, no matter what circumstances kept him out late, no matter how many times he broke it and found somewhere else to sleep, or someone else to sleep with. There was an infinite list of things Malric did to piss off his mother, and coming home late, or not coming home at all, was one of them. It was no surprise she asserted the same control over Briar, though Briar clearly didn't get the hint, or just ignored it. Not unlike Malric always had. Marie must have fucking hated it.

Malric finally sat up in the bed. He met the wirry-cow's eyes, watching as it smiled and claimed a stronger form, a more perfect visage of his mother the night she'd scared Malric the most. The night she threatened to break both his legs before letting him leave; the night he made his deal with her, knowing it might as well have been the same thing.

"Why not *go bother the kings* instead?" he urged. "I'm sure they have plenty of fears to chew on. It'll be the first and only time any piece of Marie ever gets invited to the palace, at least."

The Marie-wirry-cow smiled dreamily, and Malric almost hated how easy it was. He would have enjoyed more of a challenge. The wirry-cow just smiled, breaking eye contact and wisping away through the windowpane. Malric sighed once it was gone, flopping back onto the bed and dragging his hands down his face.

Exhaling through his nose, he gazed up at the fox constellation on the ceiling, again. A human might have thought it to be a coincidence—but the fey didn't believe in things like that. Malric knew it was a sign, a sign that Briar had manifested Malric's coming to watch over him a long, long time ago, before ever knowing the fey world existed at all. Perhaps Malric never stood a chance; perhaps he was never meant to find peace and distance from his mother at all. Not with such a powerful, passive spell drawing him in right where he needed to be. Right where Briar needed him.

14

BRIAR AND THE DINER

Briar slept in Stella's bed, sandwiched between her and Bianca, caged within his friend's giant arms that could both fling an en pointe dancer across the room as well as probably rip a tree out of the earth if she ever wanted to move the shade somewhere else.

He slept all the way until the sun rose, which was an unfamiliar experience for him. He would have liked to sleep even more, but the moment the blue light of a stormy morning peeked through the windows, he knew he wouldn't be closing his eyes again anytime soon. Not when the first flicker of recollection came blooming to life in his memory, mixing with the drunkenness still in his blood and summoning bile to surge up the back of his throat. He barely untangled himself from the couple in time to rush to the bathroom and puke in the tub. Grimacing, he turned on the nozzle to wash it down the drain, before deciding to strip down and wash himself while he was there. Unwrapping his ankle was the worst part, tempted to just cover it back up again at the sight of the swelling, the bruises. He wished he could go to urgent care, the campus physio, anything—but knew what they would tell him. *Rest. Take time off. Keep weight off it.* Even if he wanted to, that wasn't an option.

As to be expected, his conscience was a real dick that morning in the way of forcing him to relive every image from the night before at the club. The nice ones—drinking, dancing, kissing on strangers—as well as the less welcome reminders—the image of Myrtha, Marie d'Alarie, in all her white-skirted glow amongst the dancing bodies... the fey lady's threat in the alleyway... that nightmare of vines and branches bursting from his throat... how cold it was to lie there in the snow, unable to move... how Mal found and bundled him up... how Briar had embarrassed himself upon begging for Mal's help, declaring he wanted it, needed it...

Briar flushed at every memory with Mal, especially. He flushed at how warm Mal had been, how he wrapped Briar up and pulled him close, into his chest, into his heat, holding him like a pile of blankets. As if he weighed nothing, was nothing. How easy it was to sink into him and let what remained of his guard down entirely, as if Mal was actually who Briar had hoped to find him all that time...

"Hey."

Briar reeled back, screaming when a face suddenly peeked through the crack in the curtain. He sprayed it with the showerhead, summoning a spluttering curse from his victim before the curtain was yanked open.

"*Hey!*" Briar screeched right back as Mal grappled for the nozzle. Briar bashed him on the head with it, before grabbing the curtain in an attempt to cover himself. "What the hell do you think you're doing!"

"I *was* coming to check on you!" Mal hissed, rubbing the goose-egg Briar knew was laid on his head.

"When—when did you get here?"

"In the bathroom?"

"In my apartment!"

"I never left!" Mal moved like he was going to lunge again, and Briar sprayed him down a second time.

"Don't lie to me—you weren't on the couch when I got up!"

"I slept in *your* bed, dummy, so I could have a talk with that wirry-cow if it decided to come back again. I scared it off for you, so, *you're welcome.*"

Briar's fury fizzled, but he still didn't let his guard down.

"You slept in my bed?" he asked in disbelief. "F-fully clothed? On my nice sheets?"

"What, your muddy wirry-cow sheets? Calm down, I took my shoes off."

"Wh…" Briar still couldn't gather his thoughts well enough to form a full sentence, a part of him sure he had to be dreaming. He saw how Mal's wet t-shirt clung to the body underneath—all tight muscles and dips and lines of someone who trained regularly. Someone who could body Briar across a stage or onto a bed, depending on the circumstances. His face went hot, and all he could do was to spray the man down again like a rabid dog. "Get the fuck out of here, you creep!"

"Will you cut it out!" Mal growled, lunging again. He yanked the showerhead from Briar's hands and cranked the water off, leaving them both soaked and glaring at one another. Mal clearly forced himself to relax, closing his eyes and taking a deep breath through his nose. "I want to talk about… her."

"Who?" Briar asked sarcastically. *"God?"*

"What? What's wrong with you?" Mal grabbed the nearest thrifted towel from the rack, turning away for the first time and offering it to Briar. Briar scowled, but took it, yanking the curtain closed again just long enough to wrap himself up. Briar knew who Mal really meant—but he wasn't going to be the one to bring it up. He was afraid to, as if it might actually summon her to join them in the bathroom, too.

But when Mal never continued himself, and Briar started to shiver, he finally pouted his lips and asked: "What about her?"

"Last night… you asked for my help."

Briar threw the curtain open, but Mal didn't even flinch. He leaned against the counter, looking like a drenched cat.

"Not here," Briar said flatly. He meant it as a way to end the conversation entirely, but Mal just nodded and straightened back up again.

"I agree. Let's get breakfast. You owe me, anyway."

"What?" Briar argued, foot catching over the edge of the tub and tumbling into Mal's back. He regained his balance before Mal could even think to do it, himself. "I don't owe you—"

"Who scared your wirry-cow away?" Mal asked, suddenly in close, suddenly serious. Briar just stared at him, forgetting how to breathe as he was pressed back into the wall. "Who just got soaked to the bone when it's zero degrees outside?"

Briar frowned, wishing he could think of something snappy to reply, but Mal banished his thoughts like he did the shadowy thing in his room the night before.

"Fine," he finally answered through his teeth. "But you're paying."

Shoving past him, Mal barked a laugh.

"You really shouldn't shower with such hot water, bugbear! It's bad for your skin!"

"By the size of your pores I assume you learned from experience!" Briar snapped back, slamming the door behind him before glaring at his ruffled bed sheets. He went straight for them, planting his face into his pillow before reeling back again with a huff of frustration. *Fuck.* They smelled just like him.

BRIAR HAD PEDDLED PAST THE ALL-HOURS 1950S DINER a myriad of times on his way to and from class, but that was the first time he'd ever stepped inside. He certainly never expected it would be trailed by his new dance-instructor-witch-wirry-cow-exterminator, who seemed far too thrilled and weirdly reminiscent over the decor as if he'd been born during that time period. Mal couldn't be older than thirty, surely. Maybe a little less. Unless he really did know something or another about immortal skincare.

He dressed extra cute that morning, as if he thought it would earn him some mercy to use against the onslaught he anticipated on the horizon. A pastel block-color Thom Brown sweater, Christian Dada zipper pants, black Saint Laurent boots. Extremely unfortunate for him, though, was the pullover Mal stole from Stella's closet, since Briar drenched the only other thing he had—which was a pastel tie-dye Amiri pullover, a gift to her from Briar, himself. It resulted in the two of them looking like they were wearing matching colors on purpose, like couples did. *Ugh.*

Settling into one of the booths, Briar set his sights on the cardboard thunderbird muscle car holding the menus, grabbing one and unfurling it without meeting Mal's eyes across from him. He knew why they were there, he knew it might be beneficial to have the inevitable conversation that made Mal's eyes light up at the thought, he knew he'd pushed himself in a corner the night prior when he got way too cali-girl fucked-up at the club—but, damnit, he also knew it wasn't going to be *that* easy to spill all of his secrets and talk about all of his embarrassing mistakes in the past few months, whether or not the fey lady's curse tangled his tongue or not.

"Are you buying?" he interrupted Mal flirting with the waitress, the poor girl flushing so hard she might get a nosebleed. Briar purposefully avoided acknowledging how nice Mal looked, despite wearing Stella's sweatshirt and jeans that were still a little damp. Briar then purposefully avoided that stupid, smug, handsome smile Mal gave him, as if he thought Briar interrupted because he was jealous, or something. *Whatever. Just sit the hell down.*

"Anything you like," he agreed, shrugging off his jacket and laying it across the seat before sitting, himself.

"Can I get the vegan grilled cheese and tomato soup?" he asked the waitress, who scrambled for her notepad and scribbled it down. Mal just said *"same for me,"* and something about it made Briar even more annoyed.

"Can I get a black coffee, too?" he added.

"Me as well," Mal copied. His polite smile was still a little too handsome, and Briar was sure he felt how the waitress' pulse fluttered. He might have done the same if he wasn't so fucking exasperated.

"So," Mal pricked the start of Briar's waking nightmare, stretching out his arms, then tucking a finger over the top of the menu Briar was still trying to hide behind. Briar just kept avoiding his eyes. He bit down on his tongue. He pretended to be super fascinated by the dessert flier stacked next to the menus.

Mal snapped his fingers to get Briar's attention, and Briar nearly snapped them off.

"Tell me what you've done."

He said it in a way that made Briar's heart thump. Something about it was almost... seductive, and Briar knew Mal probably did it on purpose.

The waitress brought their coffees. Briar sipped at his directly, but was strangely captivated by how Mal dumped in four hazelnut cream cups and three stevia packets, until it was nearly spilling over the edge. He even leaned forward to suck some room off the top like a dog drinking lake water—and Briar didn't realize he laughed until Mal's eyes flickered up to meet his.

"I don't want to spill it," Mal said with a sarcastic smile. "Why let such an artisan brew go to waste?"

"Ah, yes, artisan—made locally, and probably five hours ago."

"You can tell that much just from one sip? What about this water, when was it harvested?"

He was being sarcastic—and Briar smirked despite himself. He hated the way Mal smiled back, equally smarmy and smug, as if satisfied to get any kind of response out of Briar at all. Fuck— that pissed him off. It made his heart race, too.

He really, *really* didn't want to talk about it.

"What is there to say that you don't already know?" Briar answered stubbornly. "I... made a deal... with someone I shouldn't have."

The inside of his mouth tingled as he had to carefully choose his words. He anticipated the moment his thoughts would twist, his tongue would go fat and numb, his throat would tighten to keep any revealing words from escaping.

Maybe Mal knew that. Maybe he understood something about it, because he didn't immediately press Briar for more details. He just looked Briar up and down, closer than Briar had let anyone do in a long, long time. It left him feeling naked, moreso than even when Mal accosted him in the shower that morning.

"You know something about those, don't you?" Briar asked, before sipping his coffee to retain an air of aloofness. "You knew what I did as soon as you saw this..."

He pulled the necklace in question from the collar of his sweatshirt, pinching the pearl dangling from the end. Mal watched his fingers as he did.

"Yeah," Mal responded with a little nod. Briar met his eyes again. "I know something about... making bad deals."

Briar waited for him to say more. When he didn't, he raised his eyebrows sarcastically in encouragement, and the little smile Mal returned was more attractive than it had any right to be. He lifted his over-sugared coffee to sip before continuing.

"... I read this book, once, but can only remember the first part," he suddenly instigated, and Briar looked at him again. "It was about... a musician, who got wrapped up with some bad people. Do you know which one I'm talking about? Can you remind me of the plot?"

Briar made a face of confusion, all while swirling through his thoughts to try and recall if he knew anything like that—but then Mal raised his eyebrows pointedly, eyes flickering to and from Briar's necklace again.

"Oh," Briar whispered as it clicked. He braced for the tangling of his thoughts, the ones that always came when discussing his deal—but that time, he didn't feel it. His heart fluttered in anticipation.

"Um... y-yeah..." he adjusted how he sat, straightening up in order to give Mal his full attention. To concentrate on every single word he chose, to form a story that was and wasn't his at the same time. "It was... about a musician who was, um... trying to find someone who could help them be... the best. Right...?"

Mal nodded in encouragement. Briar pulled a piece of loose hair over one shoulder and stroked it to keep his anxiety at bay. He sought out the right words to say, next.

"But the person who offered to help the musician... tricked them."

"That all sounds familiar," Mal nodded, playing his part perfectly, even looking thoughtful as he posed his next question. "How did they trick the musician, again?"

Sudden emotion swelled in the base of Briar's throat, and he tried to clear it. His hands on his hair agitated, until he was almost pulling it out. His thoughts didn't tangle from the fey lady's curse, but rather his own fear. But he had to say it. He had to talk about it, else he really would never escape.

"The musician made an agreement... where they only had to do one perfect performance for the person. And then the person would help them be the best."

More nodding in encouragement. Briar closed his eyes, combing more aggressively through his hair, until a hand reached out to stop him. Briar just squeezed his eyes tighter.

"But..." his voice wavered. He inhaled an uneven breath full of self-loathing and bitterness. "Every time, the person... always found something wrong with the musician's performance. Every time, there was always something wrong, even though... And then eventually... it was obvious the musician had been tricked, and the person was... was never actually going to let them go..."

Briar bit down on his tongue, breathing deep and holding it in an attempt to keep his cool. The same fingers that stopped the frantic pulling of his hair took his hand, nudging it as if Mal wanted to see the emotion Briar was fighting back against. Briar would rather die than show anything like that. Still, he grasped Mal's hand across the table, taking an unsteady sip from his coffee with the other.

"And then what?" Mal urged.

"Well... and now..." Briar struggled. He took another gulp of coffee before holding his breath, attempting to relax again. "And now... the musician is trapped, and it's ruining their life..." Briar shook his head, gazing down at where his and Mal's hands were clasped together. He pinched the man's fingers, then slowly curled each one to pop the knuckles like he always did with Stella when he'd popped his own into oblivion. Mal made a little sound of surprise, and Briar finally cracked a miserable smile.

He lifted his eyes back to the person in front of him, who gazed right back with an intensity he was beginning to expect. It summoned the words from the deepest reaches of his body, words he'd kept to himself, words he'd wished there had been anyone at all to spill across in pathetic pleas for help and relief.

"The musician never sleeps anymore," he said. "Their body always hurts, and they can't keep up in class... but the person who made the deal doesn't care, and keeps demanding more and more, and won't give the musician any breaks, or any warning when the next performance will be, and... and the musician just wishes they could disappear forever because they're starting to hate dancing so much..."

As Briar said it, he couldn't stop looking at the man across from him. Mal, the instructor, the fairy-witch, the stranger who claimed to know exactly what Briar was going through, what Briar had been starting to think would be the thing to kill him. Mal, who seemingly fell from heaven—or perhaps climbed up through the crust of hell to offer him a better deal than the one he was already in. Mal, who was too goddamn pretty, with a perfect smile that was both inviting and vicious, hazel eyes that were a little too clear, auburn hair that was a little too shiny and fell a little too perfectly around his square jaw and tan skin. If his ears had even the slightest point on the end, Briar would have run the opposite direction in an instant. The fact they didn't meant he really must have been a real person—or an angel. Or a devil. All of those options were still better than a fey lord.

But Briar knew the fey appreciated beauty more than anything else—and if Mal had truly once been wrapped up in his own deal, it made sense. He was something beautiful, after all. Briar blushed when he thought about it.

"What did you make your deal about?" he asked before realizing he did, and Mal surprised him when his arrogant facade cracked slightly. He covered it quickly with another breathy laugh and a smile to the waitress who refilled their coffees. But Briar saw it. He definitely saw it.

"I'm not that much different from you," Mal finally answered, intertwining his fingers and resting his chin on their bridge. He was back to looking at Briar as if able to see through his clothes, his skin, to nitpick every bone in his body. "The fey love dancers, don't they?"

Briar straightened up with genuine curiosity, and Mal's smile spread. Something about it reminded him of that fox-lord who attended Marie's revels, and that thing he said while carrying Briar back to the house. *Dancers have to look out for one another.* How many had Marie d'Alarie, or other high fey just like her, trapped, just like she did Briar? Perhaps old myths weren't only myths, after all—perhaps the fairy people really had been luring and trapping humans for centuries. They only grew more conniving with the times.

"Did you have to dance for them, too?" Briar asked, though it seemed obvious.

"Well—something like that," Mal answered, then took a long pause to drink from his overloaded coffee again. When he didn't add anything else, Briar couldn't wait any longer.

"How did you get away?" he asked with a little too much enthusiasm. "How did you escape?"

"Slow down, bugbear," Mal laughed, drinking back more of his coffee. "There's no single answer to anything with the fey— everything has its own puzzles to solve. Let's start with this—what did you make your deal *for?*"

Briar caught himself before speaking, realizing he would have to outwit his own curse with that explanation, too.

But—more than that, even if he could express it freely, that was the last thing he wanted to do. His *why* for making the deal with the fey lady was his biggest embarrassment. How would he ever explain he'd made a deal—just to get the attention of someone he was in love with? Someone who never saw him in the same way, enough that every look they shared was like needles in Briar's heart?

"I..." he rasped. "I... wanted to dance for someone beautiful."

He was carried back to the moment he said those words on the back of the fox-lord, too. How embarrassing it had been. He couldn't decide if it was more or less mortifying to say them to Mal, who knew more, but also had more reason to judge.

Mal didn't answer for a long time. He leaned toward Briar over the table, resting his cheek on his fingers again, looking at Briar with all the observation of someone seeing the stars for the first time. Like he had a million things to say, but at the same time, wasn't exactly sure what the correct response would be. Briar would die of embarrassment soon enough—but then Mal took pity on him, and didn't comment on that confession, directly.

"Well, I'll give you a hint," he said after another moment of silent consideration. "Most of the time, the terms you make aren't the only terms that have to be fulfilled. That's how the fey are able to trick humans so easily. The way they phrase everything is very important in allowing them to pull the rug out from under you."

Briar sighed, then nodded. He'd already figured that out, though the way Mal said it made him curious.

"Can... a deal be turned back around on a fey, too, then?" he asked. "Just like they turn it on people like me."

Mal smiled at him in a way that made him blush. It was full of what could only be appreciation, a little bit of surprise, and a strangely erotic level of *'I'm impressed.'*

"That's how you tricked them to get out of your own, isn't

it?" Briar went on, ignoring the tingling swirl of heat at the base of his stomach when Mal smiled at him like that.

"Not exactly," he smirked. Briar grabbed his hand and bent it backward in frustration, making Mal howl before bursting out laughing. "But I've learned a lot from my mistakes—enough to help poor, pathetic little fey victims like you."

"What if I can't remember the exact terms of my deal?" Briar ignored that comment.

"What—" Mal scoffed with genuine surprise. "Wait, really? You didn't write it down or anything?"

"Well—!" Briar huffed, before clamping his mouth closed as the waitress brought their food. It was only after she left that he could speak again. "Of course not! I didn't even realize what was happening at first—I thought she was just some weirdo new-age mom trying to make me feel better... And then I went and got heartbreak-wasted right after, so then the next morning I even thought maybe I had just imagined it..."

"What happened? When she approached you."

Briar pressed his lips together. He bought some time slopping tomato soup with the corner of his sandwich and taking too big of a bite. Mal just watched him the whole time. He didn't have to say it for Briar to know. *You can't keep avoiding the topic if you actually want help. Hello, dumbass, you have to say something.*

"I was... upset about something. It's a long story, but—"

"I have time."

Briar huffed again. He stole another bite of his sandwich, trying to gather his thoughts in any way that speaking them out loud wouldn't make him drop dead in embarrassment.

"You'll laugh."

"I'm not gonna promise I won't. What if it's funny?"

"Has anyone ever told you you suck?"

"Oh, yes," Mal smiled coyly. "I especially love being told what to do, just like that."

Briar partially choked, partially snorted, but either way had to cough soup out of the back of his throat afterward.

"Come on. Spill it. Let me suck all over it."

"Jesus *Christ*, okay," Briar wheezed. He took another bite. The last one to give him a chance to think. "She... she approached me after the Giselle finale, which I think I told you before. Um, I was upset, because... my friend—erm, my pas de deux partner that night, Leon, he'd just been offered a scholarship to St. Tomassin, since they were so impressed with his performance..."

"And you were jealous?"

"What? No," Briar huffed. "I mean—I wouldn't mind going to Tomassin either, maybe, but they were never going to offer me a scholarship. They already rejected me once, so I never had my hopes up like that."

"Then what were you so upset about?"

Briar's mouth went dry. He attacked his coffee, then his glass of water, but it didn't help. *You have to say it. You have to admit it. Just say it out loud, you coward. The longer you let this pause linger, the worse it's going to be. Mal is just going to say something sarcastic if you don't. You have to beat him to the punch.*

"I had feelings for him," Briar blurted, before staring in disbelief at his half-empty plate. Mal, meanwhile—actually did burst out laughing. He howled in amusement, shaking his head before coming back to earth and reiterating what Briar had just said.

"Sorry—I'm sorry, I'm not laughing because of what you said —it was your face, like you just hit a dog with your car. Like you're trying to decide if you should give it mouth-to-mouth."

"Shut up!" Briar begged, putting his face in his hands before shoving more of the sandwich into his mouth, not sure what else to do. He almost spilled about his conversation with Leon the night before, how Leon had actually asked Briar to dance with him again in some kind of dream-come-true sort of miracle—but the timing told him Mal would definitely assume he was lying to try and save face.

"So you had a crush on your partner and he got a scholarship to a different school. Then what?"

Briar swallowed his bite, but it was drier than ever. It was like sandpaper all the way down, nearly catching in his esophagus.

"That's... it," he croaked. "That's... that's really it..."

He expected Mal to erupt into more laughter—but instead, he did the only thing that could possibly be worse, which was to touch Briar's hand comfortingly and give him a look of pity. Briar almost puked. Instead, he snatched his hand away.

"Why the fuck are your fingers so clammy, freak?" he muttered, a clear defensive maneuver to avoid his own growing embarrassment. Mal considered it, then dipped his fingers in his soup to lick them clean. Briar stared at him, horrified, but Mal just kept smiling. God, what a *freak*.

"So you were in love with your partner, and they were leaving, and you were upset," he reiterated. "And the fey lady sensed your grief, and came sniffing around."

Briar didn't answer. Fuck—hearing it stated so plainly was even worse than the big, emotional mountain he'd built up in his own mind over the course of five months chained to her.

"I know it sounds stupid," he finally muttered. He hated the way Mal would just sit in silence, waiting for Briar to say something. Baiting him into saying anything. But more than that, he hated how it worked every single time. "You can laugh. Again. If you want to."

"I don't think it sounds stupid," Mal answered with surprising sincerity. "Grief is grief, and the fey don't care how big or small the stakes are. If it's important to you, it can be preyed on as easily as anything else. Someone needing a perfect score on a test is as easily victimized as someone who just lost a loved one, or someone who..." He sipped at his drink, hazel eyes lingering on Briar, "...wishes they were perfect, in order to impress an unrequited love."

Briar wanted to disappear. Meanwhile, Mal finally picked up his own sandwich, regarded it, then followed Briar's lead to dip the bread and take a bite. He wrinkled his nose instantly, though, tossing it back to the plate and sliding the whole thing into Briar's reach. Briar didn't ask questions, claiming it for himself.

"Fey get the same satisfaction out of tricking someone upset about a crush than they would over someone upset about losing a loved one. They view all human pain equally, if that makes sense."

"Because fey don't experience grief?" Briar asked bitterly, mouth full. Mal considered that question for a long time, before shaking his head.

"Fey experience grief no differently than humans do..." he answered thoughtfully. "Though they don't like to admit how similar they are to humans in the things they feel. One hell of a superiority complex."

Briar smiled sarcastically. "Right. Fey think we're just little puppies they can manipulate and train into doing what they want... by dangling what we need in front of us."

"If you're implying high fey think humans have the same capacity as puppies—well, yeah. I suppose that's fair. Though I definitely consider you more of a bird than a puppy. Flighty. Unpredictable."

Briar ignored that. He was definitely a puppy.

"And High Fey Lady Madame Marie d'Alarie would never expect a *puppy* to outwit her," Briar insisted, wiping his mouth on the back of his hand. Mal chuckled, and Briar couldn't help but smile, too.

"Then what should I do?" he went on, finishing his bowl of soup before starting in on Mal's. Mal thought about that for a moment, as well.

"If you're sure you can't recall the exact wording of your terms... there are ways to find out, but... it requires opulent techniques."

"What's that?"

"Oh, erm—*opulence* is the term used for fey magic. In general, at least."

"Oh. Is that different from what Bianca does? You called her a folk-witch, once."

"Yes, Bianca's practice is different from high fey magic. Different from veil-aligned human magic, too, which is called *Arid magic.*"

"Um..."

Mal laughed under his breath. "You don't need to know any of this to outwit a fey lady."

"Oh, good. Thank god. Can Bianca use opulent techniques to help me remember?"

"No, I don't think so. She might be able to help refresh your memory of that night, but we need the *exact* phrasing, without any chance of mistakes. You'll have to get all three branches of your deal, word for word."

"Branches?" Briar muttered, sipping at his coffee. Mal held up three fingers.

"Most formal fey deals are made up of three parts. *A request, an offer, and a consequence.* The request is what the maker of the deal wants from you; the offer is what you'll get if you give it; and the consequence is, obviously, what happens if you don't abide by the terms. You need to know all three parts, verbatim, if you want any hope of outwitting the fey lady. Hence why you should really consider the help of a friendly high fey—"

Briar reeled back. His face twisted up in disgust, then he scoffed in disgust, then smeared what remained of his sandwich around in the soup in continued disgust.

"Yeah, right—!"

"Hear me out—not *all* high fey are as cruel as your fey lady. Surely, in all your time spent on the other side of the veil, there's been even just *one* fey who has been kind to you?"

"Hell no. Not even one."

Mal frowned. He tapped his finger on the table insistently.

"Not even *one?* Think about it."

"No. Not one."

"Not even *one?*"

"No!" Briar snapped in finality. "Not a single fucking one, damnit! Stop asking like you think I'm lying, already! I've never met a single high fey who has ever been anything other than cruel to me, alright? Even those I've never met have ruined my whole life, that's how bad they are to me."

"What does that mean?"

Briar sneered. "You know the whole reason the fey lady came looking for a dancer? It was to replace her fancy son, who left to find himself or travel the world or some shit. She tells me all the time about how I'm meant to replace him, how he was *perfect*, how I should try to be just as perfect in order to properly take his place... and that if he were to ever come to a revel and see how poorly I did, he would break both my legs and leave me to rot on the edge of the—"

"That's not true," Mal interrupted with a harsh voice, sharp enough that the rest of the diner fell silent in surprise. Briar just blinked at him, before swallowing back the rest of the complaints he had queued up. Mal then closed his eyes, running fingers back through his hair before laughing, but it seemed forced.

"I was getting overwhelmed."

"Ooookay... sorry, I guess..." Briar mumbled. "Do you have high fey friends, or something...?"

"I... just..." Mal struggled to figure out what he wanted to say. Briar could almost see color in his cheeks, like even he was embarrassed for the sudden outburst. "I just hate painting anything, anyone with a broad brush, that's all. If there truly aren't *any* high fey you think can help you, though, we can figure something else out. Until then... let's ask Bianca if she can do any kind of spell to refresh your memory, and you can try to think if there's *any fey at all* who can help you until you have to go dance again."

He spoke it all with a sort of professionalism, like he was trying to sell something. Briar could only sit and listen, heart thrumming like he knew Mal wasn't telling the whole truth. Why get so defensive over some high fey? Especially over one fey lord, specifically, who Briar was specifically complaining about?

Frowning, he finished off his food as his cracked phone vibrated with a message from Stella, telling Briar to stay put because she and Bianca were on their way to join them. Briar was secretly glad, knowing the odds of the new awkwardness fading on its own were slim.

"You say no fey has ever shown you kindness," Mal went on, and Briar sighed in preparation for more of the same nagging. "Is that what happened to your ears?"

It took Briar a moment to realize what Mal meant, before touching his ear and frowning. He'd done so well to hide them since he was first attacked, strategically pinning his hair over the upper parts, pulling his beanies down to hide them.

"Yeah," he answered, though his stomach turned at the mere acknowledgement. "They... they always bother me when I finish dancing, sometimes worse than others."

"Why your ears?"

Briar pressed his lips together. He gazed down at his opposite hand clenched into a fist on the table.

"They said... the reason I'm so bad at dancing... is because I'm human. They said they were going to cut my ears into points, so maybe I could dance as well as the fey lady's son..."

Briar avoided Mal's eyes for the most part, but in the brief moment he looked up to see if Mal was listening, the intensity of the silent fury behind Mal's hazel eyes was enough to take his breath away. It cut into Briar deeply—but not in a way to hurt him. More like—to plant a seed of fear, like god help him if he ever ended up on the receiving end of such a look, himself.

"High fey believe in things like what you call *karma*, too," Mal finally spoke, grinding the words out like he actually wished to snarl them. "Those who do you harm will get what they give. The veil makes deals, too—but never compromises on its terms."

The front door of the diner swooshed open as Stella and Bianca arrived. Briar blamed the goosebumps that raced up his arms on the outside wind that swept inside—despite knowing full well, no winter breeze could chill him as deeply as the way Mal uttered those words.

15

BRIAR AND THE MEMORY

Rosemary. White chiffon. Crushed rosin. Powder deodorant. Hairspray.

Briar reclined on his back in Bianca's front room, hair combed into a pristine romantic bun and ringed with flowers. Just like it would have been on stage.

His head rested in Stella's lap, draped in the veil of white chiffon like the one he briefly wore at the beginning of Act II, symbolic to the audience of Giselle's death and waking up with the wili spirits on the other side of the veil.

When asked to wear the same slippers he wore that night, Briar didn't know what to say, and wore the slippers he danced in Coppélia with, instead. Leon had been a townsperson in that ballet, too. They had danced with one another, sort of, in that show, too. It was close enough.

All of it, combined with the low hum of brown noise in the background, a quiet replay of the Giselle score coming from Bianca's TV speakers, Stella's hands on either side of Briar's head to keep him upright—was all meant to take him back to that night. To that moment. Mal had told Bianca they were trying to recover the memory of something else, claiming the root of Briar's nightmares were all from that night and he just needed relief, and

Bianca didn't ask any questions. She was almost *too* agreeable, which made Briar suspicious. But he wasn't about to ask, just in case. He didn't want to trick himself into having to make up more lies. He was tired of lying.

It didn't help that, once told, even Stella didn't ask questions. But maybe only because, for her, there was authenticity to that claim—that claim of Briar's nightmares rooted in that night. Stella knew about Briar's feelings for Leon, she knew how badly it'd hurt to learn the news of Leon leaving, after never giving Briar the only thing he ever wanted...

Briar pushed the thoughts off. He followed Bianca's instructions, floating in the darkness behind his eyes. He smelled the rosemary and rosin, fiddled with the corner of the chiffon, sensed every one of Stella's breaths against the crown of his head. He hated that smell—rosemary. It reminded him too much of Marie d'Alarie's revel clearing; it didn't make him think of Giselle. It just made his stomach turn.

He focused on his body. On his head in Stella's lap. She'd danced as Hilarion in that same show, having to step up as Briar's own understudy at the last second when he himself rose to the role of Giselle...

"Focus, Briar," Bianca's gentle voice popped Briar's distraction. Briar squeezed his eyes tighter, exhaling through his nose.

He thought of all the practices leading up to that night. All the performances leading up to that night. How he'd just been an understudy, otherwise dancing as one of the wili spirits. Just one face amongst many. When he learned he would dance Giselle during the finale, hearing he would get his final wish of dancing with Leon on stage, just once, just one time, before Leon would learn whether or not he'd earned his scholarship... thinking if he could just stun Leon with his grace, his perfection, he might be able to convince Leon to stay just a little bit longer... to notice Briar the same way Briar had always noticed him, to finally see Briar as more than just a friend, more than just a peer... to see Briar for his talent, his abilities, his own beauty, his elegance...

Briar would never forget Leon's face as they laid in the grass together days before that final performance, watching clouds pass by as ice in their matching coffees melted and speckled with chilled dew on the outside of the cups. How Leon smiled with his perfect teeth, chin dusted with blonde scruff, laughing and teasing and talking about how exciting it was that Tomassin scouts were reportedly attending the final performance. All to determine if he'd get the scholarship he wanted, the one that would set him up for a career with a good company in the future, to have the life he really wanted, one that studying at Artemisia would never be able to provide...

"Tomassin has some of the most talented dancers in the PNW," he'd sighed, a sentiment he'd repeated a thousand times by then like a vocal manifestation, clutching his chest before throwing his arms out. "What if I get to pas des deux with Tucker Bennett? Or Ernesta Lopez? God, imagine dancing Giselle with one of them, we would one-hit kill everyone in the audience. Like, I think they would start a religion and everything. I promise to be a most merciful and doting god..."

Briar tried to laugh, but it caught in his throat. It was his heart getting in the way of the words, begging him not to say them. Begging him to just *shut up* and *don't push it* and *you don't have to make him clarify,* because his words already said it all. Still, they clung to the back of Briar's throat like thistles catch on cotton socks.

Do you ever think about if I danced Giselle *with you?*

Those same words that rang in his head the moment he was told to change into Giselle's Act I ensemble, *hurry, there isn't much time, Ashley is too sick to go on, do you remember your cues? Are you sure you can do it? Sorry for the late notice—*

How the rest of the show passed in a blur, that moment he and Leon stood on stage across from one another. Briar would never forget that initial look of surprise on Leon's face, not knowing Briar had taken his original partner's place at the last second. That look that, even months later, Briar could never decide was happy-surprised, or disappointed-surprised. A look that might haunt him more than the wirry-cow in his bedroom ever did. The look—that might have been exactly what pushed Briar into enough of a state of desperation to hear out the strange woman dressed as Queen Myrtha while crying in the dressing room long after the curtain fell.

I want to dance for someone beautiful...

"Briar?"

Stella's voice was far away, and Briar chased it too closely. He rose too fast, too close to the surface of the pool of memories where he swam, enough that his eyes fluttered open and released a few silent tears to drip down his cheeks. He released a breath he suspected he'd been holding, according to how tight his chest felt.

"Oh." The sound left him on an exhale. "Sorry, I don't... I don't think... this is working."

He tried to laugh, but Stella watched him with concern. It only made him feel worse, only made him more self-conscious, and he sat up to remove the veil from over his face. In the process, he strategically wiped the few tears on his cheeks away with the back of his hand. He asked if they could try again another time— and everyone, despite having all been told very different stories, all of them knowing some details but not others—looked at him with enough collective pity to make him sick to his stomach.

BRIAR'S ANKLE WAS THE SIZE OF A BASEBALL THE NEXT morning, as if his mood could possibly get worse.

Briar wanted to just go back to sleep. To never wake up again, not unlike his namesake. His moms used to always tease him for sleeping so much, saying he was born fast asleep, and that was why they named him *Briar*—but little did they know, all he would ever want from that day forward would be to go right back to that safe, dark place and sleep again forever and ever and ever and ever.

He was grateful to have gotten at least a little bit of practice in a few days prior, even if it was interrupted by an unexpected guest. *Damnit*—when was he supposed to meet with Leon for the first practice, again? What if his ankle was even more fucked and he had to step back? Even after possibly getting what he only ever wanted in the first place...?

Fuck. Fuck fuck fuckfuckfuckfuck. Did the universe really have to be so goddamned cruel? What about karma, or whatever? Even the fey believed in karma, according to Mal. What had he done to deserve this shit, other than having poor taste in men and a god-complex?

He wore black matchstick jeans and a comfortable t-shirt. He wrapped his swollen ankle as tightly as he could in bandages, then really entombed it within the laces of his Doc Martens for added stability—even though he couldn't entirely feel his toes as a result. The entire time, between cursing and hissing from the strain, all he could think was—was it really worth it? Was his attempt at clinging to any sort of worthiness when it came to the fey lady really worth it, if it was going to destroy his body? Destroy his life? Destroy the only thing he had, the only thing that ever provided him the love and attention he thrived on? What if he told her Leon asked him to dance, again? Would she understand, would she show mercy?

What if he just... did what she said, and offered someone else to dance for her? To take his place? Clearly she thought he wouldn't be able to ever achieve perfection, so maybe... Briar had to just... believe her? Accept her offer of mercy?

But would he really be able to live with himself knowing he'd intentionally fed someone else to the wolves like that? To those foxes at the revel?

Who would he even offer?

Because he couldn't ride his bike, Stella joined him on the crowded light rail that morning in exchange for a coffee once they arrived on campus. Smushed into one another amongst other students and businesspeople, Stella just gushed and gushed and *gushed* about Bianca, joking about how they were definitely moving in together the following week, how Stella already had her vows written, how it was just so cool and hot that she was so *smart*, how they'd done some kind of witchy sex ritual a few nights prior and Stella was sure she met god and they were gender-less and had silver locs and white eyes. It was all a little *too* peppy, especially so early in the morning, and Briar suspected it was because she could sense the thick black cloud looming over him. Her positivity did help him feel a little better, though. It was a nice distraction from everything else he carried.

To keep the mood light, he argued that all the times he'd seen god, they had giant tits and claws. Stella offered to agree to disagree—but Briar wouldn't let it go. It was then the worst thought imaginable crept in through an unguarded door in the back of his mind—

Could he offer Stella?

Allowing such a horrible thing to exist for even a second turned his stomach, made his knees go weak. He just *fwumped* into her chest and sighed while she patted his hair and told him everything was going to be alright, even though the deity he saw definitely wasn't god...

Arriving on campus, he did his best to avoid limping as they walked, not wanting her to know how much worse his injury had gotten. He looked into the faces of every single person they passed, wondering, *maybe them? What about them? Them? Them? Them?*

Most weren't even dancers; many others weren't even studying ballet, and something told him the fey lady wouldn't be satisfied with someone who only danced modern or tap or some-thing else. Why couldn't her stupid, prestigious son have been into jazz or tap dance, instead?

Briar had plenty of enemies he might consider, but none he was on medium-enough terms with to even be able to have a normal conversation and suggest they follow him into the woods.

But then, standing in line at the campus coffee shop, Briar's eyes lingered on a chalk sign that read *Artisan Brew* in swirly art-student lettering, and his stomach clenched.

Mal promised to help him understand and escape the fey lady's deal—but perhaps there was more than one way to do that. Perhaps... Briar could keep just one morally corrupt plan-B in his back pocket, just in case Mal couldn't actually deliver what he promised...

The lifespan of *that* horrible thought was only a few nanoseconds longer than the one held for Stella, before Briar kicked and punched it back into oblivion. What the hell was wrong with him? He ordered an additional sugary hazelnut coffee on top of his own and the one he promised Stella, like some kind of silent apology for a crime Mal would never, ever know he'd committed.

Snow scattered the air as they hurried back toward the ballet building, passing a group of contemporary dancers joking about how dancing naked in the snow would be symbolic of being buried alive or writhing in the womb of a corpse or something. They sneered at the ballerinas hurrying by, and the ballerinas sneered back, before laughing at one another. Funny how one sparkle of playfulness at the end of the tunnel-of-gloom perked Briar's whole mood.

Stepping into the ballet building, then the studio with only a few minutes to spare, Stella went straight for the bench and bag hooks to pull off her sneakers and exchange them for ballet flats, while Briar searched the wandering crowd for a certain instructor.

Amidst his classmates stretching, darning new pointe shoes, helping one another pull hair back into buns, one thing stood out amongst the rest—and that was Mal at the front of the room, reading something on his phone in one hand while pulling off his scarf with the other. Even that tiny movement looked like it belonged in a movie, and Briar had to gulp back the rush of idiotic desire that swelled at the back of his throat.

It didn't help that Mal wore fitted leggings and a casual top tied in a knot over his stomach, which lifted to reveal a peek of his tan skin underneath as he stretched his arms over his head, then ran his hand back through his hair like a goddamn GQ model—

Regaining any amount of sense he had, Briar made his

approach after Stella left with her drink to start stretching on the far wall. It was only when he was within speaking distance that he realized, of course, he wasn't the only one in class to notice how objectively dreamy their new instructor was, at the sight of three other steaming-hot coffees resting on the back of the piano next to him.

"Hey, bugbear," Mal grinned as Briar stepped into view, and Briar wasn't expecting how fast his face lit up in flames. He nearly doused the man in boiling liquid as he said that pet name way too loud. "Why aren't you dressed down?"

"Um..." Briar snapped back to reality for the second time. He extended his foot slightly, rolling his ankle in habit before grimacing as pain shot up his leg. "I made it mad, again."

Mal's eyes narrowed, clearly intending to ask more questions, before his eyes landed on the extra coffee in Briar's hand. He smiled in the stupidest way, like he already knew it was for him, and Briar silently cursed him.

"Is that for me?" he asked despite obviously already knowing. Reaching for it, Briar pulled it back again in annoyance.

"What? Of course not. Why would I?"

But Mal definitely knew. He dramatically threw his head back like he was swooning in exhaustion.

"That's really too bad," he sighed, just loud enough for Briar to hear. "I was brought a few other coffees this morning, but none of them are exactly what I was looking forward to... a hazelnut macchiato with extra syrup and caramel."

Briar frowned, realizing the ingredients were written in swirly sharpie on the outside of the cup. Finally, face beet red, he offered it to Mal.

"It's just... payment for offering to help me with my, um..." He trailed off. "My fairy problem. Can we meet after class to talk about it more?"

Mal nodded, clearly satisfied with his victory over the stubborn dancer in front of him.

"Ah—artisanal hazelnut. You must really like me to go to such lengths—"

"Goodbye," Briar grunted, and Mal laughed before placing the coffee on the table with the others—but set aside, slightly. Maybe so he wouldn't mix it up on accident.

Briar took his place at the back of the room, leaning against the mirrored wall and stretching his leg out. Meanwhile, Mal clapped his hands together as the day's pianist arrived and settled into their seat, starting into warmups. Ironically, Mal had critiques for them and their form, too, saying something about his siblings who played the piano and did it far differently...

Watching Mal wander the room and critique everyone standing at the bar was entertaining even though Briar couldn't hear anything he said, especially since Madame Cruz was never even that nitpicky so early in the morning. She always held private sessions set aside during class while everyone else warmed up, but Mal clearly got some sort of thrill out of scrutinizing everyone in front of the rest of the class. Briar wondered if they would ever get to see him dance, too, curiosity piquing higher when he realized... Mal didn't use many traditional words for dance positions, either because he himself wasn't familiar with them, or perhaps he weirdly assumed those in the class wouldn't know them. He never used terms like dégagé, or effacé, or en seconde—instead, it was *elongate this leg* and *widen your stance* while nudging someone's feet apart, or getting into second position himself, and telling the person to mimic and start over. Briar was once again reminded of Mal's never-ending strangeness, his mystery, his falling from the sky—or through the crust of hell—with everything Briar needed, like a gift from god—or the devil, themself.

Sighing into his coffee, Briar pulled out his phone, thinking he might search Mal's name to see if there were any performances of him online, or credits in any dance companies, or even a trail of work history—before realizing, he didn't know Mal's last name. He didn't know where Mal studied ballet, or even where he came from, only that he was friends with Bianca and knew about fey deals...

Briar pressed the warm cup to his forehead to keep the new anxiety at bay. Had he really done it again? Making agreements with people who were total strangers? Placing his last hope in one person who found him and offered the world, no differently than Marie as the queen of the wilis at the end of Giselle...?

Briar didn't know much about the high fey, except what he'd learned against his will, and those little tidbits Mal shared when alone together. One of the most notable attributes, however, was how high fey valued perfection in all things, especially the arts—which meant, if anything Mal said about dancing for them was true, he must have been a highly capable dancer. He must have been beautiful.

High fey liked humans who were particularly pretty, graceful, or otherwise talented, but not by the same standards of humans. From Briar's experience, the fey didn't favor any particular body type or physical features, or anything like that—only how one's appearance was taken care of. The story behind why they looked the way they did, or how their appearance was used to their advantage. They didn't like messy hair, or chipped nail polish, or unsightly sweat stains, or body odor, or acne, or scars, or yellow teeth, or words spoken in a tone that wasn't smooth as silk. But at the same time—all of those 'imperfections' could be 'justified', if they so wished, twisted into some self-serving romantic poetry about beauty found in hardship or disadvantageous circum-stances. How many times had Briar overheard one of Marie's guests fawning over one of their human servants with facial scars inflicted in some sort of tragic accident that made them more empathic, or submissive, or something? What about the stories of the scarred human beantighe whom the prince of something or other fell in love with despite their ugliness? The fey could find beauty in anything, they could turn any tragedy into romantic poetry—but it was never rooted in empathy or mutual respect. It always stemmed from an insatiable want to own something lovely, to commodify tragedy, and a willingness to do anything to get it —even if they were the ones inflicting the pain and suffering.

You'll thank me for this one day, the fey lady had even said the night Briar originally injured his ankle, as he collapsed within the trees with practically a scream of pain as his foot twisted beneath him. He would never forget the gentleness of her face, her touch, but how it all turned his blood to ice. His pain, his suffering, his misery trying to give her the single *perfect* dance, was infuriating in the moment—but she drooled at the thought of the romantic tale it would become once he accomplished it, or died trying. And since those were his only two options—she would, inevitably, get her romantic tragedy of the ballerina who worked tirelessly to become perfect, until they could no longer fly, until they died of heartbreak or humiliation.

Even if Briar insulted Marie's son at a future revel and they broke both of his legs, he would still be expected to dance on them. Even if it wasn't perfect—as nothing he ever did was perfect, anyway—he would still be expected to arrive at the revel on the other side of the veil and dance on snapped bones. If he didn't, if he *couldn't*—he would become as the trees, just like in his nightmares. Just like in that vision in the alleyway, until Mal found him. *To witness other dancers who would come after him, to punish his own incapability...*

Closing his eyes, Briar picked at his fingernails, suddenly able to feel those leaves again, splitting his skin beneath the strain.

He would become perfect enough for the fey lady.

Or he would escape by some miracle at Mal's suggestion.

Or—maybe he really would give Mal to her, to take his place, so that he might learn again what it was he ever loved about ballet in the first place.

Cracking open his eyes, he watched Mal across the room, critiquing Stella on something Briar couldn't hear. Saying something with all the sincerity he could muster, all while Stella smiled sarcastically like he was nothing more than a goose honking in the park.

Mal, who was handsome, tall, muscular in a way many trained dancers were. Briar was well aware of invisible disability, but the fey rarely took time to romanticize anything they couldn't see. Briar wondered what his tragedy was. What was the beautiful agony the fey forced on Mal to make his story more romantic?

OTHER STUDENTS CROWDED AROUND MAL AT THE END of class, long enough that Briar got antsy about missing his next lecture and having to leave. He made sure to take a picture of the huddle and message it to Mal with a sarcastic comment, though, just so he knew exactly how Briar felt about it. *All these mice chewing on their rat king's ass. Not worth the fight.* Mal heart-emoji reacted to that.

Afternoon classes passed slower than normal, partially because they were his least-favorite Gen-Ed courses, partially because Mal kept doing that annoying thing where he'd start typing, then stop, then start again, then wait a long time, before starting again. Briar had to resist messaging him something first. Briar was not a double-texting kind of bottom.

The winter sun was beginning to set as Briar left his final class for the day, checking his phone for any kind of message from the rat king at all, grumbling when there was still nothing amongst all the hookup app notifications and other social media pings. He almost broke all his rules and sent Mal a follow-up message just to express his annoyance, but then someone suddenly approached where he stood beneath one of the sidewalk lights, startling him.

"Hey! Sorry," Mal grinned, offering a hot drink into Briar's cold hands without warning. Briar grabbed it before it spilled all over him. On the chilly air, he smelled peppermint hot-chocolate right away, and Mal kept smiling when Briar looked at him in confusion. "You said you wanted to chat earlier. I've been waiting for you to finish class. It's about damn time. Come on."

Briar didn't have a chance to say anything, to ask what Mal

was thinking, let alone where they were going—but the man was too fast. His long legs were too goddamn *long*.

"Hey!" Briar attempted anyway, hurrying to catch up while balancing all his things, including the steaming-hot drink. It made his ankle throb, nearly losing his footing on the snow-dusted sidewalk, had Mal not noticed and grabbed him before he fell. Briar wanted to chew him out more than ever—but lost all sense of annoyance at the way Mal looked at him, still holding him upright, searching his face as if looking for anything else Briar was hiding. Briar finally pulled away, averting his eyes and shaking his head.

"I can't walk that fast," he muttered. "Will you just tell me where we're going?"

"The library," Mal smiled. "I wanted to chat somewhere quiet. Here, will this help?"

Mal bent his knees, crouching forward like he was about to push off from the sidewalk and literally sprint full-speed across campus. But then Briar realized what he was actually doing, and his face went hotter than the drink in his hand. He nearly crushed the cup in the rush of embarrassment, swallowing back a dry lump in his throat. The moment Mal glanced over his shoulder to see if Briar took the bait, though, Briar stepped forward and clambered onto the man's stupid back, hoping to crush him, but at the same time doing his best to maneuver the hot drink in his hand and not burn anyone in the process.

Unfortunately, Mal was very strong, and his back was broad, and Briar could feel all of his stupid muscles moving beneath his hands. It reminded him of riding on the fox-lord's back that night after he danced, and Briar quietly hated himself for being so pathetic.

But then Mal hooked his hands under Briar's knees wrapped around his waist—and took off running like a bat out of hell. Briar burst out laughing, unable to help it, cinching his arms around Mal's shoulders for balance as he bounced with every step. Ah—he hadn't laughed that hard in a while.

. . .

There were no empty study rooms in the old building, nor were there any empty desks without a dozen human satellites in every direction, so Briar and Mal settled on huddling on the floor between two unfrequented shelves on the very top floor. Something about it was quaint, almost romantic, like Briar was in high school about to have his first kiss... ah. He shouldn't think about that. Not when Mal was so... so...

"*Ugh,*" he mumbled while stripping his coat off and forming a nest around his hips on the hard carpet. Mal asked if he said anything, but Briar just shook his head.

Struggling to find a comfortable way to stretch his ankle in the cramped space, Briar's breath caught when Mal's hand extended to gently scoop it upward, inviting it into his lap. It was the first time Briar really witnessed the size of Mal's hands, especially in comparison to his own body—and he hated that he flushed. His instinct was to jerk away and be a brat about it, to snap at him not to touch him without asking, first—but damnit, if Mal's body wasn't warm. If elevating his ankle over the man's strong thigh didn't feel so nice. And then Mal's hand gently rubbed over the swollen joint, and Briar practically moaned in pleasure, closing his eyes and sinking sideways against the shelf. Mal chuckled under his breath, then hesitated, then risked undoing the laces of Briar's boot. Briar watched him in silence, wincing when the removal of his boot made the injury complain. He bit back more protests as Mal then unclasped the pin holding his tight bandages together, letting them unfurl like falling petals.

"Let it breathe," Mal said, both a suggestion and an explanation. "It won't heal if you're so rough with it."

"You must not really be a dancer after all," Briar mumbled, and Mal smirked at him, then pinched his big toe painted pink.

"Cute."

"Are we here to talk about fairies or my feet?"

"Hmmmmmmmmm," Mal dragged out the consideration way

too long, and Briar finally kicked him with his opposite foot. Mal just laughed more, before shaking his head and rubbing Briar's ankle a little longer. "Did you happen to remember anything from your deal? Bianca said she tried a spell on you—did it do anything?"

"Um... no," Briar rubbed the back of his head. "I actually... wanted to ask you about your own deal, again. You still haven't told me what it was... how you tricked your way out of it... I thought maybe it might give me some ideas..."

Briar recalled how Mal always avoided the topic with expertise, but he was just going to keep asking. Not unlike how Mal always *just kept asking* him about his own problems, too. Briar would just do what Mal always did and sit in silence until he got his answer. Any answer.

The problem was—Mal wasn't like him. Mal didn't fall victim to silence-induced anxiety like Briar did, and Briar quickly realized they would sit there in silence all night long like a couple of stubborn idiots if he tried to play the same dirty tricks.

"Why not?" he finally snapped, smacking Mal on the leg. "You weaseled it out of me, why won't you talk about it?"

"I didn't weasel *anything* out of you, bugbear. You told me everything all on your own."

"Stop calling me *bugbear*. I mean it."

"Wirry-cow, then."

"Oh, you really wanna die?"

"To die by these pretty hands," Mal sighed dramatically, pressing one of Briar's palms into his cheek and fluttering his eyelashes. "Would be a gift."

"I literally hate you so much."

"They would write poems about it."

"You're a creep."

Mal smiled in that handsome way he knew was handsome; that handsome way he knew always flustered Briar back into submission until his thoughts could piece back together, again.

"My deal really wasn't much different from yours," he finally said, which came as a surprise. He didn't meet Briar's gaze again, though, instead just pinching at Briar's fingers that he apparently wished to die beneath. "Compelled to dance on command, whenever asked, without warning... I can't speak the terms of my deal, either, even now, but... all it takes is to outwit them, or offer a trade. The preparation is complex, but the act itself is simple."

"A trade?" Briar asked, but already knew what Mal meant. "Um—the fey lady offered me a way to trade, too, but..."

Mal looked genuinely shocked, and then Briar was shocked that he was shocked.

"She did? What was her offer?"

"She said if I sent someone to take my place, she would consider our deal done. Is that... is that what you did? Make a trade, I mean."

Mal sighed, like the question crushed him. Exhausted him, wore him into instant dust—and Briar realized, they may have inadvertently answered their own question. The man then closed his eyes and rested his head back against the shelving, before cracking them open again to gaze straight ahead.

"Yes. I agreed to a trade."

"And?" Briar encouraged.

Rolling his head, the look Mal gave Briar was intense, but quiet. Briar bit his lip. Was that the wrong thing to ask?

"And it ruined me," he said flatly. "Which is why you're going to outwit her, instead, and not settle for anything else."

"... How did it ruin you?" Briar dared to ask, though his voice was hardly more than a whisper. Mal just kept his tired smile, edging on irritated. Briar didn't know if the sentiment was directed at him, or the high fey who'd hurt him.

"Can't talk about it," he reiterated every word.

"Not even in a roundabout way? Like we did before—with the musician."

"I'll have to think about it."

Briar knew by the constant shift of Mal's voice that they were approaching critical mass, where Mal might shut down entirely.

That wall he had, but rarely showed, was as thick as Briar's own. And while it didn't feel fair that Briar was allowing Mal to peek past his own, while being kept out in return... he couldn't blame him.

"Uh..." Briar searched for anything he could say to bring the mood back. "Um, you know, I think... I might have actually thought of a fey I can ask for help, like we talked about last time. One that has been... at least, not *as* cruel to me as the others, so..."

"Oh!" Mal's face lit up in an instant. He was going to give Briar whiplash. "I knew there had to be at least *one*. Tell me—are they handsome? What have they done to be kind to you? Be as detailed as possible so I can rub it in your face."

Briar scoffed, turning away. "They're as ugly as you are, actually, with the same dry hair and annoying mouth."

"Which part is annoying, exactly?"

"The words that come out of it. And the way it looks."

"No one has a mouth like me, I can assure you. In words and looks."

"You know, the more I think about it, the more you and him are exactly the same. No wonder it took me so long to remember he existed. Annoying and pushy and creepy, just like you."

"I think I like him already," Mal smirked, then hooked fingers around Briar's ankle and squeezed. "Think you can seduce him into helping you?"

"Seduce him!" Briar scoffed. "Just the thought makes me want to puke—can't I just *ask* him like a normal person?"

"You of all people should know the dangers of *asking* a high fey for anything. You have to make them *offer* help, otherwise you might end up in a second nasty deal, and it'll be all your own fault." He grinned threateningly, then squeezed Briar's cheeks until his lips puckered out. "C'mon, it'll be easy for you. You're cute. I'm sure you even have an ounce of charm under there, you just have to dust it off. Just don't be such an annoying brat like you always are with me."

"Hey!" Briar snapped, grabbing and squeezing Mal's face in return until they were just two puffer fish glaring at one another.

"You got nothing to say to that?" Mal stuck his tongue out. Briar wrinkled his nose, then reeled back from Mal's grip and nearly bit one of his fingers off. Mal barked a laugh, before clamping a hand over his mouth to silence the rest. It didn't matter—because Briar burst out laughing right after him.

"Sorry, but I reserve cuteness for people I like, or people I'm trying to get into bed."

Mal stared at him for a long time, waiting for a personal distinction. Briar just smirked, and Mal took the hint. His face twisted in insult, scoffing.

"Oh, I see how it is. Despite everything I'm doing for you."

"I don't know anything about you," Briar laughed. "Why should I even trust you? Maybe I need to follow your own advice and stop putting all my faith in random strangers."

"What would you like to know? I promise I have nothing exciting to offer."

"Hmmm." Briar leaned his head against the shelf, eyeing Mal up and down in curiosity. "Where did you study dance?"

"A very prestigious school you've never heard of."

"Tell me the name. I'll look it up."

"I'd rather not. I don't want you to get jealous."

Briar smiled sarcastically. "Are you really a dance instructor?"

"How else would I have been hired as one?"

"Are you really a not-a-folk-witch?"

"Yes."

"Do you have a last name?"

"I did when I joined Bianca's cell plan."

Briar pinched his lips in confusion, but Mal only laughed. His hand found Briar's sore ankle again, brushing up and down it with a sigh.

"I keep my secrets for a reason," he said. "And I appreciate you not digging."

"But why should I trust anything you say?" Briar countered,

lacking the playfulness he intended. "You haven't given me anything to believe you can actually help me... how do I know I'm not just wasting my time?"

Mal considered that for a few moments, before closing his eyes. A muscle in his cheek twitched, a sign of a clenched jaw as he thought about something intensely.

"I made a trade... for my freedom," he spoke, and Briar's breath caught. Mal just kept his eyes down, still running fingers up and down Briar's swollen ankle. "In exchange for my freedom... I promised to never dance for anyone except the high fey who owns me, ever again."

Briar's mouth dangled open in surprise, both by the confession and the horror of the words. Biting his lip, he scooted in slightly closer, touching Mal's hand on his leg.

"Sorry," he said quietly. "That's... really awful. I'm sorry for pushing you."

Mal smiled wearily, shaking his head. He met Briar eyes again, and despite the calmness of his expression, his hazel eyes were intense as ever. It made Briar smile, for some reason, in a way that almost felt like relief. Mal looked like he had something else to say, before pausing, then shaking his head and patting the side of Briar's leg. He gathered the bandages, next, propping Briar's foot on his knee for easy access to wrap it back up snugly again.

"Come on," he said as he did. "We'll be late to ice-skating with the girls."

Briar had almost forgotten. It was easier than he realized to disappear into a little bubble with Mal, whether while discussing fairy dealings or just... teasing one another. Nodding, he watched Mal's strong hands maneuver the bandage around his ankle, which looked so fragile in comparison. Mal handled it with such care, though, and Briar almost wondered how often he'd wrapped his own similar injuries. Perhaps even those brought by dancing for the fey like Briar did.

He had to fight the urge to reach out. To touch Mal's hand. To apologize again. Instead, Briar just kept quiet, letting Mal work in peace, watching his hazel eyes through lowered lashes, focusing on the work. Mal was... something beautiful.

Briar wished he'd been able to see him dance before that chance was taken away; he swore his heart even broke at an opportunity lost before he ever knew it existed.

16

MALRIC AND THE ICE

"Um, so, there's actually something I need to tell you—" Malric rasped as Bianca paid for two pairs of rental skates. The panic only amplified when they were tucked into his hands. *I don't know how to do this. I've never done this. I've been to the Winter Court exactly twice in my entire life, and once was just for a royal birthday where I got shitfaced—*

But Bianca was in too much of a hurry, pulling her skates on all while searching for Stella in the direction of the parking lot, then the line to get skates. Malric wouldn't have been able to get through to her, anyway. Gods—he was going to embarrass the hell out of himself in front of Briar, which felt particularly terrible considering the conversation they'd just finished in the library. Briar didn't actually believe Malric could dance. Did he even believe Malric's claim of not being *able* to dance, according to a fey deal? It wasn't a lie.

Despite her focus on finding Stella, Bianca was more than gracious as Malric hobbled on his skates, doing his best to keep his composure. But then the others arrived, and Briar teased the living hell out of him, even attempting to push Malric over, only for their skates to tangle up together and send them both crashing to the ground. Briar laughed a little too loud, and Malric realized there was the lightest smell of alcohol on their breath. He nagged until they revealed a little flask in their inner jacket pocket, and Malric downed the entire thing while hiding together behind a tree, all while Briar screeched at him to not take it all.

The alcohol didn't help his balance, but it definitely made playing hard to get more enjoyable—until he fell so often that one of the rink attendants offered a skating aid shaped like a penguin, which was even more humiliating. Briar went easier on him while hunched over the device, though, and even talked about how he wished he had one, too. He skated backward with his hands on the penguin's head as Malric pushed from the opposite side, grinning threateningly at one another while thinking of all the ways they could trip the other person. More than once, Stella begged them to *act like adults* whenever she and Bianca skated by holding hands, but Briar and Malric only took that as more of a challenge.

Briar shoved the penguin into Malric's crotch. Malric steered Briar backwards into the wall, where he hit with a thud and a shriek of laughter before his skates tangled in Malric's and they both ate shit. Briar stole the penguin and kept it just out of Malric's reach, which was both cruel and helpful because it forced him to tread ice upright. Briar never let him fall, though—not unless he was the one tripping him. Malric found himself attuning to the same morals without realizing, more than once catching Briar when he bumped into someone else on accident, or naturally lost his footing. It only ever ended in both of them hitting the ice together, but at least Malric looked chivalrous doing it.

When Briar eventually commented on Malric's improvement, he was the one to toss the penguin aid away and take Malric's hands. Even wearing gloves, Malric could feel the warmth of Briar's hands, so small compared to his own, but strong enough to more than once pull Malric out of a tumble-in-progress. Still skating backward, Briar moved slowly, encouraging Malric to practice propelling himself on his own. To push Briar with his own leg strength. To practice steering his body, even saying he wouldn't do any of the work and if Malric drove him into a wall again, he would abandon him in the middle of the rink. Malric did his best—if anything, just so he could keep Briar's hands in his. Just so he could win that little surprised look every time Malric did something to impress him. Briar, who was impossible to impress, except when it apparently came to learning how to skate.

"Are you impressed?" he couldn't help but ask. Briar smirked again, but differently that time.

"With what? Is this how you used to dance, too?"

"Oh—my god, you bitch," Malric scoffed, before smiling with nothing but threat. "I was a very good dancer, bugbear. I still am."

"I'll believe it when I see it."

"You're just going to have to trust me."

"How am I supposed to trust my dance instructor *and* fairy-deal-mentor to not lead me astray when I don't even know if he can dance?"

Malric laughed. He couldn't help it. It might have even been the first time any mention of his plight had actually amused him, too, which only made Briar all the more special. Malric wished it would be so easy to explain, but wasn't sure how he could without giving himself away entirely.

I can't dance for anyone except my mother—who is also the same person currently making your life hell.

If I do, I become one with the copper fauna. Of teeth and shadowed paws. Of my roots and starving for rabbits. I see your face—I'm still not entirely sure what that means, either. Remember what I said about knowing the terms of a deal verbatim? There's a good example for you for why.

Malric's eyes skimmed Briar's face, his flushed cheeks, nose, ears, his warm blonde hair spilling out from beneath a pink beanie with a fluffy pompom and cat ears. A rabbit, in his own right. A rabbit Malric wished to save rather than eat—though he might starve for them, either way.

His face warmed at the realization, though it wasn't much of a surprise. Briar was—beautiful. He was *beautiful*, but he was also —bratty. And rude. And melodramatic. And infuriatingly withholding, as getting information out of him was like pulling rusty nails from a coffin. Despite that, something about all the parts of them wrapped up in a bow the color of pink ballet silk made Malric really know how it meant to starve.

"Hey—" He started, but Briar suddenly crashed backward into another group crowding the ice. Losing his footing, he yelped, teetering backward—and Malric leapt forward just like every other time, grabbing him before they both crumpled to the ice.

Wheezing beneath him, Briar laughed, putting his hands out to grope around for Malric's chest, then his face, asking if he was alright. Malric, hanging over him, found himself in a strange daze as the look of grinning amusement on Briar's face was... captivating. Oh, gods, what was happening to him?

"I'm fine," he finally said, pushing Briar's beanie back up and out of his eyes. "Are you—"

"Oh my god, I'm sorry! Are you oka—oh! Briar!"

"Leon!" Briar exclaimed, and Malric sensed the exact moment he lost all of the rosefinch's attention.

Pulling away, Briar was already in the process of sitting up then clambering back to his feet, grinning at the stranger who'd knocked them over in the first place. "I wasn't sure if you were going to come!"

"How could I resist? We'd have bad luck, otherwise."

"Leon," someone else spoke, and Malric searched until he found a child who resembled their older brother, clinging to his coat for balance. Not unlike Malric clung to Briar for the same. Malric pulled a face at her, but she pulled one right back. Malric almost lost his composure, before realizing—Briar was still holding his hand. Perhaps he hadn't noticed, but Malric squeezed it in reaction. All the while, he scoured his memory for why the name *Leon* was so familiar.

"Hi, Madison," Briar finally pulled his eyes from the clear

object of his affection, though it didn't ease the resentment in Malric's chest. "Do you remember me?"

"No," she answered bluntly, and Briar laughed. Leon nudged and scolded her under his breath, but she just whined and pulled on his arm to keep skating. He gently shoved her away, telling her to go get some hot cocoa, he would come find her in a minute. She relented, gliding away without another word, arms crossed in annoyance. Malric gripped Briar's hand tighter, not wanting to lose to the same fate.

"Did you get my text?" Leon went on, putting his hands in his jacket. "I didn't get a reply, so I wasn't sure..."

Malric couldn't help but look the man up and down, pursing his lips as he couldn't see what it was Briar found so enchanting about him. That person, Leon, was... fine. He wasn't particularly handsome, or ugly, or tall, or fit, or unfit, or charismatic, or special... yet Briar looked at him like he was the world. Like he was the carved idol of an ancient deity who would grant every one of his wishes if he was only devout enough—

"*Oh,*" Malric blurted suddenly—before realizing it might have been more of a sneer. Leon. That was the name of Briar's pas de deux partner for Giselle, the one he made his deal with Marie over, the person he'd thrown his whole life away just to get some attention from. Malric wanted to puke. Or did he want to laugh? Maybe to laugh until he puked—

"Yeah, sorry—that practice time works fine for me," Briar answered. "Though it's been a while since I danced La Sylphide, it might take me a little bit to get back into it..."

"Nah, you remember what Madame Cruz used to always say. *You never really forget.* You know what? Let's do it right now. Come on."

"Wh—what?" Briar laughed sharply when Leon suddenly took his hand. Malric wasn't fast enough to clutch Briar's opposite grip with enough force, and his rosefinch was pulled from his grasp just like that. Malric was left staring, deserted in the middle of the ice. He might have stood there for an eternity had Stella and Bianca not skated over to ask what was going on, only for Stella to go quiet when she noticed what Malric was staring at.

Briar and Leon, weaving around one another in the center of the rink where no one else clustered. Laughing and smiling at one another, saying things Malric couldn't hear from so far away. Briar's cheeks were redder than before.

"Oh... god," Stella practically whimpered. "What is he doing here?"

Malric wanted to throw her a look. To question if she disliked him for a good reason, because all of Malric's were just petty. Not that it mattered, he never cared much to need a *good* reason to hate someone, but... considering the way Briar smiled at him *like that*, considering the history, considering the whole reason Marie preyed on Briar in the first place—Malric was hungry for any and all things he could use to further his disdain.

"Ohhh no, no, no," Stella went on, pushing a mitten over her face to disrupt loose hairs. "That's La Sylphide, isn't it? What is he doing? His ankle—"

Before she could skate off to interrupt, though, Bianca took her hand and silently protested. She shook her head, thick curls bouncing and speckled with loose snow. Malric wished she'd let Stella go. He wished he was a better skater, himself—both so he could slide in and interrupt, but also because, once he realized what Briar and Leon were doing... he wished he could be the one to touch Briar like that.

It wasn't a perfect translation of the pas de deux, of course, but—it was enough to draw attention. People slowed their circling around the ice, they paused at the walls to watch the two ballerinas perform on rickety skates. It lacked the same perfect elegance as dancing on a hard stage, but it was enough. It didn't matter. Briar was beautiful no matter what they did, how they did it, with whom they danced with. It was then Malric realized, it wasn't the veil that made Briar so beautiful in the revel clearing, at all. Briar was simply breathtaking on their own.

Malric's heart squeezed, opening old wounds he'd forgotten

about. Wounds he'd walled up and put away, in order to forget about them at all. Wounds that would only fester and poison him with resentment and jealousy and anger if he was allowed to continue watching.

But even Bianca didn't know what was so dangerous about those wounds, and what would happen if Malric allowed them to split wide open again.

Why was it watching Briar dance a clumsy version of La Sylphide on rented skates the thing that struck Malric to his core? Deep enough to split his bones, to make the muscles in his legs tremble as they fought against the roots that kept him flat-footed on the earth when he'd grown so comfortable elevated into demi-pointe?

Briar and Leon danced perfectly with one another. They danced as if sewn with experience of one another's movements, exactly as they would come and go. Briar moved with anticipation for Leon's hands, which always landed exactly where they should on Briar's waist, his arms, his back. Two dancers who knew the score despite none playing, who knew one another. Malric's heart twisted tighter, knotting up with numbing fury that left him feeling... hollow.

He... wished it was him, putting his hands on Briar's waist. Lifting him. Carrying him. Supporting him as he sank into deep leg extensions and the bending of his waist. He—wanted to be the one to support Briar's weight in his hands, as Briar crested in and out of every movement like water over sand. Like rain over leaves. A stream over stone.

Malric wished he could dance.

But since he couldn't—he could instead only wish Briar would be forced to stop so Leon would take his hands off of them.

The envy in Malric's body turned acidic the longer it took. He stared at Briar the entire time they moved, clenching and unclenching his fists, commanding them to finish—but the moment they did, Malric regretted it. The moment Briar caught

Malric's eyes watching him intensely, making them lose their focus, their balance—Malric regretted those powerful emotions channeling through him. He regretted distracting Briar for even a moment.

Briar, elevated over Leon's chest, hit the ice with a thud and a grunt, summoning a gasp from the crowd. Stella shouted something, moving to approach—but Malric was already tearing off his skates, crossing the ice on his socks alone and skidding to a halt on his knees where Briar was pushing himself upright again. He shoved Leon out of the way in the process, putting his hands on Briar's face, then searching his head, his hands, only for Briar to mumble something and swat his hands away. Malric barely felt it. He barely felt anything, barely had a thought at all, except that image of Briar hitting the ice over and over again. Had Malric done that, somehow? No, no—

"How could you drop him?" Malric demanded, leaping to his feet and grabbing Leon by the front of the jacket. "He's supposed to be able to trust you!"

"I didn't mean—!" Leon attempted, but Malric lost his footing, and they both crashed to the ice. Malric turned over to grab Leon one more time, not knowing what he would do next—but Stella reached Malric first, pulling him back hard enough that even she floundered and hit the cold ground. The surrounding crowd was shouting by then, a few strangers skating over to help Leon up, Bianca doing the same for Briar. But Briar just stared at Malric with an unreadable expression—before averting his eyes, and turning away.

"I have to..." was all they said, pulling from Bianca's hands and hurrying toward the end of the ice. Malric shoved Stella away, scrambling to his feet and racing as fast as he could in chase. He leapt onto solid ground just as Briar was wrenching his skates off on a bench, shoving their feet into boots with a wild mix of emotions on their face.

"Are you hurt?" Malric asked breathlessly, but Briar wouldn't look at him. No—Briar's face was bright red, and something told

Malric it wasn't from the cold. Malric wished to know exactly what Briar was thinking, he wanted to say anything he could at all —but Briar just shook his head, tossing the skates away and grabbing his bag.

"I'll see you in the morn—" they attempted, but Malric grabbed their hand before they could go.

"I asked if you were hurt!" he insisted. Briar finally met his eyes, and Malric saw the full range of humiliation, disappointment, agony in Briar's eyes. Malric tried to swallow the lump in his throat, but it was too large.

"I'm fine," Briar said flatly, pulling his hand away. His steamy breaths trembled with anxiety. "I'll see you in the morning, Master Mal."

Briar hurried off. They barely made it out of sight before Stella and Bianca found Malric where he stood, watching Briar go —and Stella tackled Malric to the ground, making demands. *What happened? Why did you do that? Has Briar said anything to you about Leon?*

But Malric barely heard her. He just clutched his chest, hating the miserable swirl of emotions eating him alive from the inside out.

17

MALRIC AND THE ROSEFINCH

B riar did not, in fact, see Malric in the morning. They didn't arrive at Artemisia at all that day—or even the day after. Malric tried to give Briar space, trying to take Bianca's advice so he wouldn't come across as so intense and clingy, but gods it was difficult. He couldn't get the image of Briar and Leon out of his mind. The image of Briar hitting the ice, the memory of that sound.

When he asked Stella in class, she only closed her eyes and shook her head, like to answer would be opening a can of worms. Malric recalled Briar's night at the club, and only grew more concerned, but did his best to bite it back.

At the end of the second day, Malric would have texted them to finally ask, had he not sensed that tiny flicker in the air that told him something d'Alarie related had broached the veil. It must have been his mother's magpie. He didn't waste any time answering the call, himself.

Malric's bad mood persevered all the way back home. He blamed it on knowing Leon was the reason for Briar's deal, and nothing more. He blamed it on the annoyance of Briar going silent for two days after Malric thought they were finally making a connection. There was nothing more to it. No—that twisting concern, the jealousy in Malric's gut had nothing to do with Briar. It... had nothing to do with Briar dancing with another man at all. Nothing to do with how Malric would have never dropped them like that. Nothing to do with how he had to keep his mouth shut, never able to tell Briar as much.

Arriving at one of Marie's revels for a third time in a row made Malric even more apprehensive, knowing he wouldn't be able to go unnoticed for much longer. Guests were always coming and going, that part was normal—but regular patrons were remembered, and Marie always made a point of schmoozing them most. Malric had to be more careful than ever—especially if Marie's rosefinch intended on showing him interest, just like they'd discussed in the library days prior. Oh—Malric's mood lifted in an instant at the reminder.

Collapsing into an empty pile of pillows alongside his siblings, Malric helped himself to a glass of wine as Felme and Mavera pretended not to notice him. Still, Mavera leaned casually to prop on one of her elbows, just slightly closer to the fey lord she pretended not to know next to her.

"You've recently caused quite the stir back at the house," Mavera told him, allowing her long hair to spill over one shoulder. "Without even being there. What fun it's been."

"What have I done this time?" Malric asked, hardly moving his lips. Mavera smiled to herself, exchanging a look with Felme before picking a piece of grass from her silvery leggings.

"The town oracle says you'll be back to visit again, soon. Mother's in a tizzy because her dancer has been acting up, and she wants to be sure, if you do come, everything is perfectly set up to make you jealous."

"Ah—to make me regret leaving? Isn't that what worked on Felme? When she came to see what mother's little beantighe painter had done while she was away, and was threatened by their talent?"

Felme muttered a curse into her glass, but offered no other comment.

"Maybe I should pay a visit to mother, to see what her human dancer can do," Malric said playfully. Mavera licked her lips like it was the tastiest gossip she'd heard all season.

"Should I tease mother with that? I'll tell her you stopped by the house the other night, soooo surprised to find a human asleep in your bed."

Malric considered the proposition for a long time, even as Briar emerged through the trees on the other side of the clearing. Something about watching them search the edge of the circle, eyes finally scanning over Malric and then bouncing back again, made his heart leap. That night, the necklace dressed Briar in a soft pink tutu donning gold filigree and beading, and Malric knew from the first note he'd dance the scene of Dulcinea's enchanted garden from Don Quixote. Did Briar know that one? Malric wanted to ask.

His eyes lingered on Briar's ears as they rose into starting position, healing cuts hidden beneath the glamour. He gazed down at their ankle, too, though the bandages he was sure propped the injury straight were also hidden.

"Sure," he finally said as an idea struck him. "But also mention how the dancer limps when they walk, as if they've hurt themself, somehow. How it's impacting their performance, how I would never be jealous of something forced to dance on an injury. It would only make me even more glad I left."

"What do you mean?"

"Just do it," Malric requested. Mavera made a little noise of concession, right as the music swelled and Briar began his dance. The entire time Malric watched, Briar's words echoed in his head, explaining the details of his burden.

The musician made an agreement where they only had to do one perfect performance; but every time, the person always finds something wrong. And now the musician is trapped, and it's ruining their life... and they just wish they could disappear forever because they're starting to hate dancing so much...

But—Briar was perfect. Even though Malric knew they were

in pain, their ankle likely screaming with every landing of their leaps and moments of balance on their toes, they didn't show it. Briar Hunt truly wished to be perfect, and there was still a part of him who believed he could convince the fey lady of it, even if it was futile. Malric knew it. Briar likely knew it deep down, too.

Malric wouldn't let Briar go any more days than he had to without hearing how perfect he was, even if it came from the mouth of whom he thought to be human on the other side. Even if it came from the mouth of a fey lord hidden behind a fox mask, whom he still wasn't sure he could completely trust. Even if he would one day know, it came from the mouth of the fey lady's son who he was so afraid of disappointing.

As always, when the dance came to an end, the audience members began their hunt; Malric just kept his eyes on Briar, knowing Briar knew exactly where he sat—but even so, the moment Briar sought him out amongst the crowd, his heart still thumped. Why did it excite him so much, seeing Briar's flushed, tired face looking exactly for him? He couldn't help but wonder how much Briar had thought about that moment, what they would do when it finally came, all while avoiding Mal in the human world. To know Malric had been on his mind, even under a mask...

Briar avoided the groping hands of all the other fey, and approached where Malric sat. Malric, unable to resist, rose to his feet to meet Briar halfway.

"Hello, my lord," Briar said with a breathless smile, before casting a look over his shoulder to the others he'd actively snubbed for the first time. Malric followed with his own eyes, smirking at everyone else's confused, annoyed expressions. Only Briar turning back to speak again in the most saccharine sweet voice Malric had ever heard could possibly get him to look away again. Like someone who had been raised by leanan sídhe for the sole purpose of seducing fey like him. He was definitely doing it on purpose. A part of Malric never expected him to have it in him. "Did you enjoy my performance this time?"

"I thought you danced beautifully." Malric took Briar's hand and kissed the back of it, obsessed with the look of surprise on Briar's expression. He couldn't help but fully appreciate his appearance up close—those soft, lovely features; his slender neck and shoulders; how the bodice of the tutu perfectly fit his waist before flaring out at his hips, revealing the length of his legs. "Why else do you think I come to watch you dance so often, lately? Come on, come sit with me."

"Do you like it that much?" Briar asked with a coy smile, allowing Malric to lead him back to the pillows. Malric resisted the animalistic urge to grab him, overcome with suddenly wanting to know how far he could wrap his hands around Briar's narrow middle. "You, ah... said you were a dancer yourself, before. Are you really that impressed with me?"

"You know, this is the most I've ever heard you speak," Malric teased, collapsing into the pillows—and then pulling Briar down with him by the hand. Briar made a little sound of surprise, tumbling directly on top of Malric as he lost his balance. Unfortunately for Malric, his rosefinch accidentally slammed a knee between his legs in the process, making Malric grunt and swallow back bile as Briar, in comparison, swallowed back his own burst of laughter. Instead, he asked if Malric was alright in a high-pitched voice belonging to someone trying to keep their composure.

"Yes, fine," Malric wheezed, but actively adjusted how Briar sat with him. Tucking him into the crook of his arm, Malric blinked back tears as Briar clearly still fought to hold back his amusement. Maybe he'd even done it on purpose. Malric was going to kick his ass as soon as they were back in the human world. "You weigh less than a basket of apples."

"Oh?" Briar asked, shifting slightly in Malric's arm. He was clearly uncomfortable with the sudden proximity, moving as if he wished to avoid touching Malric as much as possible, but Malric was just grossly aware of how everyone looked at them. Watching them closely. Surely, amongst the masked witnesses, Marie d'Alarie had her eyes trained on them closer than all the others, to witness their movements down to the bones. She would definitely question the identity of the fey lord beneath the mask after that night, and Malric knew his time in secret was coming to a close. It was inevitable—he only had to be intentional about it.

But all those worries melted away as, by holding Briar so close, Malric could feel the direct heat of their body. He could feel Briar's bare skin through the glamour, and the realization that Briar, beautiful Briar, was technically tucked naked into the curve of Malric's arm, his hand cupping the underside of their round ass—nearly broke him entirely.

"Would you like some wine?" he finally asked, but Briar looked instantly uncertain. Still, he bit his lip and nodded. Malric couldn't help but smile unevenly, pouring the sparkling pink wine from a carafe into the glass he'd been using for himself. "I'll make sure you don't overindulge."

Despite the promise, Briar just stared at the drink when handed to him, clearly uncertain. When Malric noticed the surface of it trembling slightly, he softened his arrogance to lean in slightly more, whispering:

"It will not trap you here," he promised. "These are not Underworld rules, dear Persephone."

"And why should I trust anything you say?" Briar mumbled in return, a clear crack in his attempt to be coquettish and cute. A flicker of sincerity, of that brattiness Mal in the library had told him to keep at bay. Despite it all, Briar was doing so well keeping it tamed beneath the surface. Malric wanted to compliment him.

"I have no reason to mislead you," he promised, instead. "Besides—if I do anything to you, that fey lady will be here in an instant to scold me, and nothing would ruin my night faster."

Briar smiled awkwardly, but still hesitated before taking a drink. Malric searched his face, before realizing what else might be bothering him. He touched the rim of the glass, making the drink inside sway to and fro.

"Has some witch in the human world warned you of the fey's pink drink? Well—no need to worry. This is not fairy wine, only sparkling white dyed pink. Our hostess could never afford the real thing."

Briar pressed his lips together. He tried to smile coyly, but it was too forced to be natural. Malric kept his smile calm and inviting, as much as he could.

"That is good to know, my lord," Briar whispered, and the formal title rolling off his tongue made Malric's insides squirm in a way he never expected. "But I'm plenty familiar with real fairy wine on my own..."

Despite his voice remaining calm, the rest of him trembled. A reminder of the extent to which Briar feared him and every other high fey in the circle, despite putting on airs of confidence and rebellion in the human world. Malric wondered if there was anything he could even say to soothe Briar's fears, being one of them. One of the things who'd trapped and tortured him for so long. Why would Briar ever trust a high fey who he'd only ever known to be tricky and cruel? Yet, like *Mal* suggested—Briar was doing his best to be brave, and Malric would be sure to reward him for it.

He reclaimed the drink for himself, downing it without another word. Wiping his mouth on the back of his hand, he let out a breath and tossed the empty glass to the blankets.

"Perhaps it would be best if you didn't," he agreed. "Perhaps I wish to know you sober, since this is the most you've ever spoken out loud."

The immediate relief on Briar's expression was both reassuring and, strangely, infuriating. Malric instinctively firmed his grasp around Briar's body, wishing he might be able to offer any sense of comfort, of protection, at all from the others surrounding them and gossiping boisterously.

"I'm sor—" Briar started, but Malric pressed a finger to his mouth to stop him short, quickly shaking his head.

"Never do that," Malric whispered. "It implies you've done something wrong—and then you would owe me something. In fact, never thank a high fey, either, no matter how kind they are to you. That's worse."

"Oh…" Briar flushed like they knew that, already.

"How much do you really know about these high fey you've made your deal with?" Malric went on, pulling Briar closer to nod toward all the others settled around the clearing. Reclining on cushions, most trapped in endless conversation, indulging in wine and cake and fruit and one another. Briar observed all of them as if it was really the first time he'd ever had a chance to do so. Perhaps it was.

"Do they always pull you to the side after performing?" Malric asked, and Briar jumped slightly at his sudden voice. He nodded.

"Have they ever hurt you?" he went on, despite knowing the answer. Briar bit his lip, fidgeting with the glamoured chiffon around his waist. Fabric that wasn't really there, manifested by the necklace for everyone to see and trick into thinking they touched.

"Well…" Briar started, but couldn't get the words out. Malric hated that little, polite, uncomfortable smile. He hated how Briar wouldn't meet his eyes. He had to fight the mental images that stormed his mind, wishing to ask more questions, wanting to know everything the fey around him had ever done to make Briar Hunt uncomfortable—but any other fey lord wouldn't have cared about that. Even Malric, had he not already had a vested interest in the rosefinch, might not have thought twice about it.

Why did that just make him angrier?

"What brings you to me, tonight?" he asked, forcing his voice to remain flirty. "You must have been enchanted by my good looks, as I am by your dance."

Something clicked behind Briar's eyes; something reminding him of why he approached. A catlike smile returned to their face, like a mask dropping over the nervousness. Malric's heart pounded like a drum as Briar touched the end of the nose of Malric's mask with a coy smile.

"How would I know, when you always wear this?" he asked,

flicking the nose with a finger, before laughing softly and going on. "Perhaps if I am forced to socialize after performing... I would much rather it be with someone I find handsome, yes, my lord."

My lord. Again, those words in Briar's sweet voice—Malric nearly combusted. He was going to burst into flames, melting his skin and Briar's both, so that they might never be parted from one another ever again. He wanted to sink his nails, his teeth, into every bit of falsely-covered flesh burning warm beneath his hands.

"Well—then that makes the both of us," Malric agreed with a hungry smile. His hand trailed down Briar's legs crossed over his lap. He forced himself to focus. To take the attention back to what he knew Briar needed to ask. It was easier said than done, though, as he continued to feel every inch of Briar's bare skin, despite seeing only the glamoured tutu and bodice. He suddenly wished to be naïve to Briar's plight, to whisk him into the dark, perhaps back to his own bed, to coax more submissive compliments from their mouth, more breaths of *'my lord'* if he could get them.

His hand drifted to Briar's ankle. His fingers trailed over the bandages.

"How often have you danced on such injuries?" he asked.

Briar flexed his jaw, as if embarrassed. Just like in the human world, where it took every ounce of trickery Malric had in him to get a single confession out of those lips.

"I always dance for Lady d'Alarie when she calls on me."

"Except for last time."

Briar's mouth dangled open, before smiling awkwardly.

"Yes, except for last time. But I learned my lesson. I will not embarrass my lady again."

Malric's hand tightened around Briar's injured ankle on accident. It was just a reflex, he couldn't stop it at those words, just recalling the sight of Briar unconscious, exhausted, partially buried under fresh snow in the alleyway behind the club. He splayed his opposite hand flat against Briar's back at the thought, reminding himself of how warm and lively Briar was right there in front of him in comparison.

"Is she cruel to you?" he asked softly. He wanted to get to the point, he couldn't resist any longer— "Is there anything I can do? As... as a fellow dancer, who wishes to look out for his kin."

Despite the clear offer—Briar froze up. His awkward, nervous smile twitched on his mouth, searching Malric's face, his mask, as if he knew it was actually Mal there under it. Waiting for his cue, for someone to feed him his line. Malric had to bite back the frustration, reminding himself of how Briar still trembled slightly on his lap.

Malric tucked a piece of hair behind Briar's ear. His eyes trailed down the length of Briar's neck, fighting the urge to place his mouth there, to leave marks that would show Marie d'Alarie she was not, in fact, the only person who could take ownership of the rosefinch she forced to dance at her beck and call.

"I'm sorry she has trapped you like this," he said without thinking. Briar smiled sarcastically, to Malric's surprise.

"I thought apologies were dangerous, my lord," he laughed softly. "Does that mean you owe me something, now?"

Those words ignited in Malric's blood, and he barely kept the flames beneath his skin at bay. He sought out anything he could say to give Briar the nudge he needed.

"I could be convinced," he smiled. "What is it that you want from me?"

Briar's eyes, like a forest pool on an overcast day, searched Malric's face. Searched every detail of his mask, of his hazel eyes that gazed through it, his mouth visible beneath it. Malric could practically see the request on his lips, silently encouraging him to utter those words they'd agreed on in the library—

"Briar."

Briar went still as stone, turning slowly to the owner of the voice. Malric followed as well, but kept the irritation off his face. Marie d'Alarie stood before them, wearing that fake, forced smile she always did when annoyed but keeping up appearances.

"Perhaps it is time for you to retire."

Briar opened his mouth to speak—then closed it again as survival instincts overpowered everything else. He offered Malric a polite, silent nod. In their eyes, Malric saw the immediate glaze of fear that crashed down the moment Marie was close-by. Malric knew it, he knew how it felt for the defenses to drop like a cage on one's self. But not a cage to trap—a cage to protect.

"Ah, I apologize for monopolizing your pretty bird," Malric said politely, shifting his body to help Briar back to his feet. "I simply couldn't stand the thought of missing another night in a row."

"You flatter me, my lord," Marie replied, and Malric was only slightly reassured when it was the same tone she used for everyone else. Clearly not recognizing him with his slightly altered voice and face hidden behind the mask. "I hope you come and witness again, soon."

"You will not find me absent at any revel where this bird performs."

"Do you hear that, Briar? Another patron who wishes to see you improve. Go on—" Marie grabbed the back of Briar's neck suddenly, shoving him into a bow. Briar made a sharp noise of surprise, and Malric had to clench his jaw to keep the rush of anger off his expression. "Thank the handsome lord for his compliment."

Briar's hands, clenched into fists at his sides, shook terribly. Even though Malric had proven himself trustworthy, it stood no match against whatever trauma Marie had inflicted. All the while, that image of his mother's hand clutching the back of Briar's neck, forcing him to bend—it made the top of Malric's own spine ache with residual memory.

"Th—" Briar choked, and Malric saw the panic on his face. *Never thank a high fey, either. That's worse.* "Thank you, my lord."

Marie finally released her grasp, and Briar bolted upright. He didn't meet Malric's eyes again, instead turning and hurrying off into the first reach of the woods he could find. Marie lingered for only a moment longer, smiling at Malric, before bowing, herself, and excusing herself to the rest of her guests. Malric watched her go, eyes locked on that open spot at the nape of her neck. His hand flexed at the thought of forcing her to bow, instead.

MALRIC NEVER WANTED TO LET BRIAR WAKE UP ALONE, again, even if Briar didn't know he was there. Was it creepy? Perhaps. But Malric would definitely come clean, one day. He just wanted to make sure when Briar fled the house in the mornings, raced into the woods, passed through the veil back to the world he knew... he would do so, safely. And then his favorite instructor Master Mal would send him a totally unsuspicious text asking if he wanted to get breakfast, or something...

Malric smirked into his drink, having spent the long night in Tyara, the city whose outskirts the d'Alarie estate sat on. A place where noble fey took holidays, owned vacation homes, enjoyed the Autumn Court's finest whiskies and beers and maple syrups. Malric never cared for it himself, always finding it a little too... polished. A little too clean to be genuine.

Leaving the bar a few hours before the sun would peek over the horizon, Tyara city remained quiet still so early in the morning, but Malric knew steam cars would soon putter down the road, illuminating the street and early morning pedestrians. He would make it back to the house before the sun even thought about rising, wanting to make sure he didn't miss a thing. He'd make sure Briar made it back through safely, with no one to bother them.

But as Malric approached the d'Alarie estate, intending on looping around to cross through the woods where no one would see him—a haunting sound caught his attention, bringing him to a halt.

Mal—Mal, wait... I just can't find them... wait, Mal, please...

Holding his breath, Malric turned to gaze through the trees to the expanse of the d'Alarie back courtyard. That place where he would be visible, vulnerable, easily spotted by anyone whose eyes he specifically didn't want chasing him.

But—that voice sounded like Briar. The moment he realized, he forgot everything else.

Emerging from the trees, the far edge of the back yard was being slowly devoured by a thick fog from an incoming cold front. Malric shivered the moment it kissed his face, but continued forward, nonetheless. Just following that ghostly call of his name, spoken like Briar wasn't completely in his own mind, like he'd been drugged, like he was hurt. Any of those possibilities propelled Malric farther into the mist until he could no longer see the house or the trees, only the grass beneath his feet. Only the edge of the woods, and the slightest peek at the edge of the revel clearing on the other side.

"Briar?" he asked gently once the voice petered off. Nothing responded, except the sound of scratching, soft grunts, uncertain breaths. Malric searched deeper, following the path into the forest, stopping the moment he spotted a white figure hunched over in the dirt between two of the trees on the edge of the clearing. Hunched, bending forward, scraping their hands through grass and soil in the initial stages of being torn apart.

"*Mal,*" Briar croaked, sinking their fingers into the soft dirt again. "*Mal, wait... I can't find them...*"

"Briar," Malric said again without thinking, the name hardly more than a breath on his lips. Hurrying forward, he almost said Briar's name again—before noticing what he wore. The front of the linen nightshirt was stained brown and green from the effort in the soil—and it was one of Malric's own. But more than that, Briar's eyes were neatly closed, eyelashes fluttering as the rest of his face hung lax. He was sleepwalking.

"Gods," Malric hissed in a mix of disbelief and relief, running fingers back through his hair. He watched Briar tear at the grass a few moments longer, before sighing and approaching from behind. He moved slowly, carefully, quietly, before crouching to the balls of his feet to see what exactly the human was looking for. There was nothing, though—only churned greenery beneath Briar's mud-plastered hands.

"Mal," he continued to beg, and Malric finally placed a soft hand on Briar's back.

"C'mon, Bry," he whispered, but Briar still didn't stop digging. "Let's get back to bed."

Briar shook his head. Malric dragged his hand down their back.

"What are you looking for?" he asked quietly.

"For the spell..." Briar trailed off, claiming two more handfuls of dirt before his breath shuddered in frustration. *"I just want them back..."*

"There's nothing in this place for you," Malric told him, and Briar finally slowed his assault on the grass. He bent over his knees for a few breaths—before falling to his side, collapsing into Malric's arms without any warning. Malric barely caught him, holding his breath until he was sure Briar was still sound asleep. He couldn't help himself, touching Briar's face with gentle fingers, tucking loose strands of rosy-blonde hair from his eyes. He was struck, once again, by how small Briar looked when he wasn't wide awake and fighting. Wide awake and spewing threats and insults—like an angry bird. It made Malric smirk, wishing him sweet dreams before pulling the sleeping creature into his chest and rising to his feet.

Briar curled up against Malric's body, breathing deeply, eyes never opening as Malric made his way back through the fog. For a moment he considered taking him and running, knowing he could protect Briar better than anyone else if he only had him alone—but knew Briar's things were likely back in the house, and Briar would just leave them there forever otherwise. Malric would just have to be careful.

Thankfully, the mist made for a perfect cover even as the sun finally cracked over the distant horizon. Malric was able to maneuver his dirt-stained rosefinch through the back servants' entrance, moving up the back stairs and out one of the wainscoting panels at the end of the upper hallway. He made it all the way back to his bedroom without anyone noticing them—though he did accidentally bonk Briar's head at least twice on the way.

Depositing someone else into his own bed wasn't particularly strange, but depositing someone covered in dirt and wearing one of his own nightshirts was definitely not his norm. Still, Malric moved with intention, resting Briar's head against the pillows, pulling the blanket up to tuck the rest of him in, though he paused at the sight of Briar's ankle. Still swollen, angry, contorting the way Briar's foot reclined on the mattress. Malric clenched his teeth—and couldn't stop his hands from undoing the bandages, moving with all the softness, all the tenderness someone like him could, unraveling the elastic to re-wrap tighter.

Tucking Briar's foot back under the blankets, he then tucked it over their sleeping body so they wouldn't get cold. He made sure to shift more hair from Briar's face as they settled into the bed, listening as they released a long, relaxed breath. Malric smiled to himself, gently brushing his fingers against the healing cut on one of Briar's ears. His smile dipped back into a frown, and then he couldn't help but see all of it. The injured ankle never given a chance to heal; the bruises on his arms and legs from trudging through the woods and tripping over undergrowth; the cuts and scrapes on his hands from digging at the soil in his sleep. What else was there? What else had there been, already healed over and gone into the place where Briar kept his most despised truths?

All Malric could do was close his eyes, leaning over the person resting in his bed.

"I will set you free from this place," he barely spoke, just loud enough for Danu to hear and take note of a promise being made. His hand trailed down the blankets to where Briar's ankle hid beneath them. "I will not allow her to hurt you any longer."

Those words were meant for more than just Briar—and Malric clenched his jaw tighter. The only thing to loosen it was leaning forward to press a promising kiss to Briar's forehead, relaxing so as to never bring anything that wasn't gentleness anywhere near him again.

It was harder than Malric anticipated to leave Briar behind. He nearly crawled into bed right alongside him; nearly stole him away. But Malric wasn't glamoured as a human. He wasn't obscured behind a fox mask. He wasn't ready for Briar to know— that he himself was the fey lady's son, who Briar thought would break his legs after dancing.

Instead, Malric channeled that anger, that frustration, toward the person who it belonged. Who gave it and should receive it, only.

Rather than exiting through the back doors like he came, Malric paused for a long time outside his bedroom door. He stood there, like the only thing between Briar and the rest of the world, letting the weight of it hang off his shoulders until he could get used to it. And then—he stepped away, turning toward the main staircase. Making his decision the moment he carried Briar's burden with his own.

He entered the dining room right as Mavera was making suggestions about the dancer's ankle at breakfast, how it would surely reflect poorly if dear Malric suddenly arrived to watch them dance when they weren't at their best...

"Who isn't at their best?" he asked with a handsome smile. Everyone in the room turned to stare at him in shock—but Malric sought out only one face among them. The one he wanted to see the panic and shock on, most. And Marie d'Alarie did not disappoint.

18

BRIAR AND THE REHEARSAL

Briar dreamed of being carried. He dreamed of the smell of cold fall mornings and tobacco and whiskey. Warmth that infiltrated his cold, stiff hands, before claiming the rest of him and tucking him away into comfort. It'd been a long time since he sank into anything so dark and safe and all-encompassing.

But then he awoke in the d'Alarie bedroom, and all sense of comfort whisked away as if it never existed at all. He just groaned softly, closing his eyes and trying to chase it down. Like a fox after a rabbit. But he wasn't fast enough, not even to remember the exact feeling of it. Maybe he just wasn't used to wanting to want to remember his dreams.

By then, Briar was used to waking up with sore feet and covered in dirt, but that morning he was even back in bed where he started. He didn't want to think about it. He was tired of dreaming of that plot in the clearing, digging endlessly and never making any progress.

Shirking off the fey lord's dirty nightshirt, he left it on the floor like he always did. He pulled on his own t-shirt, jeans, and sneakers over bare feet and bandages, which felt slightly tighter than he remembered. Shrugging into his jacket, he flung his black backpack on last, pulling his hair from where it caught down his back. Scooping his replacement rowan berry doorknob charm from the floor as he headed out, he tucked it into his pocket and hurried toward the stairs.

That morning, there were voices in the house. It wasn't completely out of the norm—but something about them was more boisterous than usual. Or maybe just enthusiastic? Briar could never tell, he still hadn't quite figured out how to determine what a fey showed to be true or false. A trick. It reminded him of sitting on the lap of the fox lord the night before, feeling every touch of his arm and hand caressing Briar's naked body beneath the glamoured ballet skirt—and his face lit up in flames. Oh, god. When was the last time he got laid, with how easily embarrassed something like that made him? He'd been so busy with Mal, with the fairy bullshit, and starting that afternoon, with Leon's dance practice at St. Tomassin—

Amidst his getaway, for the first time ever, Briar actually slowed his normally unstoppable race from the house. He took his time passing the entryway to what he knew to be the dining room, trying to guess the number of people inside based on the overlapping voices, the clattering silverware.

His timing could not have been worse. A shadow passed over the narrow gap between the doors, and they suddenly slid open. Briar found himself staring into the face of someone only seen once before in the house that morning he lost his first doorknob charm in the yard. That fey man who'd been lingering in the kitchen, who Briar raced past as quickly as he could. Briar had assumed it was only a guest, some revel patron who'd stayed the night like he had—but the moment he gazed at the fey lord directly, he saw the resemblance.

This man had the same sun-kissed skin, green eyes, amber hair as Marie d'Alarie. And while there was no other proof—something deep in Briar's most basic instincts told him it was true.

It took longer than it should have to turn and run—but that man's eyes trapped him. They petrified him in an instant, and even looked as shocked as Briar felt to find a human peeking into the dining room. Only when he moved his mouth to say something did Briar manage to finally pull away, sprinting through the house, into the kitchen, out the back door. The moment he broke through the trees, disappearing from sight, he had to stop again and dry-heave from the nauseating panic swelling in his gut.

THERE WASN'T TIME TO GO ALL THE WAY HOME BEFORE Briar's first practice with Leon, so he spent the rest of the morning in a coffee shop reading whatever was in his backpack and trying not to think about that brief confrontation that morning. That man, that fey lord—that was Marie d'Alarie's son, wasn't he? The one Briar replaced, the one who would break Briar's legs if he ever witnessed such a poor performance at the revel...

His phone pinged. It was a message from Mal, and Briar felt a brief sense of relief for something to distract him—until he saw Mal's contact picture, and his heart jumped before flattening again. Mal, with his reddish-brown hair, hazel eyes—features just similar enough to make him panic on instinct, before reminding himself, there was no reason to feel that way. Mal's hair was shorter and a little straighter. His eyes were warmer. His voice was different. He was slightly less broad, a little bit shorter. His ears were very, very *round*. Mal was—safe.

Still, Briar held his breath until he felt dizzy. He tried to force the thoughts out of his ears. When that didn't work, he actually did puke in the coffee shop bathroom. At least it made time pass quickly.

In the early afternoon, he finally packed up his things again to catch the next bus, though he secretly *despised* the idea of going anywhere near *St. Tomassin Academy of Dance for rich nepo babies,* only intensifying the closer the meeting time crept. He would even have to wear his grass-stained slippers from the revel the night before, not to mention the sweaty clothes he'd gone to and fro through the veil in, too. *Ugh*—at least the thought of seeing Leon again kept his nerves at bay; a welcome distraction, all things considered.

Briar forced himself to erase the memory of that fey lord's face from his mind. It didn't matter in that moment. It wouldn't matter again until the next time he had to dance. It might not even matter, then, because Briar always assumed there was a reason he hadn't come to watch Briar dance in all that time, anyway. Maybe he didn't give a shit. Maybe Marie was full of shit.

Sitting on the bus, Briar scrolled through his feed while constantly checking out the window to make sure he hadn't missed his stop. Seeking any kind of distraction he could find.

He'd only visited Tomassin once before, and it was while his moms were in town to tour the schools available. It ended up not mattering, because Tomassin rejected him after a brutal three-course audition.

Tomassin technically ranked higher than Artemisia, but "ranking" was always vaguely described, and usually sprinkled with a level of unspoken classism that made Briar's skin crawl. Their campus was technically newer, shinier, and therefore cost more to attend, making it inherently more "prestigious", or whatever—but the people graduating from their dance program didn't always get accepted into the companies they wanted, either. What did it really mean to be "better"? There was Briar, even, peddling onto that fancy-ass campus in search of the shimmering glass dance building, an Artemisia student invited by one of Tomassin's own to perform in their charity gala over any other dancers available on their own grounds. Maybe they could kiss his perfectly shaped Artemisian ass.

Rolling up to the doors Leon sent a picture of a few days prior, Briar didn't even bother locking up his bike as he was sure none of the rich kids would want it. He puffed up his chest, combed fingers back through his hair to make it look nice in his reflection, and grabbed the door handle while what tasted like breakfast teased the back of his throat. He really thought he'd anxiety-puked it all up in the bathroom.

The amount of money that school received was evident even in that little spit of hallway Briar walked down, demonstrated by the murals painted on the walls, the gaudy displays of every award possibly given for achievements in dance, photographs of every performance season they did—of which there were apparently *three Tomassin dance companies* putting on shows simultaneously, even just in ballet. God—Briar couldn't resist sticking his tongue out at his own reflection over the trophy case he passed.

The auditorium doors down the way suddenly opened, and Briar jumped before meeting eyes with Leon smiling at them.

"Hey, Bry," he said, motioning Briar over. "Find the place okay? Are you feeling alright from your fall?"

"Um, yeah," Briar said, tucking his phone away quickly, right as a message came through asking what he was doing that evening. He swore the attached name was Mal's. "I'm fine, you didn't even drop me from that high up."

Leon pulled Briar into a hug, and Briar wrapped his arms back around in return, embracing that familiar person he didn't realize he missed so much. It had only been a few days since skating—why did it always feel like an eternity?

Leon smelled like aftershave and shampoo. He'd gotten his ears pierced since leaving Artemisia, and that was the first time Briar noticed them up close, not in a dark practice room or on the skating rink. His scruffy face scratched the side of Briar's cheek, and Briar had to stand on his toes to really hug him all the way around like he wanted to.

Briar was in love with Leon Heller. Or, at least—he had been. Maybe even still. Just the smell of him was enough to bring back every thrilling, exhilarating, and—heartbroken memory. Briar shoved past those, just wanting to focus on the opportunity he was being given. He'd been invited to dance with Leon, specifically, in their charity pas de deux event. Clearly because Leon knew Briar was the best dancer to pair with him, just like he teased in the practice room. Perhaps he'd always known it. What if Briar danced so well, they wanted to offer him a scholarship to Tomassin, too? Would he accept it? His mind whirled through every fantasy of getting to attend with this person whose arms he fit into so perfectly, despite spending the morning considering all the things he hated most about St. Tomassin Academy—

"I'm so grateful you were able to make it. You were my only choice. Come on, we'll get you all caught up. There's no time to teach it to anyone else from the start, ha... Are you taking better care of your feet these days? I remember how you used to tape them up before class."

"Does Tomassin have it in their budget?" Briar teased. "I still tape the hell out of them whenever I can."

"I'm sure we can figure something out," Leon laughed. Inside the auditorium, it echoed off the high ceilings. "Though even if we couldn't, I know for a fact you would keep dancing, even if blood started spurting out of your slippers."

Briar laughed, too. "You know me. I'd never let a chance to be the center of attention pass me by."

Only a small part of him appreciated the size of the auditorium where they walked, though he instinctively sneered at the chandelier hanging overhead, wondering if it detached for performances of Phantom of the Opera, too. Rich assholes. Briar reassured himself that, even with all the money in the world, he and his weekly cash from mentoring kids' ballet still allowed him to dress better than all of Tomassin, combined. They probably wouldn't know Louboutins from Louis Vuitton. Ah—he should tell that one to Mal.

"The center of attention is right where you belong," Leon teased, leading Briar down the dim walkway toward the stage illuminated by overhead lights. It was then he spotted the small gathering of heads wiggling around in the shadows, and his stomach flipped in sudden anxiety. Still, he straightened up, squaring his shoulders and forming his facial features to be perfectly pretty and intimidating.

Behind the curtain, Briar finished stretching as Leon gave notice to the pianist that they would be starting soon. The choreography for La Sylphide's' pas de deux played through his mind, swaying through the first few steps on his own to warm up. He wouldn't fall that time. He and Leon would dance perfectly, just like they always did.

Stepping onto the stage, the pianist introduced the practice performance with a few notes—and Briar fell into the steps like rainwater collects and drips from leaves. Moving his arms and following with his body, lifting en pointe hurt like a bitch—but he kept it off his face, not wanting Leon to know. Not wanting anyone in the audience to notice. Just like he did at the fey lady's revels.

For familiar hands to find his waist and dip him forward, to the side, lift him lithely off his feet to float through the air, was indescribable. Even if the circumstances weren't ideal—he was dancing on stage again, and the sensation claimed every one of his senses.

They moved through the waltz without interruption, Briar hardly perceiving the real world around them. Turning romantically into Leon's arms, meeting his eyes and smiling, dipping into pirouettes and waterlike bows with arms floating to the side, Briar might as well have been made of air.

But as the accompaniment faded into the auditorium rafters, the high of the movements quickly popped at the sound of someone in the audience clearing their throat.

"Are you sure this is alright?" they asked. Leon set Briar back onto his feet, Briar just silently fighting to catch his breath as Leon wiped his forehead.

"Why not? Briar did great," Leon answered. Briar saw how the heads in the audience glanced back and forth. None of them said anything else, and the silence was tangible. He almost said something—but Leon touched the small of his back, first.

"Let's go again Briar, yeah?"

"Oh—yeah," Briar said, moving back into position as Leon

nodded at the pianist. Briar stretched and rolled his sore ankle in the few moments he had before his cue, and his eyes wandered back out to the audience. There were only ten people in those seats—but the way they talked to one another, smiling, giggling, made his skin itch all over.

The waltz began again, but that time, Briar didn't sink into the comfortable bubble of the dance. He was suddenly self-conscious about every movement, wanting to be perfect, wanting everything to be perfect for Leon and everyone watching, to prove Leon chose him for good reason.

"Everything alright?" Leon asked under his breath as the final piano note rang away. "You were stiffer, that time."

"Let's just do it again," Briar insisted. "I'm fine. Just trying to get back into it."

Again. And again. And again. They performed the dance over and over, until Briar could feel every mistake carving itself into his muscle-memory until it would soon become a permanent issue. Until he forgot how it was *supposed* to look, and only ever moved like his bones were both broken and fused together at the same time. What the fuck was wrong with him...?

No, he knew. He knew what was wrong. He heard members of the audience giggle every time he messed up again. And even though Leon never said anything, himself—even though Leon was a skilled enough dancer to pick up any slack Briar might drop —Briar couldn't snap back into the right mentality again. Not with everyone watching. Not with his ankle injury. Not with the memory of the fey lord back at the house—

He thought of the fey lady's son watching from the audience. Judging, feeling insulted at a poor excuse of a dancer, and it only heightened Briar's anxiety every time. Again and again, relentlessly squeezing him.

"Does anyone have any notes for Artemisia?" someone finally asked as another practice round ended. Briar squinted through the overhead lights to find the audience, most sitting with arms crossed and looking perturbed.

"Not really," one person finally answered.

"I wouldn't even know where to start."

"Leon, let me try it. I have the first half memorized, already."

"Briar already agreed—" Leon attempted.

"But no one's going to donate if we dance like Artemisia students."

"What the hell does that mean?" Briar snapped before he could stop himself. All the self-consciousness, anxiety, frustration grew like weeds in his chest. "Maybe the reason I can't dance is because I can hear all of you mouth-breathing from all the way up here."

The responding silence lasted only a moment.

"The reason you can't dance is because you've never had to do a real performance before," someone else said, face obscured by the lights. "How many shows does Artemisia put on in a season? Leon told us it was only one because you can't afford any more than that."

"Yeah, and you all put on a hundred shows per season, but no one knows the waltz for La Sylphide?" Briar smiled sarcastically. "Knowing the dances for every maiden and background tree in a hundred ballets isn't the same as knowing the choreo for the fucking prima ballerina—"

"What, you mean that one time you danced Giselle?" Another voice laughed. "Oooooh, a single lead, wow, we're really in lauded company."

"We've seen tapes of that performance—no wonder Leon never wanted to dance with you again."

"And—and yet here I am," Briar managed to keep the sarcastic tone, but his arrogant smile wavered. "Leon came all the way to Artemisia to find me specifically for your stupid show—"

Someone laughed. Someone else snorted.

"Leon—you told him you wanted him, specifically? Baby, you're just an understudy. No, like an under-understudy, technically. Not even second choice."

"If Keisha hadn't broken her leg, you would still be practicing your toe-raises in that old warehouse, prima donna."

"Guys, come on," Leon finally put his hands up. "We're all just stressed out because of the deadline, but it's going to be fine. Briar just needs a little more work to get back into it..."

But Briar's ears rang. He no longer stared at the audience members, but instead at Leon, who turned to him with an apologetic smile. He said something, but Briar didn't hear it.

"Sorry," he said without knowing why, before clamping his mouth shut. "I'm... just someone's understudy?" *Again?*

Leon's smile never faded, proof he didn't understand exactly why that truth stabbed Briar all the way down to the core of his being.

"Like they said—Keisha broke her leg, then Naomi had to fly home because of a family emergency. But you were the first person I thought of after that—"

"Only because they can't make a new costume in time," someone else added. "But maybe if they add some more ribbons, no one will notice Artemisia dances like a baby giraffe."

"Fuck this," Briar muttered after a moment, putting a hand to his forehead before turning to leave the stage. The others laughed, but Leon hurried after him, apologizing and begging Briar to stay. Briar just tore off his slippers, shoving his feet into his sneakers before grabbing his shoulder bag, not even bothering to pull on his jacket.

"I'll perform with you, but I won't practice with them." Briar finally snapped around to meet Leon's eyes. "I wouldn't want to embarrass you anymore. Text me if you haven't found a replacement by tomorrow."

"Come on, Briar—"

But Briar was already navigating his way through the dark backstage area, shoving through the fire door and not caring that the alarm went off overhead. It clanged shut behind him, and he walked as quickly as he could—but tears spilled down his cheeks before he even made it to his bike around the front of the building. He scrubbed them away as much as possible, grabbing his bike and yanking it off the rack. No one followed him.

He hated how the sun set so early in the winter. He hated how cold it got as soon as it was dark. He hated that he was still wearing his dirty clothes from the day before, and he hated how all those people laughing at him only made his heart pound harder and harder because it made him think about Marie d'Alarie's son and her threat of what might happen if Briar danced poorly in his presence—

He had to stop pedaling, else he would careen off the sidewalk. Grappling for the railing on the bridge where he halted, he hunched over the handlebars and fought to breathe normally, but even if he kept the panic attack at bay, the tears wouldn't stop coming. He just blubbered to himself, pathetically, wishing he could start the whole day over again.

His hand went into his jacket pocket before he really thought about it. Through blurry vision, he found the name of the only person who might understand what he was so afraid of—even if it meant admitting he wasn't okay. He needed help. He couldn't stand to be alone with all that cacophony banging around in his skull.

Help me. Help me. Help me.

"Hello?" Mal's voice was an instant balm on Briar's nerves, and Briar released a shaky, desperate laugh in reaction. "Bry? What's wrong?"

"Will you—come here?" Was all Briar could think to say.

"I'll be right there."

Briar blubbered out another wet laugh.

"You don't even know where I am."

"Doesn't matter. I'm already on my way."

"God," Briar wept, shaking his head—but unable to hold back the pitiful smile cracking through the tears. Those words, spoken in that voice—were so easy to cling to.

19

BRIAR AND THE REASON

It was both an eternity and not nearly long enough that Briar sat in the Artemisia dance room before someone else arrived to join him. Not enough time for his puffy face to go back to normal, for him to pretend like everything was actually just fine and it had all been one big misunderstanding.

Briar did not let strangers into his bed, and he did not let strangers see him cry. He'd always been that way, even before meeting the fey lady and having his life turned upside down. But as Mal stepped into the dance room and Briar lifted his splotchy face to give him an embarrassed smile, Mal could no longer be called a *stranger*.

"Hi," Mal said from the doorway. Like someone speaking into an empty room trying to find a ghost. Still, his eyes remained directly on Briar, knowing exactly where that embarrassed little spirit hid.

"Hi," Briar croaked back. "What are you doing here?"

"Gods—I've never met a bigger brat. Don't start that with me."

Briar laughed, not knowing it would only make more tears fill his eyes. He wiped them away, and finally unraveled his body curled in on itself where he sat on the floor. Meanwhile, Mal stripped off his scarf, then his snow-speckled jacket, tossing them over an empty bar and approaching. He claimed a seat on the hardwood next to where Briar sat, leaning against the mirror and bumping their shoulders together.

"Where have you been lately?" he asked. "The last time I saw you was at the ice-skating rink. I was worried about you. Did you have to go to any more revels?"

As always, Briar's instinct was to avoid the truth. He shoved through it, watching Mal's hand where it rested on his thigh. A part of him wished to grab and hold it.

"Do you remember... at the diner, I told you about this crush I had..."

"The one that led you to making your deal? That guy who football-spiked you into the ice."

Briar grimaced. "That's the one. Well, he—Leon, I mean—asked me a few days ago... if I would pas de deux with him for this charity thing hosted by his school. So... I went to do that today, and... it..."

Briar inhaled a long breath through his nose.

"They were all... just... rude as fuck, I don't know..."

Oh—he realized his misery had nothing to do with fairy bull-shit at all, and suddenly felt embarrassed for calling Mal all the way out there. For wasting his time over something personal, something so silly, something really only tangentially related to the fey deal at all. He almost pulled his legs back into his body, wanting to hide behind them— but Mal's hand extended to pat Briar's knee before he could. Something about it kept him unfolded, exposed, vulnerable. He finally gave in to the urge, care-fully taking Mal's hand. Just wanting to hold onto something. But then Mal was quiet for a long time—too long of a time, and Briar looked at him to see why.

The man was trying to bite back laughter, and Briar bent his hand back in anger.

"What!" he hissed. "What's so funny, asshole—!"

"You—you're pas de deux-ing with the person—who you

made your deal about, because—Marie d'Alarie said you needed fey help—to ever pas de deux with them again?" Mal finally blurted between bouts of laughter, despite his best attempts to keep it restrained. Briar punched him in the arm, but that only made Mal laugh harder. "Oh, fuck—oh *gods*, imagine—imagine her face, Marie's face, if she knew—you just went and got what you wanted without her! Oh, *Jesus!*"

"Stop laughing at me!" Briar shouted. "Stop it!"

"So what are you upset about, exactly?" Mal asked, shaking his head and still chuckling. "What did they say to make you so upset? You—Briar Hunt—who we both know dances better than anyone else on human legs?"

Briar blinked at him. "What?" he asked, but Mal just gave him a look of amused exasperation. Briar just looked away, hating how it made him blush. "You—you've never even seen me dance... not really..."

"You're right. Maybe you deserved to be laughed at, after all."

Briar smacked him on the arm again, but Mal just gave him a dark, encouraging smile. He nodded toward the open floor. When Briar still didn't get the hint, he squeezed Briar's hand, then lifted it out.

"Show me, then," he said. "So I know for sure."

Briar frowned at him—it may have been more of a pout—but Mal just patted his leg and motioned again for him to go and perform. Briar finally snatched his hand away stubbornly.

"Fine, but my ankle still hurts," he muttered, "so I'm not going en pointe."

Before he could fully stand, Mal grabbed his wrist and yanked him right back down. Briar laughed sharply, only for Mal to hook him by the knee and turn his body. It made Briar slump to the floor, whining and flailing his legs as Mal told him to *cut it out* and *stop it*, all while yanking Briar's shoe off to get a look at Briar's ankle for himself.

"What's it going to take to give this a break?" Mal huffed, pinching Briar's ankle and making them squeal and kick. "Do I gotta lock you up somewhere? Maybe I'll have a talk with the fey lady, myself—"

"No, no!" Briar laughed, still squirming. "It's not that bad!"

"It's the size of my thigh!" Mal insisted, stretching out his leg to demonstrate. "You're never going to fulfill your deal with a fucked up ankle!"

"I thought that's what you're here for!" Briar threatened, lunging and grabbing Mal by the shoulders, only to yelp when Mal lost his balance and fell backward. Briar went with him, finding himself straddling Mal's hips as their faces dangled only a few inches apart. Briar's breath caught, blinking a few times before laughing under his breath. Briar ignored how Mal's hands trailed up their thighs on either side, before settling on their hips. As if to keep them there.

"She offered me another way out, remember?" Briar said with feigned malevolence. "Maybe I'll offer you up to take my place dancing in the revel. Since you have so much experience dancing for the fey."

Mal smiled—but then it turned bitter, and Briar leaned back slightly.

"The joke would be on her, then," he said tightly. "But I still do not recommend taking any offered trades, Briar Rose."

"Right..." Briar muttered, shoving Mal's messy bangs from his eyes. "Because everything comes with a price."

"Good boy."

Briar flushed, then smacked Mal on the chest. "You wouldn't even know, you know. I could trick you through the veil, probably. I'm very conniving."

"I know everything I need to about the veil. As well as about conniving creatures like you."

Briar puffed a piece of hair from his face.

"I don't think she would accept me as a trade, even if you could trick me over," Mal went on, squeezing Briar's hips and making Briar's heart race.

"Why not?" But Briar's urge to tease lessened as he realized where the conversation headed, not wanting to broach the subject of Mal's inability to dance. Not even to joke.

"You would miss me, wouldn't you?" Mal asked, instead. It was mostly in jest—but there was an ounce of sincerity behind his words. Enough that Briar bit his lip, and even felt a little bad for joking about it at all.

"Why?" Briar asked. "Would she trap you there, or something?"

"I imagine so."

"Hm," Briar breathed, rolling his chin between his knuckles. "I... might miss you. A little bit."

"Only a little bit?"

"Yeah."

"But then who would keep your wirry-cows away?" Mal buried fingers into Briar's hips, making Briar yelp. "Who would hold you down so you stop dancing on injured ankles?"

"You're hardly holding me dow—ah!" Briar burst out laughing as Mal suddenly rolled, pinning Briar on his back, crushing him beneath his body. Briar squirmed, attempting to shove Mal off, but the man had to be almost twice Briar's weight. It was only when Mal grabbed Briar's wrists and pinned them over his head that the laughter weakened, replaced by blood rushing his cheeks.

"What were you saying?" Mal cooed.

"This is unfair. I could have grabbed my knife—"

"Why do you think I'm holding your hands down?"

Briar laughed again. "Alright, fine—I won't trick you into taking my place."

"Say you'd miss me, too."

"The fey taught me never to lie. You'll have to give me reason to miss you, you know, it doesn't just come auto—"

Mal tasted like cigarettes and cinnamon. His mouth on Briar's was warm and soft, and drew the breath from Briar's lungs as quickly as Mal surprised him with the sensation of being kissed. Something about it was—heartstopping, and mind-racing, all at once, in every way Briar had been denied in every one-night stand he'd ever indulged in. Even once Mal pulled away again, Briar was left breathless, and it was another few moments before he could open his eyes.

"How's that for a reason?" Mal asked coyly. His voice was low, sensual.

"I don't know, show me again—" Briar said, glad when Mal obeyed and kissed him a second time. That time, he removed his hands from Briar's wrists to hold his face, and Briar tangled his own up in Mal's hair. He sighed Mal's name, arching his back again and rolling his hips as it made heat swirl in the base of his stomach.

"Go on, Briar," Mal urged against Briar's mouth. "Say it."

"Not yet," Briar answered stubbornly. "Show me more."

Mal shifted his weight, never removing his mouth from Briar's while hooking his hands under the crooks of Briar's knees and pulling them free. Sliding his hips between Briar's thighs, he flattened Briar back to the floor, pressing into him until Briar gasped sharply—

A door clanged in the distance, making Briar jump and turn his head to search for movement. Mal, not caring, just trailed his mouth down the side of Briar's neck, biting at the golden necklace locked around Briar's throat.

"Wait," Briar groaned. "Mal, wait!"

"Why?" Mal sighed, pushing Briar back down and kissing him again to silence the words. Briar nearly tumbled right back into that delicious place—before anxiety won over his nerves, and he chomped down on Mal's bottom lip. Mal jerked back in surprise, only for Briar to grab his face and quickly kiss him once more in apology.

"I don't want anyone to walk in," he said, and Mal groaned, but sat back. Briar's legs remained nestled over Mal's hips, though, and the sight made Briar blush. He wasn't used to that—getting so embarrassed. Not wanting to be seen. Normally he didn't care so much, but something about Mal made him feel... shy. Moreso than he ever did with anyone else.

"I can't believe you bit me," Mal muttered, licking his bottom lip. "I think I'm bleeding."

"Here, just bite me back." Briar couldn't resist, grabbing Mal's face again—but that time, Mal pulled back with another over-the-top sound of complaint.

"Nooo, if I do that, I definitely won't be able to stop."

Mal finally rolled away, collapsing on his back alongside where Briar reclined on his own. Briar laughed breathlessly, closing his eyes. He extended his hand, not sure what he was looking for— until his fingers brushed against Mal's, and they intertwined.

"I won't trade you," Briar promised quietly. "Definitely not."

Mal squeezed his hand.

"You won't have to," he said, like a promise deeper than those words alone. "You'll fulfill your deal the right way, so Marie d'Alarie cannot hurt you ever again."

Briar cracked his eyes open, turning to where Mal laid next to him. He opened his mouth to ask, but the words wavered until he closed it again.

If I disappeared one day, would you miss me, too?

20

MALRIC AND THE SILVER

Malric was on his way to the revel clearing the moment he got the text from Briar, two days after their kiss in the studio. Two days that spanned a weekend, where Malric had no natural means of seeing his dancer. Two days of pure, unadulterated suffering. He hated not having what he wanted on command.

But then that text from Briar finally came, informing Mal the magpie had come for them again, just like Mal made them promise right before dropping them back off at their apartment. Malric didn't hesitate to don his mask within the edges of the veil, joining the other guests in the circle of cushions and blankets, nerves only slightly more heightened since the previous time.

There was a fair chance that that witness of Briar's dance would be the last time Malric could get away with going unnoticed, especially since his previous encounter with his family, his mother, at the breakfast table after returning a sleepwalking Briar back to bed. He'd told her, specifically, he was interested in seeing how his replacement danced—and with Mavera's comment about Briar's ankle, Malric was sure Marie would use that night as her opportunity to do something about it. Anything. She would definitely offer some sort of fey magic to help Briar finally get some relief, and to prepare them for when her son would come to watch the show the next time.

Perhaps the only thing more satisfying than the wine that night was the moment Briar emerged into the clearing wearing his glamour—and searched the guests for Malric amongst them. His fox-lord, his only friend on that side of the veil. When Briar met Malric's eyes, he even smiled awkwardly, and Malric raised a hand in silent greeting. Briar, bratty, snotty, vicious little Briar, smiled a little more and waved back slightly. It melted Malric into a puddle where he sat. It reminded him of their kiss in the studio, how Briar sank into him and pulled him closer, how he tasted so warm and sugary, how every time he allowed himself to be slightly more vulnerable, Malric fell slightly deeper in love with him—

He choked on his drink, coughing and wiping his mouth. *Love?*

Briar didn't meet anyone else's eyes upon finding his place in the grass, string instruments swelling from the side of the clearing. Malric helped himself to another glass of wine, eyes lingering on Briar's injured ankle, bandages once again obscured beneath the glamour. But he saw the way Briar flexed his foot, how he kept his weight off it when it could. He would only have to dance one more time, surely, and Marie would help him.

As the dance began, Briar became hardly more than a blur in Malric's steadily-drunker vision, dancing and leaping over the grass with movements as perfect and elegant as he possibly could be in the uneven grass. Perhaps it was the alcohol, but Malric felt a sharp spark of jealousy that Briar was forced to reserve his talents for someone like Marie who didn't fully appreciate them. Who would never assign perfection to Briar, despite it being clear right in front of them.

Just a little bit longer. Just a few more dances, and Briar would be free—

Malric heard the crunch before he saw it, Briar's ankle bending wrong beneath him. He crashed to the grass with a sharp sound of pain, and Malric jolted. Murmurs emerged from the crowd, Malric sitting up in concern as the rosefinch immediately tried to push himself back to his feet. He was—nearly panicked, arms and legs shaking in clear exhaustion as flickers of pain crossed his expression with every drag of his injured foot.

Malric hadn't consumed nearly enough wine to push down his concern for the sake of remaining unsuspicious. There wasn't enough wine in the entire world to even come close to dulling such a thunderclap of worry at the sight of Briar hurt on the ground—and without thinking it further, he leapt to his feet to hurry across the clearing.

Moving swiftly, he approached where Briar remained sprawled beneath fabric and loose hair, gently touching his arm. Briar reeled back in surprise, instinctively swatting Malric's hand away—before his eyes went wide, going still upon meeting Malric's gaze.

"It's going to be alright," Malric promised in a low voice. Briar's eyes remained wide, uncertain—but he nodded slightly. That little extension of trust that nearly broke Malric's will, nearly compelled him to tell Briar everything. Briar could trust him, Malric was the same person Briar trusted in the human world— but Malric resisted. By some grace of Danu and all her maidens, Malric resisted.

"Can you walk?" he attempted, next, but Briar hissed and whimpered the moment Malric attempted to pull him up. His heart raced, knowing everyone was watching. Everyone was witnessing him, who had tried so hard to remain in the background, rush to the dancer's aid. Marie was surely there watching, too. Recognizing his body language, perhaps finally sensing her son on the stranger in the mask.

"You took quite the tumble, didn't you?" A rattly voice emerged from the crowd, and Malric turned as quickly as Briar did to see an ancient fey walking toward them with a hard-case bag dangling off one shoulder. Malric recognized the patch on his tunic immediately, touching Briar's arm in an attempt to calm his nerves. The old man was a healer, perhaps even the same one meant to heal Briar's ankle in the first place.

Bending his knees, the healer tucked the skirt of his robe beneath him and prodded at Briar's quickly-swelling ankle as Malric leaned out of the way. Briar hissed in response, drooping his head and taking a fistful of grass in pain. The twinge returned to Malric's heart—but that time, he bit back the instinct to shove the healer away. Briar was going to get help. He was finally going to get help. His ankle would heal, he would begin the process of his escape. Malric only had to sit back and wait, while not bringing any more attention to himself than he already had.

At the thought, he glanced over his shoulder to where he knew Marie normally sat—only to find her staring right at him, wearing a knowing smile. His blood turned to ice. He turned quickly back to Briar, but a high-pitched noise filled Malric's ears, nodding blankly as the healer spoke. All the while, Briar just hunched over their fists clenched in the grass. Doing everything they could not to make a sound, not to show any reaction at all, and Malric was once again reminded of the fear in Briar's eyes whenever the fey got too close. Whenever they touched or fondled him in any way. Malric resisted another urge to reach out and comfort him, knowing it would be dangerous for the both of them, knowing Marie was looking directly at them. He just silently apologized, gently rubbing Briar's upper back as much as he could without it looking anything more than casual.

"Doesn't appear to be broken," the healer tut-tutted over Briar's ankle, before lifting his head and scanning the crowd. "You there, come and help me, please."

The random fey lord perched on the edge of the circle rose to his feet and approached. Malric recognized him as one of those who'd harassed Briar the first night Malric watched the performance, and they met eyes through matching masks.

"Hold the dancer still, their arms and their head... yes, loop your arms under theirs and back around... good, just like that. Don't want them fighting me on accident. Now, young master," the old man tapped Malric's knee to get his attention. Malric stiffened at the word *master*, knowing there was only one reason why he would choose it. He knew who Malric was—which meant Marie did, too. He only prayed Briar hadn't heard, wouldn't make the connection. "Will you be so kind as to hold the dancer's foot for me, here?"

"Of course," Malric rasped. His eyes were stuck on the way the other fey lord gripped Briar's upper body, like the healer had instructed—Briar's arms were bent upward, head bowed forward as if taking the final bow of a performance. Somehow, even held so strongly, something about him was graceful—but then Malric saw how his breaths came quickly, how his entire body shook in fright. Like a fawn caught in a trap. He watched Briar's wide eyes frantically search for an escape, wild and terrified. Perhaps the fey lord felt it, too, because he stretched Briar back over his lap, allowing him to press his nose into the side of Briar's neck with a little laugh. Briar stopped breathing, craning his head to the side in any attempt to pull away. Malric gulped. He forced himself to look elsewhere.

Sitting on his knees where the healer indicated, Malric took Briar's dainty foot into his hands. A foot he'd once massaged gently in the library, then appraised the night in the studio, appreciating the strong arches and pink polish over cracked toenails. Briar's feet were as soft as a ballet dancer's could be, and even then, Malric couldn't resist trailing his hand up and down the tendons on the front.

"L-let me go," Briar croaked, squirming beneath the fey lord's arms locking him in place, against Malric holding his foot. Malric couldn't look at him, couldn't look at how the fey lord pressed kisses to the side of Briar's neck and whispered flirtatious compliments. He just clenched his jaw, and supported his rosefinch's injured foot. *Not much longer...*

"Thank you, young master," the healer nodded, shifting how he sat. He cupped one hand over Briar's slender knee, pressing his opposite palm into the side of Briar's swollen ankle. "Hold it tight now, my lord, so we will not have to do it twice. I promise to make it quick."

The healer settled his hand around Briar's ankle, squeezing hard enough that Briar cried out and reeled back. Bending his knee, he wrenched free of Malric's grasp, only to be shoved roughly back down again by the fey who held his upper body. The healer demanded they grasp Briar tighter to keep him from moving, and even Malric obeyed in a moment of panic—but Briar only screamed, demanding to be let go, thrashing and cursing and kicking. He bent his knee back one more time, tearing free of Malric's hands—before slamming his foot back out again, crunching the nose of Malric's fox mask. Malric jerked backward with a bark of alarm, tasting blood from his nose as it instantly spilled over his lips and into his mouth. Practically snarling in a mix of pain and annoyance, he lunged forward again, grabbing Briar's ankle and gripping it harder than before.

"Be still!" he compelled at the height of the emotion, and Briar's body obeyed. Still, it trembled against Malric's grasp, muscles twitching as they attempted to fight the enchantment. Malric pushed the guilt and shame away, avoiding Briar's eyes, silently commanding the healer to hurry so it could all be over with—but then Malric watched as a drop of blood from his nose fell and splattered over the top of Briar's foot, and he realized—

His mask had come off.

21

MALRIC AND THE UNRAVELING

The world stopped around him. His heart stopped with it. He stared at the crimson spot against Briar's pale skin, before slowly lifting his eyes upward, and—meeting Briar's eyes, staring right at him. Staring at Malric, without his mask, without a glamour. The fey lady's son, who Briar had seen in the house only a few days prior. Who Briar knew to be Marie's son, the one Briar replaced, the one he'd been told—would be so embarrassed by his poor performance, would surely break Briar's legs if he ever witnessed it.

"Wait—" he started, but the healer's hands moved faster. Taking advantage of the window of peace, the old man gripped the arch of Briar's foot with one hand, hooked the other around the pit of Briar's knee, and tucked his own knee into the curve of their swollen ankle. With one smooth motion, he wrenched back on Briar's leg with one hand—and snapped Briar's ankle against his knee like bending a bow frame. It elicited a horrible *crunch*, and Briar threw his head back, shrieking loud enough to make Malric's ears ring. Malric just stared with his mouth hanging open, still clutching Briar's foot as the poor human gasped and shuddered, before tumbling into pitiful sobs.

"N-no," Briar begged as tears streamed down his cheeks, chest and shoulders hiccuping as the pain choked him. *"No, g-god— why, god— I'm sorry, I'm sorry..."*

The healer didn't respond, didn't react to the cry of agony, just brushed his hands off as if touching Briar's leg was something dirty. From the bag in the grass next to him, he then dug around to remove a lacquered box. Inside, two pieces of silver, mottled and old. The entire time the healer pressed them into Briar's ankle, shaping them until they shined with flowing, healing opulence, Malric just stared at Briar, who had gone still. He'd fainted.

"Why..." Malric croaked, and the healer let out a soft laugh.

"Opulent Silver can't heal strains alone, my lord. But if applied to a broken bone, it will heal the injury all the way from the inside out."

"You just... broke my dancer's ankle," Malric said, but his voice sounded far away. The healer nodded, tightening the straps of the cuff to make sure it was snugly in place.

"He will heal just right, and after not much time at all. It was a clean break, I can assure you. Quick and painless."

"P—" Heat flared in the back of Malric's throat. *"Painless? Did you not hear—"*

But the healer was already gathering his things. He thanked the fey lord who pinned Briar's upper body, and Briar slumped unconscious to the grass as soon as he was released. The fey lord, no longer interested in a plaything that wouldn't blush and resist, got back to his feet to re-join the audience.

"Imagine how beautiful they will be once healed again," Marie d'Alarie's voice was a death knell behind Malric, who stiffened. His mother draped herself over Malric's back, embracing him lovingly as together they gazed down at the unmoving form of Briar surrounded by grass and little flowers. His eyes were tinged pink and puffy, cheeks wet with stilled tears. If he had been oil paint on canvas, he would have been a masterpiece—but he wasn't. He was a person who Malric had drawn into the foxes' den to be eaten alive and left to rot. Who Malric had tricked into trusting him, only to betray him in the worst way he could imagine.

Was he really so much different from his mother?

Worse—the direwolf that was Marie asked one of the most dangerous questions of all, and Malric had to be careful how he answered. He couldn't show favoritism. He couldn't show disregard.

"There is something quite lovely about him, don't you think, málda?" Marie went on. Malric didn't move.

"He... must be something special, if you requested healing silver for him," Malric said, but the words barely existed. He hated the feeling of disappearing into someone he wasn't, just to protect himself. No, it was also to protect Briar. "Why him?"

Malric tried to keep his voice flat. He'd been discovered, but wouldn't let her see that that frightened him. If he showed his reservations, she would know he had other secrets being kept from her.

"I could ask you the same question," Marie whispered, and Malric's blood turned cold. "What about him made you return to watch, again and again? Do they make you miss what you once had?"

"Of course not," Malric hissed. He wasn't expecting the vitriol that stained those words, but his mother speaking so coyly made his skin crawl. *Jealous? Threatened?* Marie truly did not understand—or refused to understand—what it was that Malric was actually seeking away from her control. Driven by disgust, he couldn't stop himself from continuing—even as Briar's lips parted slightly, wet eyelashes twitching, coming to just to hear Malric's offering to his mother: *"He's not anything special."*

Words spoken in an attempt to trick Marie into agreeing, perhaps to let Briar go. Words spoken in an attempt to insist there were other reasons Malric would attend her revels outside of simple vanity and envy. But, words that Malric witnessed burn themselves into Briar's skin, like a branding, the moment they cast themselves over the dancer's ears. No, no, no—Briar wasn't supposed to hear them, they were meant for Marie alone—

But then a foot found Malric's nose for a second time, and Briar leapt to his feet to flee. Instinctively, Malric lunged to grab him, but Briar was too fast. Like a deer spooked by a boom of thunder, they took off toward the trees. Malric tried to chase— but something grabbed his arm, instead, pulling him back. He whirled around, tearing free of Marie's grasp on him.

"Don't touch me!" he snarled. "Don't ever fucking touch me again, mother!"

"Let the dancer go, málda," she said, a mix of begging and patronizing. "Dance for us instead, please—come back home, your family needs you—"

"And then what!" Malric shoved her away when she attempted to embrace him. "And then I am chained to you until I am nothing but shattered hips and feet worn to the bone? And what of the human dancer you love so much? Will they simply vanish into thin air like all the others you've used to replace us?"

Malric's voice rang out through the clearing, and the rest of the party fell silent. Marie's expression of feigned hope and grief melted instantly into something darker, something that made Malric's heart pound in apprehension.

"Is that an accusation?" she asked, voice flat. Malric gaped at her in disbelief.

"Yes," he answered bluntly. "Perhaps it is. Where are they, mother? What have you done with them? Do the kings know you're tricking low fey and humans into servitude without formally patronizing them? Only to dispose of them when you're finished?"

"How dare you!" Marie shrieked, but Malric couldn't take it anymore. He just turned and broke into a run, chasing the human dancer who'd fled into the trees. He didn't care about Marie, he didn't care about the revel, or all the guests watching, or even about what happened to all the people who came before Briar— all Malric cared about was his rosefinch, and making sure nothing of the same ever happened to them, too.

22

BRIAR AND THE RAINY NIGHT

A rush of pain—then pleasure, like fireworks crackling the bones in his ankle, wrapped up tight in a glass bottle and left at the fairgrounds to either pop or fizzle.

Pop. Briar's fireworks-in-a-glass-jar broken ankle definitely popped—straight out, into a crunchy nose. The same one he'd already smashed once before.

Marie d'Alarie's asshole son—Briar's fox-lord, his only friend in the revel clearing—barked and cursed, tumbling backward as Briar's heel made friends with his pretty face. The fireworks in his ankle exploded into the rest of his body, and he reeled back before scrambling to his feet.

He lost his footing when hands suddenly swept out to grab him, every fey in the clearing leaping to their feet with shouts and laughter as their pretty little dancer made a run for it. But unlike all the other times he shut down and let them do whatever they wanted, that time, Briar was lit up like a roman candle. He wasn't sure how many people he shouldered, kicked, punched, or how many times he ate shit and got back to his feet with a mouthful of dirt—but he just had to get away. Far, far away from the creatures who loved to torture him so much. From the creatures amongst whom there wasn't a single mercy—they who he had trusted, again, against his better judgment.

That fox-lord he'd trusted, against his better judgement, just doing what Mal insisted, with promises of there having to be at least one single friendly high fey in the entire world—who turned out to be exactly Briar's nightmare. Who did exactly as the fey lady warned, and upon seeing the embarrassment that was Briar's performance, shoved him down into the grass and broke his leg.

Tripping over his clothes in the woods, he grappled for them, pulling on his jeans and sweatshirt faster than backstage between costume changes. He didn't even tie his shoes before sprinting toward the tear in the veil.

It was raining on the Whidbey Island side, and Briar tumbled through with zero grace and zero subtlety. Tripping over a tangle of tree roots and sand, he landed face-first into the rocky beach. Something collided with his mouth, splitting his lip and coating his tongue with blood. He spit it out, attempting to push himself back to his feet, but the moment he emerged back onto the human side—the adrenaline gave way to suffocating, debilitating panic. After flight came terror, every time.

Hunching over, Briar screamed against the sand and rocks, into the beach as his body betrayed him, flooding with nauseating electricity and ice and squeezing muscles that curled him into a ball as he fought for breath between the tears and gasps. He had to get away, he had to leave that place before anyone rushed out to find him, to grab him, drag him back to the clearing, where all those terrible, cruel, heartless things waited to laugh at him and finish what they'd started—

"Hey!" Echoed in his ears, and Briar could only wrap his arms around himself, begging to disappear, begging for a rogue wave to sweep in and drag him out to sea. It would be welcome. It would be better than whatever waited for him back at the revel. But a wave never came—and Briar could only clench harder into himself as if to turn his carbon atoms into diamond. Even when hands grabbed him, pulling him over and kicking up sand in the

process, pushing hair from his eyes and touching his face, Briar still could only cry and shake and agonize because the pain in his ankle was unbearable—he could still feel the hands of that fey lord all over him, pinning his arms and chest—he could still feel the hands of Lord d'Alarie, his own friend, gripping his hurt ankle —he could still feel that man's words grip every one of his muscles until he couldn't move at all, until he was forcibly petrified, allowing them to do whatever they wished to him—

"Hey, Bry—! Hey, it's alright! I'm here, I'm right here."

Briar recognized that voice, and his defensive shell shattered in an instant. His hands flew out, gasping and sobbing and clawing at Mal's jacket, his arms, dragging him closer and closer as if he would disappear if Briar didn't pin him down fast enough. Mal's hands just scrambled over him with the same frantic movements, pulling Briar closer and closer until Briar was fully encompassed inside his jacket, inhaling his own hot, clouding gasps.

"You're safe, I've got you, nothing is going to happen to you. I'm right here."

Mal didn't ask what happened; Briar didn't ask what he was doing there. Briar just clung to him until his fingernails might have popped off, and he wouldn't have even noticed. He'd emerged on that beach so many times, all alone, by himself, never wishing someone to be there waiting for him—until that night, when Mal was. That night Briar needed someone, Mal was there. Briar wasn't going to question it.

A thumb brushed the blood away from Briar's lip, but Briar pulled away, only to grab the front of Mal's jacket and pull him closer. To bury his face into Mal's body; his warm, safe, comfortable, protective body, like a shield against the darkness, the cruelty on the other side of the trees. He just clung to this man he barely knew, he barely trusted, and cried, and cried, and cried.

Carried on Mal's back to where Briar's bike was propped up against the tree; crying softly into the collar of his wool jacket until the emotions faded into a stiff numbness, all while a light rain sprinkled them until they were both shivering. The ferry wouldn't be running for another few hours, so Mal suggested they grab a room for the night, and head to class together in the morning. Briar didn't even have the strength to sigh in frustration.

Finding the first place with vacancies; standing behind Mal while he spoke to the woman at the counter, draped in his coat and shivering; Mal making a call to Bianca to let her know where they were once they made it to the room; it all passed in a dull blur, felt only through the throbbing of his ankle. Briar had done a good enough job of avoiding the sight of whatever they did to him after breaking the bone, but he knew, inevitably, he would have to acknowledge whatever it was.

Briar didn't know exactly how or when he got there, but the next time he returned to reality, he was seated on the edge of the tub while Mal prodded at his blood-clumped lip with a piece of toilet paper and hand sanitizer. It stung like when he ripped pieces of dry skin from his lips with his teeth, but he still barely reacted. He just stared at Mal without seeing him. As the world turned back and forth beneath him.

Still, never once did Mal ask what happened. He never asked what had Briar so terrified. Briar was both grateful and put at unease by that—he didn't want to talk about it. He wanted to talk about it. He wanted to tell the one person who might understand exactly what had happened, because maybe that one person would also be the only one to comfort him that it would all be okay, after all.

After his mouth was cleaned off, Briar stood in the shower for a long, long, long time, until Mal knocked on the door and gently said his name, letting him know someone in the next room had complained about the shower running for so long. Briar lifted his hand to concede, but stopped when, instead, Mal surprised him by pushing the curtain aside and stepping in to join him. Fully dressed, the cold water soaked him through in an instant, and he barked at the chilled temperature. Turning the knob, he cranked it hotter, and Briar only then realized he was shivering.

"Let me help," Mal said, though it was clear he didn't know with what. Briar watched him in silence, before his eyes skimmed the edge of the tub in search of anything he could offer so Mal would stay. What a strange feeling, to realize he wanted this person to *stay*, even if it meant Mal would see him naked, vulnerable, miserable in the shower like a wet cat.

Grabbing a bottle of shampoo, he offered it. Mal lathered it up between his hands, and the sensation of it being worked through his long hair made Briar sigh. Knots loosened slightly in his back and shoulders, slumping against the shower wall and pressing his forehead into the laminate tiles. He closed his eyes, allowing the fully-dressed man to do whatever he wanted with his scalp.

Mal eventually took Briar by the elbow and gently exchanged places with him. Water spilled over his head, dribbling down his face, curling into his nose and making the cut in his lip sting. He just closed his eyes again as Mal worked the shampoo out of his hair, squeezing it all the way to the ends.

"Where else?" the ghostly voice came through the steam, and Briar glanced over his shoulder. Mal looked surprisingly—angry, almost, but the way his hands lingered on Briar's shoulders told him it wasn't because Briar was putting him to work. Briar's heart jumped, and his hands found one another to anxiously pick at his nail beds.

"What do you mean?" he muttered, closing his eyes when Mal traced a knuckle down the curve of Briar's spine.

"Where else do you want scrubbed?"

Briar squeezed his eyes closed, trying to fight it back, but the memories of that fey lord's hands on him crashed through any defenses he'd placed. He crossed his arms over his chest, hunching his shoulders and shaking his head.

Mal didn't wait for any instruction, instead grabbing the motel bar-soap and ripping away its wax paper shell. Rubbing it between his hands, he summoned bubbles before gliding the bar over Briar's skin. Never once did his hand itself touch, floating only on the base of the soap, and Briar imagined it smearing away any remaining memory of those unwanted touches all over him. It left him struggling for breath, inhaling water through his nose, though he clenched his jaw so hard he couldn't open his mouth for relief.

"I..." He finally croaked, though wasn't sure what exactly he meant to say. "I... I just... I hate them so much..."

Frustrated tears flooded his eyes, swept away by the shower water. He let them go, knowing Mal wouldn't be able to notice.

"They—they do whatever they want, they never... even when... They don't listen, they just... Why don't they care when I scream at them?"

The tears came faster than at first, and Briar had to wipe them away so they wouldn't make his face puff up, but it didn't matter. Every single one, pulled like a thorn from his flesh, relieving an ounce of the pressure while also knowing the prickling pain would take longer to heal. That pain of being touched when he didn't want to be.

Mal didn't answer, lowering himself to wash the small of Briar's back, then his legs. When he hesitated at Briar's ankle, Briar finally had the courage to glance down and see the silvery anklet attached over his foot. The filigree and floral engravings made it beautiful to the eye, but to him, it might as well have been the cuff to a ball and chain. Proof he was owned, proof those fey bastards could do whatever they wanted with him, without asking. Without explaining. Without permission.

"This is called opulent silver," Mal said under his breath, running his fingers over the top lip of the cuff. Briar was surprised, blinking away his tears before wiping his nose.

"You know what it is?"

Mal nodded. "They're rare, but powerful. Lots of conflicting opinions about the morality of using them, because—ah, I won't bore you with fey history. What I *will* say, though... is that, in one way or another... it's a mercy in its own way. Your ankle will heal in an eighth of the time it would with any normal human medicine."

Briar scoffed, but Mal looped his hand around Briar's calf right above the silver.

"I won't forgive them for their cruelty," Mal whispered, and Briar's anger fizzled. "But I also thank them for giving you a way to heal faster."

"They—they broke my ankle!" Briar exclaimed, finally pulling away from Mal. He nearly slipped, but caught himself on the wall. "They—! They grabbed me, and held me d-down—even that one I thought was my friend, he's actually—! He was Marie's son the entire time! And they—they snapped my ankle over their knee, how can you...!"

"How does it feel now?" Mal asked, getting slowly to his feet and never pulling his eyes from Briar's. Briar stared at him in disbelief, but once again swallowed back the vitriol. He shakily extended his leg, daring to elongate his foot to a point. Pain shot up his limb, but—it was the pain of the sprain he'd been dealing with up until that point. Not the pain of something broken.

"It feels just like it did yesterday," he argued. "Some shitty magic—"

"If it was broken, you wouldn't be able to walk on it at all," Mal finally offered him a tired, seemingly relieved smile. Flopping the washcloth in his hand over one shoulder, he turned to shut the water off. "Which means it's working, despite what they put you through. You might even be fully healed in just a few days—"

"Stop it!" Briar screamed. "What are you—Why are you talking like they did me a favor! I didn't ask for this, I didn't ask for their help—Why are you talking like I should be thanking them!"

"I'm not," Mal insisted, but Briar was already pushing his way out of the shower. In his hurry, he tripped over the edge of the tub, grabbed by Mal but already falling. They hit the floor with a crash, tearing down the shower curtain still clutched in Briar's hand. The rod detached from the wall, and it was only because Mal threw himself over Briar that it didn't crash into his head.

On his back, breathing heavily, Briar felt only Mal's weight hovering over him. Shielding him, protecting him—and it made Briar's insides turn in a rush of regret. But he bit it back, he forced it back, just groaning and putting up his hands to run fingers through the back of Mal's hair.

"Are you okay?" he asked stubbornly, and Mal responded with an exasperated sigh of his own.

"I'm fine," he said. "Are you hurt?"

"I'm fine," Briar answered quietly, pressing his lips together when Mal sat up and tossed the dislodged shower rod and curtain away. The moment he did, Briar was hit with a wave of cold air, and he couldn't stop himself from grabbing Mal's wet shirt and pulling him back in again.

"I'm sorry," he whispered, shaking his head. "I'm sorry, I just..."

Mal wrapped his arm around Briar's waist, splaying his hand over Briar's bare back to support him upright. Briar held his breath as Mal pressed his face into the curve of Briar's neck and shoulder before letting out another warm breath.

"Never, ever thank a high fey," he whispered, summoning goosebumps across Briar's skin. He said it exactly like the fox-lord —no, like Marie's son once did. "That wasn't what I meant. I hate them for what they've done to you, Briar. You don't deserve to be treated with such cruelty."

Why did those words strike him like an ax? Directly into that place at the base of his neck, between his shoulders, right where Mal kept his hand. Perhaps he knew. Perhaps he left his hand there to shield from the pain of it, just like he'd shielded Briar from the shower rod, just like he'd shielded Briar from the cold and the dark on the beach.

"I... told you so." Briar tried to smile, to say it like a joke, but it just twisted the ax in his back. Mal rolled his eyes, then pushed hair from Briar's face. Briar was drawn in by the hazel eyes looking back at him, dark and vivid at the same time, like two trains of thought fighting for dominance behind them. Both wishing to say something the other refused. It sucked Briar in, disappearing into the color of Mal's irises, the shape of his lashes, his eyebrows, his mouth.

He wasn't sure what came over him—but he sat forward, pressing their lips together. Seeking that comfort he'd felt the night in the dance studio.

Mal didn't react at first, though his expression was even more conflicted when Briar pulled away. Briar flushed with embarrassment, bit his lip, turned away, spoke the first two syllables of an apology—before Mal grabbed his arm, pulling him back and kissing him with more force. It drew the breath from Briar's chest, gasping as Mal dug their mouths against one another, breath cascading over Briar's cheek as if it was the hardest thing for him to do to not bite and re-open the wound on Briar's lip.

But—there was a part of Briar who wanted exactly that. To be bitten, torn open, given a chance to spawn new muscle, new skin, new nerves that would only recall those sensations he wished to claim and own for himself. Perhaps the hatchet of Mal's words buried into his back was more an inspiration than a punishment.

Locking his arms around the back of Mal's neck, Briar pulled him closer, kissed him harder. Mal responded in turn, and Briar fell back against the bathroom wall as Mal pressed into him. Briar bent his back, lifting himself onto Mal's lap and wrapping his legs around Mal's waist, grinding against his wet clothes enough to feel the shift in desire through Mal's mouth. It only grew hotter, hungrier, and every caught breath and grunt of resistance only made Briar want it more.

"What do you want?" Mal asked, barely separating their mouths. Briar shuddered as a hand hotter than summer grass found his chest, spreading over the expanse of skin and barely teasing one of his nipples.

"Fuck me," Briar said bluntly. Mal laughed.

"Is that all?"

"Y-yes, damnit—! Mm—!"

He curled as Mal trailed his hand lower, finding the half-hard length between Briar's legs and teasing it. Briar arched his head backward, gasping toward the ceiling and curling his toes still wrapped around Mal's middle. He grabbed a handful of Mal's hair as the man's mouth found his chest, next, swirling his tongue and scraping his teeth over the perks of skin waiting for him.

Briar could only bite back his gasps of pleasure as Mal's mouth traveled lower, curling his fingers in and out of the man's hair until a hot mouth lowered between his legs, teasing him with a tongue before tasting him entirely. He threw his head back again, moving his hips and thrusting into Mal's mouth on instinct, apologizing in a quiet laugh as Mal made a sound of disapproval. To Briar's thrill, however, Mal then cupped Briar's ass and swallowed him deeper, until his nose pressed against the base of Briar's stomach. All the while, his tongue swirled and slid up and down Briar's length, making Briar's stomach knot up and his legs contract with every drag of movement. Pain jolted up from his ankle every time, making him hiss and whine, but Mal just chuckled through his nose as if he liked it.

"I—in my bag," Briar moaned, pausing long enough to gasp as his body locked up in delight. "There are condoms in my bag—"

Mal pulled away, and Briar instantly regretted saying anything to distract him. He made a miserable sound as Mal's mouth left him, only to shudder as he was kissed up the chest and neck again, instead.

"I'll keep that in mind," Mal whispered in his ear, stroking his hand up and down Briar's length again until his fingers were wet with spit and pre-cum. Briar inhaled sharply as they then curled farther back between his legs, teasing his opening before one pushed carefully inside.

"How do you want me?" Mal's voice was low in Briar's ear, and Briar could only cling to him as even his fingers were thick, warm, overwhelming. "Should I treat you gently?"

Briar bit down on his tongue, before inhaling sharply and shaking his head.

"N—no," he rasped. "No, I hate that."

"Being treated gently?"

"Yes."

"Why?" Mal purred, inserting another finger, and then another, making Briar whine and writhe. He grabbed at Mal's wrist beneath him, but didn't pull away, just fought to breathe as Mal did exactly what he said. Pushing deep into him, opening him wider, just wet enough that it didn't sting. It hurt in the rich way it always did, in the way Briar liked, knowing it would only get better the more he was spread wide.

Mal buried his fingers deeper, and Briar gasped sharply.

"Tell me why," he demanded sensually. Briar just clutched either side of Mal's head, trying to remain upright as Mal's fingers thrust in and out of him, traveling deeper every time.

"Be-because—it—scares me," he finally babbled, before groaning and collapsing against Mal's shoulder, moaning and gasping in rhythm with the fingers inside of him, rolling his hips with want for more. "Just—fuck me like we'll never see each other —again."

"That's what you like?"

"Fuck—*yes*, damnit!" he jolted as Mal slammed his fingers all the way to the knuckles, breath tangling in his throat as the small of his back flexed tight against the rush of pressure. *"Fuck,"* he whimpered, trembling as Mal's opposite hand wrapped around him, locking him in place, only to pull back and thrust deep inside again. Briar pushed his hand between their bodies flush against one another, finally twisting open the button on Mal's pants and burying his hand down inside to find him. To find—his own hardness, straining against the fabric and making Briar's face go hot at the size of it. He stroked its length, rolling against Mal's hand again as the desire between his hips grew more intense, more demanding.

"Fuck me, Mal, please," he gasped, and Mal buried his teeth

into the side of Briar's neck, before yanking him off the floor and into his arms.

Shoving Briar down onto the bed, Mal kissed him while his hands dug through Briar's bag in search of the condoms. He found one, tearing it open and rolling it down over his length while hardly removing his mouth from Briar's at all. Grasping the travel-size bottle of lube from Briar's bag, next, Mal smirked like he shouldn't have been surprised to find it.

"I'll fuck you until you can't walk," he said like a promise, grabbing Briar's leg above the silver cuff, then opening Briar's thighs to settle between them. Rubbing his length against Briar's stomach, Briar threw his head back and softly begged. "Until you can't do anything—except to let this ankle heal."

Briar choked on the spit building in the back of his throat as Mal pushed himself inside, coaxing in and out with rolling hips in a way that was both infuriating and—necessary. Mal was—so much more than Briar expected, but in more ways than just the size of him splitting Briar apart at the base of his spine. Mal teased him, played with him, whispered such intoxicating things, and all of it combined made it hard to breathe. Hard to remain in his body, let alone in reality. Mal was, simply—nothing like Briar had ever prepared for.

He winced as Mal pressed deeper, biting back the reactionary gasp as a sweet, familiar ache twinged up his back, then trickled down the muscles of his inner thighs.

"Briar," Mal insisted, perhaps seeing the look on Briar's face before Briar masked it. Briar could only crack his eyes open in overwhelm, before closing them again and inhaling a trembling breath.

"Don't stop," he begged weakly, pulling on the blankets beneath him, rocking his hips to pull Mal deeper. "You—you're just... Just fuck me like you promised, until I can't do anything else..."

Mal edged himself deeper, another small sound escaping Briar's lips, but he nodded all the same. He wrapped his arms behind Mal's head, pulling him close as Mal moved his hips again, pressing deeper, sliding deeper before easing off again, then deeper again. Briar had to hold his breath the entire time—but mostly because otherwise, he thought he might pass out from the heat boiling his brain.

"You take me so well," Mal whispered, breath hot against Briar's ear before nibbling on the outer curve of it. He pulled back, pausing before slamming all the way to his hips, and Briar jolted, choking, reduced to a quivering pile as Mal smiled to himself—and did it again. Again and again, with long, aggressive strokes that caught every one of Briar's thoughts on a hook and yanked them back out again. Briar swore Mal pierced all the way into his stomach, pressing a hand to his navel, laughing weakly then hiccuping as Mal grabbed his wrists, pinning them over Briar's head and abandoning any sense of hesitation he had left. He dug every movement hard and deep into Briar's body, increasing his pace as Briar could only gasp and cry out Mal's name in ecstasy. Until the inside of Briar's thighs were sore and throbbing, heart pounding and hair tangling where it rubbed against the blanket beneath him. It went on for so long—Briar didn't know anyone could fuck at that punishing pace for so long —and only continued when Mal grabbed Briar by the arm and turned him onto his stomach, barely giving him a chance to catch his breath before shoving back inside again with every intention of ruining him.

Each movement of Mal's body was more demanding than the last, and soon Briar could only clutch at the blankets, bite at the cushions as drool dripped from his mouth, as his eyes watered and collected in his lashes. Mal's hands left angry prints in the curves of Briar's waist where they gripped him, interring deeper with every clutch of his hips. When they weren't gripping him, they were burying themselves into Briar's mouth, craning his head back by the chin, arching his spine so Mal could kiss him without ever breaking his rhythm. It was everything Briar needed—to tear his old skin away, to replace it, to grow new memories of how he could be grabbed and handled in the ways he wanted. How it felt for someone to take ownership without the exchange of vulnerability, to simply pleasure each other physically without any words attached. The only cracks in that perfect little bubble came every time Mal kissed him—then, in the softest voice, asked if Briar was alright. If it felt good, if Mal was hurting him. And every time, with his thoughts hardly more than steam and mush, Briar could only offer a drunken, wet-lipped smile to assert his continued, perpetual, eternal consent for Mal to continue exactly what he was doing.

The only possible way for it to command more of Briar's piety—was how it sounded for Mal to whisper, grunt, praise Briar's name endlessly in his ear, shifting flyaway strands of hair that otherwise clung to Briar's face, neck, and back with a sheen of sweat.

Briar, Briar, Briar—
You feel so good—You're so beautiful—You're everything.
You're perfect, Briar.

Briar could only smile that same overheated, sex-inebriated smile as he heard those words. Perhaps—accepting a crumb of gentleness, every now and again, was alright. Perhaps the world wouldn't break open, his identity wouldn't tumble into question, his walls wouldn't crumble and fall like Jericho.

Mal grasped him around the middle, Briar's hands gripping the headboard that rattled with every thrust of their bodies together. Grasping Briar's length, Mal kissed the back of his neck as his hand stroked, and Briar bucked, then whimpered, then came with a shudder of his body. How many times did that make it...? How many times had Mal pushed him to climax, how many times did Mal himself spill inside of Briar, or over his back...?

Briar lost count, then lost everything else. His arms gave out beneath him, followed by the rest of his strength, and he finally crumpled into saccharine, exhausted darkness.

23

BRIAR AND THE NEXT MORNING

Briar didn't dream of suffocating vines that night. Or maybe they did, but they didn't last long enough to be remembered. He hardly remembered dreaming of anything at all. Instead, he felt, sensed, breathed in only Mal's warmth, his beating heart, his skin rich with sweat and the smell of sea-salt rain through the motel window cracked open just slightly. Just enough to air out the room and make it breathable again, after Briar was devoured from every inch, along parts he never even knew a person would ever want to know of him.

Mal had done exactly as Briar asked—treating him harshly, roughly, without an ounce of gentleness, but it was different, somehow. Somehow, somehow, even with all that exchange of physicality only—it left Briar feeling more cared for than anyone else he'd ever shared a bed with. Even if Mal's hands left behind bruises, even if Briar's ass and back ached any time he turned in his sleep, even if his lips were swollen from kissing, his throat sore and scratchy from swallowing as much of Mal's length as he could at once...

So why, despite it all, did Briar feel so warm and comfortable draped over Mal's chest in the dark, sharing breaths and sleep?

Briar had always denied offerings of gentleness, whether they be from his mothers, his siblings, his friends, his brief lovers. Gentleness did not dance en pointe or perform at the forefront of Giselle or complete Odile's thirty-two fouettés or win scholarships or awards on stage. Briar had always rejected gentleness for a myriad of reasons, but mostly because he always understood gentleness as stemming from cruelty—as in, gentleness was something to provide on stage. Something to embody in front of an audience, dressed in tulle and chiffon and tights and in perfect, pristine pointe shoes. Anyone who had trained from demi to pointe knew, there was hardly any room in ballet for gentleness—and that room was reserved for moments on stage, when people were watching.

It wasn't so much that Briar *hated* being treated gently—perhaps he only wanted it from someone he knew he could trust. Someone who wouldn't use it just to rifle around in all his softest, most vulnerable parts.

Someone... like Mal, who didn't try to convince Briar a single time of their "need" for gentleness; or how Mal was the person to give it to them, like a gift. As if it would be more self-serving or chivalrous of him, or something. As if Briar was testing him and his virtue, like a knight in shining armor who would deny the princess' want to be bound and gagged and fucked into oblivion. No, Mal just confirmed it was really what Briar wanted, and leaned into it. He took Briar roughly, just like Briar asked.

Was respecting such a wish without argument not its own form of gentleness?

Briar always rejected gentleness in favor of reserving it for the stage—but something, something about Mal made him want to see what it would be like to be treated lovingly, even just once.

Briar might have slept for a century, like Briar Rose herself, had the person trapped beneath him not roused and mumbled something. If he hadn't been so tired, Briar might have quickly lifted his head in embarrassment, but instead he just wriggled slightly and buried his face against Mal's bare chest.

"Hey," Mal grumbled in response, voice groggy from sleep. He mussed up Briar's hair, before squeezing one of his cheeks. "Hey, bugbear, wake up."

"Mmmph," Briar complained, pressing his face flatter into Mal's chest before biting him like an annoyed cat. Mal hissed, grabbing a handful of Briar's hair to lift him away, and Briar couldn't help but laugh sleepily. Mal's hand in his hair didn't last much longer, instead loosening and flattening out, brushing it back, moving with care to not pull on the love-tangles left behind from their previous romp. Briar should have pulled away, should have swatted Mal's hand off, but he couldn't bring himself to do it. Something about waking next to someone without the urge to flee right away was a relief.

"How do you feel?" Mal asked, keeping his voice low. His opposite hand slithered under the shared blanket, cupping Briar's ass and making Briar laugh weakly.

"I think I can still walk."

"Then I did a poor job. Should we go again?"

Briar considered it. He *really* considered it, which was especially out of the norm for him. Morning sex was for lovers, after all—not one-night stands. Not two people trauma-bonding over bad fairy deals—but then Mal sat up to kiss him, and, ah—damnit. Briar fell right into him. He fell faster, and faster, until his body moved on his own, trailing his mouth down the man's warm bare chest, his stomach, kissing the line of hair below his navel and tasting the entire length of him until it made his gag-reflex tremble and his throat close up. Until Mal pushed Briar's head away, then the rest of his body, shoving him face down into the bed and pinning him with both hands on his lower back, sliding wet fingers inside, then the rest of him, until Briar was left gasping, moaning, pleading, clutching at the blankets and whimpering Mal's name on hiccuping breaths.

. . .

BRIAR SHOWERED FIRST. MAL OFFERED TO JOIN HIM, but Briar had already broken one of his cardinal rules—having sex with the same person more than once in twelve hours—and he couldn't handle the thought of showering and washing each other off, too. Besides—he didn't need Mal seeing how he actually *was* struggling to walk, to stand upright, not wishing to feed into his ego that was already very well fed.

Standing by the window in a towel, Briar inhaled a long drag of a cigarette, closing his eyes as the rain pattered the glass on the other side. He glanced down at the silver on his ankle for the hundredth time that morning, scowling at it and flicking ash over its shiny surface, also just like every other time. When the shower in the bathroom shut off and Mal approached from behind, Briar offered him a glance, before handing over the cigarette Mal motioned to want. Mal inhaled it, before wrinkling his nose and handing it back.

"Have you ever had fey tobacco? Way less acidic," he sighed, slicking back his wet hair. He was still naked, not even wearing a towel around his waist. It allowed Briar's eyes to travel up and down him, every inch, witnessing more than he had in the dark the night before. The muscles of his stomach, back, legs, ass. The way they moved when he spoke and shifted his weight. The small, sporadic freckles on his damp skin, next to his bellybutton, on his hip bone, on the inside of his thigh.

Briar touched Mal's face. Pulled him back close again, brushing a thumb to his lip while simultaneously inhaling a drag of the cigarette. Pressing into Mal's mouth, opening it, Briar stretched his neck and exhaled the smoke over Mal's tongue.

"Does that help?" he asked in a low voice, and Mal looked at him like he was nothing he'd ever experienced before. It made Briar's heart race, to be regarded that way. With that sort of intensity, like an animal trying to decide if it wished to nurture or gut the prey in front of it. He had to turn away before he allowed Mal to bend him in half again. He wasn't sure he would survive a third time.

"What time is it?" he asked while shirking off his towel, pulling on his underwear and jeans, then braiding his wet hair over one shoulder. Mal moved to get dressed, too, answering at first with only a grunt.

"I'm not going to tell you," he said, and Briar's eyes snapped to him. They narrowed, and Mal stepped between them and the digital clock on the nightstand—but Briar shoved past him, before practically shrieking.

"Oh, *shit!* I'm supposed to be in class!"

Shoving Mal out of the way, and Mal collapsed to the bed with a moan and a groan of disappointment, only to wheeze when Briar jumped on his stomach and screeched for him to get his ass dressed. Mal took it as some sort of challenge, throwing on his clothes before grabbing Briar's bicycle and practically sprinting with it down the hallway while Briar was still pulling his shoes on. Briar shouted after him in a burst of laughter, taking chase as the room door clanged shut behind them.

"Get on the back!" Mal invited the second they made it outside, forgoing checking out at the front desk entirely. Briar didn't ask questions, kicking a leg over the back tire, propping his feet on the spokes and wrapping his arms around Mal's neck. Mal kicked off, and they raced to catch the next ferry.

Briar was on the phone with Stella all the way across the sound, having asked to borrow a charging cable from one of the other passengers. The whole time he apologized again and again for making her worry, denying that he'd spent the night with a random hookup—but then he glanced nervously at Mal, and his eyes were apologetic.

"Nothing happened, but... I spent the night with Mr. Mal."

"*WHAT!*" Stella shrieked, but it was definitely more conspiratorial than scolding. Briar had to pull the phone away from his ear so it wouldn't burst an eardrum. "*Mx. I DON'T FUCK MY INSTRUCTORS, HUH?*"

"First of all—I've *never* claimed that," Briar mumbled. "You've seen my secret ebook folder."

"Was it a nice motel? Or was it dirty and filthy and disgusting, like in a porno?"

Briar couldn't help but laugh—but he wasn't about to give Stella any additional information so easily. A part of him was still enjoying the secrecy of his fling, after all.

"We really didn't do anything," Briar insisted, but used a tone of voice that promised he was a liar. It made Stella groan in louder exasperation. "We just got caught in the rain and found a motel, obviously~ completely innocent~"

"Was there only one bed? God. You're such a slut."

"Wh~at? No, of course there were two beds..."

"Get your ass home right now. Oh my god. I'm calling Bianca. She's going to freak out."

"Stella—!"

But the line ended, and Briar pulled the phone from his ear. It was then he realized his cheeks were warm, wondering why he was blushing. But then he realized, there was a third unusual thing happening to him that morning—and that was his night-before partner sitting there, next to him, following him home. Briar was so very out of his element.

"She's energetic in the mornings," Mal commented, pretending to be otherwise absorbed in a Puget Sound travel pamphlet. Briar sighed.

"She probably just took her pre-workout."

"Ah. Is she skipping class, too?"

"It was canceled, obviously, since our irresponsible instructor never showed up." Briar offered him a sarcastic smile. "And now everyone is going to know it's because he spent the night before in bed with a student."

"Ah, say that a little louder, why don't you? Let's see how many other freaky people are taking this early-morning ferry ride with us. Tell me about your *secret ebook folder*, too, while you're at it. I imagine it might explain how much you enjoyed my fingers in your mouth last night."

Briar gaped at him, before laughing awkwardly. He placed a hand on Mal's thigh, before shoving it between the man's crossed legs like a snake on a rabbit. Mal yelped, before shoving Briar away with a laugh.

"Don't talk to me about my secret ebook folder."

"How else will I know exactly all the things that wind you up?"

"Just ask. I'm not too shy to say it out loud."

"Hm. Clearly, you like it rough."

"No, duh."

"Bondage? BDSM?"

"Maybe a little bit; I've never had a partner to try it with."

"Edging?"

"Oooooh."

"Knife play?"

"You really know how to get a girl going."

Mal's smile was intoxicating—smug and intrigued all at once, arms crossed as he slid down on the seat to better meet Briar's eyes.

"I wouldn't mind *exploring your interests* a little further, if that interests you."

Briar smiled at him blankly, letting those words blanket him and taking all the time he needed to decide whether or not he liked the feel of it. He almost opened his mouth to answer too quickly, before swallowing the lump in his throat and finally breaking away from Mal's intense eye-contact. Everything about him was intense, and Briar still wasn't used to it when caught off guard.

"Maybe," he said, though admittedly hated how it tasted in his mouth. "I don't normally sleep with the same person twice."

"Why not?"

Briar frowned. That question wasn't as flirty or teasing as the others, it was steeped in sincerity. As if Stella had sent Mal a DM asking him to broach the subject, because Briar never, ever talked about it with Stella. Not in any detail deeper than surface-level, at least.

"Because..." *It scares me.* "Once has always seemed like enough. It's not easy to surprise me after that."

"I'm full of surprises," Mal said like a promise—or was it more of a threat?—before his hand found Briar's ankle resting over his knee, pinching that part of his leg over the top edge of the fairy silver. "Do you want to spend the rest of the day together?"

"Ah—you *are* surprising."

"What's surprising about that? Your normal one-night stands don't normally ask?"

"I'm usually long gone and blocking them by the time they wake up."

"Harsh. Well, you can't escape *me*, so why not try it out? Come on. I'll buy you something. Pretty, kinky girls love a bribe."

Briar finally laughed for real, setting his phone aside to continue charging. He gazed out the rain-speckled window at the choppy water, resting his chin in the crook of his elbow as he thought about it. As he *didn't* think about how it made him uneasy, the thought of spending the next day with someone who tasted every naughty part of him the night before. That—was what lovers did, wasn't it?

"I really shouldn't play hooky," he said, pushing away that little part of him that warmed at the thought of... what? Spending the day with Mal? Getting to know him better? No, no, definitely not—Briar really just wanted to sleep with him again, really, even if he played otherwise. "At least, not for reasons that aren't, erm, fairy-related."

"Are you sure?" Mal sidled in a little bit closer. "We could find plenty of errands to keep you distracted for as long as you want. We could even make it a productive trip, so you don't look so pale at the thought of a *date.*"

"A *date*—" Briar nearly choked, but Mal interrupted him.

"We really should do some more research about fairy protection charms... Maybe stop by a used bookstore to see if they have any reference guides... Do you need any more dance slippers? Or darning thread? I missed my only engagement for the whole day, so the rest of my daylight—and following nightdark—hours are yours, if you want them."

"It's not a date," Briar insisted once Mal finished, unexpectedly breathless.

"Fine, it's not a date," Mal relinquished, putting his hands up in defense with a smile that was just a little too shit-eating for Briar's pleasure. Still, Briar pouted his lips, crossing his arms and sitting back in his seat.

"I can't," Briar croaked. "I mean—I really shouldn't."

Mal threw his head back with a groan, and Briar regretted his refusal in an instant. But he wasn't ready for something like that —to spend the day galavanting around with his previous night's fling. He wasn't used to that. He wasn't emotionally prepared for something like that. Was it even something that *needed* emotional preparation? If not—why did his heart race at the thought? Why did he feel a little flushed and woozy as he gazed at Mal's handsome face, without even any reminder of how he'd looked in the motel room the night before? Just him, where he sat on the ferry, was handsome enough to make Briar's whole body buzz.

Briar absorbed the sight of Mal's smug half-smile, like he knew exactly why Briar was embarrassed. Briar, who had never been on a *date* before in a way he ever wanted. Briar, who was afraid of gentleness and being treated softly, who didn't go on *dates* because he learned early on, dates were just fake narratives for when guys on dating apps wanted to sleep with a dancer. It was all so much easier when Briar cut out the awkward dinner and a movie. But Mal seemed sincere in his offer, even if it was cloaked in a hundred layers of sarcasm. And... a part of Briar actually did want to spend the day with him. The regret grew stronger, but the bite on his tongue remained locked.

"What?" Mal asked when he noticed Briar's poorly-hidden gaze. Briar shook his head and quickly looked away. Still, words bubbled in the back of his throat. Honest ones, coming unexpectedly.

"I'm just... still trying to figure you out. Erm, what you want from me, I guess..."

Mal bent his elbow on the back of the seat, sweeping his hair with his fingers before shifting his legs and resting his paper coffee cup donning the ferry name on a knee. Briar knew Mal did it on purpose, trying to pose like a handsome model to dazzle his viewer. It worked, obviously.

"I'm an open book, Briar Rose. Ask me anything you'd like."

"Hm," Briar huffed through his nose. A hundred possible inquiries formed in his mind, one at a time. Questions he would never ask, not even at knifepoint. *Do you think I'm strange? What about me is so interesting? Do you think I'm an idiot for making my deal with the fey lady? Do you really think you can help me get out of it?*

Should I be afraid of the reason you keep secrets from me...?

But before he could ask any of it, his phone pinged. Briar was relieved at the opportunity to focus elsewhere—until he saw the incoming call from his mom, who pouted on the other end because he hadn't told her about the upcoming dance with Leon. Briar groaned, sitting forward and pinching the bridge of his nose, cursing Stella for being such a gossip.

24

MALRIC AND THE FEY LADY

Malric already knew Briar to be the kind to get *flustered*, but he never anticipated the extent to which it would escalate after their night together in the motel. Briar, who talked so brazenly about his one-night stands, who saw sex as just a fun activity between strangers, who blocked all of his previous, brief partners without hesitation the morning after—would blush whenever Malric smiled and winked at him in class. They would turn their eyes away with something like a pout whenever Malric met their gaze a little bit too long. Who huffed and puffed and got embarrassed whenever Malric teased them a little too much, especially when they were alone.

Briar, who, after declaring he needed a night dancing and kissing strangers, was frustrated when Stella insisted on tagging along, then brought Bianca, and then Malric joined right at the very end. Briar, who looked both *cute* and *hot as all hell* in his Moschino pleather pants and pink Miaou bustier top, who clearly intended on ignoring Malric all night while dancing with random bodies on the dance floor. Briar, who, still, kept glancing over to where Malric was relegated to the bar, not wanting to risk breaking his deal even with grinding and gyrating under neon lights.

And the whole time—Malric just watched them, too. He watched Briar dance with their body pressed against a stranger's, wrapping their slender arms around the man's neck and pulling him close. Over the rim of his whiskey glass, Malric watched hands grope up and down Briar's body, before his eyes met Briar's again in the light-streaked dark. The alcohol barely kept his animalistic envy from reaching the surface of his mind, unlike that night at the ice-skating rink when it nearly ate him alive. Malric just kept sipping his drink, not wanting to cause another scene like that one before. Not when it was so enthralling the way Briar kept looking back at him, all on his own. As if he either liked knowing Malric watched him, or was self-conscious at the thought. Malric didn't know which he would have enjoyed more.

If Briar hated it so much, he should have just ignored it. But he couldn't, he didn't—and eventually approached to ask what Malric was drinking, then why he wore such a boring shirt to the club—before pausing because he realized what the shirt was.

"Is that... Jean Paul Gaultier? 1990's?" he asked over the loud music, fingering the little padlock accessory around the neck under the white lapels. His breath smelled sweet and tangy, hints of the multiple Long Island iced teas he'd consumed since arriving; he swayed slightly on his feet; his cheeks were flushed from dancing, eyeshadow sparkling in the colorful lights. His lips were shiny and plump with cute pink lipgloss, and Malric almost missed when Briar continued speaking, distracted by the way their mouth moved. "Where did you get this?"

"I thought you said it was boring?" Malric countered with a cocky smile.

"I couldn't see what it was from so far away."

"Then you should stay a little closer," Malric smiled, just drunk enough to wrap his arm around Briar's waist, hooking against the small of his back and locking him where he stood. "I doubt any of those other people are wearing vintage designer like me."

His eyes skimmed down Briar's body with a light smile, before trailing fingers up under the bottom seam of their bustier top. "Or any designer, like you."

Briar blushed in the way Malric was growing obsessed with. His smile grew. He straightened up, nearly meeting Briar's eyes seated while Briar was standing. He curved a hand against the back of Briar's neck, almost commandingly, pulling him closer to whisper:

"You said you wanted to go home with someone tonight. Why not me?"

Perhaps that was all it really took—because Briar Hunt melted against Malric's mouth in an instant. As if that had been what he wanted all night, every night, since they first returned to land from their night at the motel. A little thing they resisted, pretending to be nothing more than an intrusive thought against everything they knew about one-night stands and breaking hearts and never repeating vulnerability with the same person. But Malric would insist on proving to his rosefinch—he was exactly the sort of person they could trust to be with over and over and over again.

FINALLY LURING BRIAR INTO HIS PERPETUAL GRASP WAS satisfying for a number of reasons—but one of them, perhaps the most important, was that Malric wasn't about to let Briar anywhere near the veil, the revel clearing, the fey world again, not after the events of the previous fete. Not after the night indulging in one another in the motel, and all the times after, where Malric finally witnessed those parts of Briar shown to so few people.

Not with every reminder of exactly what happened every time he saw the silver cuff on Briar's ankle on the ferry, on the bus, in class, at the club. Not with how Briar went stiff every time a magpie scuttled across the road or squawked from a tall tree, thinking it might be Marie's bird come to summon him again. Malric always just grabbed their hand and tugged them close, offering a distraction, promising it was nothing. Promising he was going to take care of it. *"I have a single high fey friend on the other side of the veil too, you know. I've already asked them for help, since yours turned out to be less than reliable..."*

Malric just focused on what he could control—which was Briar. Knowing where Briar was, what he was doing, how he was feeling; attending class as normal where Mal could keep an eye on him in the mornings; watching a movie on his and Stella's couch, then fucking them on the same couch when Stella left to go spend the night with Bianca. Malric struggled to let Briar go for anything longer than a few hours at a time, and when he did, he thought only of what could happen if he wasn't there when the magpie arrived again. Briar would hate knowing he was being babied, protected, shielded—but worse, if he ever discovered how Malric intended on keeping any and all of Marie's magpies far away from sight, he would ask how Malric knew anything he did, at all. Malric couldn't risk it. He'd come close enough, already. He just kept insisting his high fey friend on the other side of the veil would take care of it. They only had to be patient. That was all.

Eventually, he couldn't keep putting off the second step of that promise.

Malric was the only one who could realistically confront Marie. Malric would have to be the one to go to his mother and ask her, directly, what he needed to know. He was even sure she would tell him—she loved a game of wits—but there was a part of him that worried she might trap him there, too. Instead of Briar. Or perhaps with Briar in mind, to lure the new dancer back home.

When the first summoning magpie since the last revel did finally come, Malric woke and saw it before Briar did. It arrived around midnight, and the bird tapped its beak on the window of Bianca's sliding glass door, where Malric slept with Briar curled up next to him on the couch after watching movies together. The bird tap, tap, tapped, but it was only when Briar mumbled something and stirred that Malric realized it wasn't going to give up. He knew—that was his cue.

Gently extracting himself from that perfect, warm, comfortable place with Briar safely tucked into his chest, Malric scared the bird off.

He waited just until the sun started to rise, long after Marie's revel would have come and gone.

He left a kiss on Briar's forehead, promising he would be back soon.

Malric just wanted to get it all over with.

THE HEELS OF MALRIC'S BOOTS CLACKED ON THE hardwood, down the long upstairs corridor toward where he knew his mother would be in the late morning. He wore his nicest doublet, slack pants, boots, and even his decorative rapier for the appearance of I-am-ever-so-serious, hair pulled back into a myriad of little braids knotted off with acorns. His shoulder-cape donned the d'Alarie family crest of the fox, which would certainly put his mother in a great mood. Any reminder that their family was long-descended from a Sídhe tree, always fluffed Marie d'Alarie up enough that she would agree to anything.

If he could learn the exact terms of Briar's deal, he might be able to help him outwit it once and for all.

His mother sat in the upper gallery, classical music swirling like the sheer curtains caught in the chilly breeze outside. Despite the open windows inviting fresh air in, the double fireplaces burned at full strength, stacked high with spiced maple wood from the nearby forest. Malric had a bittersweet relationship with that scent, and knew it would only sicken him more after that very afternoon was over and done with.

Draped over one of the gaudy chaise lounges, Marie helped herself to warm nutmeg cakes and steamed honey wines. Felme sat perched on a stool at her feet, silently painting Neda reciting a poem from an author Malric wasn't familiar with. They both met his eyes as he approached, holding his gaze, looking both surprised and apprehensive. He couldn't blame them—there was no easy explanation for what he was doing there.

"*Málda*," Marie greeted without looking. Malric stopped where he was at the sound. "Come to apologize for the way you spoke to me?"

"Mother," Malric responded with perfect calm, though his heart raced. A skill learned from an entire lifetime of approaching his mother in equally terrifying circumstances. "What do you mean?"

Marie swiped her hand over the tray of snacks in front of her, sending it skittering across the floor. Malric didn't even flinch, though Felme and Neda did. Malric just watched her, watching how her hands clenched into fists before she finally turned to him. Her expression was the pinnacle of calm, but her eyes told a different story. If she could, she would tear him apart. If she hadn't been made ashen in the first season of the Moonstruck Court, she might have killed him on sight with that gaze.

"You know exactly what I mean!" she declared. "The gossip is already spreading—when I have done nothing but bring artists under my wing! Nothing but bring beauty to this court!"

"*Mother*," Malric repeated. He had to resist rolling his eyes. He was used to that speech, though—the Marie who refused to acknowledge any pain caused in favor of highlighting anything she'd done worthy of praise. "I am not here to discuss you and I."

"Then why come?" she asked. Malric turned his eyes to the foot of the chaise, and she pursed her lips before touching her hand to it. He obeyed silently, stepping around Felme and offering a brief nod of acknowledgement. Felme didn't return it, just went back to painting Neda at the front of the room.

Malric took a seat. He watched Neda's resumed performance long enough to show appreciation to his mother, though none of his brother's words actually found the comprehending parts of his mind. It was nothing but a low, long buzz. Like overhead studio lights.

"Mother," he finally said once an appropriate amount of time passed. "I wish to speak to you about the dancer."

"Ah, yes," Marie's lips curled into a wicked smile. "The one who took my offer of healing silver and ran off with it. You know, they were meant to dance for me again last night, but didn't come. Do you know anything about that?"

"No," Malric answered. "But I imagine they may be too frightened to return to any of your revels."

Her hands, crossed on her lap, twitched. Otherwise, she kept the shock of that statement hidden beneath the continued facade of a confused matriarch abandoned by one of the people she always chained close.

"Oh," she said forlornly. "What makes you say that? Do you think the dancer resents me, even after all I have offered them?"

"Like what?" Malric asked. He shouldn't have, it was a crack in his own calm, but he at least shut his mouth before going on. Marie hummed like it was a long mental list to compile.

"Well, the opportunity to dance before high fey at all is one rarely extended to humans," she said pointedly. "Not to mention the very expensive healing silver I provided, the glamour to ease their burden of supplying their own ensembles to dance in, a safe place to sleep every night, meals when they wanted them, the ongoing ability to constantly improve their craft, which was suffering in the first place... the only reason they are as lovely as they are now is because of the opportunities I have provided them, after all."

"Right." Malric had to resist clenching his fists on his knees, knowing she would notice. Knowing he had to swallow back that rage and say nothing, else the cracks in his demeanor fester deeper. She would only continue to pick at them if he showed them, and he had to remember why he was there at all. "How long did you know it was me? At your revels."

"You think I wouldn't recognize my own son?" she smiled. "I knew it was you from the first moment you crossed the circle, Malric. You cannot trick the same person who gave birth to you."

Malric knew that wasn't entirely true. Marie didn't actually know how many times he attended the revel before she noticed, otherwise she would have done something sooner. She was only hiding her own embarrassment for allowing him to slip under her nose so easily.

"Do you fancy them, Malric?" she baited, next, putting a hand on his thigh. "You held them so closely while the healer worked; you chased them when they ran off afterward... Did you ever find them on the other side?"

"The veil opening can be hard to find in the woods," Malric muttered since he couldn't directly lie. Marie might notice, but he didn't care. The less she knew about his and Briar's entangled lives, the better. "And the beach on the other side is very dark. I did have one question to ask you though, mother, inspired by a conversation I had with the dancer a few revels prior."

"Their name is Briar."

Malric grit his teeth. Proof she told everyone she possibly could Briar's name, making him more vulnerable to fey enchantment than ever. He tamped it down. Down, down, down, down, *down, damnit.*

"It seems they don't remember the exact terms of the deal they made with you, but I'm sure you worded it intentionally. Is it true they only have to prove themselves perfect to you, and then their deal is done?" he swallowed back the nervous lump in his throat. "Something so simple is dangerous, and unlike you."

Marie knew he was lying. He was trying to mislead her. Marie was smarter, more practiced in such conversations, and could smell Malric's intentions from a mile away. But something about that was a relief, somehow, as Malric didn't have to try so hard to be clever. Without outright asking, stumbling over his question would be just as effective. Marie would give Malric the answer she wanted to give him—and he would have to take it with a grain of salt, just like everything else.

But Marie was not immune to fey honesty, either, and Malric knew he could be just as clever as she.

"You learned well from me in making deals," she smiled. "As they say, *'simple leaves the firstborn.'*"

Malric grimaced. *Simple leaves the firstborn*, referencing Rumpelstiltskin's biggest mistake in singing his own name for the peasant-girl-turned queen to hear and keep her firstborn child. A story told to children as a lesson in making deals; a story that, in the human world, was a lesson of relying on cleverness and wit to overcome obstacles. To fey children, it was a show of how one's own inherent foolishness would be their inevitable downfall.

"What was it, then?" he asked. He was already exhausted by the games. He was ready to leave, to go back home to where Briar might still be sleeping the day away. Malric hoped so. He hoped to return to Bianca's apartment and collapse face-first onto the couch right next to him, pull him in close and pin him there for another six hours if he could help it.

"Are you interested in a trade, málda?" she asked, and Malric clenched his teeth. "Do you want to exchange their deal for something you're willing to offer? I may be interested—"

"Tell me the terms of their deal, first," he interrupted, not wanting to get tangled in her words. She was happy enough to oblige.

"If the root of this deal finds your pas de deux perfect, it will be done," Marie said, picking a scattered raspberry from her side table and popping it into her mouth. *"Once made perfect, any who witness your dance will bow to any request you make; any dance will be paired with the perfect partner as chosen by the veil; your dance shall enchant an entire room as a high fey enchants with their words."*

Malric waited for her to continue. There was one part of that deal missing—the consequence—and Malric knew Marie would never forget to include her favorite part of making a deal. But she just smiled at him the whole time, before claiming another abandoned berry and helping herself.

"It's quite generous, don't you think?" she asked.

"Did you see so little potential in him?" Malric heard himself ask. His ears rang in confusion, just staring at her as she continued to smile at him. Why else offer something so simple, with such a grand reward? No, that wasn't true—it wasn't simple at all. Marie could simply never declare him perfect, just like Briar said had already happened—and, Malric realized, there was the specific language of Briar having to *dance a pas de deux*. He always danced solo at Marie's revels. Even if he ever did dance perfectly, on his own...

Malric clenched his fists on his thighs. His mother really would own Briar forever, until he danced himself to death.

"I would never allow someone imperfect to perform in my name," she answered Malric's question. Malric just kept staring at her as the room undulated in the corners of his eyes. His thoughts clouded, unsure what to do next. What to say, next.

"Well," he finally said through clenched teeth, before clearing his throat. "Perhaps one day the dancer will impress you enough to earn that reward. It is indeed very generous, mother."

Her smile widened, either because she was genuinely flattered, or because she could see the growing uncertainty in Malric's eyes and it thrilled her. Malric smiled in return, before nodding once and rising to his feet.

"If you are able to convince him to return for another dance, please let me know," he said. "I would hate to miss another, especially knowing his ankle will be healed and he will be at his best."

"Once I get them back again, they will be sure to dance for me as much as I like—you are more than welcome to come and watch.." She smiled, before unpinning the fresh rosemary sprig on her lapel and pressing it to her nose. "Of all the people who can tell when he is perfect, after all, it is you, málda."

Malric smiled. He nodded, then bowed slightly, then excused himself. On his tail, he overheard Felme say something to Marie, and Marie answered in a tone that was as condescending as ever. Malric silently wished his sister luck in whatever she wanted to discuss. He didn't have time to think about it any more than that —his own mind was racing.

Marie's words haunted him all the way back through the veil. *Once I get them back again, they will be sure to dance for me as much as I like.* They pricked at him all the way up the beach, down the road, to the ferry, where he stood in line with the rest of the pedestrians and lines of cars for an hour and a half as the boat trundled over and allowed them to board.

He pushed the cycling thoughts away, and focused instead on what really mattered—the words of Marie's deal. The exact terms of the deal, where the seed of trickery waited. Buried within them, deep enough that Malric could hardly think straight. He wrote the words on the back of a pamphlet to try and clear his thoughts, tapping the end of a pen against his knee while reading them over and over and over again.

When his phone pinged, he opened it to find a message from Briar. A screenshot from another conversation, a text sent to him from Leon asking how he was doing, then apologizing for how his friends treated him at their first practice, asking if Briar would still be willing to help. *What do you think?* Briar asked, followed by: *I won't lie, I love being groveled to.*

But before Malric could answer, his heart thudded. His eyes returned to the handwritten words on the pamphlet, and he couldn't help but smirk, then burst out laughing, loud enough to startle the passenger seated next to him.

> Do it. Dance with him. Show him exactly why he thought of you in the first place.

> Show him what he's missing by taking that scholarship.

> Make him admit how perfect you are.

> i like the way you think.

Chewing on the end of his thumb, Malric could barely keep his excitement under control. He just grinned and grinned at the first part of Marie's own words.

If the root of this deal finds your pas de deux perfect...

The root of Briar's deal, and the only person he could pas de deux with, was Leon Heller.

Malric might have torn out of his skin in excitement, had a pair of shoes not suddenly entered his vision, stepping right into view next to him. He might have brushed it off as a crowded boat —but then another pair joined the first, pointed toward him. And then another. And another. And then—Malric realized what was happening, before ever lifting his eyes to meet the faces of all nine of his siblings.

25

MALRIC AND THE SIBLINGS

Like a cluster of wet geese, Malric's siblings stood there looking at him in silence, as if expecting him to say something, first. He just stared back at them in the same silence, thinking—what the hell *was* he supposed to say? His siblings—most of whom had never had any reason or interest for crossing the veil into the human world at all—??

He counted faces again, and then one more time, just in case. He squinted his eyes, then flexed the muscles behind his pupils, seeking the briefest flash of opulent magic to prove it really was them, just with glamoured, round human ears. They had no idea it took more than just moon-round ears to pass as human, damnit —and everyone on the ferry was staring.

"What... the fuck do you want?"

No—that wasn't what he wanted to say, but he was in too much shock to figure out exactly the words he meant.

"What are you doing here—" He attempted again, but stopped short when he noticed Felme at the front of the group caressing one of her hands in the other. He then realized Mavera behind her did the same, but with her entire arm. Dried tears stained her cheeks, heavy enough that even the rain couldn't whisk them away. "What happened?" he asked instead.

"We left," Felme answered weakly. "We left her, Malric. All of us."

"What?" Malric choked, lurching to his feet. "You *what?*"

"Can you help us?" Felme went on, turning back to Mavera who leaned against Maura for support. Maura just looked pale, like he was going to be sick. Malric almost blurted out for them to *go the fuck back home, gods above, what were they thinking*—but the words snarled in the back of his throat, in his lungs like vines.

Felme, the painter with the broken hand. Mavera and Maura, the pianists, one with a broken arm. Behind them, Lusia the chef; Neda the poet; Lillis the actor; Persea, Larissa, and Reta, the singers, who didn't appear injured—but he knew by their faces, they were all equally broken.

"Does mother know you're here...?" he croaked. Felme shook her head with a grimace, and Malric put his face in his hand, before collapsing back to his seat. Through his fingers, he looked at them again, as if he really thought they were just a hallucination that would vanish as soon as he focused harder. He just saw their pretty faces, their glamoured ears.

He saw their desperation. He'd *seen* that desperation, before.

Closing his eyes, he let out a long breath, before motioning for them to follow him. He led them up the side stairs to the little bistro area on the upper deck, motioning for them to shuffle into the biggest booth available, though still had to drag a table and extra chairs over so everyone could sit.

"Tell me what happened," he finally said, claiming the chair at the head of the makeshift table. On the other side of the window, the rain picked up, thunder rolling in the distance. Malric couldn't help but see it as an omen, as if that was the exact moment Marie d'Alarie realized her house, for the first time ever, was completely and entirely empty.

Perhaps the siblings sensed it, too, because the silence was heavy. They all just looked at one another in a way that told Malric what he already assumed—they'd all agreed to leave, but not all of them were confident in which direction they came.

Malric let out another breath, trying to find a tone of voice that would be more reassuring.

"I have friends on this side who can help you," he said, thinking of Bianca first and foremost. But there were others in Los Angeles, in Edinburgh, a small village in Russia, another in Mexico... Some were better friends than others, but all were safe places for high fey to go and hide. Malric could promise that much. "There are lots of high fey hiding on this side of the veil, too. There are resources for people like us displaced to the human world, for one reason or another. I'll help you land on your feet—but first, you have to tell me what happened."

He clenched his teeth, realizing there were unspoken words attached to that request.

Tell me if Briar is in danger.

Like a bottle of champagne shaken to bursting, Maura speaking first popped the invisible cork blocking all of their mouths at once. A shared, family cork, hammered into place by one person who taught her children when, how, and to whom they could speak. To reel that cork out without restraint... Malric wasn't surprised, but still felt like he'd been punched in the chest.

"Felme told us what happened at the revel the other night, with the dancer and their ankle—"

"It was because of what you did at the revel when she broke the dancer's ankle."

"You talked back to her and then ran away!? I didn't think that was possible. She didn't even chase you..."

"—even though you went after the dancer by yourself, and then neither of you came back that night."

"And then you came back and confronted her again, just now —is that true?"

"We can assume you found them, right? Are they safe? Are they okay?"

"Do they know you're Marie's son? Or do you wear this human glamour with them?"

"We all thought if you ever came back home, mother would

definitely chain you up in the house—but then today, you came, and then... you left. Just like that. Why didn't mother try and stop you?"

"Doesn't that frighten you?"

"It would have been easier to grab you while you were there, instead of charming the veil opening to repel the dancer's necklace..."

"She commissioned the town oracle to place the charm as soon as you left, which is why—"

Malric interrupted the chorus of conversation. "She what? With Briar's necklace? And the veil?""

The siblings returned to silence, biting their lips and glancing around to one another. Beneath them, the ship rocked on a turbulent wave, as if it was also impatient to hear what they had to say. Malric thought he might burst as the silence stretched into eternity. *Is Briar in danger? Is Briar in danger? Please—*

"Mother has gone too far this time," Persea finally broke the silence, motioning to Felme's injured hand, to Mavera's arm. His voice was quiet, but in Malric's ears, it rang with volume. That might have been the very first time any of them ever spoke poorly of their mother without fear of her overhearing from behind the walls of the house, and a frightened reverence fell over the d'Alarie children. Persea went on in a whisper, but, nonetheless, went on. "I've never seen her physically hurt one of us—but the moment she did, it was clear she knew she's losing control. I think when you shouted at her in front of everyone, and then you chased after the dancer like you didn't care what she would do, broke something inside of her."

"Her realizing you've attended her revels in secret multiple times did, too."

"And the way you didn't fall for her charms while there visiting, just today," Felme croaked. "It was... it made me realize... gods, what was stopping the rest of us?"

"We should have known when we learned about the wirry-cow, but..." Maura added last.

"What?" Malric gasped. He stared at his brother, who squared his jaw and gulped, before glancing at his twin's injured arm resting gently on her lap. Malric had to insist, fearing Maura might never finish: "The wirry-cow?"

"The... the wirry-cow," he croaked. "She was the one who sent it to haunt Briar. She hoped they would realize how soundly they slept in the house in comparison, and eventually never leave the fey world at all..."

Malric knew that. He almost said as much, but Mavera added weakly:

"She hates that her dancer always goes back home the next morning."

Maura continued: "But the wirry-cow told mother it'd been cast out by someone, and couldn't go back."

"She's always wanted to keep Briar on her side of the veil, no matter what," Neda, the silent poet, interjected, finally getting to the point. The siblings fell silent once more, gazing down at their hands on laps, at the table, as if the words weighed heavy on every one of them. "She's intended to charm the veil opening for a while now; she's going to use the necklace Briar wears as an anchor. You rejecting her might have been the final straw... If Briar goes back to dance for her again, I don't think..."

The ringing in Malric's ears grew louder. Overhead, a voice crackled through the intercom announcing their approach to the other side of the sound.

Neda didn't need to finish for the words to ring in his ears, in his head.

If Briar goes back to dance for her again, I don't think they'll ever be able to leave.

Once I get them back again, they will be sure to dance for me as much as I like...

"Felme tried to confront mother about charming the veil and trapping Briar, right after you left this afternoon. That's when she got angry, and hurt her," Mavera added. "I tried to step in, and mother broke my arm, too..."

"That was when I knew we had to leave," Felme reiterated, shaking her head. "Mother broke my hand—and said nothing, even though it's the hand I use to paint. I guess in a way it's a blessing. My first thought wasn't how badly it hurt—but how I wouldn't be able to paint for her any longer..."

Malric put his hand out, touching Felme's shoulder. He wished he had more to offer, especially in that moment, to ease his siblings' combined pain.

"I'm friends with a folk witch in Seattle who can help with your hand, and your arm," he said, nodding to Felme then Mavera. "Or at least find someone discreet who knows fey healing. If not, there are plenty of other veil tears around here, you can jump back through without mother ever noticing and find a healer—"

"No." Felme shook her head. "I won't go back. Not for a long time; maybe ever."

"You have to," Malric insisted. It was on instinct, the words tasting bitter even as he said them. Even as he continued to speak. "None of you know the human world like I do—it's not something you can just join without thinking, without preparing ahead of time. You all *look* like godsdamn fey, even with round ears."

"Anything will be better than going back to that place," Felme whispered, and the silent agreement from all the others was loud as before. Malric searched their faces, one by one, sitting in a circle around the laminate table as rain pummeled the window next to them. He recalled what Felme said that night Malric drank with her in her room.

Some mornings, Maura and Mavera's fingers are too stiff to even hold a fork...

Lusia grows more malnourished by the day...

Neda is hardly present, always staring off into space or sleeping the day away...

Lillis doesn't leave the house...

Persea, Larissa, and Reta hardly speak at all...

I'm slowly losing my eyesight. It's irreversible—unless I reduce the strain on them. Which is out of the question, because who then will provide work for mother to present in her galleries across the Autumn Court...?

Malric stared at his siblings; most of whom had never had a chance to recover from Marie's demands, others who had escaped only to be lured back. Only for their replacements to vanish into thin air, just like Briar would if Malric ever broke and went back home, too.

"Won't she just replace all of you?" he asked hoarsely. "With more innocent people, who she'll work until they're dust..."

"You accused her of illegally patronizing human beantighes, remember?" Mavera smiled wearily. "Gossip is already spreading. She'll at least wait a few days before searching out some other creature whose grief she can prey on."

"We just have to make sure her current dancer doesn't answer any of her calls, in the meantime..." Neda said softly, clenching his fists on his knees. "I can't imagine if they get trapped over there, and none of us ever know..."

"I'll know," Malric said like a promise, before closing his eyes and furrowing his brows. "Still, I can keep him away for as long as I can."

"Are you close with him? In the human world, too?" Neda asked softly. Malric bit his lip, skirting the truth.

"We know each other, but we could be closer. He won't know I'm keeping the bird from contacting him."

"There'll be punishment," Maura muttered. "If the dancer doesn't answer mother's calls..."

Maura trailed off, as if he wished to declare what that punishment was, but just like Malric, he had no idea. No one did, except Briar and Marie.

"I know," Malric still said, nodding.. He dug around in his jacket pocket, removing the ferry pamphlet where he'd transcribed the exact terms of Briar's deal with Marie—missing only what those consequences were. Still— "Little does mother know,

Briar is already on the verge of meeting the terms of their deal even without her help. And then..."

"She'll have nothing," Felme whispered. Why did those words make Malric's heart skip in a rush of adrenaline? Or was it enthrallment?

"Nothing," he repeated.

"Nothing." The word echoed from a chorus of exhausted mouths.

Marie d'Alarie, who was known to have everything, or who could wring it from her children like water from a cloth—would finally know what it was like to have nothing.

Malric could hardly bite back his vicious, satisfied grin.

26

BRIAR AND THE SPLINTER

Why did it feel strange, that time, to wake up alone? Briar half expected to open his eyes to a stranger's room, where he would begin his normal ritual of disappearing into the dawn—but instead it was his own ceiling overhead. It was his own sheets he felt as his hand extended to the side, as if habitually searching for someone. He quickly reeled it back in again with a frown, rubbing his eyes, stretching every limb until his joints popped.

His phone pinged, and he groaned again. Upon seeing who the message was from, Briar hated how fast he sat up to unlock the screen.

> Bianca is on her way to your apartment to deep clean.

> Come to your window if you wish to escape.

Briar blinked at the messages a few times, before biting his lip and kicking the blankets away. Wearing only a pair of boyshorts, he leaned toward the window, unable to resist smiling at the surprise of Mal standing in the alleyway down below. He waved his phone in greeting, and Briar waved back awkwardly. Mal made another motion toward the fire escape, and Briar bit his lip again, before nodding. Something about Mal climbing the rickety steel to where Briar stood on the other side of the window was a little too Romeo and Juliet, and Briar had to swallow back the instinctual urge to despise the way it made him feel. Fluttery, mostly.

Briar unlocked the window latch as Malric reached him, sliding the pane upward and shivering as a wintry wind attacked his bare chest.

"Get dressed," Mal said with a flirty smile. "Or don't, but you might get weird looks on the street. I, personally, like you exactly how you are."

"Where are we going?" Briar asked, ignoring that flirtiness.

"Anywhere you like."

They gazed at one another in silence for a moment, just long enough for Briar to absorb those words.

"Why?" he finally asked.

"Because I don't want to be roped into cleaning your bathroom, either. C'mon. Wear something cute."

"Everything I own is cute," Briar insisted, and Mal nodded like he already knew that.

The man sat on Briar's bed as Briar rummaged around in his dresser, his closet, showing Mal a handful of options before finally settling on something—an off-the-shoulder Maje crewneck flannel, black jeans, and shiny Yves Saint Laurent heeled boots with point toes—and together they crawled out the window to freedom. Right as Mal was helping Briar through, Stella knocked enthusiastically on the bedroom door, inviting herself in, then inviting Briar to help with the deep-dive under the sink and in the tub—only to bark at them as Briar laughed and shoved Mal toward the stairs to hurry. He was still laughing when they reached the alleyway at the bottom, where Mal took his hand, and they ran.

They went to old bookstores, hopping on and off the train, walking until Briar's feet hurt and he had to be carried on Mal's strong back. Mal bought him a scone and coffee at Briar's favorite cafe on the corner. They had street ramen downtown surrounded by standing heaters as snow tried to fall from the thick clouds overhead.

Briar told Mal more about the dance lessons he taught on weekends for extra cash to buy his clothes, but how otherwise, his moms paid for his rent and groceries, though only enough for him to get by—and only if he kept his grades up.

"That explains why you wouldn't play hooky with me the other day," Mal sighed, tossing a gyoza into his mouth. Steam puffed on his breath, warmed by the food and the sake. "Are you top of your class?"

"Not even close," Briar grimaced. "My moms only expect me to get a 3.5 GPA. I can go as low as a 3.0 if I dance one of the main positions in the winter or spring shows, though. My grades always drop as soon as casting is announced for that reason."

Mal laughed, like he actually thought Briar was funny. In a way that was strangely comforting, like Briar could rest assured there were parts of him that were actually charming and likable. More parts than just his ass and legs, at least.

But—also Briar's legs and ass, which was also flattering. A slightly-buzzed Mal even squeezed Briar's knee, then hooked a hand under it to lift Briar's foot onto his lap so he could examine the healing silver still clamped in place. He flicked it with a finger, releasing a sharp, musical note.

"How does it feel?" he asked. "Better, lately?"

"Yeah, I guess," Briar mumbled, unable to resist flirtily pressing his expensive shoe between Mal's legs. He bit back a smile when Mal grabbed the foot with a dark smile of his own, squeezing it until Briar made a noise.

"When it's all healed, I want you to dance for me," he said, then stroked his hand up and down the side of Briar's leg, giving Briar goosebumps. "Like you're meant to dance. Unhindered. Perfect."

"Perfect," Briar muttered with a bitter smile, before sighing

and stirring his chopsticks around in the spicy broth at the bottom of his bowl. "I wish…"

He trailed off, but wanted to say it. He wanted Mal to know, even if it was… embarrassing.

"I wish… you and I could dance together, sometime." The words left him, sadder than Briar anticipated. It did sadden him, more than he ever thought something like it would. It was almost as upsetting as when he heard Leon had taken the scholarship for Tomassin, and Briar had to accept he might never get to dance with him again, either.

Briar didn't realize he was avoiding Mal's gaze until a finger curled under his chin, nudging his face upward. Briar found Mal's thoughtful expression, the ghost of a reassuring smile on his lips like he wasn't sure he wanted to show it or not.

"One day," he said, but it lacked the same resolve as every other promise he'd ever made. "Let's promise to dance together, one day."

Briar took Mal's hand, even surprising himself. He squeezed it.

"After my deal is done… I'll help you with yours," he said. "To get out of the consequences of making your trade with the fey, or whatever. It's not fair. And I… I want to see you dance. I want to pas de deux with you."

"You do? That badly?" Mal smirked, sliding to the edge of his stool and pressing his legs into either side of Briar's. Briar leaned closer on instinct, though his heart raced nervously. Small movements like that, the way Mal kept holding Briar's hand even after the declaration was made, how Mal's opposite fingers brushed a snowflake from Briar's cheek… that was all tenderness, wasn't it? That was the gentleness Briar had always hidden from, gentleness he'd always been afraid to accept?

Mal was the last person Briar should be allowing to touch him like that, with anything except passion and roughness. Mal, who had so many secrets of his own. Who came out of nowhere, who might disappear again into nowhere once he was ready to move on. Mr. Mal, who didn't have a last name, who was cursed to never dance again. Who apparently had a tumultuous past around fey deals just like Briar did, and knew exactly everything to do in order to break Briar from his own, but who wouldn't—or couldn't—talk about how he earned all of that experience in the first place.

Briar should not have accepted even a brush of gentleness from someone whose protective walls were as high and as thick as his own were—but perhaps that was also what made Mal so easy to find comfort in. Someone who hid behind walls must have known the same roughness Briar allowed himself to have; they must know how delicate an offering of tenderness was. That to break it might break the person who accepted it.

Briar couldn't stop himself from taking hold of the front of Mal's jacket, pulling him into a slightly drunken kiss that was warm and spicy and soft. It wasn't perfect, it wasn't from the movies, Briar could taste miso broth and sake on Mal's tongue— but he'd learned from his time with the fey lady, perfection was subject to the beholder. And, maybe, Briar really did find Mal to be perfect.

MORE DAYS PASSED THAT WAY. QUIETLY, CALMLY, punctuated with Mal's mouth or his hands on the couch, in Bianca's shower in secret, between bookshelves in the library, in the dance studio after class when everyone had gone. Once Briar finally allowed Mal to touch him again that night at the club, it was endless, and Briar couldn't ever find himself fully satisfied with what he received. Sometimes it was enough to just kiss him, to feel Mal's strong hands trail up Briar's back from the base of his spine to his shoulders, rippling the fabric of Briar's shirt and brushing fingers against bare skin. Other times, skin was all there was. Skin on skin, mouths devouring and silencing one another so no one would hear, so they could keep that moment all to themselves.

The more time that passed without a visit from Marie's summoning magpie, though, the more nervous Briar grew. Still, he never mentioned it to Mal, not wanting to worry him; not wanting to pop their little bubble of peace, for as long as they could have it. Briar knew the fey lady would come calling again soon, and he would know the moment she did. He only wanted to enjoy every moment of Mal's distraction until then, like walking brain fog made of rose oils and sedative nectars luring him into a state of only peace and delight.

Gentleness. Tenderness. Briar was learning to like it; he was learning how to accept it without a racing heart or spiking anxiety. Maybe it was alright to be doted on, just a little bit, just sometimes. Especially from someone like Mal, who was both rough and careful, Briar only grew more eager to accept anything he offered the longer they got to know one another.

At the end of a whole week without sign of the magpie, Briar returned home from a particularly demanding fuck on Bianca's couch and slept the rest of the day away. But it was in those quiet moments alone in his room that he found himself growing anxious again, waking up from dreams that evolved from uncomfortable to awful, sometimes thinking he saw the fey lady's silhouette in the corner of his room again. Always wondering when the bird would come again.

It was only his anxiety from the silence, he knew—but there wasn't enough alcohol or meds to ease his worry, especially when Mal wasn't there to emotionally sedate him. He just tried to refocus his nervous energy into something more productive—like waking Stella up at 3 AM while practicing on that worn-down spot in his room. Or again at 4 AM while scrounging around in the fridge for something to eat or something to drink, whichever came first. Or at 5 AM when he was up doing crafts because he couldn't stop worrying that the magpie had tried to summon him at some point, but he'd just been too distracted by Mal to notice. Especially the following morning in class when he plucked a splinter from under his fingernail, he couldn't stop worrying about everything at all.

He didn't know if the spinning in his chest was relief or impatience. He knew Marie d'Alarie would never just let him go, so where was she? What would happen if she never called on him again? Would he still fall victim to her curse of the trees if she found someone else to replace him, on the literal grounds that he no longer danced for her...?

He just had to keep finding distractions. Focusing on his healing ankle. Allowing Mal to do whatever he was doing in the background, knowing Mal was definitely going to help him, definitely had something planned...

But then the splinters in his hands grew regular enough to stand out, and Briar could hardly keep the panic out of his chest every time he dug for another wooden passenger burrowed inside his finger that refused to let go.

Rolling up to the bittersweetly familiar Tomassin doors after a week of peace, Briar remembered what he was so nervous about again. He fixed his hair in his reflection, let out a long sigh, and grabbed the handle—only to find it locked. The flashing red light on the card reader next to the hinges made him frown in further frustration.

Pulling out his phone, he typed out a quick message to Leon that he needed to be let in, but someone suddenly came up behind him and asked, *"Locked?"*

"Yeah—oh! Wh-what are you doing here?"

Mal looked like he wanted to smirk, but kept his expression flat. "You sure we're in the right place?"

"'We?'"

"I saw you were headed this way... my sis—erm, my friend and

I were getting coffee down the street, I thought I'd see what my little bugbear was up to."

Briar frowned. "I decided to keep practicing with Leon... for the gala..."

"Ah," Mal said, then lifted his eyes as Leon hurried to the doors from the other side. Smiling and apologizing, he pushed them open, before giving a look of surprise at Mal, then passing it to Briar.

"Um, Leon, this is—"

"Mal. Briar's boyfriend," Mal interjected, and Briar stared at him. Before Mal could shake Leon's hand, Briar shoved it away.

"He's just a friend. He loves to joke."

Mal frowned at him that time, though it was more of a pout than anything. If Leon hadn't been there watching, Briar would have punched him. Instead, he just screamed through his eyes—*you can't just say whatever you want!*

You let just anyone do those nasty things to you? Briar swore he read behind Mal's eyes, but that might have been his own projection. His own embarrassment. He'd never had a *boyfriend* before —the word alone scared the shit out of him.

Grabbing the handle, Briar said nothing else and followed Leon inside, smacking Mal with the door as he went. Mal grunted, but followed on Briar's heels all the same. He tried to grab Briar's hand as they made their way down the hall, but Briar snatched it away again with an annoyed look. Mal offered the same look right back. Briar wanted to kill him.

Upon reaching the auditorium doors, Briar attempted to smack Mal with those ones, too, but Mal was prepared. He snatched it out of Briar's hand and bonked him in the head, instead, before hissing a laugh and grabbing him to apologize when Briar groaned and rubbed his nose.

"What are you doing here!" Briar hissed under his breath.

"I'm just keeping an eye on you."

"What for?" he argued, yanking the door from Mal's hand just on principle.

"I also just like spending time with you, you know."

"We've been spending all our time together, lately."

"I thought you liked it."

"I do—but not if you're going around telling people we're boyfriends!"

"Aren't we?"

Briar wanted to scream. "I don't want to talk about this right now."

"Then stop giving me such snotty looks."

"Then—! Just go away!"

"I'm already here."

"Mal, if you want to sit with everyone else..." Leon interrupted as awkwardly as ever, and Briar flushed before shoving Mal away and hurrying toward the stage. Mal let out a breathy laugh, thanking Leon before telling him to *take good care of Briar, he's fragile*. Briar was going to kill him.

Mal took a seat in the padded audience chairs with most of the same faces Briar recognized from the last disastrous attempt at practicing, but he was confident that time it would go differently. His ankle was nearly healed, he knew what to expect. They would have nothing to critique him over.

Mal, on the other hand, Briar didn't know what to anticipate. It made him nervous in a way he wasn't expecting.

Briar followed Leon up the side steps of the stage and behind the curtain, where he stripped off his jacket and scarf and kicked off his sneakers to replace with a pair of pointe shoes. Blood rushed to his cheeks when he realized that would be the first time Mal would actually see him dance. Like, genuinely dance, not just in class. Not to mention, hand-in-hand with Leon, who Mal clearly had some sort of feelings about considering his *boyfriend* comment.

"So... boyfriend, huh?" Leon asked while rubbing the bottom of his demi slippers in the box of crushed rosin next to the curtain. "Um... isn't he the guy who almost punched me at the ice-skating rink? Guess that explains it..."

Briar's face rushed with heat. "*No!* He's not my boyfriend. He was only joking."

"Ah," Leon chuckled. "I'm not surprised, for the record—you just never dated anyone when we were hanging out. I thought maybe you weren't into that."

Briar raised his eyebrows. "I mean... I don't know," was all he could think to say. He fought against that little impulse in the back of his mind implying things that definitely, definitely weren't true about why Leon chose to phrase it like *that*. "I've just... never met anyone I wanna go steady with, I guess."

"Really, no one?" Leon laughed. Briar focused harder on his ribbons.

"Not when they were also interested in going steady with me, at least."

"Well—Mal seems nice enough," he said, despite the fact the man had, in fact, tried to assault Leon at the ice rink. "Handsome, too. Is he a dancer?"

"Um... used to be." *Until a fey deal made it so he's cursed to never dance again, or something. It's a long story. Kinda funny, actually, because I, too, did something really stupid in terms of my dancing and the fey...* "He's an instructor at Artemisia right now, though."

"Oh—you still got a thing for instructors?"

"'*Still?*' No!" Briar cried, and Leon laughed, and then Briar laughed, too. It was way too easy.

"Well, maybe he'll have some good critiques for us, today."

"Let's maybe not encourage him," Briar mumbled, before shaking his head as the following silence was awkward as all hell. He cleared his throat. "Are you—are you seeing anyone, Leon? Last I heard, you were dating that one girl, um... Tricia, or something?"

"Oh, yeah—we broke up a few months ago. Just kinda dating around right now, not interested in anything too serious with graduation only a year away. You never know what company you'll get into and if you'll have to move away, you know?"

"Yeah, definitely." Briar didn't know. "Well—if you want any recommendations for places to meet people, um... I'm kind of a pro at getting around."

God, he was so stupid.

"Your boyfriend doesn't mind?"

"He's not my boyfriend!" Briar cried, and Leon laughed.

Briar shook the thoughts away. He coated the bottoms of his shoes in rosin, pretending not to notice how Leon put his hands out in case he needed help balancing. Just like he always used to.

Briar squeezed in a few final toe-stretches as the pianist settled into their place and played the introductory notes. He and Leon emerged into the lights of the stage, and the waltz melted like wax over their movements with all the ease and fluidity as it should have the very first time. Briar was over the moon with how his ankle felt beneath the choreography, how he could actually disappear into the dance, how it all felt so natural again. A strange resurgence of what he ever loved about dancing in the first place, that little piece of champagne in his soul that Marie d'Alarie had nearly taken away...

But then the music faded, and Briar's elation was cut short at the sound of Mal clearing his voice from the audience.

"Do you mind if I share some feedback?"

Briar turned to him immediately with a bitter expression, but Mal must have anticipated it, because he kept his eyes on Leon standing to Briar's side on the stage. Leon, breathing heavily with a few drops of sweat on his forehead, nodded and welcomed anything Mal had to say. Mal wasted no time getting to his feet and, to Briar's disbelief, climbed the stairs to the stage.

He circled around them like a vulture, examining every detail as if their practice outfits had anything to do with the dance, itself. He continued to avoid Briar's gaze the entire time. *Briar was going to kill him.*

"When you move across the stage, your legs need to extend longer and wider to be more elegant. You're doing a sort of three-quarter step that looks rushed. When you lift and return your partner to the floor, as well, you need to follow the movement through all the way instead of completing it when Briar's feet touch the ground. Can I show you?"

That time, Mal looked at Briar. Briar glared at him, but clenched his teeth and nodded. Mal's hands found his waist, and he was lifted into the air. Briar panicked at first, worried it would come back to bite him—before seeing how Mal did the bare minimum, nothing that could be considered *dancing*. So instead of worrying, Briar purposefully flopped his arms and legs like a stubborn fish, only to then flush with embarrassment when people in the audience snickered and whispered to one another. Right, he forgot—he was performing for Leon's peers, too. A class of perfect dancers who already thought Briar didn't belong.

Mal returned him to the floor, but Briar touched his arm.

"Try again," he mumbled without looking at him. "I wasn't ready, before."

Mal did. That time, Briar moved like he was supposed to—but the whispers still didn't stop. He frowned, landing heavily because of the new distraction. His fingers pinched together in a habitual search of his spinner ring.

"Right," Leon answered with a polite smile. "Let's go again Briar."

"Yeah," Briar said, hurrying out of Mal's reach as Leon nodded to the piano. Just like the first time—their second dance was worse. Their third attempt was *worse,* and Briar could only mentally curse Mal endlessly for ruining something he'd been so happy to have again.

"Don't you have any notes for Artemisia?" someone finally asked as another performance ended, Briar nearly tripping over his feet as he lost focus and landed awkwardly, again.

"Not really," Mal finally answered, then flipped a piece of hair from his eyes. "Briar's technique isn't the problem."

"Seriously?" someone else mumbled. Briar took a step back from Leon, who just smiled and chuckled nervously like he hoped they could still play it all off as friendly teasing. Briar could barely think through the steam in his brain.

"Guys, we talked about this," Leon begged as politely as possible. "Briar's still our best chance. Besides, he's recovering from an ankle injury right now—right, Bry? You'll be fine by opening night."

"I never would have guessed it was his ankle by the way the rest of his body moves. Check his spine and shoulders too, Leon, maybe the doctors missed something."

Briar stared at them—then stared at Mal, who no longer had anything to say. Briar clenched his fists by his sides, before pressing his lips together.

"Going to storm off again?" someone else mocked, and Briar deflated in an instant. No, definitely not—but then two of the audience members leapt to their feet to rush the stage and insist they could do it better, and Leon sighed in frustration before giving in and waving to the pianist to start the waltz from the top. Briar just took a few steps back out of the way, watching the first performance, and then half of the second, before he couldn't stand it. Knowing he just looked stupid standing there watching.

No one noticed when he slipped back through the curtain, finding his bag and throwing it on over his shoulder, not bothering to pull on his coat or even change his shoes. No one said anything as he hurried down the stage steps in the dark, because they were all too busy watching Leon attempt the pas de deux with other potential replacements, since Briar couldn't seem to get a handle on it.

But that wasn't true—Mal had ruined it. He'd been bitchy and sarcastic like he always was, but that time, it wasn't funny. It just made Briar feel *stupid*.

He meant to make a clean getaway, except his bike was security-locked to the pole for illegal parking without a permit. Briar stared at it with wet eyes, before his face twisted in anger and he lunged, slamming his foot against the tire again and again until the whole bike tumbled onto its side with a dramatic crash.

Gasping for breath, Briar then scrumbled the cuffs of his sleeves all over his face to wipe the tears away, but more replaced them in no time.

"Hey."

Briar turned. He met Mal's eyes. Mal looked at him with nothing but pity, and Briar's heart erupted into enraged flames. It was all his fault—how could he look at Briar like it wasn't?

"What!" he screamed. "What the hell do you want from me!"

He slammed his heel into the bike between words, again and again until even the magic silver couldn't keep the ache of his weakened ankle at bay.

"You must have thought it was hilarious! You must think it's hilarious—to watch them all laugh at me—when I finally get to dance with him again! You must think it's fucking hilarious that I'm still just a fucking nobody to him, even after everything I've done—! Every stupid choice I've ever made, all because I was in love with my pas de deux partner—who never even looked at me—!"

The words caught in his throat as he whirled to verbally assault Mal face-to-face, but Leon was suddenly standing at the corner behind him. Mal turned, too, when he saw the look of horror on Briar's expression.

"Briar?" Leon asked. "I just... wanted to make sure you were alright. I told everyone to knock it off. They were just joking around, so..."

Briar stared at him, before a crushed laugh bubbled out of the back of his throat.

"Is that it?" he asked after letting the silence linger a moment longer. Giving Leon any additional chance he needed to acknowledge what he'd just overheard. "There's nothing else you want to say?"

"Briar, not like this," Mal attempted, but Briar just combed fingers back through his hair, then turned on heel to walk away. Mal chased after him—but Leon didn't. Briar should have known that would be the case. Leon had never chased after him before then, either.

There was no way to make sense of the churning in his gut, his chest, his heart—and all Briar knew to do was run away. That's all he ever did. Normally it worked—but then he met Mal. Mal, who hardly ever left Briar alone to dwell in his misery and self-hatred and embarrassment. Who always chased and found him, to tease the misery away. To smile at him and make him laugh and—

"Oh, god," Briar croaked, clutching the front of his jacket as he swore his heart was about to fail. He was mortified—he was heartbroken—he was lost, and confused, and all he could think was of Mal's face as Briar screamed at him. Shouting those things about Leon that he didn't even know if he himself still believed anymore, things he'd carried for so long because they were all he knew.

Crossing onto the busy bridge over the river, a chilly wind blew over him, whipping his hair sideways. A part of him hoped he might be swept away by the incoming storm, to disappear somewhere not even Mal would be able to find him.

But then he stopped short. He forced his legs to stop fleeing, even if it meant they would snap beneath him. Fisting his hands at his sides, Briar clenched his teeth hard enough he swore they cracked—and then forced himself to turn around. If Mal wasn't there, if Mal wasn't actually following him, he would have his answer, he wouldn't have to feel so guilty or confused or—

Arms found him in an instant. Wrapping him in a warm, protective embrace, and Briar burst into tears like a giant baby. He cried and cried all the tears he'd repressed since first developing feelings for Leon, all those times he was reminded Leon never saw him that way, and never would. He cried the tears held back when he learned Leon wanted to transfer to Tomassin, how he talked so excitedly about who he might be able to pas de deux with one day, never once speaking Briar's own name despite sitting right next to him. He cried as hard as he only ever did after waking from dreams where he saw only that look on Leon's face while emerging onto stage during the finale of Giselle, when Briar couldn't tell if he was thrilled or disappointed to find Briar dancing toward him.

And the whole time, Mal just held him. Mal just rubbed his hand up and down Briar's back, never saying anything, only keeping Briar's ghost pinned in his body so it wouldn't get caught on the wind and torn away like a kite.

Briar was still in love with Leon—but at the same time, he wasn't. Maybe he hadn't been for a long time. Maybe Briar simply held onto that sentiment, because to admit otherwise would kill him. He would die. He would die to know—the person he threw his whole life away for, who never noticed him and never would, was no longer a person he was interested in noticing him, anymore.

The only person he cared about anymore—had followed him. Held him. Comforted him. Without being asked. Without having to sell his soul to a demon to get a taste of it. Mal gave that freely, willingly, and Briar cried harder as he realized it.

Compelled to something like anger, Briar suddenly bent over, roughly ripping off one ballet slipper—and throwing it over the railing with ferocity. He tore away the second one and threw it, too. He watched both of them silently as they hit the waves below, floating on the dark surface before falling victim to the rough tide and sinking into nothingness. Mal must have seen how Briar's chin quivered, because he inhaled a sharp breath before exclaiming *"hell yeah!"* and bending to rip off his own shoe—and throw it over.

Briar screamed, leaning over the railing as a perfectly good Jimmy Choo loafer slapped the water before disappearing into it. Briar only barely turned and grappled Mal's arm as he raised the second one to sacrifice, next, in so much shock he choked on his tears, then begged Mal to show mercy. But Mal was stronger, reeling back and hucking the second shoe into the river with a howl of excitement.

God—Briar laughed. And then he cried more, pounding his

fists against Mal's chest and shouting about how those were $300 shoes. How he was so stupid, he was so goddamn stupid—and he made Briar feel everything. Every single emotion a human could, in all the ways no one had ever made him feel, before. In ways that were frightening, and intimidating—but something about feeling everything with Mal there didn't scare him so much.

"Are your shoes in your bag?" Mal asked next with a laugh, pushing hair from Briar's wet face. Briar nodded, chuckling miserably as Mal reached around him and unzipped the bag hanging off Briar's shoulder. He yanked out a pair of familiar Converse sneakers, kneeling down and gently patting the outside of Briar's right ankle. Briar put his hands on Mal's shoulders for balance, lifting the requested foot. Mal slid it on, then did the same with the next. When he straightened up again, Briar didn't know whether to smile or cry some more.

"Do you think I'm pathetic?" he asked in the interim, hardly any louder than the wind. Mal frowned. He shook his head, then tipped Briar's chin and kissed his cold lips in reply. Upon pulling away, Briar lingered with his head outstretched, eyes closed, letting the warmth linger on his mouth.

"I think you're perfect," Mal breathed, pulling away only enough that when Briar opened his eyes, he could see every emotion swirling behind Mal's. Guilt, regret, rage, bloodlust, pride, appreciation. Briar didn't know what kind of face he wore in response—but whatever it was compelled Mal to kiss him again.

"I'm so sorry," he insisted, taking Briar's face next and kissing his forehead, then his cold nose. "I am a selfish creature. I'm greedy. I like to keep things all to myself—but that's no excuse for making you uncomfortable. For singling you out in front of everyone else—especially when I did, actually, have plenty of notes on your form. Just, for the record."

Briar groaned and rolled his eyes, fwumping into Mal's chest. Mal patted the back of his head, then nudged Briar's face back into view in order to kiss him again. Briar inhaled as much of the warmth as he could, kissing Mal as long as he could get away with. Every moment washed the grit from his veins, like cleansing a curse with salt, until soon he wasn't sure what he'd been so upset about.

"Also know that I am five seconds away from leaving you here to go back and slaughter every person in that auditorium for how they treated you," Mal whispered with only an inch between their mouths, voice dark and serious.

"You would do that for me?" Briar teased. "Kill a whole audience for laughing at me?"

"Without hesitation."

"Wow, you really are a romantic," he said weakly, before shaking his head. He pressed his forehead to Mal's, looping his arms around the back of the man's neck even though it forced him to hunch. "They're just... they're all just such pricks... They talked to me like that last time, too, but... I don't know, maybe I shouldn't have gone back..."

Mal bit his lip. Briar touched his thumb to it in question, a silent request to know what he was thinking.

"You know—a while ago, you said something about how maybe dancing with Leon would be enough to cancel out your deal with the fey lady. The more I think about it... the more I think it's true."

Briar smiled in exasperation.

"But you're still jealous."

"Out of my mind, really." Mal smirked. "But I understand. I think I can survive watching you perform one, single, perfect dance with someone like Leon, if it means you'll be set free, afterward."

"Wow, my boyfriend is so generous."

Mal reeled back with a gasp, then a grin, and Briar just rolled his eyes.

"I was being *sarcastic,* you dope."

"No, I don't think you were—I heard sincerity in your voice. Briar—my boyfriend, Briar!"

Briar argued, then shoved Mal away as Mal threw his arms out to pull Briar in and squeeze him until he nearly popped like a balloon. Briar squealed and swore at him, but Mal didn't let go. He just held Briar close enough that Briar felt nothing else except his warmth, his comfort, his—gentleness.

BRIAR AND THE CHARM

That night, Briar dreamed of worms slithering through his veins. He dreamed of being buried alive, unable to move with his eyes wide open and staring at a rainy sky overhead. Lowered into a dark grave as the people he loved wept over him around the edge of the surface. He wanted to scream at them to look at him, meet his eyes, check one more time that he was really dead—but he couldn't move. He couldn't even blink. He could only watch as, one by one, the people all left, until only Mal remained leaning over the edge. Briar stared at him; Mal was meeting his eyes. Did he know? Did he know Briar was still alive? Why didn't he say anything?

From heights Briar couldn't see, shovelfuls of dirt suddenly cascaded over him. Landing like heavy fists against his stomach, his chest, before scattering over his face and infiltrating his mouth and nose. He inhaled the soil until his insides felt like sandpaper. Until he understood what it was like for a tree to inter its roots farther into the earth in search of water and life.

He tried to scream, but the dirt spilling over him never stopped. It just piled and piled and piled, until even his eyes were blocked out. Until his mouth was full of dirt. Until he couldn't breathe without the rough grating of soil throughout his entire body.

He woke with a start, but only in the deepest parts. His heart slammed against his chest, his fingers twitched, but his eyes didn't open. He only realized why after his soul returned to its physical form, finding his eyelashes tangled together in a way that was unusual. As if sticky sap glued them shut.

Sliding the hands of his soul into his fingers like putting on gloves, he managed to reattach the rest of himself into the corporal vehicle. He groaned under his breath, throat scratchy and dry just like in his dream. He must have a cold coming on.

He lifted his hands to his eyes, rubbing away the sticky film that kept them shut. His knuckles scraped against his cheeks like he always hated in the middle of dry winters, and he wondered if it was because he'd exfoliated them too roughly in the shower the night before. Perhaps he didn't have any skin left.

Something was lodged in the back of his throat, furthering his assumption he'd caught something. Coughing into his hand, he finally managed to sit up and blink through his blurry eyes, groaning softly as his entire body was stiff like an artist's drawing form. He must have slept deeper than he thought.

Whatever scratched the back of his throat refused to detach no matter how much he rolled his tongue around or coughed, and he finally shoved his scratchy fingers into his mouth in an attempt to dig it out as a last resort. His fingers closed over something flat and papery, and he internally rolled his eyes wondering if he'd inhaled something while sleeping...

But upon plucking it out, upon his vision finally clearing enough to see it in detail, Briar just stared. There was a fresh green leaf in his hand.

And his hand—was punctured by a thousand more little splinters emerging through sore skin.

He nearly screamed, throwing the leaf away and kicking his feet to scramble backward. He kicked too far, tumbling over the side of the bed and hitting the floor with a heavy *thud*. It barely fazed him—he was too distracted by the callous feeling of his hands, how there were round protrusions like spring buds pushing out from under his fingernails. How the rough skin was forming on the tops of his feet. How he swore he could see—thin, winding root systems crawling under his skin.

His mind reeled.

If you ever refuse me, you will become as the trees to witness the perfection of another; to learn what you yourself couldn't do.

"F—" He croaked, wincing as his voice was hardly more than a rasp. His breath fluttered something deep in his chest, somewhere he would never be able to reach. He thought of the leaf he'd plucked from the back of his throat. He thought of—

He grabbed a pair of sewing scissors from his nightstand, and hooked the blades over the largest protrusion from his thumb. He snipped it away, then found the next one. And the next. And the next. Then he frantically snipped at anything emerging from his toes, the tops of his feet. He snipped and plucked and pulled out anything his fingers trailed over, not unlike how he stripped away any part of his cuticles that stood out a little too much while riding the bus.

When he was done—he stared at himself in the vanity mirror, wearing only his underwear and the fey lady's charmed necklace. His ears rang, staring at the delicate chains of gold, the single drop of a pink pearl between his collarbones. A necklace that glamoured him every time he entered the revel, with magic strong enough to make the visions tangible under his hands.

Staring down at the scissors, he trembled, but a single prick of hope, or maybe relief, stabbed him in the center of his chest. It had to only be the necklace tricking him into thinking there were leaves growing from his skin. It was impossible, otherwise. He would have died in his sleep if trees truly rooted in his body.

But—he hadn't seen any magpies in days. Why would...?

It had to be only a glamour. Some sort of trick. Just like in the alleyway that one night Marie cornered him at the club. He only had to counter-charm the glamour, somehow—

He recalled one of the shops he and Mal had visited that day they fled Stella's cleaning-trap. He thought of their wall of herbs and crystals and charms wrapped up in tulle bags dangling from hooks. He thought of nothing else from there, just dressed as fast as he could.

They hadn't spent a lot of time in that shop the first time, but Briar knew exactly where to go to find it. He even remembered exactly how it smelled inside, that cozy, velvety sort of incense smell that only witchy occult shops had. The same scent that Mal said gave him a migraine, so they had to leave after only perusing the crystals and some of the hex bags. Briar remembered how Mal kept his hands behind his back the entire time, as if worried any accidental touch really would curse him. Briar should have teased him more.

Briar wasn't long in the store before someone noticed how out of his element he was—or maybe how sweaty and anxious he was, like a preteen winding up the courage to commit their first petty theft—and after explaining his plight as vaguely as possible, Briar watched as the associate worked behind the glass counter to pour him his own custom protection bag. According to them, it would not only lessen the effects of glamours, or 'psychic attacks,' in the room where it was nailed over the door, it would also protect him from demonic entities, nightmares, and other hexes weaker than it was. Briar just nodded and smiled frantically whenever he could, adding in more requests on top of the first when he spotted other buzzwords written on cards that he felt like he needed. Healing. Strength. Good vibes. All that shit. They talked him into buying some rose quartz while they were at it, and he put it on his credit card with silent apologies to his mom when she saw the bill later.

"Briar?"

Briar jumped, then turned—then turned to stone at the pretty face looking at him with raised eyebrows. Their features were just slightly different from how Briar recognized them in the fey world, including newly-beveled ears as if the tips had been taken off in a grinder. But Briar would recognize someone so beautiful anywhere. He would recognize their dirty blonde hair and rounded features, green eyes looking back at him in a mix of surprise and uncertainty. No—that was Briar's own reflection in Neda's eyes. It had to be. He had to be the one wearing that face of disbelief, it wouldn't make sense otherwise.

His heart lumped in the back of his throat, making it impossible to speak, almost impossible to breathe. His hands twitched at his sides, and all he could think was—he wished Mal was there with him.

"What..." he attempted, word escaping as hardly more than a rasp. "What are you... doing here, Neda? Are you—"

"We left home," Neda said, not meaning to interrupt and blushing in embarrassment when they realized they had. They averted their eyes, shaking their head and rubbing the back of their neck. That was when Briar saw the nametag pinned to Neda's sweatshirt, donning the store's logo and the false name *Ned*. No, not just a false name—a human one.

"You... left?" Briar asked weakly. "What do you mean? Isn't she—won't she—"

Neda put their hands up, uncertainty growing as Briar's did.

"Didn't Malric explain everything to you?"

"Who?" Briar snapped as the agitation in his body climbed higher. "I don't know who that is."

"Oh—my brother! The one you replaced—erm, ah, he's actually right in the back talking to the store owner. He's the one who helped me get the job here. Hold on, I'll go grab him, alright? He can explain what's going on."

Briar said nothing as Neda smiled politely, then turned to scurry behind the counter and through a back door. Briar just watched them go. Briar's ears rang with earsplitting alarms. Briar's mind was nothing but shrieking howls. Neda's brother, *Malric*. The one Briar replaced. The one whose nose Briar smashed with his foot, who Marie always threatened would break Briar's legs if Briar didn't perform well enough... who had already broken his ankle, and might have done more if given the chance...

Briar grabbed his protection charm, and ran from the store. He hit the door out so hard the glass inside vibrated, slamming the bells dangling from the upper corner into the wall with a horrible noise. Briar barely heard it. He barely felt the person he crashed into on the other side, barely realized how hard he hit the sidewalk and scraped up his hands. He didn't feel himself getting back to his feet and running as fast as he could back home, before anyone could see him at all.

28

MALRIC AND THE DARKNESS

"*Help me—he's going to find me, please, please help me...*"
Malric had never moved so fast. He should have known when Neda spoke to him in the back of the shop, talking about how Briar had been there, how Briar was in the front waiting for them, only for it to be empty. Malric assumed Neda was just confused, just mistook a stranger for Briar, instead—but then that phone call came a few hours later, and Malric knew something was wrong. Something had happened. All he could think was of Marie's threat, that he would know as soon as Briar returned to the fey world.

He had to resist tearing his own holes through the veil to snap directly to Briar's apartment, but it would have been too risky. It might have taken more time in the long run, since the veil wasn't so predictable. Riding the bus was torture. He couldn't get his legs to move fast enough down the sidewalk without breaking into a full run. He tried to call Briar back again, but it rang and rang and rang until going to voicemail.

All the way to Briar's building, up the stairs, to the apartment door where he knocked as frantically as he could without scaring Briar more. When no one answered, his mind went blank, calling Briar again as he hurried back down and around the side, searching the alleyway until he found Briar's window a few stories up. It was dark, but Malric still hurried up the fire escape. The call went to voicemail, but right before it did, he saw the glow of Briar's phone screen lit up on their bed. The bed was empty otherwise, though, and seemingly so was the rest of the room, and Malric nearly punched a hole straight through the glass.

He forced himself to focus. He closed his eyes, breathing through his nose and touching his fingers to the upper edge of the sliding panel. Briar had invited Malric inside once before, meaning Malric had a level of pull on the manipulation of the lock. A little bit of opulence, a little bit of cunning fox magic, and he was able to twist the lever just enough to shimmy the window upward and climb inside.

He almost called out Briar's name, but held it back. The room was silent enough to give him chills, flexing his hands at his sides before straining his eyes into the ability to search for his rosefinch in the darkness, just like at the club. His heart pounded hard when he was reminded of the club, and he nearly snapped—but then the trail of Briar, while luminescent throughout their entire room, pinpointed at the closet door.

Keeping quiet, he approached the dark corner. He hooked fingers through the metal inlet and slid the door to the side, where he found Briar huddled on the ground, curled into a tight ball and struggling to breathe. It was like someone had kicked Malric in the back, knocking the air out of him, a silent wheeze escaping his lungs as he dropped to his knees and gently touched Briar's shoulder.

"Bry?" he asked gently, and Briar whimpered, petrifying in an instant, before barely lifting his head from where it was pressed behind crossed arms. His messy hair draped over his eyes, but Malric could see the faint reflection of tears on his cheeks.

"Mal?" they asked pitifully, and it broke Malric's heart.

"What happened, Briar?" he demanded, inhaling sharply when Briar just sobbed and shook his head quietly, before putting out his hands to grapple at Malric's coat. Malric didn't hesitate, putting his arms around Briar's tiny form and holding him closely, pulling him firmly into his body, like a shield against the rest of the world. He crawled into the closet right alongside his dancer, using his foot to slide the door shut again so he wouldn't have to move his hands. He held Briar like something he treasured, kissing and stroking his hair as Briar fought to breathe normally between wordless, trembling sobs. Malric tried to coax the words out of him one, then two more times, only for Briar to moan and shake his head, burying his face into Malric's stomach. As if he feared speaking it out loud would summon whatever frightened him so much. Malric just pulled him closer.

When Briar's fears finally petered out, they still didn't sit up. Malric still didn't stop stroking his hair, didn't push the closet door open even though the air inside was getting muggy with heat.

"Do you think I'm pathetic?" Briar asked, hardly more than a ghost on the wind, just like on the bridge after practice with Leon. Malric frowned. He tipped Briar's chin so they could look at each other, brushing hair from Briar's puffy eyes.

"I think you're perfect," Malric breathed. Just like on the bridge. He expected a grimace or a smirk from Briar in return—and something about the lingering fear, the exhaustion on his expression only made Malric's insides squeeze tighter in desperation. He sat forward, kissing Briar with all the delicacy he could, worried the person resting on his lap might break if he was too rough.

"You're perfect," he repeated. "You'll always be perfect."

Briar laughed weakly, before taking the back of Malric's head and pulling him into another kiss, as if they didn't want to hear it anymore. As if they hated those words, even if Malric meant them with his entire soul.

If Briar wouldn't use his words to explain, Malric wouldn't force him. Malric would respect that, even if it tore him apart not knowing what was horrifying his perfect dancer so badly. But Malric didn't need to know as much as he simply wanted to be there, to provide comfort and a sense of safety, so he followed Briar's lead. He gave what Briar requested without words, kissing him, kissing him, kissing him, until he finally kicked open the closet door and carried Briar out again.

TIME MOVED SLOWLY. LIKE THICK YARN THROUGH THE narrow eyelet of a needle.

It was the first time Briar had ever pulled Malric into his bed like that, and Malric wasn't going to waste it. He wanted to show Briar exactly what he thought to be most perfect about him—everything. Everything was perfect, and he would be thorough. He would take his time, even if it cost them an eternity.

There was an equal desperation from Briar, but Malric caught Briar's hands every time they tried to touch him, first. He caught Briar before he could kiss any lower than Malric's stomach. Malric wanted only to worship Briar, so that he might never forget, even when on stage performing in front of people who might never appreciate him as much as Malric did.

Kissing down his neck, swirling his tongue over pink nipples, tasting the soft skin of Briar's navel, he bathed in the sounds of Briar's catching breaths, his moans, how he begged Malric's name softly.

Briar Rose was not like fey, or even other humans Malric had had his hands on in all his years of living. Of course, making love to fey and making love to humans was, in so many ways, exactly the same—but at the same time, entirely different, in such small ways it was hard to describe. Malric hardly had a preference between the two, either—until that moment. Until that moment, even still fully dressed, even with only his hands on Briar's waist and his mouth on Briar's skin, Malric knew he had a preference.

His preference was Briar Hunt.

Briar Hunt's skin was soft, somehow silken and velvety at the same time, smelling of rose powder and cucumber soap. Briar Hunt's breaths caught with every single sensation, even the smallest stimulation from Malric's tongue, despite being the most thick-skinned brat Malric had ever met. Apparently Briar's weakness was a mouth that knew what it was doing—and gods knew Malric was going to learn every sound his rosefinch could make.

Shoving the jumper Briar wore over their head, Malric tied it off around Briar's wrists, then bodily dragged his slender, petite frame up the height of the bed to tie off the extra sleeves to the headboard. Briar's breath came shaky the entire time, occasionally dappled with breathless laughter in all the ways that drove Malric crazy. Tiny sounds of approval, tiny sounds of consent and enjoyment without ever having to say as much. It was erotic in its own way, to know his partner well enough to hear and understand those little moments, to be able to make adjustments to his own approach at a moment's notice if he had to. He would make Briar feel everything he wanted—and leave him unconscious on the bed just like the first time. Just like the way Briar liked.

Malric's eyes lifted as he trailed his tongue back over Briar's navel, then tickled the fine peachy-blonde hairs growing in a line below his belly button. Briar watched him through flushed, heavy eyelids, straining against the bindings on his wrists every time he fluttered with pleasure. It took everything in Malric not to rush. He wanted to show Briar how it felt to be worshiped like an angelic thing formed from perfection. Just like Briar had worked all his life to achieve as such a beautiful dancer. He'd worked so hard to be something perfect, and Malric would commend him for it using only his mouth.

Pulling down the waistband of Briar's black leggings, Briar rolled his hips and whispered Malric's name in desire. Malric smiled to himself, meeting Briar's eyes just long enough to memorize that face.

Pulling Briar's leggings away, Malric dumped them on the floor. He then crawled to hang over Briar's body stretched long beneath him, appreciating the flush of color anywhere his mouth touched, between his thighs that trembled with anticipation.

"Gorgeous," he whispered, kissing below the belly button

again before tugging on the waistband of Briar's boyshorts and coaxing them down. Briar, despite being so confident and smug in the daylight, turned and buried his face into the crook of his restrained arm as soon as he was exposed. Malric laughed under his breath in response—then lowered himself between Briar's legs, and took him into his mouth.

Briar bucked with a gasp, then a choking moan, arching his back as Malric pressed a hand to Briar's stomach to push him back down to the bed. Coaxing up and down with his mouth, he tasted every inch, teasing the tip with his tongue before pressing it all the way to the edge of his throat. He teased Briar's navel with the tip of his nose as he went down on him flush to the base, obsessed with every clench and shudder of thighs, every twitch of the length against his tongue, every single little breath and sound of pleasure Briar made while tied off to his own headboard.

"You—" Briar's voice hitched. "Mal—take your clothes off, damnit, I can't be... I don't want to be... the only one."

Malric offered Briar a few more long, sensual strokes of his mouth before finally pulling away, a thin string of spit trailing from his lips.

With Briar's legs open on either side of Malric's waist, Malric straightened up and pulled off his shirt over his head, showing off the shape of his torso and the muscles of his stomach that always made Briar's eyes sparkle. Briar watched him the entire time, looking a little feverish and drunk, especially once Malric tossed his shirt to the floor and Briar smiled to himself at the sight of his bare chest.

"Hot," was all he could think to say, before clearly hating himself and slumping back into the pillows. "Oh, god, Jesus, lord —you're so fucking hot. Shut up, just—*ah!*"

Briar jumped as Malric hooked hands under his knees, curling his back as his legs were lifted open over either one of Malric's shoulders.

"Oh?" Malric asked, kissing the inside of Briar's thigh before practically bending the rosefinch in half to return his mouth between Briar's legs. They clenched against Malric's shoulders, then squeezed his head in delight as Malric felt the climax edging closer and closer. He just stroked with his tongue, his lips, teasing the center of Briar's ass with his thumb as Briar gasped and speckled with beads of sweat on his forehead and chest.

"I'm—!" Briar begged, unable to keep his eyes open or his mouth closed. Malric waited a moment longer—before pulling away, and laughing as Briar almost screamed as the peak was suddenly withheld from him. "You fucking—asshole, god, fuck you, *ugh...*"

"Did you like that?" Malric asked, smiling as Briar groaned beneath his weight, back curling further as Malric pressed his shoulders into the backs of Briar's thighs to push sweaty hair from his eyes. "Do you want more from me?"

"Yes," Briar moaned without hesitation. "Just—just put it in me, Mal, please..."

Without removing Briar's legs from his shoulders, Malric reached to the drawers of the bedside table. He removed the bottle of lube he knew to be there—and the look on Briar's face when he realized Malric could assume such a thing was enough to make Malric laugh. It didn't last long, though, as he spilled a line between Briar's legs, then stroked and coaxed a finger inside. Briar's expression fell entirely, practically melting off his face as his lips parted in overwhelm and he sank back into the pillows.

"Just—do it," Briar begged weakly. "Don't make me wait."

"I don't think so," Malric whispered, his opposite hand taking a hold of Briar's thigh and squeezing. "You're so small—I might hurt you."

"Oh, *fuck,*" Briar moaned like that was the hottest thing anyone had ever said to him. Malric just smiled to himself, easing his finger in and out gently, before introducing another, then another. He focused on Briar's breaths every time, listening for any change in rhythm, for any hint it was too much. But the longer Malric took to be careful—the more impatient he grew, too.

"Do you want me to wear a condom?" Malric asked, before huffing because the phrasing *definitely* made him sound like an asshole. "I mean—"

"Mal—just fuck me already, *damnit!*" Briar cried out, straining against the sweater pinning his arms and rattling the headboard in declaration.

Malric removed his fingers in an instant, and Briar jumped, biting his lip in surprise. With a command like that, Malric wasn't going to wait any longer, he wasn't going to continue to coddle the creature in front of him—Briar would just have to bear it if he couldn't handle it. Malric couldn't wait any longer, either, about to tear through what clothing he still wore.

Undoing the button and zipper on his pants, he slid his length up and down between Briar's legs, as if to remind him what he was begging for.

"Do you regret not letting me warm you up?" he asked in a low voice, but Briar just shook his head. Teasing it between Briar's legs, Malric shuddered at how, when flush between Briar's hips—it reached within a few inches of his bellybutton. Despite the demands, just like every other time, Malric would still have to be careful.

"Briar," Malric said seriously, leaning forward to take Briar's chin to ensure they met eyes. "If it doesn't feel good, you can stop me. I'll take care of you, so just—don't just endure anything that doesn't drive you crazy."

"Everything you do—drives me crazy," Briar moaned, rolling his hips and inviting Mal closer on his own—only to cry out in pleasure when Mal finally pushed himself inside, caging Briar against the bed as the dancer's wrists strained against the sweater keeping them restrained.

He left Briar's wrists tied even as he thrust inside, hanging over him and bracing one hand on the headboard. Moving his hips in and out with intention, he memorized every shift of pleasure crossing Briar's delicate features. He burned each flicker of passion into his memory, how it differed from the rabid heat of the first time and all the times after, how every smooth stroke of his hips made Briar's eyelashes flutter, his cheeks flush, his lips part as if searching for breath despite not being crushed. Suffocated by pleasure only. By the pleasure Malric provided him, and would continue to provide him until he evaporated into a misty afterglow.

Malric had never felt more powerful, more domineering, than in those moments he watched Briar's expression change with every movement of his own hips. How even the most gentle of movements could summon the most enthralling, wanton looks from someone so demanding—to reduce them to nothing but moans and sharp intakes of breath, giving way to anything and everything Malric did to him without complaint, only compliments in the form of Malric's name falling from his kiss-bruised mouth wet with spit. Malric's muscles quivered with want to break him in half—until, eventually, he nearly did. Clutching Briar's body into his chest and slamming deeply into them, holding them close as they gasped and trembled, climaxing hard enough their breaths tightened into whimpers.

Malric loved Briar into what could only be described as a *coma,* and reveled in his own fine work as his rosefinch slept amongst buckled pillows and a nest of messy hair. He couldn't resist tucking strands from their flushed, dewy face, resting his chin in his hand and smiling to himself as if he gazed upon something rare and invaluable. Perhaps that was exactly what it was. He leaned down to kiss Briar's damp forehead, tucking loose strands away, swearing to never forget how it felt for Briar Hunt to be his.

MALRIC SLEPT DEEPER THAN HE KNEW POSSIBLE, knowing it definitely had to do with where he rested, with whom he rested, nestled together on Briar's lavender sheets that smelled like him over every inch. On the pillowcases just worn enough from use, and the rhythmic ticking, tapping, whooshing of wind out the window and Briar's little trinkets throughout the room.

For the first time in a long time, Malric slept without a single fear at all.

He slept until the sun rose, filling the room with a cozy, romantic, overcast light, the kind that only came with a blanket of fresh snow on the ground outside. It was his first view of the bedroom in the daylight since the very, very first time he visited, and something about that was... charming. He couldn't help but smile as his eyes fluttered open, patting the bed next to him to find Briar missing, but the sound of the shower down the hall answered that question before he could ask it. Instead of getting up to join him, Malric just closed his eyes again, sinking back into the blankets with a contented sigh as he rubbed his eyes.

Briar would dance at that gala with Leon in a few more days, and everything would be fixed. He would never return to the fey world—and Malric never would, either. Neither would any of his siblings, who were finding all the help they needed with underground resources to help people exactly like them on the human side. Resources, education, assistance for high fey displaced by war or unrest or—well, abusive mothers working them to the bone.

When the shower cut off in the other room, Malric called out Briar's name, singing for him to hurry back to bed before Malric went and got him, himself. The sound of Briar's laugh from the bathroom made butterflies fill Malric's stomach, and he grinned at all the thoughts of what they might do that day to pass the time. He had a suggestion on his tongue right as Briar came racing into the room—only to stop short, eyes going wide as they landed on Malric still in bed.

Malric made a face of confusion, trying to figure out the joke. He sat up on one elbow, motioning with a finger for Briar to join him back under the blankets—but Briar didn't move. He'd gone completely still, petrified, right where he stood. Malric nearly asked what was wrong—but the tiniest peek of sun poked through the clouds outside, beaming through the window, illuminating his reflection in the mirror on Briar's vanity. Malric couldn't help but look—and his heart stopped. He stared at the person who stared back at him, and his worst nightmare unfolded faster than he could stop it.

Pointed ears. Perfect, angular features. Smooth skin. Shiny, tousled auburn hair that hung a few inches longer than that of Mr. Mal, the dance instructor.

Over the door—Malric spotted a charmed bag embroidered with a clover, a stalk of wheat. An anti-glamour charm, gone unnoticed by him in the dark. His real face, gone unnoticed by them both all night long.

The towel in Briar's hand flopped to the floor. They still didn't move, didn't blink. They didn't even breathe, just—staring at him. Briar might as well have been a million miles away. Despite being so close, despite the heat of their body still coating the blankets where Malric still reclined—Briar was both there, and gone. Malric saw the exact moment it clicked behind the rosefinch's eyes. That moment he realized—exactly who Malric was, and who he had been the entire time.

"Bry—"

"You—" Briar croaked, like he'd been punched in the chest. No other words followed them, though Briar's mouth dangled open in wanting to say more.

Malric just stared at Briar as his thoughts raced, searching for anything at all he could say, but he kept getting caught in the tangle in his mind that wouldn't allow him to move forward. One not placed there by a fey deal, by his mother—but by Malric's own horror in what came to light in front of him. His own trickery, his own lies.

That was his opportunity to tell Briar everything. To explain everything, to reassure him Malric never meant him any harm, he'd only been trying to do what was in his own power to protect him—but he knew from the look on Briar's face, it wouldn't matter. Those walls were back, those walls Briar hid behind the very first time they met. They were back, and they were thicker, heavier than ever. Just like that.

Malric could see it so clearly written on Briar's expression, he didn't even have to speak the words out loud for them to ricochet off the ceiling and bang around in Malric's skull.

I trusted you.

It all moved too quickly for Malric to react. He never got his chance to come up with the perfect thing to say to, at the least, dump water on Briar's explosive reaction. No, there was only yelling. Screaming. Crying. Briar rushed Malric in the bed, grabbing and yanking him from the blankets. He slammed his fists against Malric's chest as tears spilled from his eyes, cheeks shiny in the low light of the apartment as Malric fought to speak over him. But Briar wouldn't listen, Briar just shoved Malric's clothes into Malric's arms and shoved him back. Back and back and back, until he hit the front door. And then Briar shoved him out of that, too, slamming and locking it in Malric's wake.

Malric dropped his clothes and pounded on the door. He shook the doorknob and begged Briar to unlock it, to listen to him, to let him explain, but there was no more sound on the other side. Only the distant, short-lived scream from farther into the apartment—and then silence. Silence so sudden, so chilling, it made Malric's ears ring.

"Briar?" he croaked, shaking the knob again. When someone down the hall poked their head out and cleared their throat, Malric turned, only then remembering other people existed in the reality he shared with his rosefinch. He moved robotically, ears buzzing like they were full of crickets as he yanked his pants and shirt back on. He didn't have his shoes. Even if he could glamour some, his feet would still be bare to the cold outside.

Why did it suddenly go so quiet on the other side of the door?

Why did Briar have to shove Malric out without his phone to call Bianca for help?

Why—did Malric mislead someone so fragile for so long? Did he really think it would never come to a head? How could he have let himself be so arrogant to think he really—could control both his own fate, and Briar's at the same time?

Was he any different from Marie, who grasped Briar by the

throat every time she called him for another dance? Satisfied by his obedience, just as Malric had been every time Briar took one of his hints and delivered it back across the veil, thinking he was scheming with two people who cared for him?

Two people, whittled to one, then burned until, as far as Briar knew, there was nothing. There was no one. There was no friendly fox-lord. There was no handsome dance instructor. There was only Malric d'Alarie, the son of the woman who'd destroyed Briar's life.

29

BRIAR AND THE TRICK

Briar couldn't move his hands. No—he couldn't move any part of his body at all. He could only stand in the doorway to his bedroom, staring at the sheets where he and Mal had slept piled on top of one another. Safe, warm, unbothered. He just stared as that same person pounded on the front door of the apartment, begging Briar to let him back in. To unlock the door. To listen to him.

Briar lifted his stiff hands and pressed them to his ears. Harder and harder and harder until his wrist popped under the strain—but he could still hear it. The pounding on the door, the panic in Mal's voice—the sincerity in Mal's voice as he told Briar how beautiful he was the night before. Mal's hands pounding on the door—that had held Briar lovingly in the dark, bending and caressing him, leaving bruises on his thighs and his waist, never giving Briar the gentleness he hated, always giving him the care he craved.

How could Briar have let it happen, all over again?

How could he have fallen for the same trick all over again?

How could he have let a high fey sniff out his grief—and take advantage of it, so easily?

The humiliation dropped like a hundred rocks on his back, in his stomach. He bent his knees beneath him, crouching to the floor with his hands still over his ears—and screamed.

THE DAY PASSED IN A HAZE.
The day passed in a haze.
The day passed in a haze.
Staring at the wall where he sat on the floor, unable to stomach crawling into bed.

Sitting on the couch with Stella and watching movies, smiling and laughing and making conversation as if someone else had taken control of his body. A demon that felt nothing, while Briar's ghost dangled in the upper corner of the room, looming, floating, feeling nothing.

If he felt nothing, there would be no grief. There would be nothing for anyone else to sense and prey on. Mal might lose track of Briar entirely. He might find someone else to pamper then rip open to see what was hiding inside. Briar was tired of being opened up—but he was more tired of offering them a penetrable person to open in the first place.

He wouldn't do that anymore. Briar wouldn't feel grief, he wouldn't open to anyone. Briar would just watch movies with his best friend; listen to her chatter about her girlfriend. He would eat dinner with her, then sit on the couch when she left to go to her girlfriend's place for the night.

He would sit on the couch until the sun came up, then eat breakfast without tasting it. He would spin and spin and spin on that worn spot in the hardwood at the foot of his bed, with the full-body mirror turned away so he wouldn't have to look at himself.

He wouldn't remember getting dressed, pulling on a coat and boots, grabbing his wallet and keys, and leaving the apartment. He wouldn't comprehend climbing on the bus, the light rail, and walking into the first building he knew to have loud music and bright lights and overpriced drinks.

He wouldn't realize what he was doing until it was too late, with his phone out and a message already sent. Waiting for a reply. The way he felt nothing when a response came was the first time he fluttered back into his body, just for a moment, and questioned what he was doing at all.

> single again.

> wanna meet downtown for a drink?

HE DRANK MORE THAN HE USUALLY DID, MOSTLY TO ease his nerves. Leon, somehow, kept up with him—until Briar couldn't ignore the way Leon looked at him. With something like curiosity, something like... surprise, as if it was the first time he ever actually noticed Briar at all. Sitting at the bar together, dancing together, then—kissing in the club bathroom, before tumbling into a cab.

Briar used to fantasize about what it would be like to kiss Leon Heller. He thought Leon might taste like... pine, or something. Pine and honey and old leather, like in romance novels.

But when he finally had his chance, Leon just tasted like a mistake. Well, a mistake mixed with lots of expensive club drinks and weed, as Briar couldn't resist what Leon's roommates were smoking once they made it to the apartment.

Leon didn't taste *bad*, but he didn't taste *good*.

Leon's hands drunkenly groping him in bed wasn't *bad*, but it wasn't *good*. The compliments Leon gave him in the dark weren't *bad;* they weren't *good*. Briar's orgasm wasn't *bad* or *good*. It was all, simply... nothing. He felt nothing.

Well, at first he felt nothing. The longer he went realizing there truly was no real spark between himself and the person he threw his life away for, though, the more disappointment turned into dread, and then misery, and then pure agony after he came and couldn't stop the humiliating panic attack that left him screaming and crying into Leon's pillows as Leon showered off down the hall.

Fuck. Briar had really thrown his entire life away for nothing. For literally nothing.

He pretended to be asleep when Leon came back. But Leon never joined him in bed—he just peeked into the bedroom. Left a glass of water and Tylenol on the side table. Adjusted Briar's blankets. Then—left, maybe to sleep on the couch.

Briar wanted to tear out of his skin.

Something rapped on the window the next morning, waking him. Was it the meteor he'd manifested coming to destroy the planet? Ah—no. It was Marie d'Alarie's magpie.

Briar stared at it for a long time. That bird he knew maybe better than he should have, who could find Briar literally anywhere. In the middle of shopping, in class, on the bus, and, apparently, in the bed of his most recent night of disappointment. He'd even come to befriend the animal somewhat, occasionally inviting it into his room when it arrived during a thunderstorm and feeding it pumpkin seeds before unfurling the fey woman's summoning. But that morning, despite the fluffy snow tumbling from the sky, Briar didn't move when he met the bird's eyes. He normally addressed it right away, so the hesitation appeared to even catch the messenger off guard. It tilted its head in confusion, then papped its beak against the glass again, as if thinking Briar hadn't heard it the first time.

But the thought of accepting another request to dance... made his stomach turn over. What if Malric was there again to humiliate him? What if everyone there knew how Briar had trusted the fey lord just like the fey lady, how foolish he was, how he'd looked so stupid and embarrassed himself so badly?

Briar... didn't want anything to do with them, for more reasons than just because he regretted the deal he made.

Briar wanted to disappear from them. From the world. From

any place where any fey creature could lay a hand on him or even whisper false promises into his ear.

The bird pecked the glass again, and Briar snapped. He leapt off the bed, rushing to the window. He threw the pane open, flailing his arms and shouting for it to leave. It squawked and flapped backward, tumbling into the railing with a clang before scrambling away into the sky. Briar only felt a little bit bad.

Foolish. So fucking stupid.

He made it back home with enough time to spare for a shower before his first class that morning—and he spent it in a fugue state snipping new, imagined branches from under the skin of his palms, sprouting from his elbows. Maybe he needed another charm bag. One for every room. One to wear around his neck. He tugged on the golden necklace as he thought about it, stomach turning over when he was reminded of how he'd rejected the fey lady's summon for a dance that morning. It would be just like that time in the alleyway—a dream. Only a dream.

As he plucked sprouts from under his skin, even as he clambered out and rubbed moisturizer across his face, Stella blocked him in the bathroom as she gave him her most intense big-sister-mom-friend glare.

"What?" he snapped, but she just pinched his cheek until he swore at her.

"Did you fuck him?"

"Who?"

"Well—Leon. You sent me the weirdest text last night, saying you were with him."

"Does it matter?"

"I'm only curious. Was it everything you ever hoped it would be?"

Briar frowned. He puffed out his cheeks, then pouted his mouth and averted his eyes toward the steamy mirror. Leon hadn't even left any hickies on him. His mouth wasn't sore and swollen from being passionately crushed beneath someone wanting to eat him alive. His scalp didn't throb from his hair being pulled. He barely ached in his ass or tailbone.

"It was whatever," he mumbled, and Stella let out a breath like a wheezing dog.

"Oh, god, you're kidding me—he was only *okay?*"

Briar flushed, pushing past Stella who immediately chased him down with more questions, searching for gossip.

"Is he big? Is he a good kisser? What's he like in bed? Is he rough? Or soft? Did you guys listen to music while you did it? Does he shave? Wait, who topped?"

"I hate you," Briar complained, but Stella followed him the rest of the way into his room to sit on his bed while he pulled on clothes for the day. His head spun, face still boiling with heat though he genuinely didn't know why. He was normally open about telling Stella everything, since sex wasn't anything for him to be embarrassed or shy about—but something about admitting to his best friend that sex with the person he'd obsessed over for so long was more embarrassing than if he told her he'd puked all over Leon's sheets, or something. Maybe he should have lied about that, instead. Something about it was easier to swallow.

"He's... average," Briar started in a low voice. "He kisses fine. He was fine. He wasn't rough. We listened to Hozier. He doesn't shave. He topped. I came exactly one time, and so did he. We used a condom. He showered right after, then slept on the couch. He offered me a bowl of cereal this morning before I left, but I said no. He told me to text him when I made it home."

Stella stared at him like she'd just sucked on a lemon, but was in that transition period where her tongue didn't know if it was sweet or sour. Like she was waiting for something else. For anything else. For any kind of further emotion or reaction or expression to cross Briar's face.

"Oh..." she finally trailed off, then bit her lip like she was trying to hold back her laugh. Briar smiled at her weakly in encouragement, silently telling her it was fine to find it all so very funny. She finally broke, bursting out laughing and tumbling back onto the bed. "He's average! He's vanilla! He's just a nice, simple guy you can take home to mom! Oh, you poor thing."

"Really unfortunate," Briar mumbled, but the sarcastic smile lingered. He pulled on a pair of forest plaid Burberry pants and an Isabel Marant crop top knotted at the waist. He pulled on his boots, next, just grateful there was no dance practice with Mal that morning. He didn't want to think about it. He wanted to stay far, far away, especially if the fey lord was still wandering around on campus for one reason or another. Briar... didn't want to know.

"Leon will be someone else's prince charming," he finally said while braiding his hair over one shoulder, then pulling on a thick winter coat. "Someone who likes to be fucked gently."

"Lovingly?"

Briar almost responded sarcastically, but it caught in the back of his throat.

"I don't know," he whispered. Whatever it was he did with Leon the night before—it wasn't cruel, but it wasn't *loving*, either.

Leon never thought Briar was anything special, and that was fine. It was just a casual hookup. Two friends finally fucking because they were a little drunk, and why not. So why was he so frustrated by all of it?

He's nothing special.

Briar's stomach turned. He let out a long breath through his nose, closing his eyes and shaking his head.

"Come on," he mumbled. "We better get going, or we'll be late."

30

BRIAR AND THE ROOTS

The following afternoon, Briar and Leon finally had a private practice, away from all the rude, judgemental eyes of Leon's classmates. It went better in that way—but worse in others. Briar was growing glamoured vines inside of him. He was growing branches under his skin. He just wanted to get it out of the way, in order to race back home again to cut them all off and drink a bottle of wine and pretend none of it was happening at all.

Pretend he'd never made his stupid deal in the first place.

Pretend he hadn't fallen for Mal's trick not once, but twice.

Pretend Leon didn't keep trying to bring up their night together, to which Briar always found a way to change the subject because he just couldn't stomach the thought of *re-hashing* a one-night stand with someone as nice and simple as Leon was.

Pretend there wasn't enough cortisol in his body to make every muscle hurt; and to pretend like he didn't keep finding splinters growing out from under his nails, deep and thick enough that he thought his nails might pop off; pretend he hadn't already seen exactly what was happening to him in every nightmare leading up to that moment, and how there was nothing he could do about it, and how there was a small part of him that knew it might not just be a glamour at all, and knowing Mal was the only person he ever could call to possibly help him, only for the thought to bend him over the gutter outside Tomassin and puke until he couldn't breathe. Nausea that made the world spin while he kicked his bike home, hating how his ankle barely ever hurt, anymore. Stomach-churning agony that nearly made it impossible to even lift his bike up the front steps so he could go home. He just wanted to go home. He just wanted to go to bed and disappear and pretend, pretend, pretend—

Briar slammed the door shut behind him. He stripped his bag off, then his coat, meaning to throw them onto the bed but missing and slamming them to the floor. He barely realized.

Approaching his vanity, he dug through the clutter for a pair of tweezers. Pinching them over the tip of the biggest splinter under his nail, he wrenched it out in one swift movement—only for a cry of pain to break from his mouth as it felt attached to the bone in his thumb, ripping away with barbs and leaving him bleeding. His heart pounded, staring at the bubbling blood that came instantly, then moving his eyes to the splinter—and stopping short.

It wasn't just a splinter. It wasn't just a glamour. It actually had... roots. Little, hairlike roots splitting from the bottom like a sapling searching for water deeper in the earth. They weren't a glamour at all. They weren't a psychic trick. They weren't just a dream. Briar really was—becoming one with the trees.

But it had started before he ever denied the fey lady's magpie summons, unless—unless that hadn't actually been the first time. Unless, the reason Mal had been spending so much time with Briar, the reason Briar never witnessed any of the birds, the reason he found splinters before ever denying anything, himself—was because Mal had been doing it for him, behind his back. Mal had cursed him, first.

His hand shook, accidentally dropping the root, but it didn't matter. He heard only the pounding of his heart in his ears, turning his hand back over again to find another. To pull it out from the base instead of just cutting off the head and assuming that would be enough.

He winced, pulling out a second one. It wasn't as thick, as barbed as the first, but still pulled from deep within his skin.

Searching for more, he found a third in his opposite hand. A fourth in the curve of his thumb.

He used the tweezers to flay his skin apart, one after another, biting back tears as he burrowed the pincers into his skin—but when he really looked close, there were more dark spots freckling the palm of his hand than he could count. More speckled down his wrist. Up his forearm.

Stripping off his shirt, he threw it to the floor. He kicked off his shoes and socks, next, shoving his legs from his pants and searching the rest of his body. There were spots on his toes, too. On the tops of his feet. Spreading up his ankles, before fading within his shins.

His thoughts boiled, but he managed to grab a damp towel from the night before and rush to the bathroom. He turned the water on as hot as he could, using a newer pair of eyebrow tweezers to hack at his skin and rip out more of the fibrous invaders. It was just like plucking arm and leg hairs. That was it. In fact, that's probably all it was. Clearly the stress just made his body hair grow in thicker and darker. He just needed to set up an appointment to get waxed. Maybe that would help him feel better all around, like a newborn baby. Like a fresh thing. Like a person who knew nothing of scratchy hairs or splinters or ferns tugging on his bare legs as he walked through thick undergrowth into a revel clearing—

When his fingers and hands were too swollen and painful to dig any longer, when he could no longer hold the tweezers between open, pinpricks of sore spots, he bit back frustrated tears and clattered them to the lip in the wall. Then, he scooped a handful of his most expensive body exfoliating cream and slathered it all over himself, biting back curses as it stung upon meeting any open wounds. And then—he scrubbed. With his sore nails, with his loofah, with the scratchy washcloth he normally used to scrub away backne. He scrubbed and scraped until every inch of his skin throbbed with his heartbeat, burning hot despite the water from the nozzle tempering out as he took way too much time.

He was alright. Everything was alright. He hadn't slept well in a few days, he was only seeing things. It might still only be a glamour. Just his imagination. A hallucination from the stress. He just needed to lay down and rest. He had to stop picking at his skin. There were not tiny branches... growing from under his skin.

His knees wobbled, and he buckled to the shower floor as it was suddenly hard to breathe. His whole body hurt, like a sunburn devoured every inch of skin. The steam in the room collected in a thick cloud, because he forgot to turn the fan on. He was—exhausted. His heart shouldn't be pounding so hard when he was so tired, when he hadn't slept, when he was so panicked by what he thought he saw—

The world wavered, as if underwater. His head sank to the side, resting against the cheap laminate wall tiles. Oh—it was all spinning. It wouldn't stop spinning, and Briar couldn't get a hold on to anything for support.

The bathroom door suddenly opened, and someone rushed inside. Briar's blurry vision made him think it was Stella at first, but then the sweeping scent of a bittersweet cologne struck his nose, and he almost puked.

Mal said his name pleadingly, scooping him off the floor of the tub before grabbing his hands and asking what was happening to him. Briar just fought to regain any ounce of composure he had left, pushing out of Mal's arms and nearly stumbling back to the ground again had the fey lord not caught him.

"No... fuck off," he whimpered, but Mal was already pulling him from the tub and tucking a towel into his hands. Briar took it, barely registering how his grasp left red pin pricks all over the fibers. "Let go of me... get off me... don't touch me..."

Stella stepped in, but not in a way she meant to shove Mal

back in aggression. She gently coaxed Briar from Mal's hands, and Briar took his chance to stumble out of the bathroom as she and the man—the fey lord—exchanged tense words. Briar just followed the hallway, dragging his hand down the wall until he reached his bedroom, where he slumped inside and locked it behind him.

The fresh air was crisp, bringing him back to his body in no time at all. Though, as soon as his mind swirled and settled again, he almost wished to go back to the flurry of heat and sweat as he heard Mal's voice on the other side of the door, saying something to Stella. To Bianca. Briar just squeezed his eyes closed, flattening his hands to his ears and shaking his head, begging Mal to leave. To go away. To disappear.

Leave me alone. Leave me alone. What else could you possibly do to me?

Briar dragged his throbbing, raw body to the bed. He collapsed into the blankets with a heavy breath, completely naked. He pulled the blankets around himself, sinking into them like a rock in a lake.

31

MALRIC AND THE CONFESSION

Days after Briar witnessed Malric's truth and shoved him out the door, Malric paced back and forth on the sidewalk outside of Briar's apartment until the sun went down. He'd done his best to give Briar space, to distract himself with his siblings, to keep just a close enough distance so Briar wouldn't answer any of Marie's calls—but, damnit, the silence was driving him mad.

But Briar didn't answer the door. His window was dark. Malric didn't want to panic—but he did. Of course he did. He broke his own biggest rule first, calling Briar over and over again. Then he called Stella. Then he called Bianca. Why wasn't anyone answering!?

It was freezing by the time Bianca and Stella stumbled around the corner, laughing and leaning on one another, at least a little bit intoxicated with big booming clouds of steam bursting from their mouths.

"Hey!" Malric snapped as they came into reach. As if on instinct, Stella suddenly lunged forward to put herself between Malric and Bianca, thinking it was a stranger about to rob them— but then she narrowed her eyes as the recognition crept through her drunkenness. Malric didn't have time to wait for her return greeting. His nerves only heightened when he saw Briar hadn't been out with them all night.

"Where's Briar?" he asked. "Do you know? Have you heard from him at all today?"

Stella still took a moment before answering, then straightened up. The way she squared her shoulders told Malric she had, indeed, heard something, despite her vague reply.

"Did you and Briar get into an argument or something?"

"Stella, by Danu's mounds, just *tell me if you know—*"

"Briar's fine," she interrupted him, and Malric's mouth clamped shut. He frowned at her, breathing through his nose and waiting for her to continue on her own. He wouldn't hesitate to push the issue more if she didn't. "He told me to tell you to leave him alone. Wouldn't tell me why, though, but now I'm beginning to think—"

"It's nothing," Malric was the one to interrupt that time. "It's *nothing.* Just tell me where he is so I can—"

"Nah." She shook her head. Bianca finally stepped out from behind her, frowning at Malric like she was disappointed in him for something. He pulled a face of exasperation right back at her. She didn't know what had happened, and neither did Stella, and in many ways neither did Briar—Malric just needed to talk to him. To explain as much as he could.

"Just leave him alone for now," Stella continued with a sigh, digging into her coat pocket for her keys.

Malric lashed out to grab Stella's wrist before she could open the door to the building. She retaliated, grabbing his wrist in return and twisting it in self defense. If Malric had been just another human, she might have snapped his arm backward entirely—but he wasn't human, and Stella must have realized as much as soon as he only grunted beneath her onslaught. She stared at him for a long time, before putting her hand to her face again and shaking her head.

"I must have had more to drink than I thought..." she mumbled, and Bianca finally stepped in as the buffer between them. She put her hand on Stella's arm, asking if it was alright for Malric to go upstairs with them to at least warm up before kicking him back to the curb, again. Stella sighed, rubbing her forehead with pinched brows before giving Malric a pointed look.

"*Fine.* But if Briar is home, don't bother him, okay? Or I'll throw you right back out the window."

Malric nodded. If he wasn't already a fey prone to trickery, he would have crossed his fingers behind his back.

Upon walking through the door to the apartment, there was no question whether or not Briar was there. The shower was running. Malric had to resist going straight for the bathroom and inviting himself in, just like he had once before—but Bianca eyed him closely, threateningly. She never pulled that gaze the whole time Malric sat at the laminate table with her while Stella brewed tea and they ordered dinner to be delivered. Briar remained in the shower. Malric kept his eyes on the bathroom door.

He was going to tear out of his skin. That person who'd been avoiding him, who he'd been trying so hard to give space, was right on the other side of the wall. Malric just wanted to see him, wanted to speak with him, wanted to do and say anything he could to prove he wasn't as evil and cruel as his trick made him out to be—

But then he heard something thump to the floor, and his ears perked for a different reason. Even Stella stopped speaking for a pause, glancing toward the bathroom. Malric got to his feet without any further prompting, and no one stopped him. His vision tunneled, his focus sharpened. He went straight for the door, not thinking about what he would say upon opening it— but then, in a cloud of steam and the smell of shampoo, Briar was slumped in the tub. Malric's heart exploded, and he rushed in.

Throwing his arms into the basin, Briar was wobbly and disoriented from the heat—

No, not the heat, Malric realized in horror. Every inch of Briar was pricked with a thousand red spots, tiny cuts, speckled with debris like dirt and broken leaves. In the bottom of the tub—

more leaves, bark, scattered twigs, whisked toward the drain by the pounding water from the showerhead and clustering to clog the gap. Malric's breath caught. Oh, what—

What the fuck was going on?

He scooped his arms under Briar's naked body, lifting him from the tub with a soft gasp of his name, asking if he was alright, what was going on—but Briar just pushed back on him, shoving away, mumbling for Malric to fuck off. To leave him alone. Malric couldn't breathe.

The rest came in a blur. Stella entering the bathroom, asking what was going on; Briar escaping in the middle of the confusion. Out of Malric's reach, despite whatever was happening to him. No, no, no—why wouldn't Briar look at him? Why wouldn't Briar talk to him? Malric—might be able to help, Malric might...

But Briar was already gone. Vanished into the hallway, into his bedroom, behind another door.

Stella shuffled Malric from the bathroom, mumbling under her breath in question when she saw the state of the bathtub. Bianca took Malric's hand and pulled him up the hallway, calling out to Stella that they were going to wait for the food delivery down on the curb. She didn't even give Malric a chance to pull his coat on.

His ears rang as they left through the door. Down the outside hallway. Down the stairs. Through the main door, before halting on the sidewalk outside. He couldn't completely remember how he got there. He only saw Briar in the tub. Only smelled the steam and the shampoo. Only recalled that look on Briar's face in the brief moment they met eyes, how he looked—broken, and scared, and empty, all at once.

"Why don't you tell me everything?"

Malric turned to her. She gazed straight ahead, like she didn't want to look at him. He couldn't tell if she was angry, or worried, but neither would have been ideal. Malric almost decided to be stubborn, to be difficult, to ask what she was talking about—but then he glanced back at the building. Briar's bedroom window wasn't visible from where they stood, but Malric wondered if they were still awake. If their light was on. If they'd gone to bed. If they were...

Closing his eyes, he dug a cigarette from his pocket. Lighting it, he inhaled a long, hot breath.

Malric told Bianca everything, everything he possibly could, even the things he should have only ever kept in his heart. Things Briar would beat his ass for revealing, but were too heavy to hold back as soon as the landslide of words found its velocity out of his mouth.

It's like I said at the club that night—Briar made a fey deal with my mother and has been dancing for her for months. I followed him here, through the veil. I pretended to be a dance instructor at Artemisia. I tried to help him, but every time I did, it only hurt him. All I ever do is hurt him, Bee, and this last time was the worst betrayal of all. I don't know if he'll ever speak to me again. He might never look at me again. What am I supposed to do now?

Bianca didn't know everything about the fey world, she'd never even visited, herself, but she knew enough for the blood to drain from her face as Malric laid everything out. More than once, she opened her mouth to say something, to ask a question, before biting her lip and holding it back.

"Briar... is back to his old habits, these past couple of days," she finally said, voice quiet. The steam was thick on her breath. "Going out, drinking, finding somewhere else to spend the night. Stella's worried sick, of course, but he's at least communicating this time around. I didn't see what happened in the bathroom just now, but... he's... *fine,* all things considered. He even spent the night with Leon a few nights ago, so maybe this is just how he's coping. In his own way..."

Coping. *Coping.* Malric had done that, hadn't he? Pushed Briar—to need to *cope* with anything at all, hadn't he?

Malric d'Alarie, despite having good intentions, was as selfish and cruel as his mother was. As self-absorbed, obsessed with getting everything he wanted, no matter the cost. And Briar had found himself crushed between the two of them. Crushed from both sides, pulled in two different directions, back and forth until his bones and soul snapped into a million pieces not unlike when that fey healer snapped his ankle with ease. Without a single flinch from himself, or anyone else in the revel clearing. With only Briar left screaming and crying, with no one there to help him, even the person who, right on the other side of the veil, declared every promise he could think of just to make Briar trust him implicitly.

"Fuck," he croaked, pressing his palms into his eyes as his entire being trembled. Why did that memory, the taste of those words, strike him like lightning?

"Fuck." He grit his teeth. "Oh, fuck, fuck, fuck, gods, fuck—"

Bianca rubbed her hand up and down Malric's back, as if to comfort him. But he didn't deserve it, he didn't deserve that gentleness.

All of it combined with that additional thought that crushed his heart in all the ways he wasn't prepared for—that additional thought of what Briar had done with Leon. What they talked about. If Briar opened up to him, told him things he'd only before trusted Malric with. Things Malric had taken, and held, and used against them without meaning to. Trust that was broken after only given once earned.

He wondered—if they indulged in one another. If Briar saw that Leon would never, ever treat him like Malric did—

But wasn't that better? Wasn't that better, for Briar to find and cling to someone who treated him exactly how Malric didn't...?

Malric, who hurt him. Who hurt him beyond belief, but wanted a single chance to explain, to beg for forgiveness even if Briar wouldn't give it. Just so Briar would know how desperate he was, enough to beg on his knees. One of the most dangerous things a high fey lord could do.

Malric just—hadn't been able to tell Briar enough. He hadn't been able to explain *enough*, in the exact right way, how he thought Briar was perfect. He needed Briar to know. He needed

Briar to *know*, in the deepest reaches of his being, how Malric felt about him—

But even if he had managed to string those flawless words together—it would have all crumbled the moment Briar saw who he'd really allowed into his bed. Into that one place he never brought home strangers to share with him. He'd invited Malric into the one place he was the most vulnerable, and Malric thanked him by tearing his trust into bloody shreds.

By leaving Briar on his own, to seek comfort elsewhere, anywhere he could find it—until littered with bleeding pockmarks across his body, more on the verge of poking through his skin, a trail of leaves and twigs behind him on the bathroom floor and in the shower. A fey curse. A fey trick. One Malric should have seen coming, should have warned him about, somehow—

But Malric had waited too long. Malric had left Briar to suffer alone for too long—and to see Briar's face, one of terror so different from that they wore the morning they realized who Malric really was—

Malric would never wipe that image from his mind, for as long as he lived.

3 2

MALRIC AND THE CONSEQUENCE

Malric sat on Stella's couch, catatonic, for hours, staring at Briar's door the entire time. Barely breathing, barely moving, as Stella and Bianca shared quiet conversation in Stella's bedroom after eating dinner in silence. His phone lit up constantly with messages from his siblings, asking if everything was alright, because he had been supposed to meet them, earlier. He'd completely forgotten. He'd forgotten everything the moment he saw Briar limp in the bathtub.

Leaves and twigs emerging from Briar's body, all over him, like saplings from freshly-tilled earth.

Malric pressed his face into his hands, dragging them down and nearly suffocating himself. What had he done? What had he done...?

The sky grew dark through the windows, Stella and Bianca grew quiet in bed, and it was only when the apartment fell into complete silence that Malric heard the telltale *thump* of a body hitting the floor. Only Briar was left to make such a noise, and Malric was on his feet in an instant. Just like the first time.

He hovered outside Briar's door, listening. He held his breath, closing his eyes to focus every sense on his ears. Through the wood—there was the sound of quiet groans. Dragging limbs. Gasping and choking. Snipping scissors.

Malric grabbed the doorknob, but it didn't budge. That tiny, final denial of his help shot fire through his muscles—and without meaning to, his hand clenched tight, crumpling the metal between his fingers. He could only shakily pull away with a sharp breath, before shaking his head and shoving his way inside.

Searching the bedroom, it wasn't clear right away where Briar was. Malric slowly closed the door behind him, not wanting Stella or Bianca to accidentally see if there was something terrible on the other side—and only then did Malric spot the scattered leaves, the twigs, the freckles of blood on the hardwood floor, on the opposite side of the bed. The closer he looked, he finally spotted a foot, next, and his heart leapt into his throat. He rushed forward, only to reel back again with a sharp gasp.

Briar turned to look at him from where he sat, eyes glazed over in a mix of exhaustion and fear. His mouth dangled open, wobbling, before words escaped between his lips and ripped Malric's heart from his chest.

"What's h-happening to me, my—my lord?" they asked the fey lord in front of them, stripped of his glamour by the charm nailed over the door.

Those words, spoken beneath a veil of terror and agony and someone who had carried too much in silence for too long. Hair messy and loose and knotted over bumps as if a crown of twigs had gotten snarled. His hands, swollen and gnarled with fresh blood oozing from every place he ripped each piece of wood. That deep flutter in his voice, the wheezing of wind through thick tree branches, as if they slowly infiltrated his chest as well as they did under his skin.

Malric's rosefinch—was being eaten from the inside out, faster than he could keep it at bay, and had been for a while. He kept it to himself, until on the verge of being swallowed by bark and leaves, even fighting Malric off hours prior when he finally saw it for himself. But Briar could no longer hide it—he could no longer keep it hidden.

Malric took a step closer. Briar just watched him, crimson-wet hands hovering slightly off his lap as if it hurt too much to even lay them flat. His eyes were swollen and pink from crying, cheeks glistening with tears and mouth hanging open against a sob that would break at any moment. Every breath was haggard. Every breath was forced through branches tangling inside of him.

That must have been the punishment Maura warned him about on the ferry, the one Malric wondered of when visiting his mother to inquire about Briar's deal. The one he should have pushed harder to know, the one he'd left without ever learning.

Malric—had done that, too. He'd allowed that consequence to unfurl, all those times he scared Marie's bird away, thinking there would be time. He'd allowed himself to be arrogant, to think no consequence would come before Briar could have his final dance. He'd—never even thought to ask Briar, themself, what would happen if they refused Marie's bird. Whether they knew it or not.

How could he have been so inconsiderate?

Sinking to his knees in front of Briar, Malric's hand shook as he tucked a strand of messy hair from Briar's face. Up close, he saw all the pricks of scabbed blood where Briar had snipped too close to the skin of his cheeks, his forehead, his neck, in a desperate attempt to halt the growth poking through him. He must have been in agony.

"I'm... sorry," Malric whispered, and Briar's expression crumpled. His lips pressed together, head lolling heavily forward as his shoulders moved with exhausted sobs. Tears dripped between Briar's bent knees, mixing with the scattered blood spots and broken twigs.

Malric just kept his hand on Briar's hair. He combed it back, before flattening his hand to gently pet him. Beneath his touch, he felt a myriad more buds poking through Briar's scalp. On the verge of bursting through with leaves and knots.

"I'm sorry, Briar," he went on, voice cracking. "I'm so sorry, I'm so sorry, for everything..."

Briar didn't say anything, just weakly shook his head. He had no more fight in him, no more sarcastic replies or arguments. Malric hated it. It felt so wrong. Briar should have screamed at him, clawed at him, hit him and cursed him.

But the person in front of him—had been left on his own for too long. Malric had waited too long for someone who was too proud to ask for help, from anyone. He should have known Briar would never reach out to him, anyway—the person who betrayed him the worst. The person he knew better than to ever trust again, even with what was happening to him.

"... I read this book, once," he croaked. Briar stiffened beneath him, barely lifting his red eyes to meet Malric's in the low evening light. "It was about a musician... who thought he could save the person he put in a terrible position, but in reality, couldn't even save himself..."

Briar lifted his eyes slightly more. Malric never blinked, fighting to keep his expression calm.

"The musician ran away from home, because the music he loved was being used against him in a way that he started to resent it. He agreed to never play music ever again, so long as he could live freely.

"The musician was replaced by someone else who played the same music. And that person was being used in the same way he had been."

He tucked another piece of hair behind Briar's ear.

"The musician thought himself... clever. He thought he could outwit his mother into letting the new musician go, perhaps before they, too, came to resent the thing they were so good at...

"But the moment the musician stepped back into the web, there was nothing but pain. Nothing but tricks. Nothing but... hurting the other musician he was trying so hard to save, no matter what he did. Because he thought he could... he *should* do it all by himself, because... he believed... it was his fault the new musician was trapped at all. Because he'd run away and left a gap for someone else to have to fill. But..."

His hand trailed down to Briar's leg bent closest to him, brushing his thumb over the rough skin that had once been soft as silk.

"All he did... was hurt the new musician, who didn't understand what was going on. Again and again, the newest musician kept getting caught up in what the old musician wanted to control... The musician pushed, and pushed, and pushed against the powers that be, thinking he could save the new musician eventually, but—in many ways, he thought it was like saving himself, instead. And he lost sight of the new musician entirely, and how badly he hurt them every time he tried something new, until..."

The words caught in the back of his throat. Briar's stormy blue eyes never left his, though every inch of him trembled.

"The musician... hurt the very person they were trying to save, beyond forgiveness."

The final words came in a choked whisper, and Malric finally turned his eyes away from Briar's. He couldn't stomach it.

"But it was all selfish," he croaked. "It was selfish to think... I could have everything I wanted, exactly how I wanted it... that the person I cared for would do whatever I said, whatever I wished, without asking any questions..."

He lifted his eyes again, brimming with emotion.

"Doesn't that make me just as bad as her?"

Briar's chin quivered—and then he burst into real tears. Gasping and sobbing and choking on breaths attempting to be stolen by the curse in his lungs. He collapsed into Malric's body, and Malric immediately embraced him. Pulling him close, Briar cried into his shirt. Malric could only cling to him tightly, wishing to give him the breath in his own lungs if it would ease the pain.

IT WASN'T FORGIVENESS, NOT REALLY. PERHAPS JUST enough to trust Malric to hold him while lying in Briar's bed, stroking the back of his head, down his spine, feeling for every shaky breath that came and went. Malric knew it wasn't the forgiveness he wanted, he needed, because—the Briar he knew would not have folded so easily. Would not have accepted his repentance without more of a fight, or at least not without expressing his own feelings about how stupid and fucked up Malric was. The fact Briar closed his eyes after sinking into Malric's arms, didn't argue when Malric lifted him into bed, and then even crawled in alongside him—told Malric his rosefinch was too tired to fight. Too tired to be angry. He didn't feel anything except fear, and pain.

Malric held him close. He never closed his eyes, even as the sun fully set, even as the street outside grew quiet as midnight ticked by. He wouldn't. He was too busy ensuring Briar continued to breathe, one after another, all while feeling how the nubby branches grew from his skin despite being picked and ripped away. Malric knew they would only continue to grow until he ended the curse. One more day. Just one more day. Briar would dance with Leon that next night at the charity performance, and he would find the relief he'd been seeking for so long. He would hear those words he'd been seeking for so long, from the mouth of the person who rooted Briar's deal into existence. From the mouth of someone beautiful—

You were perfect.

But then something shifted in the corner of the room, and Malric sought it out. His heart pattered in an oncoming fury, thinking it must have been that wirry-cow returning to harass Briar into another sleepless night—but before Malric could see it clearly, something came over him. Something thick and stinking of sap, something that pressed him heavily into the bed and glued his eyes closed, choking the wakefulness from his body until he had no choice but to concede and sleep.

When he woke again in the morning, Briar was gone. Only a sprig of rosemary laid on the pillow where his head had been.

33

MALRIC AND THE FOX

Racing through the veil, Malric tore through the underbrush, the trees, the ferns, rushing straight for his mother's revel clearing—but it was empty. Dark and still, only the smell of rosemary surrounding the edges stinging his nose. In his grasp, the small sprig he'd carried from Briar's pillow was hardly more than bruised leaves and dripping oils staining the inside of his hand.

Where were they? Where had Marie taken them?

Malric had to find him—Malric always found him. Briar would be waiting for him, Briar knew Malric would come, and they were right. They were right. Even though Malric couldn't use his fox magic, smothered by the thick stench of rosemary in the air, Malric would find him. Briar would be waiting.

Bursting through the trees into the estate's backyard, Malric went straight for the house. Overhead, thick clouds clustered in the sky, blocking out the sun behind a wall that made the world dark and colorless. Fog kissed the grass, stuffed like cotton between the trees of the surrounding forest, making it impossible to see every inch of the yard Malric hurried across. It didn't matter—there was a light in one of the upper windows of the house. His room; the room where Briar slept after dancing. They had to be in there. Waiting for him. Knowing Malric would come. Malric was almost there, Malric would be there in only a few more moments.

Shoving open the back door of the house, it was as dark and empty on the other side as the yard had been. Malric's every movement echoed off the rafters, and for the first time, Malric was filled with unease at the lifelessness in front of him. There were no lights. There were no servants, no food cooking on the stove, no distant chatter of his siblings, no ghosts floating between the walls and leaving whispers of air in their wakes. There was simply —nothing.

Briar was waiting for him. He didn't hesitate, hurrying through the kitchen and ignoring how his boots on the hardwood floors echoed as if being chased by a dozen others. He went for the main staircase and ascended two at a time, then cut to the right down the first main corridor and directly to his bedroom door. There was light peeking out from underneath. Briar was right on the other side.

Malric grabbed the knob and pushed the door open—but only a single candle on the windowsill moved. He held his breath, heart beating in his ears. He blinked, then searched the room one more time—but it was empty.

"No," he whispered, hurrying forward. He went to the bed, but the duvet and pillows were all untouched, in place where they'd been tucked. He checked under the bed; under the writing desk; on every couch and cushioned chair. He opened the door into the bathroom and searched the bathtub, the small linen closet. He crawled his hands over the bed one more time. He stared at the single flickering candle in the window, but even on the other side of the glass, there was nothing. Only dense fog.

"Briar knew what would happen if they denied me."

Malric snapped around to find Marie standing in the open doorway, holding a candelabra donning three candlesticks, though only one was lit. It illuminated her face, clammy with sweat, claw marks raking down her cheek and neck. Mud was smeared down the front of her gown, drawn in lines like five fingers clinging to her. Tearing at her. Fighting.

Malric's whole world crashed.

"Where are they!" he roared, lunging at his mother and shoving her backward. She stumbled a few steps before catching herself, only for Malric to grab the front of her collar with one hand and wrench the candelabra away with the other. The base of it was damp and caked with mud, spotted with more smeared, dirty fingerprints. "What did you do with him, you witch! Tell me where he is!"

"It's too late, Malric," she told him, trembling in exhaustion —or was it fright? As if whatever Briar did to fight back compelled her enough to experience a single emotion that wasn't pure, unbridled arrogance. "What's done is done. I gave them plenty of chances. I gave them so many opportunities to save themself. They could have made the exact deal you did, if they only swallowed their own pride and brought me a replacement— they chose pride over my grace, just like all the others!"

Malric slammed Marie into the wall, pinning her by his forearm.

"Tell me where he is," Malric snarled. "Or I'll break your jaw, just like Felme wished of me."

For the first time ever, Malric saw unease in his mother's eyes. Staring at him, mouth dangling open as she struggled to find the words. The look of it incited nothing but pure, hot elation to swell in his muscles. She of all people should know, a chained fox bites. A released fox remembers. An enraged beast protects what's theirs.

"... the others," she finally muttered. Malric thrust her against the wall again, and she hissed. "He's with the others! In the clearing! There's nothing you can do for them, now, málda—Briar made their deal. You can't get in the way."

"The oth—" Malric started, but vomit raced up the back of his throat as he realized mid-breath what she meant. *The others.*

The others. Felme's voice cracked like lightning in the back of his mind.

I got curious about the people she chose to replace me when I left those two times.

I tried to find out. And then I tried to find out about the ones who replaced Neda and Lusia, too.

I can't find much about any of them.

It's like they disappeared, or never existed at all.

His memory flooded with every image of Briar decorated with leaves, twigs, branches; the feeling of his once-soft skin turned rough and raw as bark formed down his arms and legs. The way tears filled his eyes as he gazed up at Malric in defeat, hands bleeding, covered in sores and open wounds in all the places he'd cut and pricked and tore roots and new buds from his skin. The whistling of his breath with every inhale as branches festered in his chest. The scratching of leaves unfurling through his hair, tickling the side of Malric's face as Malric just clung to him as he slept, praying he would wake up again. Praying, if he dreamed, it would be comforting. Just a moment of comfort for someone burdened with the curse of a dryad.

"You..." he rasped. "You're the only person you can ever treat with such cruelty, now—and I will sleep soundly knowing you'll die where no one will notice or care."

"Mal—"

But Malric was already pushing away from the wall, and running as fast as his feet would carry him. Down the hall. Down the stairs. Out the door. Into the fog, across the grass, until he saw the silhouettes of those perpetual spring trees standing tall in the mist.

He was too scared to count them, that time.

34

BRIAR AND THE DRYAD

Briar wrapped the plush white scarf around the bottom half of his face, around the back of his head, tucking it into the front again. To protect his nose, his mouth, his ears from the biting cold of the nighttime air, illuminated by lanterns around the skating rink punctuated with the scattered clacking of blades on ice. He couldn't recall how he got there, let alone what he'd been doing before arriving—but Stella didn't look worried. Maybe he'd gone on another bender, blacking out everything that came before—but clearly in the interim, he'd performed well enough to not raise any suspicion.

The more he followed his friend toward the ice, though, the more he noticed how *stiff* his limbs were. As if his bones were replaced with thick icicles, like the ones that grew over the eaves of old houses. Long and pointed, making his joints ache as they poked at his tendons, his muscles from the inside out. Still, he kept it off his face. He didn't want Stella to worry.

Approaching the ice, he paused again, that time accidentally allowing his confusion to crest through his controlled expression. It wasn't the ice rink he was used to in the city—it was Possession Sound, awash with smooth glass over the surface, reflecting lights and the faces of those who skated on its smooth top. The ice *thunked* and plucked like guitar strings with the added weight of patrons, but otherwise didn't shift. It didn't even crack, despite the ominous noise. Briar almost stopped to ask if it was really such a good idea to skate on the sound like that, wondering where all the cargo ships were going to go, what the tide must be doing underneath the surface—but Stella was unfazed. She just smiled and motioned for Briar to hurry, they were going to be late. There were people waiting for them.

Sure enough, near the edge of the water, Briar's heart leapt at the sight of Bianca and Leon. Bianca grinned the moment she saw Stella, racing into her arms, embracing her, kissing her. They skittered off onto the ice hand-in-hand without another word, leaving Briar and Leon staring at one another in the near-darkness. His friend's familiar face was nearly obscured with every one of Briar's breaths, exhaling thick steam as the air that seemed to only grow colder despite his scarf and thick coat.

"Hi," he finally spoke, first. Something about facing Leon after what felt like so long, just the two of them in the low light, churned Briar's soul like a water wheel in a river. His heart raced, like there was more he wanted to say, but he didn't know exactly what those words were supposed to be.

Only one thing stood out amongst the rush of heat attempting to warm him from the inside out—and that was the unexpected urge to turn around and... search. As if someone was missing. Even though Leon was the only person Briar would ever want to see, right there, waiting for him, offering a hand to hold... Briar wondered if it was warm. He wondered if it was exactly as warm as he always dreamed it would be.

But then Leon smiled, and it was different than he remembered. It was handsomer than it should have been, and Briar suddenly thought he'd never seen anyone so lovely before in his life. It was an ethereal sort of handsome, inhuman, unlike anything that should have ever held out a hand for him. The kind of handsomeness they warned about in stories of vampires, demons, devils, creatures who only meant harm to unsuspecting humans crossing paths on the road. But Briar couldn't resist him —Briar would never be able to resist him, especially when he smiled like *that*.

He put out his hand, finding relief from the cold as soon as they touched. Leon's hand was so warm, it chased away the bitter nibbling of icy needles on Briar's skin. It cured the stiffness in his limbs, melting the ice taking place in his bones. He fleetingly hoped they didn't melt so much he lost the ability to stand at all.

He couldn't remember putting on skates, but Leon pulled him onto the smooth ice without another word. Briar followed after him, gliding over the surface on two blades biting perfectly into the frozen top. Like a porcelain ballerina in a music box, they floated over the mirror beneath their feet as the rest of the crowd melted away into the darkness. Until it was only them, only them, only them. Only Leon's warmth, his smile, his touch that made everything that had ever hurt in Briar's body melt like ice beneath the sun.

Briar didn't realize what he was doing until his body was already floating in sync with the movements. Leon, without a word of prompting, had pulled Briar into the opening steps of *Giselle*. Even the scenes where only Albrecht danced, or Giselle conversed silently with her mother, their movements ebbed and flowed as if the entire dance was always meant for two people. As if, the entire time, every single person on stage danced with someone no one else could see.

The flow of Briar's skates on the ice helped his movements when the rest of him felt too stiff. It carried him with ease, as if he were a bird on wings rather than a dancer on blades. He rose en pointe, he shimmered his feet across the glass, all the while gazing at Leon whenever he could. Whenever they stood face-to-face, chest-to-chest. Briar only ever turned away when the plucking thrum of settling ice was too loud to ignore—but Leon just touched his face and brought him back. To gaze at him, nearly close enough that they might touch lips. Nearly brushing noses. More than once, Briar closed his eyes, wishing to feel the heat of

Leon's mouth, finally. To finally, finally feel it, to be reminded why he ever swore to dance at that fey revel night after night after night after night until his feet were nothing more than bloody bones and his limbs had stiffened to ice—

Thud. The ice vibrated beneath Briar's feet, echoing off the distant shores as if moving on skates of its own. Briar turned to search the glossy ground, but saw only the dark blackness of the ice. Licked beneath the surface by the velvety blue of the sound's ocean water.

Leon summoned him back, and Briar sank into his gentle, commanding dance once more. The steam on his breath grew as they went. The stiffness in his body intensified as they went. Soon, even Leon's warm touch wasn't enough to scare the petrification away.

Still—Briar didn't think about it. He didn't want to think about it. He wanted only to disappear into that dance with Leon, where it was only him. Where Briar was the only person for Leon to see. To adore. To applaud and appreciate. That was all he ever wanted, from the very beginning.

Thud.

Briar turned to search again, but Leon took his face sooner, that time. Briar disappeared back into him—

Thud. Thud.

Briar's eyes flickered open, meeting Leon's only a few inches from his own. They enchanted him without words. Wind combed through Briar's hair as their feet swept around in a gliding arch on the ice. His scarf fell away, but he barely noticed. The ice bit at his ears, his nose, his mouth. If Leon would only kiss him, the frost on his lips wouldn't ache so badly—

Briar!

Briar's breath caught. He tried to turn again, but Leon claimed his attention. Again and again, commanding him back with touches gentler than Briar had any right to take for himself. Touches that caressed his chin, his cheek. Touches that carefully undid the buttons of his coat, shirking it off, letting it fall to the ice between movements. Briar had no chance to bend and reclaim it, locked in the choreography he'd memorized months earlier, determined to be absolutely perfect. Perfect enough for Leon to remember him, even if he left Briar's side—

The cold licked at Briar's skin, his bare throat, his forearms, his shoulders, his back. Beneath his fingers, floral-applique tulle fluttered with every turn, and he recognized the feeling of a long bell skirt. The same one he wore that night he danced Giselle with the person there with him, the only one keeping him warm on the ice of Possession Sound—

Briar, come back!

Please, come back to me!

Thudding echoes gave way to shredding, then snapping. Cracking, tearing, like old oak trees giving way beneath their own weight, rotten trunks buckling beneath heavy branches.

Leon took Briar's face again. Briar vanished into it—before catching his breath, and pulling away. Enough to feel a rush of frozen air, breaking the spell just long enough to search the ice, and see something floating beneath it. Hands splayed against the bottom, tearing at the ice from the depths of the ocean, ripping away fingernails and turning the glassy surface pink.

He gasped, stumbling backward. Leon caught him before he could fall, coaxing Briar back into the familiar choreography again. Cooing reassurances, begging Briar to just *focus on him, focus on me, Bry—don't leave me, Briar, I want to finally give you what you want. Stay with me, come with me, dance with me—*

Briar, open your eyes!

This is the last dance we'll ever get together, don't throw it away—

Don't leave me! Come back!

You'll never dance again after this, so stay with me—

Please, Briar, I'm so sorry—!

Briar's ears rang. He attempted to pull free of Leon's grasp, heart pounding as he knew, he *knew* who that second voice belonged to, the one under the ice, the one calling out to him, calling his name with such desperation. Briar knew, but he couldn't place it. Why couldn't he remember their name? Why didn't Leon hear it—or did he? Why did he ignore it?

The ice shelf cracked again. Like the twang of a harp. It struck Briar in the back of the neck with an invisible hand, and he jolted away from Leon—only for the ice on the air to claim every inch of his skin in an instant. But that person, that voice—he wanted to go to it. He wanted to find them, to pull them from the water. Briar wanted to find them, to follow them. To assure them he was fine, he was alright, he was only dancing, he was only—

Teeth chattering, Briar turned to search the ice, only for his skates to vanish beneath him. Replaced with satin slippers, he lost his balance on the glassy surface, crashing to it with a gasp and a cry. Whimpering as the chill clawed at his bare skin, he pushed the thick skirt of his tutu away, wiping his numb hands over the glossy surface in search of those pressed from underneath. He wanted to find them, he wanted—he wanted to touch them. To hold them. He wanted to warm them, to see the face of the person they belonged to. It pulled him from the root of his heart, the center of his ribcage, like an invisible thread he'd forgotten about.

Here, Briar! I'm here, I'm right here! Open your eyes, bugbear, please—

Briar's heart pounded, but none of the blood ever reached his limbs. It froze in his veins before saturating his skin, slowly losing its color as the winter air took hold of him. Traveling up his hands, his wrists, his forearms, his elbows. Searching on his hands and knees, the cold dried and split his lips, frosting on the inner walls of his throat, making every breath heavy and ragged. Heat built at the base of his neck, but it wasn't the warmth of comfort —it was the warmth of his body pleading for relief. His vision wobbled. His breaths came heavier, sticky and thick as if inhaling clay.

Glancing weakly over his shoulder, Briar searched for Leon, wishing he would help, wishing he might offer his warmth for Briar to use again—but Leon stood right where Briar had left him. Motionless. Blank. Clutching Briar's white scarf that waved in the frozen breeze. Leon's eyes, glazed over, stared at him—as someone stood behind him. Dressed in white, clutching a rosemary branch of the Wili Queen.

Come back to me, Leon's voice said in the brittle air, though his mouth didn't move. The shadow behind him hunched slightly, draped in the same leaves and blue flowers as the thrush in her hand. Myrtha, the Wili Queen that resurrected Giselle from her grave—Briar had seen her before. Briar knew her, somehow, despite also knowing she was only a character. A role in a play.

"Come back to me," Leon's voice rang out again, but that time, the words came from his mouth—only to simultaneously emerge from the fey queen standing behind him. Her hand tightened on the rosemary branch as Briar just stared. Beneath him, something thumped against the ice again, and he felt it beneath his hand.

"Come dance with me, Briar," Leon, the fey lady, begged. "This is your last chance, Briar. You will never dance again. Come and dance with me for eternity, we will never stop, so long as you stay with me."

Bry—I found you. I'm here.

"Don't you wish to dance for me?"

There, there. Yes, Briar, it's me—please, open your eyes. Come on. I'm right here.

Briar's mouth dangled open. Empty, wordless. His heart drummed, though felt suffocated beneath tendrils of ice wrapping around it. Keeping it from pounding, from feeling anything more than the cold, more than a want for warmth. Leon was warm; the ice beneath his hands and knees was cold. It hurt his skin, it burned in that horrible way only ice could.

But—Leon was no longer the only reason Briar had to dance. Briar couldn't remember—he couldn't remember why, but— somehow, he knew, there would be other reasons to dance that weren't to simply impress the one person whose affection he'd obsessed over for so long.

"No," he finally whispered. A word so small, said so softly—but the moment he uttered it, the rosemary branch in the fey lady's hand snapped in half.

The ice gave way beneath him. Briar plunged into the clawing, inky depths of the sound, vanishing beneath the glassy sheet in an instant. He might have thought himself dead—had he not plummeted directly into the arms of someone waiting for him right below the surface.

Briar wanted to embrace him. Briar wanted to throw his arms out, to pull Malric into his body, to breathe in his fresh scent and bury his face into his soft hair, to steal his warmth and hear the sound of his name from those lips he'd fallen prey to so many times—but his arms wouldn't move. The ice clung to him, burying hooks across his skin and wrenching tight like a marionette on a string.

Briar, Briar, Briar. I'm here. I'm here for you. Open your eyes.

But Briar no longer had his puppeteer. He no longer had the strings that told him how and when to move. When to dance. When to bow. When to say *thank you* and nod his head. The person in that bitter water with him was no puppeteer—they might as well have floated on cut strings no different from Briar's. But then how did they move?

How did their hands, warm as a spring sun, caress his face and melt the permafrost building beneath his skin?

Briar wanted to touch him back. Briar wanted to see him. To speak his name. To chase that warmth, to learn how to dance without strings all over again. To lift himself from his own grave, rather than hope the Queen of the Wilis offered him grace.

Malric. Malric. Mal—

"—*ric,*" he murmured. The hands cupping his face moved. A thumb brushed over his mouth, followed by the sound of someone pushing through thick foliage.

"Yes, yes, Briar—gods, yes, I'm right here. Open your eyes. Come on."

Briar chased that voice calling out to him. In the icy water, it drifted on the tide, summoning him deeper. Down into the dark depths, away from that single source of warmth he'd been given on the surface. Away from his friends, away from the air, away from Leon's perfect pas de deux. But even in step with him, Leon hadn't been able to give Briar all the heat he needed. All the warmth he wanted. Briar still moved stiffly. Briar still slowly froze.

"Malric," he heard his own voice. It was strained, syllables whistling like a breeze through leafy branches. He chased it. He said it again, raspy and thin. The hands on his face pulled him deeper into the darkness, plunging down farther and farther, until Briar was sure he would eventually sink all the way to the bottom, never to emerge again—

Warmth kissed him, instead. Warmth and the smell of freshly turned soil, just like he learned while gardening with his mom in the spring. He felt the earth beneath his fingernails, crunching between his teeth, scratching the inside of his throat where frost had been moments prior. His arms dangled heavy, weighed down by a hundred anchors buried in his skin. He couldn't move his legs, wrapped together with braided twine.

No—not twine.

No—not anchors.

No—not soil.

Bark. Twigs. New buds unfurling into leaves, piercing through his skin as if rooted in his bones. A wheezing sob escaped him, searching for the comfort of those warm hands again.

"It... hurts," he pleaded, hardly recognizing his own voice as it was choked by the branches growing inside of him. "It hurts, it hurts—"

"I know—I know Bry, just hang on. I'm going to cut you free. And then—and then I'm going to take you home. You're going to pas de deux with Leon. There's still plenty of time to make it to the gala. You're going to be perfect. And then this will all be over."

Briar wanted to argue, knowing Malric was lying, wanting to accuse him of being the only high fey who could lie—but he choked on the words as Malric snapped the first branch away. As if a single string of his own nerves had webbed through the growth, Briar felt it like a dagger piercing his skin. Again and again, he cried out as Malric snapped branches, twigs, plucked leaves from Briar's skin. As he pulled vines from the back of Briar's throat, like unspooling yarn from a skein. Briar gagged and choked as Malric just begged for his forgiveness between telling him everything was going to be alright.

As the bark was ripped from his legs, Briar swore every movement took skin with it. It was only when he finally opened his watering eyes to see his legs still intact that everything spun, then crashed down on top of him, and he went limp in shock. Malric pulled Briar into his arms, against his chest, caressing him as he finished removing what else he could of the curse growing from Briar's flesh.

Finally lifted from the earth that wished to claim him, Briar's heavy eyes dangled open. He realized where he was without having to see it clearly—he may have even been able to figure it out by the scent, alone. Marie d'Alarie's clearing, with her unique, perfect trees intermingling with the wild ones. There he was, right in the spot where he'd once buried his own ballet slippers to make his deal with her. Where he'd planted the seed of his own grave without knowing it; without knowing he would, one day, claw his way back out merely at the beck and call of another high fey whose voice he would chase until his last living breath.

"You came," Briar wept into Malric's shirt, pulled closer to Malric's chest as the arms supporting him curled tighter. "You found me."

"I will always find you," Malric said like the first offering of a fey deal. "No matter where you go, I will always find you."

It was easier to breathe without the crushing tangle of branches in his chest, though Briar knew more remained inside. Other growth rooted too deep even for Malric to tear out, like weeds taking hold in concrete. Still—Briar couldn't help but smile. When Malric smiled back down at him in the low light of the Autumn Court's moon, Briar even exhaled a tiny laugh of relief.

"You found me," he repeated, as if still in disbelief. "You... thought of me."

Malric chuckled. He pressed a kiss to Briar's forehead, and Briar's eyes grew heavy and sank back closed, as if blanketed in a fey lord's spell to ease his pain.

"I never stop."

BRIAR AND THE SCISSORS

Briar eased in and out of consciousness as Malric carried him back through the woods, the veil, onto the ferry as the sun set on the horizon. He didn't have the strength to speak, to fight back—not that he was sure he would have, if he could. He wasn't sure what he would have done if in his right mind, in his right state of being. He just thought about how in that dream, he'd chased Mal into the ice. He'd chosen Mal, over the safety and predictability of Leon.

Briar didn't know what that said about who he was, what he deserved. He'd once told Mal he didn't like being treated *gently*, after all—because it scared him. Was that why it was so easy to fall back into Mal's arms without any fight at all? To even chase after him, after that person who had never treated him gently...?

No. No, no, no, no, no—that wasn't true. That wasn't true at all. Mal had treated him more gently than anyone else ever had, even when Briar told him all his most embarrassing secrets. Even when Briar confided his most mortifying truths. Mal had treated him with gentleness for every single moment, even in those brief ones after Briar realized who he really was. Those brief moments of passing, where the gentlest thing Mal could do was keep his distance and let Briar breathe.

"Is your name really Mal?" he asked weakly, resting on Mal's lap as the ferry bobbed on the water beneath them. Mal tucked some hair behind his ear.

"My name is Malric," he said. "But some friends call me Mal, too."

Something about that was strangely reassuring. Mal, Malric, hadn't misled Briar entirely. He even gave Briar his real name, as much as he felt like he could.

"Are you going to hurt me?" Briar asked, next. His voice was flat, but it summoned a reaction from Malric, whose heart pounded loud enough for Briar to hear through his chest.

"No," he said with an intensity Briar didn't expect. "I never, ever meant to hurt you, Briar. And once this is all over, and only if you want to—I want to tell you everything. I'll explain myself. I'll apologize on my knees."

Briar rolled his eyes. "Fey don't do that."

"Do what? Apologize?"

"Yeah."

"They do when they know they've done a terrible thing to someone they care for."

Briar scoffed. "You care for me..." he mumbled. It wasn't a question, but perhaps it should have been. He felt Malric lean closer, pressing their foreheads together.

"I care for you so much, it makes me foolish," he whispered. Why did Briar smile when he heard that? "And foolishness made me cruel, without knowing it."

"It's in your nature," Briar mumbled. He cracked open his eyes for the first time, seeking out Malric with blurry vision. He wore his human disguise again, and Briar wrinkled his nose. "It was a charm I got from that one shop, to take away fey glamours. Neda was working there..."

Malric shifted Briar's weight in his arms, grimacing before laughing awkwardly.

"They left my mother," Malric said in a low voice. "They were tired of seeing how she treated you, so... they left. I've been trying to find places for all of them to go."

"... Neda was still way too pretty."

Mal let out a chuckle.

"Most of them haven't ever been to the human world before, they don't realize how hard a convincing glamour can be. All of us... have special talents, and Marie took advantage of them for all of our lives. This is the first time they've ever had a real taste of freedom."

"They're still here? In the human world?"

"Oh, yes. There are actually quite a few fey, high and wild, both, roaming around in the human world. Some of my siblings already have jobs; others are learning how to love their talents again. All of them are in therapy."

Briar laughed, and it demonstrated how sore his throat was from inhaling all the soil he did. "A magical fairy in therapy... sounds like a kid's book."

"Maybe," Malric smiled softly down at him, before shaking his head. "If you want, too... I'll introduce them to you. Properly. They owe you their freedom, in a way."

Briar smiled weakly again. He closed his eyes, leaning against Malric's chest and listening to the relaxing pace of his heart.

"Do you really think dancing with Leon will set me free?" he asked airily, before coughing as he swore he felt another vine stretch out between his lungs.

"If the root of the deal finds Briar perfect, they will be free," Malric answered in a breath. "Does that sound familiar? It's the exact language of your deal with my mother."

"Oh... yeah, I guess it does..." Briar sighed. "Leon is the root of my deal, then."

"Yes, I think so."

"Good," Briar nestled into the crook of Malric's neck. "One more dance, then I finally get to rest. Right?"

"Yes," he promised. "You can rest for as long as you like."

"Will you wait for me?"

Malric was quiet for a long time, before exhaling what Briar could only describe as a month's worth of relief held hostage in his chest.

"I'll wait any amount of eternity it takes."

Briar smiled unevenly. "Good. Maybe by then... I won't hate you so much."

"I'll hold you to that."

In many ways, Briar had no choice but to trust him. Mal, Lord Malric d'Alarie, that person who hurt him, who betrayed him, who broke his heart when he didn't even know it had been entrusted to him. But his confession while they knelt on Briar's floor echoed through his mind the entire journey back to the city; the memory of how Briar chose him in his dream, which he knew had been only his subconscious mind calling out for him to listen. Despite the restlessness of the few pieces of sleep he could claim all the way to Tomassin, draped in Mal's familiar arms, he still drifted longer and deeper than the days prior.

"I'm going to help you get ready," Mal whispered through Briar's haze of exhaustion. He didn't know when exactly they arrived at the school, but Briar's eyes cracked open to blurrily make out the dressing room backstage. They were off to the side of the others, nearly in the shadows, and Briar was grateful. The other dancers would surely see the leaves and buds growing through his skin, otherwise.

Mal crouched in front of him with a pair of nail clippers, snipping away whatever growths had emerged from Briar's skin since the last time. Briar almost asked how bad it was, but could hardly speak. He could hardly breathe. The roots spreading through his lungs had only expanded into a thicket that barely let a breeze through.

It hurt far less when Mal handled him than when he'd done it to himself, and Briar was even able to close his eyes and sink back into the cozy energy of backstage atmosphere. Every now and then Mal would touch his face, summoning his eyes to open, as if testing to see if Briar was still alive. Briar just smiled at him weakly, sarcastically, each time, before sinking back into that soft relief all over again.

When Mal coaxed him back to the land of the living once more, it was after Briar's feet and legs, hands and arms, and even parts of his shoulders and neck had been addressed by gentle hands. In fact, the longer Mal touched him so softly, so delicately, with so much care—the less the fires of contempt burned inside of him, as if begging for forgiveness to come less with words, and more with those actions. Those shows of gentleness, the same ones Briar once said he hated. But even as his emotions swirled in a muddy cloud of confusion, Briar couldn't resist taking Mal's face and kissing him weakly. Mal gently cupped a hand beneath Briar's face and kissed him back with restraint, so as to not hurt him any further than he already was.

"You're going to be alright," he promised, taking Briar's hand next and kissing his knuckles. "You'll dance with Leon tonight, and that will be the end of all of this. You will be perfect. I know it."

Briar managed to smile weakly, but couldn't find his eyes to open again. As badly as he wanted to look at Mal directly, to reassure himself those words might finally, finally, be true—it scared him too much to be proven wrong again. To be embarrassed again. Briar would much rather cling to the hope that maybe, that time, Mal was telling him the truth. He wasn't sure he could do the opposite and still find the strength to stand on stage with Leon that night.

"Are you looking forward to it?" Mal asked while gently combing Briar's hair, next, and braiding it back into a romantic bun.

"To what?" Briar mumbled, head lolling forward. He coughed suddenly, cracking open his eyes to find the tiniest splatter of red on the back of his hand. He quickly wiped it away.

"To dance with Leon again."

Briar smirked, then shook his head weakly.

"I... don't care about that anymore," he whispered. "After tonight... I'm only going to ever dance for myself... for once."

Mal chuckled, and Briar glanced back at him. The way he smiled was so satisfied with himself, and it made Briar smile sarcastically.

"You made your deal... on the basis of *dancing for someone beautiful*," Mal whispered. "And as far as I'm concerned... you're the most beautiful thing to ever exist."

Briar wanted to snap back with something bratty, but it caught in his mouth. Instead, he just blushed, turning away and shaking his head. He glanced down at his calloused, bark-rough hands decorated with spots of red where the branches had been cut away.

"Not anymore," he whispered. Mal tugged lightly on his hair.

"High fey can't lie," Mal responded. He let the words linger, and they struck Briar down to his soul.

Frustrated tears filled his eyes as he realized—if he had never been able to dance with perfection previously, how was he supposed to while his muscles were run through with oak roots?

Was he really going to die?

Was there any point at all?

Had he really thrown everything away for a selfish wish of wanting someone he couldn't have? Was it really going to end so quickly, with a whimper and cheeks wet with tears?

He wanted to say something. He wanted to ask Mal for reassurance, one last time, that everything was going to be alright—but could he really trust the same person who'd strung him along for all those days? When he had just as much power against Marie d'Alarie as Briar did? And Briar—was only a human. A vulnerable, defenseless, pathetic little creature. If even Mal didn't stand a chance, what did he?

Pressing his lips together, he shoved all of the thoughts away.

Even if he died, even if the branches suffocated him from the inside out, he would at least get to dance one last time. To dance one last time—and for it to be for himself, only. For Leon, for Mal to see that he had it in him despite everything else. Even if it wasn't perfect. Even if he was stiff and broken like a doll with rusted hinges. Even if he made a fool of himself—he wouldn't die until he finally danced for himself amongst all the times he'd been used, otherwise.

Mal coaxed Briar to his feet, helping him stretch out his limbs until they bent as normally as possible, as they made their way to the queue of other dancers ahead of them. Mal found him a place to sit, commenting on the mess of leaves they'd left on the dressing room floor and how he should hurry to clean it up. Briar watched him go, only for his attention to move as Leon spotted where they sat and hurried over.

Briar knew, in that instant, he wasn't going to get what he wanted so easily. Not when Leon's smile dropped instantly at the sight of him, having to use the wall to sit upright, freckled with pricks of blood where leaves had been snipped from his arms, his neck, his chest, his face. He was sure rogue leaves poked through his hair, clustering around the base of his romantic bun. He was sure, by the time their turn to go out on stage came, there would be even more growth already emerging.

Leon looked at him with uncertainty. With wide eyes of disbelief, as if the Briar who sat in front of him was the exact last thing he was hoping to see.

"It's fine," Briar promised, knowing what Leon was about to say, not wanting to hear it. He just smiled, putting his hands out, but Leon pulled back slightly. He shook his head.

"Bry…" he whispered, next words hovering as he just looked Briar up and down one more time. "What's going on? You're… not okay. You're sick, Bry—I knew it the last time we practiced, and you just look worse, now. You—you have to go to the hospital. Come on, I'll take you myself—"

"No!" Briar grabbed him, begging. "Just let me dance, Leon, it's fine—!"

"I'm not going to dance with you when you're this sick!"

Leon grabbed Briar's shoulders, before reeling away in surprise when he felt the branches spreading beneath Briar's skin. His eyes went wide, staring at his hand, and then back to Briar's face.

"What's going on?" he asked weakly. "Briar—just wait here, alright? I'll go get changed. I'll get your things, and I'll come back for you. I'll take you to the hospital, alright? Just wait here."

"No!" Briar pleaded, but Leon stepped out of his reach again. Briar shook his head pleadingly, softly begging Leon's name again and again, but Leon looked at him like he was something to be frightened of. And then—he turned and left. He left so swiftly that Briar couldn't even try to keep up with his stiff legs.

He lost his footing, caught just before he hit the floor by two strong arms that swept him upright again.

"What's going on?" Mal asked, but Briar only stared in the direction Leon had raced off to. It took everything in him to hold back tears of frustration, and disappointment, and embarrass-ment, and—rage. Pure, hot fucking rage, that he would be denied his last chance to dance because of the curse the fey lady placed on him. That his relief was right in reach—only to be shrugged off so easily.

He shoved out of Mal's arms, but Mal stretched out and grabbed him again stubbornly. Briar attempted to push himself free again, fighting Mal's strength as all the swirling emotions swelled like a noxious gas in his chest, threatening to blow him open into nothing but debris and broken branches after a storm.

"He won't dance with me!" he finally cried. "Because—he's afraid of me! He thinks I'm sick, he says he won't dance with me—!"

The effort, the exclamations knocked the air out of him, forgetting his lungs were compromised by the roots in his chest. He bent over, gasping and heaving for breaths that came in haggard and strained. Mal rubbed his back, before pulling him close.

"I'll..." he trailed off, before clenching his jaw. "I'll go find him. I'll talk to him, Briar. You'll get to dance, I swear it. I promise you, no matter what it takes. Just be ready to go on stage when it's your cue, alright? I'll make sure of it."

"No, no..." Briar shook his head. The thought of Mal failing, of Briar stepping out onto stage in all his stiff awkwardness, to perform the first few notes of a pas de deux that was supposed to be beautiful—the thought of Mal failing to convince Leon to join him, leaving Briar all by himself in front of all those people, to be laughed at—

Mal grabbed Briar's face—and kissed him. Harder than before, stealing any and all of Briar's thoughts at once. Just for a moment. Just long enough to claim his entire attention upon locking eyes.

"I will not let you dance alone again." He swore it. "Ever again. I will not leave you alone, ever again. No matter what it takes, someone will join you on stage tonight."

Briar wanted to trust him. Briar wanted to believe Mal really, truly, had his back that time, but—how many times had he already thought that?

Mal saw the thoughts behind Briar's eyes. He must have, because he kissed Briar once more, silencing the growing chorus of doubt for a second time.

"I swear it," he said between their mouths. "I swear it, Briar Rose. Just once more. Just give me your trust once more. I will not let you down. I will not squander it again. I swear it."

Briar pressed his lips together. He fluttered his eyelashes, attempting to blink the tears away before they could ruin his makeup.

"If I'm left out there, all by myself..." he whispered weakly. "I don't know what I'll do."

"I won't leave you," Mal insisted intensely, pressing their foreheads together. "If you are left alone on stage, my heart will stop in an instant. This I declare as a geis between us two. I will not leave you alone."

Briar didn't have a chance to argue any longer, because Mal kissed him one last time before disappearing in a rush into the darkness of the back stage. Briar just watched him go, hands extending outward in uncertainty, but—just like when Leon left him, Mal escaped his reach too quickly to chase.

Briar slowly bent his hands into his chest. He felt like his heart was going to stop, gnarled too deeply within the branches claiming him bit by bit. What if Mal left, just like Leon did? What if he didn't intend on keeping his promises, just like all the other times?

What if...?

Briar... wanted to believe him. Just one more time. He could extend his trust just... one more time.

He would die, either way. The branches would take him before the humiliation did, either way.

At least, if Mal was telling the truth—Briar would get his last wish, before giving up the ghost.

THE COUPLE QUEUED AHEAD OF HIM DANCED THE PAS de deux for Giselle. He watched with glazed eyes, as if the rest of the world had gone silent except the live orchestra, the overhead lights, the rhythmic *pap, pap, pap, thud, drag* of pointe shoes and ballet flats hitting the floor throughout the choreography.

It took him back to the season finale, prior, where he did the same with Leon. Dancing in perfect sync with one another. Briar even found himself nodding his head slightly every time the performers in front of him tapped the stage with their shoes, or the music indicated the pace of the movements.

He could feel Leon's hands on his waist. Lifting him, then setting him down with perfect fluidity. He could hear his own heartbeat in his ears. His own heavy breaths, though no one in the audience would ever, ever notice it moving in his chest or shoulders. He heard every inhale and exhale and soft grunt as Leon clenched his muscles and lifted Briar overhead, how his arms trembled just slightly with strength as he was lowered again like water. How, even with the live orchestra right at the foot of the stage, Briar barely heard their strings and flutes over his own feet echoing off the hollow stage.

When the dance in front of him came to a close, he barely noticed. His ears just rang. His body burned hot. He thought he might faint.

The presenter stepped out, politely clapping before repeating the names of the performers and which school they attended, and reminding the audience members to cast their donations via the app or the submission card they were given upon arriving.

The announcer said his name, next. They announced it with Leon's. *Our next performance is the pas de deux from Les Sylphides...* Wrong. That was the wrong ballet. It was from La Sylphide, not Chopin's non-narrative dance. In any other circumstance, Briar would have been furious, he might have even danced out on stage in the middle of the announcement to correct them —but he only heard the ringing in his ears.

Briar did not normally get stage fright, but he hardly felt attached to his own body. His own body, that slowly shifted to eventually belong to the trees. A body that would slowly no longer be his at all.

The announcer stepped away, and a familiar prelude swelled from the orchestra pit.

Leon should have danced out onto the stage, pantomiming his character flitting through the woods with curiosity. Briar would have joined him only a few moments later, to meet at the back of the stage and dance-step toward the audience, then part again, then continue through the movements of two people who never touched, until the very end.

But Leon wasn't there. There wasn't anyone there.

Briar just thought of Mal's words. His promise that Briar wouldn't be left all by himself. He wouldn't be left alone. Mal swore it. He declared it.

Briar closed his eyes. He flexed his stiff hands, bending his joints and snapping any treelike tendrils that had spread in those moments he stood frozen. He turned his eyes to the floor—and emerged from the curtain exactly as he was supposed to, had a partner been waiting for him on the other side.

He didn't want to look. He didn't want to know. He could technically dance the entire thing by himself, as he didn't need a partner for any lifts or tall jumps. But—then everyone would see. They would see how stiff and awkward and broken he was, as that pas de deux specifically focused so much on individual skill and craft—

He would just dance. He would dance with his eyes closed, if he had to. He wasn't there to dance for Leon, or even for the audience. He was there to dance for himself, one last time. One last time, before he lost the ability to dance at all.

On cue, Briar found his place at the back of the stage, moving his arms and legs, keeping his eyes low so he wouldn't have to see how Mal had let him down once again—

But at the very last moment, someone rushed out to meet him.

❧ 36 ❧

MALRIC AND THE DRYAD

I will not let you dance alone again. Ever again. I will not leave you alone, ever again.

Those words rang inside Malric's head. They bounced off the inside of his skull, bruising his brain and leaving cracks in bone like the gong of church bells. Louder and louder, earsplitting by the time he found Leon wiping away his makeup in the dressing room. That very moment—the world went silent, and Malric watched his reflection in the mirrors move. He hardly recognized himself.

He rushed Leon. He grabbed him by the shoulder, turning him around. He took a fistful of the man's collar, slamming him back against the mirror hard enough that it split on impact. Leon grappled for his hand, staring at him with wide, terrified eyes.

"Hey!" he cried. "Hey, I'm sorry! I don't want any trouble, Mal—look, if this is about Briar—*urk!*"

Malric rammed Leon against the mirror a second time, ears ringing as shards of glass broke away from the frame and clattered to the vanity.

"Why won't you dance with him?" Malric demanded. "It's all he wants!"

"Because—!" Leon clutched Malric's hand, eyes wide.

"Because he needs to go to the *hospital!* Didn't you see him!? He looks terrible! I was going to change back into my clothes and take him—"

Malric stared at him, but couldn't place a name on the surge of emotion radiating from his chest. It wasn't anger, or even shock, it was—*it was*—

Horror. Horror as he realized—Leon truly was never a villain at all. He never truly set out to break Briar's heart. To lead him on and leave him wanting. Leon really, truly, was simply—a man. Just a simple man who had no idea about fey, fey deals, what Briar did for even a chance to get Leon's attention. Which meant Leon would never understand exactly how painful it was for Briar to be rejected by him, one last time, as his insides were slowly being claimed by gnarled bark and wood.

Briar knew all along Leon was a simple man, too—which was exactly why he went to such lengths to captivate him. Because Leon wasn't withholding affection to be cruel, or even out of inconsideration—he was simply unaware of Briar's feelings at all. Somehow—that felt worse. Everything Briar had ever done suddenly pieced itself together, explaining him, explaining how lost and easily-manipulated he was all that time—and how cruel Marie had been to prey on him when she likely knew very well the reason Leon didn't love Briar back.

"You..." Malric attempted, but his throat was tight. The word hardly vocalized at all. "Just... just dance with him, Leon. Just once. It's only one dance. Not even ten minutes—"

Leon surprised him with a twist of his expression into anger. He shoved Malric away, breaking his grasp.

"What the hell is wrong with you?" he hissed. "Do you not care about Briar at all? He needs a doctor, not this—"

"No, Leon, you don't understand what he needs—"

"He doesn't need to dance!"

"*Yes, he does!*" Malric roared, grabbing Leon again, that time with both hands. He shoved Leon into the broken mirror again, making the entire row of glass rattle. "This last dance will cure him, Leon—it'll save him! It's the only thing that can, it's the only thing I can do!"

Leon stared at him, clearly at a loss for words. Through the walls, the previous pas de deux accompaniment descended to a close. Malric gripped Leon's tunic tighter, finding it harder and harder to breathe. To find his composure.

"Just one dance, godsdamnit," he hissed. He practically begged. "It's all he's ever wanted from you, damnit—just one more dance. Just to be noticed by you. You have no idea what he's gone through—just to get one more fucking dance with you!"

"What—" Leon croaked. "What are you talking about? Briar can get any dance partner he likes, he doesn't need me—!"

"Briar just wants you to think he's perfect!" Malric shouted, spit flying from his mouth. "That's all he's ever wanted, you selfish prick!"

"Mal!" Leon yelled back, gripping Malric's arms that held the front of his shirt. "I—I do think he's perfect, damnit! I even told him so! Why else would I ask him to dance with me? He's all I had!"

Malric stared at him. "When?" he asked hoarsely.

"What?"

"*When,* damnit! When did you tell him that!"

"I—I don't know! At our last practice!"

No, no, no—he didn't understand, he didn't *understand*—but the music from the stage simmered, and petered off. The applause was loud enough to be heard even all the way in the dressing room. Malric's hands on Leon's tunic trembled, clenched tight enough that his fingers locked.

What was he supposed to do?

He could compel the man—but would that negate Marie's terms of setting Briar free? Was there anyone else to take Leon's place? Anyone at all, just so that Briar wouldn't be left alone. So Briar wouldn't be forced to dance alone, ever again, just like Malric promised. They could figure out what to do, next, after the dance was done. Malric just had to keep his promise that time, and then they could confront Leon again afterward. Malric would force Leon to declare Briar's perfection, formally, with a knife to his throat, if he had to.

But—he didn't know anyone else to ask. What was he supposed to do? Who was he supposed to shove on stage to pas de deux with Briar, since Malric himself couldn't? Malric, who could never dance for anyone, else he face the consequences of the trade he made. Malric, who had given up dancing for, with, in front of anyone, and everyone, for a taste of freedom. Freedom that was bitter and sad and pointless until he met Briar Hunt and swore to set him free, too.

Malric swallowed hard, but the lump in his throat was covered in nails. Those nails that burdened him whenever he knew there was a decision to make, one that would result in his own loss. His own misery.

Marie made that trade for a reason. Marie knew Malric wouldn't ever find anyone he would be willing to give up his life to dance with—

But Marie never anticipated the way falling in love with Briar Hunt was all the taste of freedom Malric ever needed; and even if it was cut short, even if Malric couldn't be there for Briar's final redemption, Malric wouldn't leave Briar alone to dance.

Shoving away from Leon, Malric raced through the door toward the stage.

La Sylphide's pas de deux had already started. Malric searched his memory for the steps, finally finding his place at an opening in the curtain. On the opposite side, illuminated beneath the spotlight, Briar was already there. Approaching the back of the raked stage, moving stiffly, but still somehow perfectly. He had his eyes turned downward, as if he didn't want to see. As if he would rather stare at his own feet than see himself alone in front of an entire audience, who would laugh at him and his awkward footing.

But Briar was perfect. He was breathtaking, even at his lowest. Even trussed with branches growing inside of him, beneath his skin, petrifying his limbs and his lungs. Briar Hunt, of all people, deserved to dance for himself and no one else. Briar Hunt deserved to be free. Briar Hunt deserved to love ballet, and be loved by it back.

Malric glamoured himself in an instant, and rushed out on stage.

DANCING WITH BRIAR HUNT, HIS ROSEFINCH, HIS object of obsession, was like nothing Malric could have ever imagined. Even though Briar stared at Malric in shock at first, and then concern, always with words on their lips that couldn't be spoken. Words of panic, knowing Malric—couldn't be there. Shouldn't be there. Malric wasn't supposed to dance for, with, alongside anyone except the fey he'd made his deal with—but Malric wouldn't allow Briar to dance alone, even if it meant taking the risk he did.

Danian scholars claimed dance was what first teased the veil into opening; a human and a high fey, fingertips brushing without knowing, without any awareness of the mirror's edge on the other side.

The veil, so enamored by the two of them alone, wished to know how it would look if they danced in one another's arms, instead. The veil, desperate to witness such a lovely visage, rent itself apart, to allow aridity and opulence to enmesh with one another for the first time. Two magic spells of opposing sides, combining in perfect harmony.

Malric used to dance with the intention of rending open the veil for himself. He wanted to find that other dancer promised for him, destined to be the one to enmesh and harmonize with his every movement—only to reach adulthood, and make the choice to forgo dancing altogether in exchange for freedom. Freedom he saw echoed in Briar Hunt; freedom he saw stolen from Briar Hunt. Freedom that didn't feel quite so appealing without the thing that brought him joy, brought him hope, brought him the chance to reach harmony with someone else.

But on that stage, where the lights fell away, where the audience ceased to exist, where even the string instruments playing at their feet fell silent—Malric finally understood what it meant to meet and know someone's movements in every entirety. To anticipate every breath, to act on every slip of their hands and feet. An ascension from dancing alone, or even waltzing with a partner—he and Briar Hunt, hand in hand, would rent the veil apart irreparably. It would never separate them, ever again—or so it felt in those very moments Malric touched Briar's hands, his waist, as Briar draped over Malric's arms with ease and all the grace of the veil, itself.

A dance that Malric wished to live in for every single moment of the rest of eternity, to memorize, to taste and feel until the day he died—but a dance that came to an end far too quickly. A dance that came to an end not soon enough, as Briar suffered through every single moment of it. Perhaps that was why Malric barely felt the passage of time, why he couldn't enjoy every single moment the way he was meant to. The person he danced with was in agony —and that wasn't the way Malric wished to recall his first dance with Briar.

Briar, who as the dance concluded, buckled in Malric's arms, releasing an agonized gasp that clutched Malric's heart in a vice grip. Malric simply pulled him upright, into his chest. He supported every inch of Briar's body, lifting him to his toes without allowing him to put any weight on them. Holding that small, fragile, indestructible person flush to his chest with one arm wrapped under his hips, the other curved around his upper back. Safe, where he might rest for just a moment after completing the most magnificent performance any human ever could. One beautiful enough to open the veil and draw Malric straight to him. One of someone in agony, who thought they would die with every step, who wished only to feel the pleasure of dancing one last time.

Malric touched Briar's face as the crowd applauded. He wondered if Briar's family was amongst them, cheering and clapping to show their adoration.

"Do you hear them?" he asked softly, unsure if Briar could. "They think you're magnificent."

Briar just fought to catch his breath. He put his hand to his chest, gripping the front of his bodice in a fist. Malric leaned his head forward, kissing Briar's forehead before nestling his cheek against Briar's flushed with the effort.

"You danced perfectly."

Briar's entire body shuddered. Malric clutched them as they contorted, throwing their head backward with wide eyes toward the ceiling as their mouth dangled open in overwhelm. Malric held his breath, just staring at Briar, before gritting his teeth as he felt the nauseating sensation of his insides churning. Reaching their own tendrils outward, toward his arms, his legs. Racing down them, through the muscle like roots. Like lightning searching for the earth.

Malric held it back as long as he could, for as long as his own defensive opulent magic would let him—until soon, his glamour couldn't hide it, and he lost his ability to even maintain his ensemble.

His nails grew into points, burrowing into Briar's newly-softened skin. His ears perked, his vision brightened, and all he saw was the fear on Briar's face. The pounding of Briar's heart as they frantically pulled Malric off the stage, voice muddled by the banging in Malric's skull.

Dance for anyone other than me, ever again, and you shall become one with the copper fauna. Of they behind whom we hide our faces; of teeth and shadowed paws. Of your roots and starving for rabbits.

37

BRIAR AND THE FOX

La Sylphide was one of the world's oldest-surviving romantic ballets. The story of a man seduced by a sylph, and their love that could never be.

The man, forbidden from holding the sylph he loves in his arms, obtains a magic scarf from a witch that will allow the lovers to embrace. But upon placing the scarf on the sylph, her wings dissolve and she crumbles to dust, leaving him alone.

Their pas de deux narrates the beginning of Act II, where the main character follows the sylph into the glade where she lives for the first time, and she shows him all the lovely things to find there.

Briar was hardly able to pantomime the movements of gathering flowers and presenting them to Mal, who never broke character. He moved habitually, knowing the steps by heart, hardly having to think of what his stiff, miserable body did all while his mind screamed with every passing moment. Every moment Mal remained on stage, watching him, dancing with him. Terrified of what would happen if he stayed there. If he continued to dance with Briar just out of reach.

The two lovers, never meant to touch, else the narrative be broken. Mal was meant to extend his hands for Briar playfully each time he came within reach, where Briar would flit away with a coy smile and the audience would chuckle.

But Briar barely lifted his leg into the midpoint arabesque when his ankle gave way beneath him. He nearly buckled to the floor, before Mal was suddenly there, sweeping him into an elegant turn and gently lifting him into a floating jump. Without even a hitch in his step. Without anyone in the audience, except those who knew it was wrong, to even notice. In fact, Briar swore he heard small gasps of delight.

They were never meant to touch—but from that moment onward, Mal never let Briar go for even a moment. Even though Briar was meant to flutter around the stage on his own, Mal never left him. Even in those moments where he removed his hands and allowed Briar to move freely, he still never pulled away far. And any time Briar's rooted limbs strained beneath him, fighting back against every movement, Mal seemed to sense it even before Briar did. As if he could anticipate exactly which movements, which leaps, which toe-lifts would be too much for him, and he was there to ease Briar through every single one.

All the while, Mal danced like no one Briar had ever seen. Not like Leon, or any other perfect specimen from Tomassin. Not like anyone he'd ever witnessed in ballet tour groups performing the Nutcracker at Christmas. Not even those prima donnas dancing for the New York Ballet or the Russian Ballet. Briar couldn't even specify what it was about Mal, specifically, that made him so captivating to watch, to be touched by, but—

Briar suddenly understood why Marie d'Alarie had never declared him perfect. Because compared to Lord Malric, there might never be anyone who danced so flawlessly.

Briar's vision was going blurry by the time the dance came to an end, though his body moved on its own. Knowing every step, every turn by heart. Even if he didn't, Mal would have guided him with ease.

When the final notes of the orchestra swelled, Briar found himself in the final high-arabesque where the characters canonically touched for the very first time in the entire dance. Where the man embraces the sylph's waist and dips her into the lift with ease and care, holding the position as the final note cascades over the stage and the lights dim.

The second they did, Briar's leg gave way beneath him. Mal threw out his hands, gathering him swiftly in a cloud of tulle skirts and wire wings at the small of Briar's back.

Briar couldn't breathe. His entire body was going tight, clenching and convulsing at the same time as he just gasped for breath. On the other side of the dark stage, the audience cheered and clapped as the final ring of the music faded.

Mal touched Briar's face. He turned it upward, meeting his eyes. They were only a hair's breadth apart, breathing heavily as the world fell away. Until it was only the two of them left.

Mal's mouth curled into a satisfied smile.

"You danced perfectly."

The gold chains of the fey lady's necklace—snapped from around Briar's neck, tumbling to the stage. Heat erupted in his chest—instantaneously scorching the roots and branches overwhelming him. He nearly screamed at the rush of heat, throwing his head back as the lights lifted again and whispers crossed the audience, having expected the two performers to have left in the darkness. But Briar didn't perceive them, burying his fingers into Malric's arms for support as he felt every inch of the dryad's curse turning to ash within his limbs.

The moment it finally faded, as quickly as it came, he lifted his head between gasping breaths to meet Mal's eyes in confusion. He almost asked what was going on—but then Mal's own expression suddenly clenched, and he hunched his back.

Briar gasped his name, grappling for him, asking what was wrong—but the words caught when Mal's own fingers dug into Briar's arms, and Briar could only hold back his shriek of alarm as claws tore through the ends of Mal's fingers.

"Mal!" he shouted, grabbing Mal's face and forcing it to lift upward—but the eyes that looked back at him were no longer the warm hazel-green he'd come to know. They were burnt orange, like autumn leaves. Like a smoke-choked moon. And in the center of them, irises closed into pinpricks, all while the fey lord's teeth clenched hard enough to tremble beneath Briar's hands.

Briar heard the whispers of the audience, but didn't turn to them. He just grabbed Mal's shirt, stumbling backward to pull him off the stage.

The moment they tumbled out of sight, Mal lost his footing, crashing into Briar and throwing them both to the floor. Briar lifted his head, vision spinning as he sought out his partner in the dark, only to find him still hovering on his hands and knees where he'd fallen. A low rumble emerged from the back of Malric's throat like a growl—and Briar watched as his hands darkened, creeping up to his forearms. His fingers bent inward, snapping away at the knuckles. His knees crunched backward into hind legs, evoking a guttural snarl from Mal's throat. Briar grabbed his face one more time, watching as his teeth elongated into canines, and—sharp ears, like horns, suddenly spawned from the crown of his head, not unlike the fox mask he wore to all of his mother's revels.

"Malric!" Briar begged, clutching Malric's face even as fur spread over his cheeks, the bones beneath snapping and warping. Behind them, someone called Mal's name and came searching, Briar turning quickly to find Bianca and Stella just as they raced into view. Stella grabbed Bianca instantly, pulling her back with a bark of alarm, but Briar just whirled back to look at the man in front of him. By then, he was unrecognizable—replaced by a gnarled fox the size of a great dane still taking form.

"*No!*" Briar cried, throwing his arms around Mal's muscled neck, burying his face into the thick copper fur tearing through the collar of his shirt. Even as Mal snarled and whipped his head back and forth, froth dripping down the back of Briar's neck. "No, no, no, Mal, please—!"

"He danced for someone... other than his mother," Bianca croaked. Briar just clung to Mal harder, begging him to stop, to change back, but Mal finally wrenched himself free of Briar's arms and stumbled backward. He thrashed his head, then shook out his body to knock what remained of his torn clothes away. He then met Briar's eyes one last time—and bounded through the hanging clothes next to them, crashing into something on the other side and tearing through the emergency exit.

Briar leapt to his feet to take chase, but Stella grabbed him before he could get far. Briar fought against her grasp, just staring at the door hanging ajar, begging to be let go—until Stella's voice boomed, only covered by the orchestra's next performance.

"Somebody is going to tell me what the FUCK is going on! NOW!"

Bianca touched Briar's shoulder, summoning him back to the moment. He pulled away from Stella in a panic, grabbing Bianca by the shirt, instead.

"You know what that was?" he begged. "You know what just happened? What can I do? How can I help him?"

"Him? What about *you?"* Bianca's voice cracked, hands scrambling up and down Briar's arms, then touching his face, and Briar was reminded—the branches were gone. The leaves forcing themselves through his skin, the roots, the splinters were all gone. He could breathe normally. His heart pounded without the weight of bark crushing it.

One of the stage hands tapped Briar on the shoulder, holding out a hand. Briar, in a daze, opened his palm to accept whatever they had—only for his breath to catch as the fey lady's necklace poured like golden water into his hand. Snapped in the back, no longer as bright and glistening as when perpetually around his neck. Proof that the deal was done. The deal was broken.

But then—

That meant—

You danced perfectly.

Briar stared at Bianca, ears ringing. It meant—Leon had never been the root of Briar's deal at all. Malric had. The fey son who revoked his right to dance, who left an opening in the revel, who planted the seed that would become Briar's opportunity to make his deal in the first place. The root.

"He..." Briar croaked. Did Malric know? The floor turned under his feet. "He... he saved me, but he... he had to dance with me, first..."

The room spun. His vision blurred around the edges. He thought it was panicked tears, at first—but like a tree falling in the forest, Briar's exhausted ghost flickered, detaching from his body enough that his knees buckled and he sank to the floor.

38

BRIAR AND THE SIBLINGS

Briar really thought Malric would come back on his own. Malric, who was smart, and cunning, and full of surprises. But the more days that passed without sight of him, without any contact at all, even Bianca beginning to look worried—the more Briar began to panic, too. What if he didn't come back? What if he *couldn't?* What if Briar had just—abandoned him, wherever he ended up, as that foxlike creature? What if he wasn't even in his right mind, what if he was lost?

What if he didn't remember who he once was? Who Briar was?

There was only so much Bianca could tell him; she'd done well to maintain boundaries with Malric for their entire friendship, only ever learning what she absolutely had to about him, his family, the fey, fey deals. Not wanting to get wrapped up in them, herself. Not like Briar had. Her middling knowledge was exactly enough to stay safe, and stay sane.

What she did tell him, haunted him.

"Malric has been forced to dance for his mother for his entire life. When I met him, he was in the worst part of it. His hips were beginning to give out. He was going to dance himself to death.

"I convinced him to finally leave. He stayed on my couch for a

few weeks before journeying off elsewhere to keep his mind busy. He always came back at least once a month, though. I thought he was doing better—not well, *but better. And then he heard about you, and what was happening to you... and it lured him right back in, didn't it?"*

She didn't say it like an accusation, like it was Briar's fault for Malric tumbling right back into his mother's web. She said it like she should have known better. They all should have known better. Marie would do anything to get Malric back, even when no one could expect.

"I know his siblings are here, in the human world," Briar told her, and Bianca looked surprised. "Can you take me to talk to them?"

"I don't know if..."

"Bianca," Briar asserted, squeezing the pearl that dangled from the golden chains wrapped around his wrist. "I think I can help him. But I need to talk to someone who knows better, first."

ONE, TWO, THREE, FOUR, FIVE, SIX, SEVEN, EIGHT, NINE.

Briar knew there was a godawful number of d'Alarie children, though he'd never seen them all in the same room, before. For the first time, being surrounded by high fey—even glamoured ones only pretending to be human, didn't frighten him. For some reason, it only made him angrier, once he finally understood exactly what Marie d'Alarie had done to them. All of them.

The ones named Mavera and Maura worked at the coffee shop where they all sat, wearing brown aprons tied around their waists and baseball caps donning the shop name. They were still way too pretty. All of them were, in fact, but Briar wasn't there to give them lessons on being human. They might have even been doing it on purpose, considering the way the tip jar at the register overflowed as Mavera flirted with every patron who came through, and then Maura flirted with them again as their drinks were left on the counter. Briar remembered those days. He pulled the same stunt working at Starbucks in his freshman year at Cal State.

Mavera and Maura at the coffee shop; Neda at the witch store; Lusia at a greenhouse; Lillis at an after-school program; Persea, Larissa, Reta, Felme at a local art gallery. Some pursuing their passions in small ways, others taking a break from them entirely. Briar wanted to give them all hugs. He wanted to get them all drunk so they could spill their guts all over the floor and cry it out. Maybe, later. They were missing one person who should be there.

Sitting at one of the two shop tables pushed together, Briar sat at the head feeling like a mafia boss. With Stella as his bodyguard and Bianca as his advisor, maybe that wasn't entirely unusual. Stella, however, was not her normal self, looking a little shell-shocked at her tea as she was still trying to comprehend the reality of there being at least two different worlds—human and fey. Bianca tried to gently include places like heaven, hell, limbo on top of it, only to stop before Stella puked.

"Tell me what's happened to him," Briar started, only after taking a long breath to try and calm the anxiety making his hands tremble. "Tell me where Malric is."

"We don't know the terms of his deal—" Neda attempted.

"Bullshit," Briar said through his teeth, before clamping his mouth shut and taking another stiff breath. "You know your mother. You might not know the exact words—but you know what kind of trick she would play. He turned into a giant fucking fox in front of my eyes—tell me what Marie would make him do, next."

"A fox?" the oldest sister, Felme, asked weakly. All the others turned to her, but she just stared at Briar. Briar held her eyes. Her mouth dangled open in shock, before nodding slowly. "Oh... gods."

She glanced at Neda, next. And then Lusia. All of them stared at one another. Neda looked emotional, like he was about to cry.

"Paint..."

"Write..."

"Cook for anyone other than me, ever again, and you shall become one with the copper fauna."

"Of they behind whom we hide our faces; of teeth and shadowed paws."

"Of your roots and starving for rabbits."

Briar's heart pounded in his chest.

"Are those the exact words?" he asked, recalling how Mal taught him about the importance of detail in any fey deal. The others nodded, looking embarrassed. Briar wondered at first why they'd never discussed that shared experience—before realizing, perhaps they didn't know. Perhaps it was too embarrassing to discuss leaving home at all, so they never spoke of the details to their siblings.

But if they were the words used with them back then, then they must have also been the words Malric heard before he left home, too. The ones that tangled in the back of his throat forbidding him from speaking them, just like Briar and his own. Briar swallowed back his own tangle of knots, different from those placed by the fey lady.

He could outwit them. He could outwit her. Just like Malric did.

"It's because he danced with me," he admitted. "He was—he was the root of my deal, he..."

"She... did it on purpose. All of it," Neda said like a fact. "Malric was the only one who could set you free, but he would have to pas de deux with you, first. It makes sense..."

"How did she know Malric would find you?" someone else asked. Briar wasn't sure which one, staring down at his drink.

"She made Briar his replacement," Felme whispered. "Of course he would find them."

"It was all on purpose."

"She never anticipated Malric choosing his consequence," Bianca interjected, and all other eleven faces looked at her. She looked frustrated with all of them, like it was taking everything not to erupt into shouts. "She never thought he would take that part of the deal! She thought she would have Briar forever, or Malric would return on his own. She probably never expected Malric to give up his life for Briar!"

The others went quiet. Briar continued staring down at the coffee in his hands, running his thumb over the outside of the cup. Drawing lines in the condensation. Malric... sacrificed himself for Briar. Just to save Briar...

Squeezing his eyes closed, he inhaled a deep breath. Briar had to do something. He had to do *something*, he couldn't just leave Malric to whatever Marie wanted to do with him. Especially since he was the only d'Alarie child left. He was the only one she had, anymore, and it was all his fault the others abandoned her, too. Briar's heart pounded with a rush of fear, desperate for anything at all he could do to help—but gazing at the faces surrounding him, he realized with a thud of anxiety... they were all looking at *him*. As if he was the one with the answers. He straightened in his seat. He almost snapped at them to stop fucking looking at him— but the words caught in his throat as he picked anxiously at the skin of his nails. At that place where splinters had grown out of him, from the inside out.

If the root of this deal finds your pas de deux perfect, it will be done. He mouthed the words under his breath, furrowing his brows. Those words he'd known the entire time he'd danced for her, but only Malric had provided them in their entirety. *Once made perfect, any who witness your dance will bow to any request you make...*

He jolted upright, scaring the others. He stared straight at Felme, who stared right back.

"I... I know what I have to do," he said, voice hoarse. Even though it terrified him, even though his instincts screamed and kicked and flailed and tried to beat it all back down again. It would mean—going back. It would mean finding her on his own. It would mean—returning to the web, the revel clearing, even though he knew she might try and keep him there forever.

But—Malric had returned to it to take care of Briar, too.

Malric had returned to the web just to save Briar, too. Briar had to return the favor.

And the moment he decided—he couldn't help the tiny, satisfied smile that quirked the corner of his mouth.

Any dance will be paired with the perfect partner as chosen by the veil.

39

BRIAR AND THE FEY LADY

B riar waited until Stella and Bianca were asleep before he left the apartment. If he hurried, he would make it on the last ferry to Whidbey Island.

It was freezing that night, but he knew it would be warm amidst the veil. Just like it always was. It would be warm, and there would be someone there waiting for him to come. Waiting with equally comforting arms as soon as Briar set him free from his curse.

Briar would not let Malric wander alone, one with the copper fauna, of teeth and shadowed paws, of his roots and starving for rabbits. Briar would find him, just like Malric once found him amidst the agony of the consequences of a fey deal gone wrong.

BRIAR NORMALLY SPENT THE JOURNEY PICKING HIS nails, gazing out the window, searching the sky for his magpie friend who would flap down and give him a second note that said *on second thought, the revel was canceled, tonight.*

That night, he just focused on the opposite side of Possession Sound creeping closer with every minute. He fiddled with the broken charmed necklace that once shackled him to the revel clearing, wrapped around his wrist. In his bag was the ensemble he'd worn in La Sylphide, snatched from Tomassin's backstage as he still had a passcode for the lock. An outfit not unlike the one worn by Giselle in Act II—an outfit to match the one he would dance with Malric for Marie d'Alarie to see. To bring his deal full circle. To show her how he never needed her at all.

To claim his perfect partner from the veil, just like she promised he could.

That time, Briar wasn't invited. He didn't know if there would be people there to witness him dance, like all the others—but it didn't matter. There was only one person he wanted to dance for—and he would do it with perfection.

Arriving on the other side of the sound, Briar kicked a leg over the seat of his bike just like he always did. He turned his shoulder bag to bounce against the small of his back as he pedaled in the dark toward the beach. As he left his bike leaning against the same tree he always did, hiking up in the beach in search of that migrating mirage that would suck him through to the other side. The fey side, where he would dress himself in Giselle's skirt and bodice; where he would dance with his hair down, wearing dirty pointe shoes dug up from where he'd planted them months prior.

THE REVEL CLEARING WAS ALIGHT WITH LANTERNS, BUT didn't slow his approach. At least, not until he realized—there was no string accompaniment in the air. There were no chattering voices or boisterous laughter of a drunken high fey audience. There was only the lantern light, the stench of rosemary, and, as he crept closer from the shadows—a single person seated on the cushions at the head of the circle, her fox mask pushed up out of her face as she tipped back a glass of wine into her mouth. Marie d'Alarie, seated alone at one of her own fetes. Briar had never seen the clearing so empty—it was almost ominous.

Something crunched in the brush behind him, and he snapped around to look—only for his breath to catch as, a few yards away, eyes reflecting the lantern glow gazed back at him. A shadowy creature the size of a wolf, with ears perked upright, head bowed in curiosity.

"Mal," Briar whispered. The animal's ears twitched, but it otherwise didn't move. Briar had to resist racing to throw his arms around them, still not knowing if Malric would be in his right mind in his animal form—or if it was even Malric at all. God knew, there were trickier things in the fey woods.

"Stay with me," was all Briar could think to say, a small plea for his fox-lord not to stray too far. "I'm going to need you, soon."

The animal still didn't react—except Briar swore it nodded its head slightly in acknowledgement. He couldn't help but smile, before taking off through the darkness to where he recalled his burial plot to be. Keeping within the shadows, he dropped to his knees on the edge of the overturned soil where Mal had exhumed him only a few days prior, burying his hands into the soil and tearing through it with vigor he never had while asleep. Dirt churned into hardly more than earthy foam, easily rifled through as the roots of his own body had softened it. It made gathering his slippers easier than ever before—an irony not lost on him.

Stripping off his clothes, Briar scanned the darkness as he was naked in the trees, spotting the fox's curious eyes again. He smiled at it, before shaking out his hair and pulling on the white bodice. It was a pain in the ass to snap the hooks in place on the back by himself, jumping when he swore he felt cold hands touch his spine to try and help. But upon turning, there was nothing. Only the fox's shadowy form in the bushes, only the misplaced trees surrounding him. Briar gazed at their fingerlike branches for a long moment, before shaking his head and twisting his arms back to continue clasping the bodice together. Pulling on the romantic tutu, last, Briar had to stop and close his eyes, breathe in a long inhale as his heart pounded harder and harder. He placed a hand over his chest, inhaling, exhaling through his nose, forcing himself to relax.

He breathed in the smell of rosemary. The smell of the forest. The smell of babbling creeks and that sharp, warm, minty scent of the nearby veil opening. He listened to the crickets, the nighttime birds, the sound of the forest all around him in every direction. Things he'd never paused to appreciate a single time when called to dance for Marie, things he resented, things that made his anxiety spike as they were associated with his waking nightmares.

But that time, he forced himself to focus. He forced himself to feel the cool breeze on his bare skin, his arms, his legs, trailing through his loose hair like fingers. He felt the dirt under his nails, he felt the cold, still shape of the pointe shoes on his feet, a muddy pink from their time interred in the earth and speckled with holes where roots had grown from them.

Something brushed his hand. He swore it was another, grasping for him, intertwining their fingers, but that time he didn't look. He kept his eyes closed, holding his breath. He didn't know for sure—but something told him it was Mal. If anything, it was who he wished would touch his hand gently in that moment the most, to give him the courage to perform one final dance.

One final dance, for himself. For his own sake. To save someone he loved.

Opening his eyes, Briar emerged into the clearing. Marie's eyes turned to him. She pulled the glass of wine from her mouth slowly, raising her eyebrows in question.

"Why have you come here?" she asked, loud in the emptiness. She looked different from all those other times—her bright red hair was faded, growing in at the roots, proving it to be dyed. Her face lacked the same color and perfection Briar had come to know, like a glamour had failed. Her eyes looked heavy, miserable.

Briar curtsied as elegantly as he could. Marie's accusatory expression softened somewhat. She looked surprised to see him there—but not because she knew his curse had been broken. Not like she knew he was even still alive, after being buried in the earth.

"I'm here to provide one more performance," he said upon straightening back up. "Now that I have been declared perfect, I would like to demonstrate it for you, my lady."

Marie's mouth twitched. She turned the wine glass in her hand, glancing around the empty revel circle as if a part of her wondered if it was only her imagination. As if all of it, the emptiness of her fete, was all just a cruel trick of the forest's magic. She looked at him—as if she truly still thought him to be dead. Briar, dressed as Giselle's ghost, come to perform for her one last time.

"Alright, then," she finally agreed with a breathy voice. "One last dance for me, to demonstrate the perfection I have given you."

Briar bowed again, keeping his eyes low.

"You may recognize the score I've chosen, my lady. It's the same one that brought you to me in the first place."

Marie cleared her throat. Still uncertain. Still unsure if she was witnessing Briar or just the echo of him. He saw how her eyes kept flickering to where his tree should have been, as if she hadn't thought to check and see if Malric had ever dug him back out of the earth.

"A fine choice," she rasped. "And who will be your partner?"

Briar smiled back.

"I do not know yet," he said with a small, coy nod. "But, according to our deal—as I have been made perfect, the veil shall choose my partner for me."

Marie just nodded. Briar bowed slightly more in acknowledgement, before finding his place in the clearing. His place on the stage, where he'd once met hands with Leon, hoping to perform so beautifully it would change his mind entirely. Leon would want to stay at Artemisia with Briar; Leon would want to only ever dance with Briar.

But it was arrogant of Briar to wish for something like that. He wouldn't make that mistake, again—he would, as Marie offered, let the veil choose who he was meant to dance with.

There were no string musicians to play for him that night—but Briar heard the notes in his mind. Notes he'd memorized for years, in class, at home, during all those times he practiced en pointe in the garage, backstage, on that worn spot in his bedroom. He knew that score down to every single breath—and he sank into the movements as if written for him.

He danced as a call to the veil, which would see him and know exactly who he needed to join him. He danced like he did at the start of La Sylphide, with his eyes low, avoiding the urge to search. His partner would come. Surely, his perfect partner would come the moment it was his turn. Briar just focused on his feet, his arms, his movements, the sound of the forest in every direction, the memory of the music in his mind coaxing each step from his body.

Something rustled in the shadows between the trees. Briar just melted through the movements as he knew best. Those movements, one by one, that carried him closer and closer to the moment—

The exact moment he anticipated, when Albrecht and Giselle touched—and warm hands found his waist. Briar couldn't stop himself—he jumped, foot falling out of line to catch his balance, turning quickly to look. His heart swelled and lifted the moment he met Malric's eyes, gazing down at him with the same intensity they always did. He stood naked in the clearing there, a handsome high fey lord, chosen for Briar by the veil, itself.

A smile of pure relief found Briar's mouth. He extended a hand to cup Malric's cheek, and Malric's eyes closed, leaning into it. Turning his face and kissing Briar's palm with a soft exhale through his nose. Briar's smile grew, turning en pointe and wrapping the golden necklace chains from around his wrist.

"Here," he whispered. "My Albrecht..."

Draping the chain around Malric's neck, it did exactly what it had always done for Briar, glamouring him in the dance ensemble he needed. Malric let out another soft breath, still not speaking a word, only keeping his eyes locked on Briar. As if an animalistic part of him remained, still trying to gather his bearings. Still trying to make sense of what had happened to him. Briar just touched Malric's face again, pulling him down and pressing their foreheads together, gently.

"Dance with me," he beseeched softly. "Will you?"

Malric's hand found Briar's against his cheek, pressing it flush, before cupping it gently.

"There's no one else but you, Briar."

Briar smiled to himself. He met Malric's eyes again, resisting the urge to rise onto his toes and kiss him. Instead—Malric lifted him with ease by the waist, and their dance continued from the moment it left off.

Briar's pointed foot returned to the earth as Malric settled him down, holding his breath as the choreography allowed him to slowly turn like a porcelain figure in a music box, only to sink into his partner's arms. Giselle's spirit seeking comfort from Albrecht, who sought her ghost at her forest grave. Giselle, indulging in the feeling of his arms wrapped around her, promising that despite everything, she still loved him dearly.

Briar sank into Malric's body. Malric wrapped his arms around Briar's bare shoulders, breathing heavily and smelling of dirt and verdant plants, as if he'd run full-tilt to the revel clearing from wherever he'd been. Briar took his chance to lift his eyes to Malric's, smiling at him in reassurance as Malric just gazed back down at him in awe. As if Briar was the loveliest, most cunning thing he'd ever laid eyes on.

The choreography pulled them apart again, though their hands clasped in the middle. Briar bent back into an arabesque as the music elongated into something sorrowful, Malric's hands knowingly traveling back to Briar's hips, then his waist, turning him with all the elegance of a breeze rippling water.

Draping backward over Malric's chest and shoulders as the movements demanded, Briar was lifted and swept and turned in exactly all the movements he had been, once, with Leon—but with Malric, they carried him to another world entirely. It was a conversation, a song, an entire lifetime exchanged in movements perfectly in tune with one another, without any misplaced steps or hitches of breath. It was a flawless exchange of their bodies, their words, without ever speaking anything at all. It was Briar knowing he could trust to find Malric's hands there to support him when he had to dip blindly backward or forward; it was Briar trusting Malric to lift him with ease, and return him like a breath back to the grass. It was always knowing exactly where Malric was, even when Briar wasn't looking directly at him.

It was—every element within Briar's body, his soul, reaching out to meet Malric's and cling to it, until they might as well have shared the same mind.

In the final draw of silent music, Briar traveled on his toes to the center of the clearing where Malric knelt, placing a hand on his shoulder and ending the performance with an elegant foot raised, like two pieces of art lingering as the curtains fell. But as the performance ebbed, Briar didn't pull away. He bent lower, wrapping his arms around Malric from behind, then finding Marie d'Alarie's eyes where she sat at her place on the edge. Marie d'Alarie, who watched them both in what Briar could only describe as disbelief, as someone flushed with horror, as if that was the first moment she realized, what she witnessed dancing in front of her was, in fact, very real.

"The veil has chosen my partner for me," Briar said, never taking his eyes from her. "And I will be taking him with me."

Briar dragged his hands up the front of Malric's glamoured tunic, feeling both the fabric and the bare skin of his chest. Feeling how the fey lord shuddered beneath his hands, trembling with heavy breaths of both exhaustion and his own cresting emotions. Briar kissed the back of Malric's head, letting the moment linger a heartbeat longer, before coaxing the man back to his feet, taking his hand, and rushing him across the grass. Wanting to whisk him away, to steal him, to rescue him from the queen of the wilis, just like Giselle did Albrecht in the woods—

"*Wait!*" Marie shrieked, and Briar only realized he'd been

compelled when his feet stopped against his will. Malric grabbed him before he could fall, pulling Briar into his body before turning to confront Marie himself.

"Your deal is done, mother," he snarled, a spark of fiery life finally emerging from his shock. Goosebumps raced down Briar's arms at the harshness of his voice. "There is nothing left for you to give or take. Rot in your isolation with dignity."

Marie, on her feet, didn't say anything at first. The wine glass in her hand trembled, spilling red drink down her fingers and dripping over the cushions.

"Málda—please, don't leave me here alone. Tell me what has happened to my children, tell me where they are so I know they're safe—"

"I no longer pity the likes of you," Malric interrupted. "Your children have grown, mother, they no longer need to rely on someone like you to find a reason for being. Take this time to dwell on your own consequences."

Marie's nostrils flared, shoulders hunching in a rush of anger. She threw the glass to the ground, where it shattered against the earth. "If you insist on keeping my children from me—so be it. I will simply find more to take your place, as I always have. More— like your dancer. You and your siblings may be able to hide from me, Malric—but he can't. I've stolen him once, I can do it again."

Briar's resolve cracked at those words, as well as the compelling enchantment on his body, taking an uneasy step back, sidling slightly closer to Malric who stood between him and the fey woman. Malric's hand in Briar's tightened, almost hard enough that it might snap. The rest of his body, muscles clenching like diamond in the earth, trembled with tempered fury.

"Make a deal with me, mother."

"No!" Briar cried, grabbing Malric's arm as those words made his world crash. Malric didn't look back at them, just flexed his hand in Briar's, like it would be enough to soothe Briar's panic. But after everything they'd done, after everything he and Malric both had gone through, not to mention Malric's siblings—to make another deal with her? To offer another deal with Marie? Was that really all high fey knew how to do, damnit?

"... No," Marie spoke before Briar could argue further. He glanced around Malric to where she remained at the opposite end of the clearing, not expecting to find her eyes staring right back at him. Smiling. Briar's blood ran cold. "I will not make a deal with you, málda—but I will make one with the dancer, if they so wish."

Malric stiffened. He stared at Marie a moment longer, before glancing down to Briar. His eyes overflowed with emotions— anger, rage, desperation, panic—but he said nothing. Briar tried to read his thoughts, tried to see what exactly Malric was thinking, but there was only white noise between them. Perhaps that was only Briar's own panic settling in, after his defensive walls plummeted the moment Malric was back within reach once more.

"I... I can't," Briar whispered, shaking his head. "I don't know how, I can't—"

"Yes, you do," Malric turned toward him, taking Briar's opposite hand, holding both. "You know plenty about fey deals, Briar —from your own, and what I've taught you."

"But I'm not—!" Briar tried to insist. Marie made a sound of impatience across the clearing, and Briar's head snapped to look at her—only for Malric's fingers to curl under Briar's chin and pull his attention back.

"You're just as clever and conniving as any high fey," he whispered. "You got the veil to thwart my mother's own curse on me."

"That wasn't—"

"Just think, Briar," Malric whispered, pressing their foreheads together and closing his eyes. "Don't rush. You remember the three parts of a deal, don't you?"

Briar whimpered, squeezing his eyes closed. Still, he nodded.

A request. An offer. A consequence.

Briar's hands found the front of Malric's tunic. He dug through the glamour for the heat of his chest, spreading his hands against the warm skin found there. He felt Malric's heart pounding harder than it should have, proving he was just as frightened as Briar was. For some reason, that was comforting. Briar took a deep breath, before turning back to Marie.

He did what Malric said. He took his time considering every option, every way he could phrase each part. Like a high fey would.

A request—

Just fuck off. Never come back. Never hurt another human or fey person, ever again. Leave these poor people alone.

An offer—

I won't chain you to one of these trees to be eaten alive by worms.

A consequence—

If you ever hurt anyone ever again...

Briar glanced at the place he'd once buried his slippers. That place he planted the last thing that had given him hope, a seed to take root and eventually claim him when he failed. He glanced at the trees surrounding that plot, out of place, not belonging in the fey Autumn Court with the rest of the forest. He thought of every dream he'd had of digging up the earth.

Briar's stomach turned, realizing a truth he might have already known, but was still too afraid to even mentally vocalize. His eyes flickered to the necklace Malric still wore, still glamouring him as they remained right on the inner edge of the circle of pungent rosemary.

A request. An offer. A consequence.

He reached up, unclasping the gold chains from around Malric's neck. He gazed down at them as the words formed in his mind, skittering in and out of order, snapping in and out of place like searching for puzzle pieces.

"Alright," he whispered, more for himself than the fey who could hear him. He lifted his eyes to Marie, who grinned viciously at him, foaming for a chance to hear what he would say. To find all the ways she could outwit him and his offer. Briar swallowed back the lump in his throat, delicate chains between his fingers trembling as he held it outward.

"Marie d'Alarie...my request—*you will not trick anyone else into performing at your revels. Um, my offer—any time you set foot inside the circle of rosemary... your children will be compelled to return and perform for you.*" He held up the necklace. "The—the consequence—*you have to wear this charmed necklace, which will only glamour you as a revel hostess when within the clearing—but only you, yourself, can remove it. Outside of the clearing... you will witness perfection in the same manner you promised those who have come before.*"

Marie's eyes bulged, grinning wider than Briar knew possible.

"Agreed," she announced, practically rushing across the grass to where Briar extended the necklace. She snatched it from his hands, tying it around her neck in an instant before barking a laugh. She called Briar an imbecile, a fool, a naive little moon-ear for offering something so simple, so easily owned. She never wanted to have to trick others at all, she only ever wanted her own children to perform for her, and Briar gave her exactly what she wanted, anytime she wanted it. She only had to step back into the circle again, and every d'Alarie child would be forced to return in an instant.

Malric's shaking hand touched Briar's shoulder. Briar didn't look at him, not right away. He just kept watching Marie, who tromped back across the clearing to the opposite end. Straight through the circle of rosemary, exiting with every intention of crossing right back into it again—

But her foot caught on something, and she fell with a grunt. Briar jumped, holding his breath. His eyes flickered to those out-of-place trees again. He gulped through the tightness in his throat —and offered them a tiny nod of encouragement. Those who came before him, who died by the curse of the dryad like he almost had.

Marie attempted to claw back to her feet—but one of her hands was stuck in the grass, pinning her. Right on the edge of the circle, partially hidden behind the wall of rosemary. She cried out in alarm, demanding to know what Briar had done—but Briar heard only the fey lady's own words echoing in his ears. *You shall become as the trees, to witness the perfection of another.*

You will witness perfection in the same manner you promised those who have come before...

"Did you think I meant your fey audience, you bitch?" he whispered as Marie screeched and thrashed, tearing at the leaves emerging from her skin like an incoming tide over a beach; like storm clouds obscuring the sun. Enveloping her, piercing through her skin and taking root in the fresh soil where she stood. Anchoring her right on the edge of the circle, just out of reach. Petrifying her limbs and hardening her skin, until branches grew like long tendrils from her mouth, solidifying as unnatural hands reaching desperately for her salvation on the other side of the circle. Never getting close enough to grab it.

To become as the trees.

Malric tugged on Briar's hand after nothing short of an eternity passed, watching the woman grow into just another tree at the edge of the clearing. A tug on Briar's hand, a pull into the shadows, feet meeting the familiar pathway through the woods toward the d'Alarie estate. The only place they would be able to find peace, silence, comfort as soon as they both needed it.

Briar kissed Malric the moment they crossed through the door into his bedroom. Malric lifted Briar off his feet, carrying him to the bed where they reveled in one another's bodies, breaths, whispers of affection and thanks and promises of forever. Where Briar pressed Malric onto his back and opened his legs to straddle his hips, riding him with soft breaths while clinging to the headboard. Kissing him between rushes of pleasure and adrenaline, disappearing into him and everything he could summon Briar's body to still feel. To share in one another's exhaustion, to exchange it in the darkness, to release all the pent-up anger, grief, relief of all that had come to pass into one another, to gasp promises made before, but never spoken out loud enough.

I will always think of you. I will always find you. I will always have you.

40

THE FOX AND THE DRYAD

Three Months Later

Malric was put on Hunt-family duty, which meant keeping track of two over-the-top moms and four little sisters who screeched and ran back and forth around in the parking lot while the adults waited in line. The youngest wore a swan costume; the twins wore matching, home-made Odette and Odile tutus, and the oldest, barely in high-school, leaned against the building with her phone dressed as Prince Siegfried. Malric didn't know there was going to be a dress code. He would have dressed up, too. Maybe as Rothbart.

But Malric was also on Bianca duty, technically, though she was a thousand times less of a handful, especially in her state of catatonia. Staring straight ahead without blinking. Just fiddling with the box in her pocket. Speaking with short answers and a flat tone of voice like it was all she could do just to not pass out in anxiety.

Briar's moms—Lynn and Joyce—were as conniving as their oldest child, still bitter that Briar hadn't given them enough time to plan a trip for his performance with Leon months earlier, still intent on getting their revenge with the big-ass flower bouquets draped over their arms. There was nothing like making Briar think he was about to be rained over with flowers, only for them to go to Stella as congratulation gifts, instead. Little did they know, all of Malric's nine siblings were standing a hundred yards down the entry line, each holding their own bundle of flowers of peonies and baby's breath and everything in-between. Briar's ego was going to be completely fine.

"Hey, Master Mal!" Leon's voice grabbed Malric from an amusing conversation between the moms, turning quickly to nod and smile. "Oh—hey, Lynn! Joyce!"

Leon gave Briar's moms a far-more enthusiastic greeting—and hugs—than he did his own new dance instructor, but Malric tried not to take it personally. He would just work the man to exhaustion in practice on Monday, and then laugh about it with Briar later at dinner. Like always, since Malric took that position at St. Tomassin teaching their advanced class. A little bit of healthy distance from Briar at Artemisia, while still pursuing that thing he realized he loved so much while stalking the rosefinch in the first place. Gods, Malric liked critiquing bitchy dancers on their form.

Finally shuffling into the Artemisia theater building, Malric herded the Hunt family through the crowd toward their seats. A line of nine inhumanly-beautiful non-humans followed like chicks behind their mother hen, practically shoving their way through the other guests in order to catch up. The number of times the d'Alarie children had almost started a fight in public, still trying to get their fey personalities in human skin under control—Malric might need another intervention.

Briar had danced as Odette and Odile in every one of Artemisia's spring show performances leading up to that night, and Malric had attended every single one. It was only that night, the finale, that he had a whole additional crowd of adoring fans joining him, and more than once he had to remind his siblings to mind their manners and not hoot and holler whenever Briar came on stage—only for Briar's moms to shriek and cheer on the opposite side of him. Briar on stage kept his expression perfectly under control, though Malric could see the way his cheeks reddened in embarrassment.

Since fulfilling their deal with Marie d'Alarie, since finally being offered a chance to rest, to recover, to find a balance in his life again—Briar became even more perfect on his feet. Dancing the way he was always meant to, in ways far more dangerous than when Malric first witnessed him at the revel. Had Briar performed so beautifully that time, Malric surely would have torn to his feet, grabbed the dancer around the waist, and disappeared into the woods in an instant. Perhaps Briar's subdued grace had been a godsend for them both, all things considered.

Malric had watched Briar dance on stage an innumerable number of times since then—and still, each time, it left him breathless. On the edge of his seat, hypnotized by the way Briar moved, the loveliness of his steps, his expression, everything about it. It may have been a result of Marie's deal, that Briar would be able to enchant everyone he ever danced for—but something told Malric, such wasn't entirely the case. Briar was simply...

"Perfect," he whispered, watching his white swan sweep around the prince with flirty movements.

"You know, I sewed Briar's first tutu, just like that one," Joyce leaned over to share, and Malric grinned.

"You don't happen to have old videos, do you? Briar refuses to show me any."

The woman's eyes lit up, a stark contrast from the evil smile on her mouth.

"Oh, honey. Thousands. From the day he first watched Swan Princess all the way up until now. Right, Lynn?" she nudged her wife with an elbow, and Malric leaned forward to find Lynn perched with her phone upright and recording every moment. Malric had to bite back more laughter.

"Stella looks so handsome, doesn't she?" Lynn went on, smiling playfully at Bianca, who remained petrified in the seat on

Malric's opposite side. She only nodded slowly, eyes glazed over, unblinking as Prince Siegfried-Stella lifted Briar off his feet and spun him around like he weighed as much as the feathers pinned in his hair. Malric just patted his friend's leg, though Bianca inhaled sharply in surprise and almost choked.

"It's going to be fine," he whispered. "You told me yourself, she's expecting it."

"Mama is going to kill me," Bianca croaked. Lynn immediately whispered about how *if Bianca needed a new parent who loved and accepted her for who she was, no matter who she married*—but Bianca just turned to her, pale, shaking his head. "No—because I promised I wouldn't get engaged until at least a year."

"Four and a half months is close enough," Malric reassured. Someone behind them made a shushing sound, but Lynn leaned over Malric's lap and kept speaking.

"You know, sweetheart, Joyce and I got engaged after only two weeks."

"Yeah, and only because some of our friends were fostering baby Briar, and we wanted him for ourselves."

Malric and Bianca both turned to them in shock, but the women just snickered like playing a secret game of *two truths and a lie*. They only didn't get the truth because the little swan wriggling in the seat next to Joyce complained about needing to use the bathroom, and Joyce scooped them up and over a shoulder to obey. The swan squealed and giggled and kicked the whole way down the row, while the oldest sister hid her face behind her hand in embarrassment.

Malric liked them. No—he loved them. The Hunts were what he'd always imagined a family to be—and even more than that, they were a family of chosen members. All five children, adopted by two mothers who were in the process of applying to foster more since Briar was out of the house. Mothers who loved and adored their children more than anything—who supported them in whatever they chose, who sewed homemade tutus and booked flights at the last minute to watch a show because their prima-ballerina forgot to tell them about it, again.

They, who during the ballet's Act IV climax, cried as Briar danced Odette choosing to die rather than live betrayed by her love. Who, before the curtains even closed, launched to their feet and clapped, shouting *encore, encore!* like they'd learned from the movies. All of Briar's siblings joined them, even the easily-embarrassed oldest sister, who jumped onto her seat and shouted Briar's name between cupped hands until someone hissed at her to sit down. Thank god—Malric was watching Maura and Mavera witness the excitement, scooching to the edges of their seats to join it before it was all cut off. That was Bianca's cue to go, and Malric patted her on the leg, and then smacked her on the leg to snap her out of her fugue state, where she leapt to her feet like a rocket and scrambled over all nine d'Alarie children blocking her way to the exit.

Briar's family erupted all over again as soon as the curtains parted once more for the final bow, and eight fey-thrown bouquets found Briar's feet on the stage. Briar searched the audience, squinting through the lights before finally setting eyes on the entire row of people there to cheer for him. His composure finally broke, putting a hand over his mouth and turning beet red before hurrying off the stage with all the grace of a prima ballerina.

When the entire cast fluttered back out for the final bow of the night—Stella was surprised to find Bianca taking her hand instead of Briar at the front of the line. Bianca, who looked like she was going to puke, or maybe pass out into the orchestra pit. But, just like she and Malric had practiced, she instead dug around in her pocket, and got down on one knee. Stella stumbled backward a step, hands over her mouth in shock as the audience cheered, blocking out the words Bianca shakily said to the person she loved. Exactly how it should have been—words for Stella, only. Even Malric's eyes flooded with tears when Stella nodded fervently, sweeping Bianca off her feet and spinning her, before kissing her for everyone to see.

MALRIC RAN AND SCOOPED BRIAR OFF THE GROUND just like every other time, making Briar laugh and kick his feet as his tutu was crushed between their bodies. Malric littered him with compliments, kisses, nuzzling their faces together and mussing up Briar's hair as Briar whined the whole time, only to pull on Malric's ear to finally get him to lay off. Malric only conceded as the rest of the group caught up, crowding Briar with half the bouquets available, fawning and swooning over Stella and Bianca with all the others.

But Malric only saw Briar, his rosefinch, his dancer. He tucked away some of the hair he'd misplaced in the onslaught, before pressing a soft kiss to Briar's forehead.

"How did I dance?"

"Hmmm," Malric considered, before saying those same words he always did. "I think I'll need a closer look."

Briar smiled at him with a knowing glance. Malric had to put them down just long enough to address his family, his friends, Malric's siblings, compiling plans to meet for dinner downtown in an hour. Malric waited patiently, watching the audience vacate their seats in tandem.

Once the crowd was gone, once Briar's family and the others had gone to change in the dressing rooms or find their car in the parking lot, Briar found Malric behind the curtain again. They took his hand, just like every other time. They pulled him onto the stage—and Malric took his place where he would have rather been. Where he was the one to witness Briar's movements up close. To hold his waist, turn his body, lift him overhead and bask in the ease and grace of their movements. The one Briar and Stella had just performed on stage for all to see, danced again just for he and his rosefinch. A promise made to never go a single day without a pas de deux, as Briar once requested before they had the freedom to do so.

"You danced perfectly," Malric whispered as the waltz came to an end, lingering in each other's arms, mouths hardly an inch apart while catching their breaths. Briar smiled up at him in that perfect way he always did, forehead shiny with sweat, eyes bright like a stormy sky. Perfect. Perfect—Briar Hunt was perfect.

"I'll get to say that to you, soon," Briar mused in return, referring to Malric's own upcoming role in Tomassin's company performance of *Romeo and Juliet*. "I need to practice my choreography for after curtain."

"I'll teach it to you," Malric promised, before tucking a finger under Briar's chin to kiss him. To melt into one another, exhausted and brimming with life at the same time. "I want to dance every pas de deux there is with you, both human and fey, until they're perfect."

"That'll be easy," Briar smirked. "Everything with you—is always perfect."

"You're easy to please."

Briar giggled. He pulled Malric into another kiss, holding him, pressing their bodies together and trailing fingers back up through his hair.

"I'm not," he promised. "You're just everything I've ever wanted, my lord."

Malric smiled, laughing under his breath. He took Briar's hands, holding them to his chest, before kissing Briar one more time on the forehead.

Some Danian scholars claimed dance was what first teased the veil open.

A human and a high fey turning, twisting, floating in tandem with one another, unaware of the mirror's edge separating them.

Malric used to dance with the intention of rending open the veil for himself, to find they who danced in his reflection. He once thought himself having to be perfect in order to earn it—until he met the one who fit perfectly into his arms, with whom Malric fell perfectly in step with, and he realized—

Perfection was only found in exchange for gentleness. Perfection was only given with promise of gentleness.

And no one would ever worship the perfection of Briar Hunt, or provide him all the gentleness of the world, the way Malric d'Alarie would. For so long as he lived.

Secrets are kept for a reason. Whether it be long-hidden truths or the history of Morrígan Academy, perhaps exhuming centuries of cruelty is exactly what Saffron needs to protect the people he loves most.

Rowan Blood Terms to Know

Arid/aridity: Used to describe the innate magic of humans in relation to the veil and the fey world.

Ashen: Used to describe high fey who cannot perform magic (opulence) due to manipulation of the veil.

Beantighes: Term used to describe human servants working in the fey world.

Compelling: Fey magic used to enchant humans into obeying spoken commands with or without their consent.

Folk Witch: Used to describe someone who performs magic unrelated to specifically the fey world or the veil.

Glamour: Used by the fey to disguise their physical appearance and other attributes. An opulent skill.

Opulent/opulence: Used to describe the innate magic of high fey in relation to the veil and the fey world.

Revel: A party (or fete) hosted by the fey.

Sídhe: A class of high fey families capable of performing higher levels of magic/opulence, including specialized magical skills; the oldest families in the fey world who make up the majority of the highest nobility in the fey world.

The Veil: The middleground separating the human world and the fey world, as well as a source of magic for both human and fey.

ACKNOWLEDGMENTS

My one simple peace, Mo, who continues to be my biggest supporter, my co-creator, my sensational cover artist, and the love of my life. Every day I get to do this with you is a blessing I will never feel like I deserve. You are everything I could have ever asked for in a partner; everything I write is a love letter to you. Point me where you want me.

https://morlevart.com/
Twitter: @morlevart

My friends and close peers, who do so much for me before, during, and after the process of writing and publishing. The industry is difficult, especially self-pub, but you all make it so much easier to find enjoyment in the process.

And a giant, special thanks to **Elle Porter** who did the fastest beta read ever on the shortest timeline ever and provided some amazing feedback! Go find their work here: https://www.porterotica.com/

The Rowan Blood Fandom, full of people who amaze me with their creativity, passion, and personality that make all the hard work worth it. Your support means the whole world to me, and I can't wait to continue discovering Alfidel (and beyond) together.

ABOUT THE AUTHOR

Kellen Graves (they/them) is a queer indie writer and artist from the Pacific Northwest, where they live with their partner, two cats, and crystal collection. They also enjoy digital illustration, photography, collecting planners, and disappearing into the ocean.

You can find more info about this release and upcoming releases, see their art, and connect by following Kellen on social media or checking out their website.

TWITTER: @SKELLYGRAVES
INSTAGRAM: @SKELLYGRAVES

SKELLYGRAVES.COM
SKELLYGRAVES.CARRD.CO

ALSO BY KELLEN GRAVES

ROWAN BLOOD

PRINCE OF THE SORROWS (VOL ONE)

LORD OF SILVER ASHES (VOL TWO)

HERALD OF THE WITCH'S MARK (VOL THREE)

VOLUME 4 (2024)